The Winter Witching

Emma Steinbrecher

CONTENTS

This one is actually for me.
(sorry to everyone else)

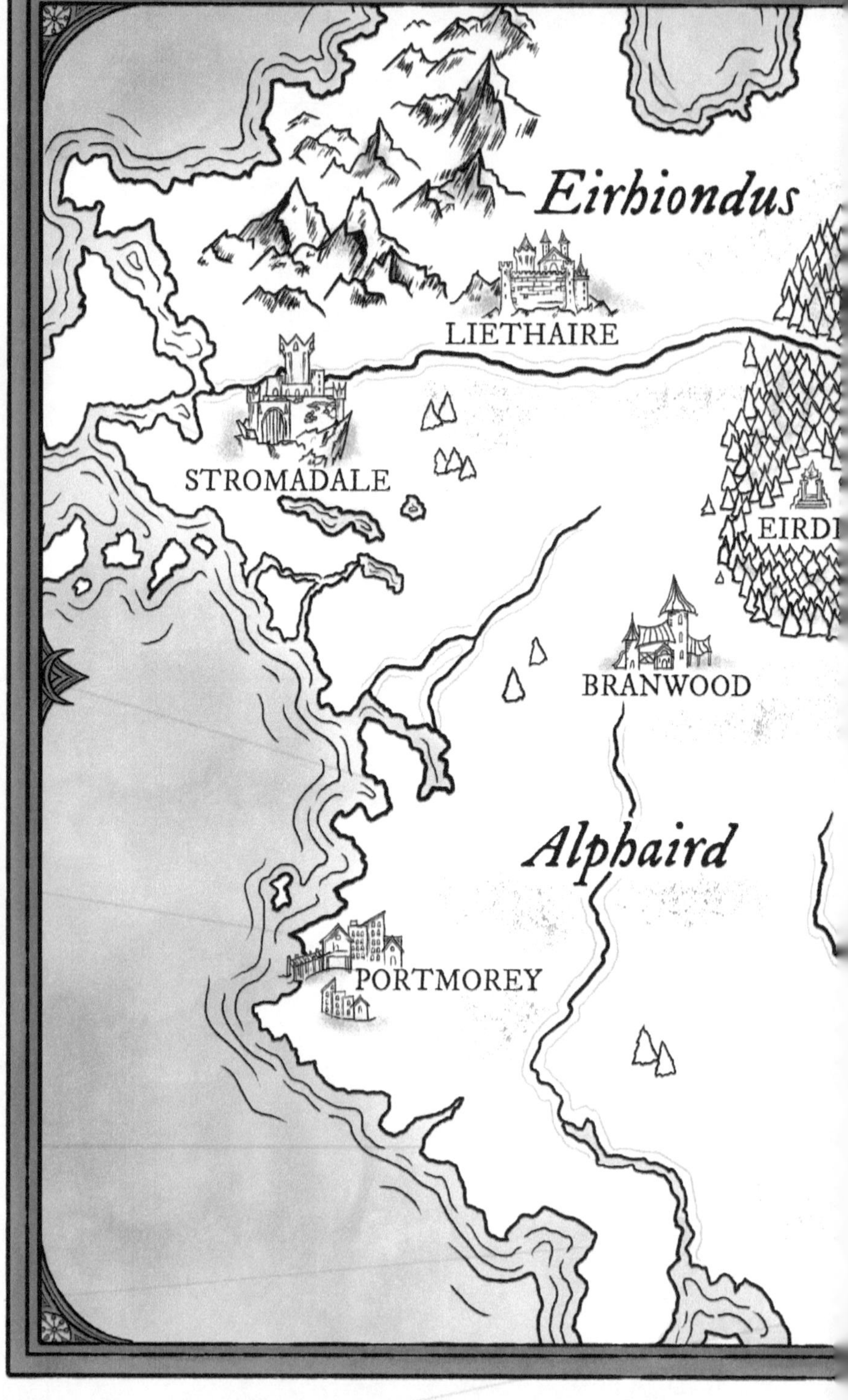

Eirhiondus
LIETHAIRE
STROMADALE
EIRDI
BRANWOOD
Alphaird
PORTMOREY

ONELIA
The Waldwood
ARAXIE
ABELLONA
CYRA
KESLOW
MARMERE
MAHLEGH
N
W
E
S

TRIGGER WARNINGS

Trigger warnings for this book include: graphic violence, blood, gore, sexual assault (off page/implied), death, war, corrupt government structures, sexism/misogyny, cursing, and sexually explicit content.

If you feel any triggers are missing from this list, please feel free to reach out.

Be kind to yourselves.

Pronunciation Guide

Characters:

Rialey: Ray-lee

Eryx: Air-ix

Theron: Th-air-un

Caius: ky-us

Verena: ver-aye-nuh

Places:

Alphaird: Al-faird

Marmere: Mar-meer

Eirdis: Air-dis

Eirhiondus: Air-ee-on-dus

Leithaire: Lithe-air

Part One

That year, the snow came, and it did not cease.

The cold never left.

That is, not until they started lighting the fires—burning the
witches of the Waldwood forest.

Burning the magic from our world.

They wanted to conquer it all.

But unfortunately for them, witches are not so easily slain.

Chapter One

Rialey

The rage of women burns cold.

Maybe that's why the empire can't burn the witches out of existence. It's like the embers refuse to burn hot enough to suffocate the magic the kingdom fears so greatly.

Sweat slicked the back of my neck as I descended the stone steps into the palace dungeons, every careful step pulling me deeper into the darkest part of the kingdom. The jagged walls seemed to tilt inward, threatening anyone who dared enter the dungeons' depths—guards, executioners, even the king's own witch hunter. At the bottom step, I steadied myself against the wall, feeling the rough, wet scrape of stone against my calloused fingertips. The sconces cast ominous shadows through the narrow hallway.

When the clanking of keys drew my attention to the left, I shrank back against the wall. The rough stone scratched through the fabric of my clothes, marking my flesh with every shallow breath I attempted to keep quiet.

I wasn't supposed to be in the dungeons.

Not at night, anyway.

Holding my breath, I tapped into my magic, careful to only use enough to cast my illusion—to blend into the wall. I'd seen witches burn out before—spiking a fever as the well of their magic overfilled and consumed them. Tip the scales beyond exhaustion, and you'd never see King Wineslowe's pyres, but you'd burn all the same. I could not afford that fate.

I *could not* die.

I looked to the fire across from me, careful not to make a sound as it danced and taunted.

I wasn't fooled by my fleeting position of power—not in the slightest. In the kingdom of Alphaird, witches would always know fear—so beneath the suffocated moonlight in the heart of the dungeons, amidst the fires burning along the roughly carved walls, I sent up a prayer to whichever goddess would listen—hoping the king's wrath would not find me.

There were a million different reasons King Wineslowe couldn't quite rid the soil of such despicable magic, but when it came down to it, it was my belief that weak men were only masters of one thing.

Appearing more powerful than they truly were.

My heart sped up despite the departing guard as I slinked into the side hallway and into the tunnels. My boots tapped on the damp stone floors, water droplets dripping from overhead and splashing the ground.

The cells began on either side, iron bars caging every one of King Wineslowe's prisoners.

Most of them were accused of one crime alone.

Possessing magic.

I walked straight through the labyrinth of cells, the cold rage burning in my chest the entire trek to my section. Iron bars cast shadows across the floor with every sconce I passed, but the fires did little to break through the consuming darkness beyond where my footsteps landed. Although the moonlight didn't reach this far below ground, I could feel the night air against my limbs. The black tunic and pants did nothing to warm against the frigid winter.

As many times as I'd been in the dungeons, I couldn't escape the unsettling promise of creatures lurking in the dark—anxious in the pursuit to shove my secrets into the light.

I stopped, the sconces on the walls now lighting only the main tunnel. Beyond the iron bars, shadows cloaked the prisoner. I could feel her presence, though—as viscerally as the magic coursing through my blood.

Her rage was as cold as mine.

"Witch Hunter."

Her brittle voice arrived just as her face reached the light—brown hair matted to frame the sharp angles of her face. The gray tint to her pale skin—the smell of rot—all reminded me that this woman was a prisoner of the Kingdom. But nothing solidified that fact like the bone cuffs circling her wrists—keeping her magic at bay.

"Verena," I replied, a smile slashing across my face, my daggers ready and waiting in their sheaths at my belt.

"You bother to learn the prisoners' names?" she questioned. Her brown eyes hardened as she cocked her head to the side in challenge. *Good. We haven't broken her.*

"It's more rewarding," I answered, and the temperature seemed to drop.

Verena scoffed, her thin dressing gown stained and torn at the thigh. I kept my eyes elevated, refusing to look at her appearance too closely. There was no room for pity in the palace—not when I had a part to play.

"I can't imagine why you're here, Hunter," she gritted out, her chapped lips shifting as she spoke to reveal cracks painted in blood. Verena's hardened eyes traced the scar marring my left cheek, then followed in a trail to the loose black hair hanging down to my waist, the daggers strapped across my body, and the old leather boots planted on the damp, stone floors.

"Why do you say that?" I tilted my head to the side to match hers, questioning.

"They don't execute witches at night. Think we're more powerful." Her lip peeled into a snarl. "Something about the moon and our goddesses." Verena's gaze burned with anger. "Or maybe they just like to watch the fires burn with an audience."

"I'm not here to drag you to your execution."

Her chin tilted upward, and her eyes widened slightly—the only sign that what I said surprised her. She quickly smoothed her features into something more akin to bitterness. "Isn't that your job?" she asked, her tone biting.

"The one I'm known for."

Gold flashed in my vision, my body heating at the magic running through my blood. I grabbed hold of the glittering streaks, only visible to me, and molded my illusion—cloaking us in darkness. To the other prisoners—the guards—we no longer existed.

I snatched the keys from my belt, clasping the cold metal in my fist to keep them from jangling. My illusions only stretched so far—failing to mask sound or smell.

When I slipped the rusty key into the hole, I unlocked the witch's cage.

My mask slipped, the urgency pumping through my veins as I lowered my voice; the smirk falling from my lips.

"You have to be silent," I whispered. My breath misted in the frigid air, mingling with the scent of rotting flesh and death. It didn't matter how many times I did this; the panic was all the same. Sweat-slicked skin, and an anxious heart I tried hard to hide.

Verena's cell swallowed the light behind her, obstructing my view of the conditions she'd been in these past weeks. I was thankful for the small mercy of not seeing it with my eyes—the image of her gaunt and wasting away would be enough.

I shifted my focus to my purpose—my reason for sneaking into the dungeons after dark when there were no pyres to light—no witches to burn.

"Your cuffs will be removed when we get outside of the palace grounds," I began, "and a trustworthy guide will help you to the edge of the city." I kept the emotion out of my voice. It would always be better that way. I needed distance from the prisoners where I could have it.

Not everyone could be saved. Many would die.

Some by my own hand.

The corner of my mouth tugged upward—just slightly. "I hope you know how to get to the Waldwood Forest."

In the quiet of the dungeons, I could almost hear her heart beating along with mine—feel her shock as she stared at me.

Panic washed over her face, hollowing her cheeks even more than the weeks of starvation. "Won't someone see?" Verena's voice was breathless, her steps hesitant as she moved just outside her cell. Her stiff movements came slowly, muscles clearly sore and atrophied. It wouldn't serve her well, but beyond the initial escape, she wasn't my problem.

The gold seeped into my vision again, and I grabbed hold of it, my cheeks warming as I crafted an illusion, one I'd used time and time again. Verena's eyes widened as my hair turned a stark shade of white.

"You—" She didn't finish the sentence, but there was no doubt in her tone. She knew what I was.

The rattling of keys. Sharp footsteps along the floors of a darkened hall.

I whipped my head backward, clinging to my magic in the hopes we'd blend in with the dungeons.

"We have to go." I let go of the illusion coloring my hair, keeping us cocooned in our own darkness—our own protection. "Quiet steps," I warned.

Verena leaned toward me, her bare feet bloody. "What will happen when I don't show up for my execution?" she whispered as I turned to walk through the long tunnel of the dungeon. I stopped, turning my head toward her to look over my shoulder.

Water dripped from the jagged stones overhead, splashing onto the ground and keeping time with my heart pumping.

"What do you mean?" I asked.

"When I'm executed," she pressed. "How will you explain that I am not there?"

I chuckled low, cocking an eyebrow as I turned fully to face her. "They'll see exactly what they want to see." I offered. "You just worry about getting out."

Her wild eyes darted to every shadow or whispering movement of firelight. With trembling hands, the bone shackles around her wrists rattled, her lips now parted in fear. The long chain of ivory and magic connected the two cuffs and would do nothing to help her cause if she kept shaking.

Like a frightened fawn standing in the forest, she didn't step forward—didn't follow when I urged her onward.

With another echoing step from a guard off in the distance, the thread of my patience snapped. I grabbed her wrists to halt their shaking, the dripping of the dungeons splashing the scar on my cheek when I crowded her space.

She'd be her own demise if she couldn't control herself, and the near-painful grip I had on her wrist told her how pertinent it was that her demise did not happen.

"Control yourself," I hissed. My fingers tightened around her wrist until I could feel her pulse fluttering like a deer stalked by a wolf. Prey. She was prey in this kingdom—as we all were, but unless she could master her own fear, she'd be nothing but carrion left on a dungeon floor. That or ash billowing in the wind. "You walk in silence, or you don't walk at all."

Verena nodded, her bare feet padding over dirt and stone behind me.

My focus narrowed on every step—every movement toward the deepest parts of the dungeons. Darkness encircled us as I clung to my illusion, vaguely aware of the witch following, her hands now white-knuckling the ivory chains of her shackles to keep them silent.

I twisted around the corner where the ceiling pressed lower—those jagged pieces of stone hungry for blood. My heart raced as I stepped over a muddied depression on the floor, catching sight of the guard that had been prowling down the corridor, his lantern gripped in one meaty hand. His expression was a severe mask. The two swords crossed at his back stuck out over his shoulders, and I was certain those weren't the only weapons carried.

I felt for the knife strapped to my waist. When I glanced back at Verena, I could see the heightened fear in her wide eyes. The deer now caught in the sights of a true hunter.

I nodded toward the iron bars to our right, encouraging her to tuck in and pressing her back into the cold metal.

The guard wouldn't see anything aside from darkness, but he could certainly walk into one of us unknowingly.

Best we waited it out.

With my heart hammering in my chest, I closed my eyes, envisioning that golden thread, and taking hold, doing my best to cast the image of the cell we stood before. If the corridor swallowed the light from his lantern, he'd know something was wrong. This image had to be crafted carefully.

There were things the kingdom didn't know about magic, but they weren't stupid.

Verena trembled next to me, vibrating the iron bars.

I opened my eyes, giving her a warning look.

Don't, I thought, as if it would stop her.

The guard's footsteps slowed, his boots scuffing against the rough floors. His threatening chuckle matched the menacing sneer on his face when he held his lantern aloft, turning toward one of the cells.

"There's my pretty little witch," he growled, and my stomach recoiled.

It wasn't like I didn't know the horrors of the palace—the realities of guards and corrupt kingdoms.

Still. It didn't make it any easier.

I swallowed the bile in my throat, the rancid taste of it burning all the way down. I knew full well who he was leering at. It was my job to know these dungeons like the back of my hand—and sometimes I wished I had been very incompetent at my job.

"Fuck off," the woman spat, her body still cloaked in darkness. His lantern light didn't quite reach her.

When the shaking of the bars at my back turned frantic, I knew we would have to leave before anything worse could happen.

I nodded to continue, noting the skepticism in Verena's gaze. She probably wanted to be noble—wanted me to *do* something, but I was no hero. I had to pick my battles and not ponder the consequences.

We moved, my boot scuffing on the floor and drawing the attention of the guard, his lantern flashing to my carefully crafted illusion.

The predatory look in his eyes sent my heart pounding painfully in my chest. I could almost hear its rapid beating as I held my breath, praying to the gods he wouldn't walk near us.

My life hung in the balance—if I were discovered, I would not only lose my position, but I would lose my life and my ability to help prisoners escape right along with it.

My parents had died to protect me, and I'd sworn not to waste the gift I'd been given.

"What was that?" the guard asked, slowly stepping forward, using the lantern as protection.

On instinct, I reached back, clutching Verena's thin fingers in my own. Her clammy skin dampened my own, chilling like the eternal winter raging beyond the palace walls. It seemed the cold had seeped into her bones too—becoming a part of who she was.

A creature to be hunted—preyed upon—*burned*.

Squeezing, I tried to reassure her as the guard loomed closer—too close.

"Come out, Little Witch," he said, as a smile stretched across his sweat-slicked face.

When he leaned in so close, I could smell his breath—taste it. Bloodlust and foul liquor made me want to gag, and I leaned back.

Don't get any closer.

Verena tugged gently at my hand, but I didn't move, closing my eyes and holding that golden thread as a lifeline.

"Hm," he said, turning back to the cell he'd been tormenting.

We didn't stay long enough to learn what would become of that witch. I simply nodded, urging Verena forward. Keeping her hand grasped in mine, we moved like ghosts through the dungeons—phantoms haunting the halls with memories of the kingdom's darkness and hatred burned like a brand into our souls.

Chapter Two

Eryx

S he was late.

CHAPTER THREE

RIALEY

The long-forgotten cell tucked at the end of a narrow hallway in the dungeons provided easy access to the tunnels beneath the palace.

As Verena and I made our way beneath the palace grounds, slowly creeping toward the old door that would lead us to the sewers beneath the city, I couldn't stop thinking about the witch still locked in the palace—forced to sacrifice her body and life for whatever the Kingdom of Alphaird wanted.

When they chose me as the king's executioner two years ago, I'd entered the running with one thought in my head. *Fight. Survive.*

I hadn't realized the horrors I'd see in the years following—hadn't understood that watching King Wineslowe's soldiers run through my entire village would only be the beginning.

There was no escaping the prison of Marmere's palace—not for me, anyway.

My stomach recoiled, nausea making me feel uneasy as we prowled toward our destination. Verena's fervent shaking rattled the bone chains between her wrists, her teeth chattering when greeted with the cold's embrace.

I didn't bother halting her hands, didn't spit warnings at her about the sounds she was making. With my illusion gone, the hum of my magic settled beneath my skin. We would not need to be hidden when we were the only two souls surrounded by darkness.

I held the lantern aloft to light the tunnel ahead, noting the long crack across the ceiling that signaled the end of our walk.

Eryx would surely wait for us on the other side.

Looking at Verena now, I noted how frail she appeared. Two months in the dungeons had whittled her down to nothing. Her feet were still bare; blood and dirt streaked over the thin skin there.

I looked up to catch her gaze, brown eyes wide with what appeared to be fear and the subtle spark of hope.

"What gave you away?" I asked, keeping pace.

She blinked, long lashes dusting her pale cheeks. "What do you mean?"

I smirked, one corner of my mouth turning upward—the expression gentler now that we were out of the dungeons. "How did they know you were a witch?" I asked. "When the hunters brought you in, they said you'd been working in a tavern when they caught you using magic. How did they find out?" I leaned closer to her. "What did you do?"

Her jaw clenched, the furious chattering ceasing as she gripped the chains at her wrists. The quiet overwhelmed us as Verena's gaze hardened. "Used my magic on the wrong man," she admitted before her eyes hit the stone wall of the tunnel, and her hands released the chains—her teeth chattering once more.

I nodded, saying nothing else as we made it to the hidden door.

Setting the lantern down, I thought about that damn witch again, trying my best to forget about it. I fumbled with the lock on the door, pushing as the metal groaned before we crawled through the small circle leading to a dark corner of the sewers.

My boot hit the wet floor, and I winced, thinking about Verena's bare feet behind me, trekking through human waste and gods knew what.

We ascended the iron ladder, and gold flashed in my vision as I held onto my magic, cloaking us in darkness while I pushed up on the sewer grate.

The city of Marmere became more ominous at night. A light dusting of snow decorated the narrow, cobbled streets. Most of the lanterns had been put out, keeping us hidden in the shadows.

I gripped Verena's hand to pull her up and into the alleyway, slowly covering our access to the sewers before nodding toward the small alcove tucked between buildings.

A seed of doubt gnawed in my stomach as the moon peeked through the clouds overhead. Eryx had waited at least an hour for our arrival. I'd never been *this* late before, and despite everything I knew of Eryx, I didn't know where his limits were.

Relief washed over me when I saw him waiting in the shadows. His hood was pulled low, his face shielded by a black cover save for his blue eyes—deep like the ocean's depths.

I'd never seen more of him than that—didn't know what his life looked like in the light. Yet, I knew him. You couldn't watch someone treat the kingdom's condemned with such quiet kindness night after night without glimpsing their soul.

"You're here," I whispered before reaching to grab Verena's bicep to drag her forward. Her feet dug into the dirty street, causing her step forward to stutter. I closed my eyes and inhaled deeply before looking at her—the fear plain in every tense muscle of her thin body.

Eryx was here—he waited.

"It's okay," I said. "He's a friend."

Eryx looked her over, eyes pausing on every scratch, nick, or bruise painting her skin. I could see his wince, as if he, too, imagined the horrors the witch had endured. There was compassion there—not pity, but something gentler. It was the kind of gaze that made you feel understood. His eyes caught on her feet, now worse off than they'd been before.

"I couldn't get boots this time." He looked at me, and my heart ached. She'd walked all this way—spent months in the dungeons, and now we were releasing her through the streets just to abandon her at the edge of the city with no shoes and tattered clothes.

"Fine," I said, setting the lantern down and holding my magic to keep us cocooned in darkness.

I knelt on the stone, my black breeches doing little to soften the rough scrape of the street and the cool dusting of snow that seeped into the fabric. My hands worked the laces of my boots until I could shuck them off, dropping them at Verena's feet. "They might be too big," I admitted, knowing I was at least three inches taller than the witch. "Better than too small, I suppose."

I looked at Eryx, my socked feet now soaked with cold dampness. I supposed it was better than the snow that typically covered the kingdom—the snow Verena would find in the Waldwood forest to the north.

She needed the shoes more than I did.

"Did you at least get a cloak?" I asked.

Eryx reached behind him, lifting the thick black fabric from the small bench in the alcove, and handed it to Verena.

"You really should trust me more," Eryx scolded. His eyes crinkled at the corner—amused.

"I trust you plenty," I admitted. The words felt like a confession. Of all those surrounding me in the palace, Eryx was the one I trusted the most.

Pitiful, but I couldn't risk anyone else knowing my secrets.

Verena gripped the cloak in her chained hands, brows furrowed. "I can't put this on."

Eryx chuckled, digging in his pocket, before placing the bone key into the hole of her cuffs. I watched, knowing the key he used came from the same animal they'd killed to bind her. It was the only way cuffs like that would open.

Old witch magic—the kind that someone who didn't have magic coursing through their blood could replicate.

It made my stomach churn knowing the Kingdom was willing to use all they hated about us to hunt us down and kill us.

The chains released, bone cuffs hitting the cobblestones with a hollow sound as Verena made quick work of the cloak.

Eryx looked at my feet, then at me. "You're going to walk like that?" he asked.

"*She* walked like that already. I'm sure I'll be fine."

Small crinkles formed at the corners of his eyes again, the only sign he was smiling. "What will you do if you get stopped in the palace without shoes?"

I grabbed hold of my magic, the warming sensation pleasant against the cold as the illusion of shoes appeared at my feet. Cocking a brow, I smirked. "Like I said, I'll be fine."

Eryx chuckled before glancing at the sky, the threat of dawn taunting us. "We should go," he said before picking the bone cuffs off the ground. He held them out, my fingers brushing his. Despite the gloves shielding his skin, I could feel the warmth there—the *something* inside of him that made his convictions match my own. It was the very thing that propelled him to action—the thing that made Eryx get the witches out of the city.

I looked away from the cuffs, nodding once at Verena before turning to make my way back to the sewers.

Shit and piss-soaked my socks completely by the time I got to the tunnels.

As I entered the dungeons, I padded slowly through the darkness, passing cells filled with the withering accused.

A broad figure appeared before me, so large he took up the entire hallway, almost blocking the light from his lantern.

He turned slowly, a wicked smile on his face as he looked at me. "Miss Rialey," he said, my name on his lips making my skin crawl. Glancing down at my feet, his brow furrowed before he looked back up.

My magic warmed my skin.

"I didn't even hear you walk up behind me," he said, smirking.

I chuckled, resting my hand on the hilt of my dagger. "Well," I started, smiling sweetly. "Easier to be quiet when you're smaller."

His eyes lit like a predator spotting its prey. "Of course."

I could almost hear his voice earlier, the taunting hidden beneath his words. The *little witch* made my chest burn with frigid anger as my gaze flicked to his chest, the spot where his heart pumped blood through his veins.

The slide of my dagger from its sheath hummed against my skin, and I lunged, shoving the blade upward until it made contact with his chest. I pushed past the resistance until the cracking of bone and squelching of flesh satisfied my bitterness. Holding firm, I braced myself against his large form, relishing in the shock painted over his features—the echo of his gargling breaths against the stone walls just before his eyes glazed over.

I made quick work of removing the belt at his waist and wrapping it beneath his arms, grunting as I yanked the buckle as tight as I could manage. I gripped the leather at his back and heaved, my breath coming out in harsh pants as his body slid against the dirty dungeon floors.

My muscles ached as I dragged his body through the dungeons, opening iron bars to an unlocked cell and pulling him into the depths of the darkest corner—the corner right next to the sleeping woman in the cell over.

The *little witch*—barely nineteen—knelt in the dirt, tears cutting paths through the grime on her bronze skin.

I blinked, catching my breath as I watched her—the guard's lifeless form slumped next to my feet.

When I found my way back to my rooms, dawn had broken over the horizon.

I scrubbed my skin, changing into a new set of leathers, and found an old pair of boots tucked at the back of my wardrobe.

When I laced them up from the chair in the corner next to my window, a knock sounded on the door of my bedroom just before a plump figure entered the room.

"Visha," I said to the middle-aged woman who entered the room with a fresh set of linens.

She smiled first, before the expression dropped when she glanced at my bed. The sheets were untouched from yesterday; the image pulling her lips into a frown.

"Did you even sleep?" she asked, her tone biting.

In terms of palace help, Visha was my favorite. During my two years at the palace, she'd been a constant, taking requests and tidying my rooms throughout the day.

Despite that, she didn't know what I was. No one in the palace did. It would be too dangerous to divulge such information, risking the very thing I spent my time doing. In fact, the only soul that knew about my magic was Eryx.

"Restless night," I answered, tying the lace of my second boot. "Anyway," I began, "Can you get a new pair of leather boots ordered for me? The quicker that can be done, the better."

Visha glanced at my feet, noting the worn leather, the hole in the side of my left boot, and the way one sole pulled away at the heel. "Remarkable," she said. "How long did this pair last? A month?"

I chuckled before standing, grabbing my cleaned dagger and sheathing it at my waist.

"Give or take."

Visha nodded, her light hair framing her soft features as she placed the fresh linens on the nightstand. "I'll be sure to have that done, Miss Rialey." She set to work stripping the bed, and I glanced out the window. The city square came into view beneath the rising sun. In the center, the pyres loomed in the distance, unlit and waiting.

When I left, I felt the aching of my muscles and the burning in my chest as I prepared to light the fires.

Fires that would burn a witch who did not exist.

As far as I was concerned, Verena was gone.

Chapter Four

Theron

The town square bustled with excitement and nervous energy, voices rising in fevered whispers. The glowing fires flickered in the distance, bright against the overcast sky stretching out over the city of Marmere. The acrid scent of pitch and kindling curdled my stomach, but I tamped it down.

I adjusted my collar; the nerves making my skin feel too tight, my mind racing.

Lord Renwick's balcony hovered at the south side of the town square; stone railings intricately carved to detail kings of the past. If I were being honest, Renwick merely longed to flaunt the gold that lined his coffers and impress my father by giving up the space for royal spectating. And King Wineslowe certainly loved to spectate.

Especially when his kingdom was burning witches.

"You were late this morning."

I turned as the door clicked shut behind my father. His spiked crown rested atop his hair, a mix of black and grey slicked back and hitting just above his shoulders.

He certainly looked the part of a king, cold and menacing—an imposing presence even around his son.

Clearing my throat, I folded my hands behind my back, straightened my posture, and bowed ever so slightly. "Apologies," I muttered. "I've not been sleeping well as of late, but I assure you, I've asked the palace healers to provide a tonic that may remedy the situation."

His brows hung low, a permanent frown painted on his lips as he scowled at me—clearly displeased. "You still suffer from nightmares."

It wasn't a question. In a moment of weakness, I'd admitted to my father that taking part in the witch hunts to the north of our kingdom had given me dreams too nefarious to repeat.

He'd called me weak then, and thought me weak now. I was sure of it.

"I will not be late again," I offered, hoping it would placate him.

King Wineslowe grunted, moving toward the throne of black velvet and gold that he occupied once a week at these burnings. When he sat, he folded his hands across his lap, gazing out at the crowds gathering around the pyres.

"You should wear your crown, Theron. You are the prince of this realm, after all." His low voice, rough like gravel, made my muscles tense.

"In the future, I will remember to dress more appropriately." My hands were still clasped at my back as I watched my father's executioner, Rialey Dagon, appear riding along a horse-drawn cart that had entered the square. Her braided hair hung down her back, brow furrowed in concentration as she walked to the back of the cart and yanked the lock from the latch.

Employed by my father for two years, Rialey was fierce, if not somewhat of a mystery.

My father offered rooms in the palace in exchange for her services. While he deemed the provisions far beyond necessary, he'd been convinced that offering luxury would ensure loyalty; especially to a woman who had no title to her name. She did, however, have access to training rooms, fine linens, clothing, and whatever delicacies the palace kitchens had to offer.

It was a luxurious life in exchange for burning the witches taken prisoner by my father.

We watched as she escorted a resigned figure from the cart, her grip rough on the woman's arm, pulling her toward the blazing fires.

The authorities took in the witch after an incident at a local tavern, where they caught her using her magic against one of my father's guards. She'd sat for two months in the dungeons beneath the palace, knowing her fate. There were no trials for witches in our kingdom, only the promise of death.

"A dungeon guard has gone missing," my father interrupted, drawing my attention back to where he sat perched on his makeshift throne.

I raised a brow, feigning interest in the story he was likely to tell me. I did not care for the dungeon guards. In fact, I did not care for the palace dungeons at all.

"Shouldn't be a problem." My father grunted, shifting in his seat. "Weakness is not rewarded under my rule." His blue eyes were pointed when his gaze met mine, eyes so like my own—hardened and swimming with malicious intent.

"Of course," I responded, nodding before returning my gaze to the dark-haired woman practically dragging the body of a witch up the steps. The stone structure had been built for this very purpose, elevated above the flames so that once at the top, witches could be tossed to the fire, their magic burned like the outer edges of the Waldwood forest at the start of my father's reign.

He'd tried to burn it all, but the magic had been stronger.

His only accomplishment being the eradication of their queen—her execution.

According to the witches, one could only be chosen by their gods, and no such thing had happened in my lifetime.

My father believed he had won.

When Rialey got to the top, she snarled something in the woman's ear, her brown hair matted at the back of her head, slightly shorter than I remembered it being upon her arrival to the dungeons. My head cocked to the side, watching as Rialey pushed her forward, her feet losing their bearings on the stone structure.

When the witch fell onto the fire, I looked away. My jaw clenched until my teeth ached, stomach churning with discomfort as the scent of charred flesh and magic permeated the air. Bile rose in my throat, the copper tang of blood coating my tongue.

I need a distraction, something to ease the discomfort slicing through me like a sharpened blade.

I looked toward my father, schooling my expression the way I'd been taught my entire life. "The girl," I began. "Your executioner. Will she be in attendance next month?"

I chose my words carefully, knowing that if I revealed too much, my father's wrath would find me. I could not show interest in the woman, could not show that I knew anything about her at all, even after she'd lived in my home for two years.

My father's scowl deepened. "In attendance of what?" he asked. "The ball?" He chuckled, a sharp and vicious sound that made my back straighten. "You are meant to pick a *wife*, Theron. While I give that bitch what she asks for in exchange for her services to the kingdom, she'd make no wife for you. This interest in her is misplaced."

"Forgive me," I said, tipping my chin downward. I fought the urge to run a pale hand through the blond strands on my head, hoping they were not too mussed from my *activities* prior to this attendance—the reason for my tardiness. "I merely asked out of curiosity. Her status is valued by the kingdom, and I believe it pertinent to keep her comfortable as she is adequate at her job." I gripped the fingers behind my back tightly—the sensation nearing pain. "You, of course, know that I am considering Renwick's daughter as well as the other from the east."

Each major city in Alphaird had a lord to rule over it. My father, often busy with policies that encompassed the entire kingdom, insisted he did not have time for civil debates among commoners. He would pass those responsibilities and any he found unfavorable off to the men he'd hand-picked for the lordship.

"Bloodbane's daughter?" my father scoffed. "That girl is far too old, Theron."

"She is twenty-eight, same as myself, is she not?"

My father tapped a finger on the golden arm of his chair, his nose wrinkling in disgust. "Bloodbane's daughter is your age, yes, but you know how these things work. She's far too old to be married off to royalty. Better to consider Renwick and his kin. He's done far more for the kingdom than Bloodbane."

I didn't have it in me to emphasize that Renwick spent his time betraying all in the name of my father to hold his position. He was not a useful lord unless sucking my father's metaphorical cock was the only requirement.

I also had no interest in his daughter or marriage. Though I'd never admit that to Wineslowe.

"I will consider what you've said when choosing who to dance with." I turned, the tension keeping my body stiff, made worse by the chilling breeze that swirled around the balcony.

"As for the executioner," my father began again, "I may consider extending the invitation. You are correct in your thoughts. She should be kept happy as she has contributed to the eradication of much of the kingdom's vermin." He sighed. "Of course, the poor bitch would require a dress. We've plenty to spare." He shifted again in his chair, straightening as the shouting died down from below, the crowd parting now that there were no more witches to burn. A light day, I supposed.

My father grunted. "She will attend," he decided before waving a hand in my direction. "You are dismissed, Theron. Go take a ride on that expensive horse of yours or find a book to occupy your time in the library. Whatever you do, do not produce a bastard heir before you've chosen a wife." His gaze slid to mine, knowing and cruel. "And don't be late again."

"Yes, Father."

I turned on my heel, my body aching as I descended the steps of Renwick's large home, a castle, really, praying to any god that would listen that Renwick's daughter would be nowhere on the premises.

As luck would have it, she was not. Giving me the freedom to return to the palace.

Chapter Five

Verena

My lungs burned, breaths rattling in and out as the cold air stole all feeling from my limbs.

I hadn't gotten the name of the man who escorted me out of the city of Marmere—or maybe I'd just forgotten. I'd struggled to keep my mind right, desperately trying to hang onto whatever pieces of sanity I still had. My vision vacillated between reality and the dreams and images that plagued me in the palace dungeons. The forest, once a comfort to me and my magic, felt as if it were haunted by shadows—vicious villains lurking in the dark and eager to see me dead.

With boots too large for my feet, I trudged through thick, powdery snow. The sharp sting of wind bit at my fingers like razor-sharp teeth, the frigid chill seeping its way through the threadbare wool, into my bones, until my teeth chattered.

I felt weak.

Half alive.

Calling to the memory of those cursed bone cuffs hitting the ground, I attempted to feel the gentle pulse of my magic, low and simmering—barely a flicker.

My hand scratched against the rough bark of a bare tree as I allowed myself the briefest pause. Snow started falling around me, glittering despite the long stretch of overcast sky. There was no end to the oppressive cloud cover, and I couldn't help but imagine it stretched to the far reaches of the kingdom—an omen of darkness.

Closing my eyes, I breathed deeply, trying to find enough of my magic to bring some comfort. I didn't know how I'd make it to the Waldwood forest—not like this, anyway.

There was nothing—not a glimmer of the power I once held as it finally left me completely. It wasn't as if that power had served me well back in Marmere, but the little I'd had felt like a lifeline—even when it had gotten me into trouble.

I'd been careless in that tavern—made too many mistakes when handling the miserable guard who'd fallen asleep in the corner. Anger had burrowed its way beneath my skin, driving me into action—into danger.

He'd been handsy and forward—drunk, I supposed. And I was hurting. It wasn't difficult to place my tray on the bar top—to reach into the depths of my being and dredge up the magic that allowed me access to the sleeping man's mind.

Revenge tasted sweet until I realized there was no hope for a woman like me. A witch. I was cursed to begin with. No amount of power or retaliation would change the opinions of evil men.

He'd awoken, eyes locked with mine across the room, a hardened and knowing sharpness to his dark gaze.

I forced myself forward, glancing at the treeline for any hint of life. I knew where I was headed—mostly.

Maybe if I'd been more careful, like the witch hunter, they wouldn't have thrown me into the dungeons.

The witch hunter. Another person whose name I was unfamiliar with, despite owing her a life debt.

She'd made her magic clear. Of the three types of witch magic, she'd controlled the color of her dark hair shining in the dim light of the dungeon. I could still remember the hope that flickered in my chest as the black strands shifted to a brilliant white before my eyes—white like the snow underfoot.

Powerful. Her magic was certainly powerful, though not so much as the dream-walking magic I possessed. My chest ached at the realization that *I* was powerful.

At least, I used to be.

Parted from the Waldwood, we all settled for a permanently weakened state, but adding the fact that I'd been kept in the dungeons?

My magic felt like barely a whisper.

And after trekking alone in the wilderness outside of Maremere?

There was nothing left.

I stumbled over a snow-covered log, my limbs sore and aching despite the soft padding of snow. My feet were bleeding in the witch hunter's boots, but I'd long since forgotten how that felt with the cold numbing my flesh.

When I looked up, my arms shook as I knelt on all fours in the forest's late afternoon light. A shadow appeared overhead, and my gaze flicked upward as an owl descended onto a bare branch—watching with curiosity as I felt my body fading.

I took a deep breath, thankful for another small break. My heart pounded slowly, a steady rhythm reminding me I was, in fact, alive.

The pyres were lit earlier in the day—or yesterday. I couldn't remember how long it had been since I had left the city. All I knew was that King Wineslowe didn't get the chance to throw me on the flames and burn me alive, and for that, I was grateful.

A spark of something flickered in my chest—something I'd avoided for the last two months.

Hope.

Pushing off the ground, I trekked onward, wandering through the forest. This wasn't the Waldwood. There was no magic buzzing beneath the soil. The trees merely swayed in the breeze, with bleak creaking sounds echoing from their branches.

My vision narrowed, dark spots forming on the very edges of my sight, and I knew I wouldn't make it any further without stopping to rest—to recover.

Looking through the trees again, I longed to find a sign of what I was looking for—the cottage I knew sat amid these trees—my saving grace.

I knew she'd help—she had to.

The only problem was that my vision became slower to return, and I barely felt the cold anymore. What good was it if the witch hunter risked her life for my escape, and I didn't make it to the Waldwood? I could lie down in the snow now and rest for a while until my sight came back.

The chill of winter would surround me as the snow continued to fall, burying me until the earth swallowed me up.

I knelt, the idea so tempting it overwhelmed me. It could all be over, and maybe then, the pain of my past would disappear. The forest could eat my magic, or whatever was left of it. Satisfied with the power of a dreamwalker, the trees may become part of the Waldwood forest. I'm sure the ground would be thankful for the magic of a witch who could enter the minds of the slumbering.

I looked up, gasping as I saw the faint stretch of smoke in the distance. Standing, I propelled myself forward as my lungs burned and my legs shook. I was pushing my frail body past its limits.

The world swayed before I'd even made it a few steps, my vision swimming as tears pricked my eyes, threatening to fall onto frozen cheeks.

My voice was breathless—weak.

"Keep going," I whispered, urging my failing body forward. "Keep moving."

I chanted, even as I felt the snow pad my landing. The thought remained even when I let my head settle in the cold, the smoke a mere memory.

Maybe I was right. The forest *did* want to swallow me up.

Keep moving. Keep moving. Don't give up, Verena. Keep moving.

I closed my eyes, my vision darkening as I sucked in a final icy breath.

The snow was gentle—kind and welcoming as it begged me to give myself up to the forest.

An icy tear stung my cheek before everything went numb.

That last spark of hope flickering out.

Chapter Six

Eryx

I clutched the boots in my hand, the new leather stiff as I watched the door from a chair in the corner, my pulse hammering in my throat. From the chair in the corner, I tucked myself deep in shadow, every creak in the wood outside the door making my muscles coil tighter.

My gloved hand rose to my face, ensuring my eyes were still the only visible feature as my heart pounded. If I were caught in her rooms—if anyone else walked through the—

The door clicked open, Rialey tugging at the leather piece around her braid and running her fingers through the soft strands to separate it. The black hair fell like a curtain around her just before her gaze met mine.

She gasped, her hand drawing the dagger from her belt before I could blink. With precision, she threw the dagger straight for my head as I leaned to the side. The blade buried itself into the wood around the fireplace at my back.

I lifted the boots, one corner of my mouth turning up beneath my mask.

It had been a risk entering this part of the palace the way I had. I didn't mind, though. Somehow, when Rialey Dagon was present, I felt the desire for rebellion tug at my chest.

My smile widened, though I was certain she couldn't see it as I wiggled the boots suspended in the air. "I brought you these."

CHAPTER SEVEN

RIALEY

"How did you get in here?"

I tugged my dagger free from the wood and sheathed it at my waist, the fear slowly dissolving as I watched Eryx stand from the chair. The boots he'd brought now sat on the ground, and my eyes flicked from the black leather to his deep blue gaze.

The sun had set, moonlight seeping into my bedroom from the window behind him. He'd never been in my room before, though I didn't have much to my name when I'd come here—nothing I could bring that wouldn't reveal me to be exactly what King Wineslowe loathed. A mahogany wardrobe stood as tall as the four-poster bed; all matching with simple carvings. The lantern flickered in the corner, the fire in the hearth crackling and casting him in a gentle orange glow.

I frowned. "And I am fully capable of securing new boots for myself."

He glanced at my feet, clearly unimpressed by the old pair. "I can see that," he said, his voice light. "Those boots look just as fine as the ones you gave to the girl. How dare I risk my life to deliver a nicer pair."

I fumbled with the buckle of my belt, dropping it onto the untouched bed along with my dagger. My body ached, exhaustion pulling at my muscles and begging me to lie down. "Risking my life too," I pointed out as I knelt to unlace the old pair of boots.

"Isn't that what we do?" he asked. "I'm not putting you in any more danger than you already put yourself in."

He wasn't wrong.

I shucked off my boots, my arm brushing his when I passed him to look at the pair he'd brought.

Supple leather, well-made, and clearly expensive, I ran my finger along the side. There wasn't much I knew about Eryx as it pertained to his life outside of what we were doing.

This was the first time he'd been in my room.

"Thank you," I muttered, my eyes connecting with his.

My chest tightened as he stared at me. Whatever possessed him to buy these—

If he bought them, that is.

"Well," he began, folding his hands across his chest. "Try them on. See if they fit."

I sat on the chair he'd occupied when I entered the room, eagerly stuffing my socked feet into the new shoes. When I worked the laces, I glanced upward. "You never answered me," I said. "How did you get in here? How did you even know which rooms were mine?"

"Same way you get the witches out, I imagine." The smirk was evident in the way he spoke, and for the briefest moment, I longed to see it. Eryx and I had spent the better part of a year getting the witches out of the city. One hundred twenty-three witches, to be exact. I blinked up at him, wishing I could know what he looked like—who he was.

The nature of my job required secrecy. I couldn't risk being discovered, and I certainly couldn't risk condemning myself to the same fate—not when I had the power to help. While I was still on a leash, my leash was longer, and I intended to use that in any way I could.

It wasn't a far stretch to want to know *something* about him. Despite our distance, Eryx was the one soul in this wretched kingdom that knew the truth. Somehow, he knew more about me than anyone I interacted with daily, and that I didn't know him in the same way felt cruel—lonely.

He shifted where he stood; the firelight flickering around him, warming my room from the cold and bitter night. "And as for knowing which rooms were yours? I have my ways."

"Very specific."

I stood. Testing the fit as nerves spiked in my blood. Any of the palace staff could walk through the door unknowing. And what would they think if they found him here? Masked, dressed in black, and carrying weapons, Eryx's presence would be questioned. It wasn't safe.

"You shouldn't be here," I said, my voice more hushed.

Glancing around the room, I couldn't help the way worry crawled into my chest, making its home in the rapid beating of my heart. Eryx couldn't get caught here. And how would he get out? Through the window? How did he even get this far into the palace, to begin with?

"Why?" he asked, his tone still light. He looked around, making a show of his perusal. "Is there a lover somewhere in these rooms I should be aware of?"

My frown deepened. "I'm being serious."

"As am I." Eryx uncrossed his arms, clearing his throat as he clasped his hands at his back, quickly undoing the motion and walking to the corner of the room to run a gloved finger over the carvings of my wardrobe. "I'm actually here for a reason," he admitted, his back still towards me.

I stood still as he made himself busy, his boots scuffing on the stone floor when he moved and took in the paintings hanging on the far wall.

Clearing my throat, I stepped forward just as he made it to my nightstand, gently touching the handle of the top drawer. Withdrawing a hand, he turned, all humor leaving his blue gaze.

"I won't be available for a while," he began, his hands now clasped behind his back once more. "I have responsibilities to attend to over the next month. Unpleasant, but necessary."

I nodded, my chest tightening. Guilt swarmed in the pit of my stomach, weighing me down until I felt as if I could hardly breathe. If Eryx couldn't help, there was little I could do.

Alone, I had only so much power. My magic could only do so much, and despite the way bile rose in my throat, I knew I would have to shove it down. Witches would die.

He had to know that.

"Okay," I said, nearly a whisper. There was no sense in begging him.

Eryx exhaled long and low, the stiffness of his stance washing away with the release. He stood more casually—naturally when his eyes found mine. "I'm sorry," he said, hurt evident in the gentle rasp woven into his voice.

His apology—the sincerity of it—didn't stop the sting. I couldn't blame him, of course, but as I thought back on the face of the witch I'd seen just one night prior, my heart ached.

"I understand," I said, forcing a weak smile to my lips.

The fire crackled, moonlight sprawling over the floors of my room, a reminder that Eryx was somewhere he very much did not belong.

"Thank you, again." I wiggled my foot. "For the boots I mean. Your thievery must be rather impressive." My smile turned more genuine. "I'm sure you have created quite the name for yourself in the city of Marmere."

Eryx chuckled, nodding in agreement. "You are right, though. I *should* go. We can't be caught."

I nodded, glancing from the door to the window and wondering how he would leave—how he got here, to begin with, and if a pair of boots was really worth risking his life.

I turned, my eyes burning as I thought about what I would have to do—the witches I would have to kill in his absence.

The tears trickled down my cheeks as I knelt and worked at the laces of my new boots—boots I didn't deserve, as the warm firelight flickered from the hearth, I'd sacrificed my morality to have.

Warmth kissed my back as his presence moved closer, his body a shadow blocking out the firelight. "Rialey," he whispered, his tone soft. It almost made it worse.

Tomorrow, I would harden myself. Tomorrow I would deal with the fate I'd carved.

I didn't speak; the pain slicing as I hastened to the other shoe, his body still looming over me. For a moment, I thought he'd touch me—step closer and offer the comfort I wished to receive from the only person who knew the truth about me.

Instead, the warmth disappeared. I closed my eyes, expecting to find him across the room when I opened them, but when I stood, Eryx was gone.

Chapter Eight

Verena

I blinked slowly, the crackling of a fire making my head pound.

My stomach felt hollow, lips cracked and peeling painfully as my blurred vision came into focus. The small cottage boasted of dried herbs and warmth. Bathed in light from the fire, the entire room had been decorated with plush blankets and blankets knitted from fine wool. Cords held the thick curtains open to reveal the depths of the night outside.

Moonlight reflected on the fallen snow, now deeper than when I had been wandering the woods alone. I squinted, trying to clear my vision as I wondered how long I'd been asleep while the world buried itself in deep winter.

I felt the blankets covering my body and realized someone had put me in a clean nightgown, one without rips and stains from the palace dungeons. When I pushed against the mattress, trying to get a better look at where I had ended up, my head spun. I shut my eyes against the harsh pain at my temples, lying back on the pillows and listening to the steaming kettle that sounded over the fire in the hearth.

A chilled breeze entered the room, followed by a slam of the door on the other side of the one-room cottage. That cold brought back memories of the snow—the overwhelming urge to lie down and dissolve into the earth forever.

"Damnit."

I blinked, watching as a man plowed through the room, grabbing a towel from a wooden hutch set by the small kitchen. He gripped the kettle's handle beneath the towel and placed it on the butcher block surface of a long table in the corner.

His dark hair had been shaved short, and stubble dusted his jaw. He was shorter than the man who had led me out of the city, a darker complexion, too.

My hands fisted the sheets, nerves coursing through my blood. If I had to escape, I didn't know if my body would fail me again, so I remained quiet as I watched him.

His fingers fumbled as he procured a cup hanging overhead and then tapped each jar from the hutch as if assessing exactly what he'd need.

Herbs, I assumed.

When I slowly brought my hand to my chest, feeling the beating of my heart, I breathed in slowly. Tears threatened the corners of my eyes as I realized what that pulse meant.

I survived.

"You're awake."

The deep voice startled me, and I gripped the sheets again, pulling them higher up my body as if it could produce a barrier between me and the man. My throat felt dry as I stared at him, taking in the way his brows lowered, concern drawing a vertical line on his forehead. He turned and grabbed another cup.

When his fingers pinched at the herbs in the jar, the door sounded again, a short woman carrying a bundle of logs as she looked around the room.

"Not that, Caius," she scolded, looking between me and the man. "The girl has been out for a day and a half; she's going to need a different blend."

The woman dropped the logs by the door, letting them tumble to the ground before hurrying to the jars in the hutch, selecting one with sure fingers and passing it to the man.

Caius, I thought.

Her umber skin matched that of the man in the room, though the subtle wrinkles around her eyes informed me she was older. When her dark eyes pinned mine, I couldn't look away. My throat was still dry, refusing to cooperate as I tried to speak.

"Who—" The word barely left my lips, rasping and unfamiliar as I attempted to sit up again, fighting the pain slashing through my skull.

"Careful," the woman warned, scurrying to the bedside to place gentle hands beneath my shoulders.

I flinched despite the care she took in helping me sit up, moving the pillows so I could lean against them.

My head pounded, and I closed my eyes, trying to bring myself to the present. Normally, I'd be more cautious. I'd make a plan of escape. The kingdom of Alphaird was not kind to witches, and I'd spent years hidden in the city of Marmere, avoiding detection. I couldn't muster the energy to do the same here. I was far too weak.

"Here," Caius handed the woman a cup, and she took it graciously, pushing it toward my dry lips.

"You'll need to drink something. Eat something too." Her dark gaze softened when I flinched away from the tea. "Now, stop that," she scolded, but there was no true bite to her words. "We're not in the habit of burning witches around here, and you're not in a position to question us. Drink up."

My gaze hardened as I raised my stiff arms to grip the cup, bringing it to my lips and drinking down the bitter liquid. The tea coated my throat, easing some of the dryness as they watched me. Caius stood with his own cup in one large hand, his dark eyes curious as they roved over my face.

"Didn't think to make me a cup, Caius?" the woman said.

He chuckled, turning away to return to the kettle. "Sincerest apologies, grandmother. I was a bit distracted when I realized our guest had awakened."

The woman tsked, looking over the fire where a cast iron pot remained hanging next to where the kettle had been. "Stew should be done soon," she said before looking back at me. "I'd take it slow, though. You don't want to overdo it."

I nodded, lowering the cup and holding it on my lap. The cup warmed my hands, the tea soothing my throat enough that when I spoke again, it sounded less strained. "Who are you?" I finally asked.

The woman smiled again, warm and welcoming, just like their little cottage tucked away in the woods. "Ahvi," she said. "And that's my grandson, Caius. He's the one who found you nearly two days ago. Brought you back here with skin as cold as ice."

I nodded, looking at the nightgown and thumbing the cream-colored fabric. My stomach knotted up with discomfort.

Ahvi chuckled. "Now that," she began, "was my doing. No need to worry there, Dear." She patted my hand gently, her skin warm despite the time she'd spent outside.

Walking to the door, Ahvi gathered the firewood and brought it near the hearth, carefully throwing another log on the flames before checking the stew.

Caius leaned against the long table by the wall beneath the teacups, his dark eyes still staring at me as I shifted beneath his curious inspection.

Looking away, I took another sip of tea. "How did you know I was a witch?" I asked.

"I'm not one, myself," said Ahvi, "but I'm no fool."

I nodded again, assuming my question had confirmed her suspicions. If she wasn't certain before, she certainly was now.

"Where were you headed?"

The low voice startled me, and I looked up to see Caius still sipping on the tea as his grandmother prepared the soup, gathering bowls from the hutch, and dipping a ladle into the food.

"I—" I cleared my throat, the action near painful. I debated lying, but there was no use. I thought myself dead before—what were a few more days. "The Waldwood," I answered.

"Quite the trek." Caius set the cup down, gathering two bowls before he moved to the chair near the bed. He set one bowl on the nightstand and gently gathered the cup of tea I'd been nursing, his fingers brushing mine as he did. When he set the cup down, he handed me the bowl of soup. "You won't make it that far north like this."

I dipped the spoon into the stew, moving a potato around the broth. "I should be fine."

Ahvi chuckled from the corner, but Caius kept staring at me, his face a serious mask as he studied me. "Unlikely," he remarked.

"You're welcome to stay as long as you like, Dear." Ahvi gathered her own bowl, sitting at the small table in the center of the room. "The Waldwood will be there. Not even King Wineslowe could burn her down, so I assume those trees will stand another day."

I brought the spoon to my lips, the salty stew soothing the groaning emptiness in my gut. I swallowed it down, gathering another spoonful and swallowing that down, too.

Caius watched, picking at his own dinner next to me.

Nausea struck me suddenly, souring the soup in my stomach. I nearly tossed the bowl on the nightstand, leaning over the bed to expel the little bit of food I'd consumed.

My vomit covered the ground, splattering up onto Caius's boots.

He didn't stand, just placed his own bowl next to mine, and sighed. "Tea it is, then," he said, handing me a rag and my cup. Standing, he dug in a bin below the long table in the corner and brought a bucket to the bedside as well as other supplies.

My face flushed after I wiped my mouth. I sipped on the tea again, watching as the strange man knelt—cleaning the mess from the worn hardwood floors.

Chapter Nine

Rialey

When I had found myself employed by the king, I stopped going into the city of Marmere. Aside from the executions, I had isolated myself in the palace. Especially after I had tried to get my first witch out of the dungeons.

That first attempt resulted in death, and though I'd been no stranger to the concept, the girl had died on the streets of Marmere because of me. When I had led her in the wrong direction, I'd barely outrun the guard's arrows myself—watching her go down in a dark alleyway—the life leaving her eyes.

The only good thing that had come out of the incident had been running into Eryx. He'd helped me get back to the palace undetected and under the cover of darkness. That first conversation had been rushed—punctuated by the pounding in my chest and the fear that had washed over me.

I'd killed many witches on account of my job, but I'd saved many, too. And if I were to continue saving them, sacrifices had to be made—though every ounce of blood on my hands made my stomach roil and drew up the images of that first witch with an arrow sticking out of her chest—her blood dripping to the white dusting of snow below.

With guilt embedded in my very being, I knew I couldn't go out into the city. Being the king's executioner would make it far too easy to recognize me. Even as I kept my distance, my face would be known among the masses, and the opinions of me would be mixed. To some, I'd be a hero, and to others, a villain.

I supposed both were true.

If I kept my distance from Marmere during the week, my chances of discovery decreased greatly.

But after three weeks of throwing women into the fire during Eryx's absence, I could no longer tolerate the evil I'd taken part in—carried out with my own hands.

I sat in my bathing chamber, my back to the ornate tub I hadn't earned. My eyes felt heavy—my head swimming as I dreaded the execution set for the following morning. Normally, Eryx and I would have planned to meet tonight. We would have gotten the girl out of the city, and I'd be hunting some evil man from a back alley, dragging him to the fire masked as a witch and relishing in the scent of his scorched flesh.

I didn't know what that said about me, but I hardly had the energy to pick the sentiment apart further.

Closing my eyes, I could see her eyes again. The witch from last week, who had realized who I was—what I was before I tossed her onto the pyre and betrayed my own kind.

I stood, running to the chamber pot in the corner and expelling the contents of my stomach as a gentle knock sounded at the door.

Wiping my mouth, I turned, noticing the hardened look on Visha's face.

"You're sick," she said—her tone biting.

I pushed my hair away from my shoulders, straightening and clearing my throat. The flush of embarrassment still worked its way to my cheeks. Visha didn't know the truth—she couldn't.

"No," I said, and she raised a scolding brow.

"Pregnant?"

I scoffed. "No." I shook my head. "You would know better than anyone how empty my bed is."

Visha walked to the tub, delicately placing a plush towel over the rim. "I've noticed you don't even make your way to your own bed," she said. "You very well could be warming another."

I rolled my eyes, walking to the basin in the corner and wetting my hands. "I have neither time nor patience for a partner."

My gaze found hers through the mirror, and Visha nodded, clearly biting back whatever she had been wanting to say.

"The king's general sent you this," she said, holding out the neat envelope—the same one that appeared in my chamber every week—either hand-delivered or placed on the vanity in my bedroom. "This week's execution," she informed.

I walked up to the woman, snatching the envelope as my stomach twisted, and I tore through the paper. One name had been scrawled at the top of the parchment, followed by a detailed summary of the woman's crimes and a cell number.

The cell number gave me pause.

It was the girl hounded by the guard I killed when Eryx and I had gotten Verena out of the palace.

I couldn't do it.

"Thank you," I said, my voice smaller than I would have liked. Visha cocked her head to the side, pity written plainly across her rounded features.

"Hm," she said. "You must be ill. I've cleaned that chamber pot enough this week to know. Maybe we could postpone—"

"No," I snapped. "The king will not accept such a thing, and you know it. I will be there tomorrow morning."

Turning, Visha made her way to the door, looking over her shoulder just before she exited the room. "You know," she said, "forgive me for feeling so bold, but all of this death cannot be good for you, Rialey." She turned more, her eyes blazing as she lowered her voice. "Not for you and not for the kingdom."

My stomach churned, the vomit threatening to rise again. "Best keep that to yourself," I said.

And when she finally left, I found myself hunched over the toilet for the second time in less than an hour, making my mind up on the matter.

When I'd finished, I would find my way down to the dungeons—consequences be damned.

The dungeons, dark and damp with stale air that swallowed sorrows, stretched out in front of me as I kept my dagger close.

The palace dungeons were patrolled more heavily during the day, but my presence wasn't unexpected. I nodded at a guard whose name I hadn't bothered to learn, keeping my posture relaxed as I lurked in the darkness—a hunter in my own right.

King Wineslowe's guards had found the dead guard two days ago, but the stench still lingered in the air. They'd believed this witch had killed him despite her shackles and the way she had been behind bars. While it had initially made me nervous for her, I'd soon come to realize that the guards stood clear of her cell—too afraid to get close.

That served me well.

Gold appeared in my vision, and I molded my illusion to suit me, casting myself and the entire cell into darkness where I saw a figure, hunched and broken on the dirt floor, her hands shackled together, her hair dark and matted at her back.

"Soraya," I said, keeping my voice low.

My heart fluttered like that of a rabbit nearly ensnared—as if I were the one being hunted.

Her head slowly turned until her round eyes peered at me, glassy and fighting off tears. Her full lips remained sealed, dry cracks of blood decorating the bluish tones of them. Her bronze skin had lost its luster, and my chest tightened.

"Have you come to kill me?" she asked.

I took a deep breath before grabbing hold of my magic and changing the appearance of my face. My features, usually sharper, had softened. The scar beneath my left eye had faded, replaced by smooth skin a shade paler than my own.

"Oh," she said, before turning back to the wall.

Her resignation felt like a punch to the gut. I didn't know how I'd convince her to leave her cell—to *do* anything.

"They think I killed him," she whispered, and I pulled out the key from my pocket, unlocking the iron bars with a small metal groaning sound. I halted, glancing down the hall and praying to all the gods no guards waited for us—listening to the familiar sound of a cell door opening.

Once I found the hallway still blessedly empty, I stepped forward, my gaze narrowing on the girl. "You didn't."

She turned again, her eyes closed, and a fat tear sliding down her cheek. "Maybe I did," she whispered. "I wanted to."

I knelt near her, placing a hand on her shoulder and noting the way she flinched away—hating myself for not having the forethought not to touch her.

Something stirred in the pit of my belly—vicious and gnawing like a caged beast. I wanted Soraya to fight—I wanted her to make it to The Waldwood more than I craved my next breath. That festering desire snapped something in me, and I seized her shoulders, forcing her eyes to mine.

"You have to want this," I bit out, my tone icy. "I can get you out of the palace, and I *may* be able to help you out of the city. But if you aren't willing to fight, Soraya. There is nothing I can do for you."

Her dark eyes held mine, bottomless in their depths as I kept my hands on her shoulders. It felt as if everything inside me had been screaming. I was screaming for her to run, to hope, to *feel*.

When Soraya nodded, I stood up, more determined than ever.

Exiting the dungeons had proven easier than I anticipated. It was the streets that sent my heart rapidly beating again, the image of a slain witch dying in the moonlight on my conscience.

"Keep up," I whispered before lifting my hands to the sewer grate. "You won't look the same, but some of these guards seem to smell magic. They'll do anything to bring in the next victim of the kingdom, so you best be on guard."

Soraya, who hadn't said a word since we left her cell, nodded.

When my fingers touched the cool metal of the grate, I heard voices and sucked in a breath, kneeling further into the darkness.

I turned to Soraya, holding my finger to my lips as every ounce of my being screamed at me to run.

"He'd traveled all the way to the northernmost city just to invite one of the lord's daughters," a man spoke, his voice a deep rasp. Aside from that, the only identifying features I could make out through the grate were his muddied shoes and the slick slush on the streets from the earlier snow.

"Oh, please," another man said, though I couldn't see him. "The little shit has gone around the entire kingdom, inviting every available whore. Daddy's probably been pressuring him to hurry up and find a wife—stop dicking around with the servants."

"I heard the King of Eirhiondus wishes to marry. Maybe the prince is competing against him. I'm sure an alliance between the kingdoms would be favorable."

The second man scoffed. "There will be no alliance with Eirhiondus."

A roaring sounded in my ears, my blood pumping quickly on account of our near discovery. The rest of the conversation sounded as if I were hearing it underwater until the very moment the two men had cleared the alleyway, leaving me doubting if we'd be able to crawl up to the street undetected.

"Better be quick," I said, pushing the grate aside. I hauled Soraya through the small hole, quickly covering our tracks before we turned down the alleyway, finding our way to the busy road filled with street vendors and the smell of spices. I kept my magic close, hiding us as best I could beneath unassuming disguises.

When we neared the edge of the city, the large wall loomed over us. Guards patrolled the top of the stone structure, and the edges of my nerves frayed. I'd need to hold onto three detailed illusions at once. One lapse in focus could result in our demise—especially because Soraya's hands were still shackled by bone cuffs beneath her cloak. If she were asked to move in a certain way—

"Papers?" A lanky man with a trimmed mustache said, his expression bored.

Gold wrapped around me, and my hand found the paper I had shoved in my pocket. I forced them to him, recalling everything I could to be sure I'd left no stone unturned in casting this particular illusion.

The man held them to the dim light from the overcast sky, squinting as he read details of our false identities.

When his gray eyes found mine, I felt my knees shake. "Your father is a merchant?" he questioned.

"Yes," I said, lowering my gaze.

"And you're both sisters?"

"Correct. We are merely traveling for a visit. We will be meeting a friend one town over and continuing on, using her horses."

The guard stared at us as carriage wheels sounded on the street behind us. The clinking of metal, the sound of footsteps prowling, it all slowly faded to nothing. It was as if time had stopped, just as I held my breath while the guard considered my honesty.

It *was* odd for us to be leaving Marmere on foot. Certainly not impossible, but odd.

He nodded, and relief washed over me like a heavy rain.

"Have a safe trip," he said, and I fought the urge to look over at Soraya.

I'd gotten her out.

CHAPTER TEN

RIALEY

It took an hour to walk around the outside of the city undetected and find my way to a different gate for re-entry. My magic had exhausted me, and my muscles ached. I didn't know if it had been the act of getting Soraya out or if I was just exhausted from the adrenaline.

Re-entry proved easier, and I quickly found my way to the market center, no longer disguised and donning my true features.

Many glanced in my direction as I walked the cobbled streets back to the palace, hoping my return would be uneventful. Aside from the hushed whispers, it was, until a horse halted in front of me. Fear struck me as I followed the horse's legs up to a boot, and then further to the last man I wanted to be seen by.

"Miss Dagon." The prince, with blonde hair and a dusting of stubble on his jaw, sat astride a large mare. His blue eyes light beneath the overcast sky.

I stared.

I hadn't spoken to Prince Wineslowe despite residing in the palace. My quarters were far closer to those of the palace staff, and I'd never found a need to introduce myself to the man. Complacent and starched, he was everything I loathed. How someone could sit back watching their father kill hundreds, I didn't understand.

A sharp pain slashed through my chest.

I had killed, too.

Frequently.

Prince Wineslowe's gaze trailed over my body, burning everything it touched with a fiery rage. I fought to control my expression, though my jaw was clenched and my fists balled at my sides.

When he finally looked at my feet, one corner of his mouth turned up. "Nice boots," he said smugly. "A gift from my father, I assume?"

My heart lurched. The boots Eryx had left me with were more worn now—broken in from a few weeks of use, but still new in their appearance. "Yes," I answered through gritted teeth, dropping my gaze. "A gift."

Prince Wineslowe cleared his throat, forcing me to look up at him. Oddly enough, the prince was handsome. Something that would serve him well in his pursuit of a wife. I'm sure there were hundreds of court ladies ready to lie down their autonomy for his charm.

"You'll be in attendance next week?" he asked.

Right.

Soon after Eryx's departure, I'd gotten word from King Wineslowe that I was to be invited to the upcoming ball. Of course, an invitation from the king was not something that would afford me a *choice*. I would have to attend, regardless.

"I am grateful for the invitation," I said, clutching my cloak tightly around my body to ward off the breeze that was picking up.

Prince Wineslowe cocked a brow, his eyes practically glittering. "And you have a dress?" he asked.

I fought the urge to scoff.

"I will wear a gown previously given," I answered. I had no shortage of clothing in the palace.

His gaze burned hot again when he tsked, his eyes tracing over every hidden curve beneath my cloak. It felt as if he could see right through me. And that—was dangerous. It would be no good keeping company with anyone perceptive. I could end up losing my position as executioner—end up losing my life.

"Nonsense," he finally said. "There will be many women fighting for my attention. Surely, you'd require a new gown for such an occasion."

The way my teeth ground together sent pain shooting through my jaw. I could almost hear the implications—the rude way he'd implied I'd want anything to do with him at all.

"I," I began, "unlike those *many* women, am not fighting for your attention."

His brows rose, and I curtsied, turning on one heel before taking my leave.

Before I had left completely, he called after me. "I'll have something sent to your rooms," he said. "Have a nice day."

I didn't bother looking back—consequences be damned. That prideful piece of shit didn't deserve my allegiance. He deserved nothing—especially not from me.

The box sat taunting me from the bed as I sat in the corner chair of my room. It had been waiting for me upon my return to my quarters after dark.

How Prince Theron pulled off delivering a dress of this caliber in that amount of time, I couldn't figure out.

The green dress plunged at the neckline, nearly dropping to my navel, where the delicate beading continued from the bodice and down into the beginning of the A-line skirt. The thin straps were delicate when I thumbed them, too stunned to say a word.

The dress looked as if it had been inspired by the Waldwood. The beading resembled vines and branches stretching above and reaching for an overcast sky.

As I nervously ran my finger over my lip, staring at the open box on the comforter of my bed, I couldn't stop the nerves that buzzed in my body, making me feel on edge.

It was foolish to believe the prince knew anything about my heritage—to think he knew what I was.

Not a soul beyond Eryx knew the power I held, and I intended to keep it that way.

CHAPTER ELEVEN

CAIUS

The axe was heavy as it slammed against the wood, cracking the center of the log, and sending an echoing sound bouncing off the trees.

I swiped at my brow, sweat beading despite the cold, and threw the last few logs on the pile. The past week had been warmer, causing the snow to melt and turn to mud, but with the dropping temperatures and the overcast sky stretching for miles, I knew snow would come again soon.

It was the cycle of winter—set forth by King Wineslowe himself.

I yanked on the twine, tying the logs together before hauling them back to the cabin and trying to tamp down my bitterness.

I remembered the days before winter. Though I had been very young, it was a place I often went to in my dreams—a reminder of what the king had done to Alphaird—done to those I cared for.

When I opened the door, a gust of wind rustled the papers littering the bed where Verena had been sleeping. Typically, Ma would sleep in the bed, and I'd take the couch, but with our new guest, I had since become accustomed to the floor of our small cabin.

For the last three weeks, the woman had spent most of her time help-ing my grandmother cook, cleaning every inch of dust from the wooden baseboards, and drawing when the physical work became too much. She was frail—worn down by her past in the way that most witches were. Our kingdom was not kind to them, and it was evident in the gaunt appearance Verena had appeared with—though she'd filled out considerably since then.

The gray tone of her skin had all but disappeared, leaving pale skin and a smattering of freckles. Her figure seemed fuller—healthier, and despite the number of papers lying on the bed, she'd been drawing less and working more. A sure sign that her strength was building.

"What did you draw this time?" I asked, nodding to the parchment before dropping the logs by the fireplace and stacking them carefully. The wooden floors creaked beneath my weight when I knelt, tossing one log on the fire and grabbing the iron to stoke the flames.

"Trees, mostly," Verena answered from the corner of the room where she poured three cups of tea and carefully set them out on the table.

"Ma won't be back in time for that," I said, standing and wiping my palms on my black pants. "She won't be back until tomorrow, actually. Stopped by our friend's a few miles east to borrow a horse before going to Marmere. She doesn't travel once darkness falls, so I assume she will stay before returning."

I eyed her warily, wondering how much she could see through the small lie—how much she knew of the rebellion brewing just under the surface.

Lately, Ma had been traveling more for meetings—gathering with those like-minded individuals who wished for a better tomorrow.

Her healing talents—knowledge of herbal medicine—were invaluable, especially in the parts of the kingdom where famine and poverty touched us all.

She'd passed that knowledge along to me, and while I wasn't as good at identifying herbs, lacking practice on account of the snow, I'd gotten fairly decent.

Good with a sword, too.

Just in case.

Verena hummed, sliding the third cup across the wooden table until it sat next to her own. "Two for me, then."

I chuckled, pulling back the chair and joining her at the table. "Thank you," I muttered, lifting the tea before taking a sip. The liquid warmed me from the inside out, fighting off the cold air beyond our cabin. "Why the trees?" I asked.

"What?" Verena's brown eyes cut to mine, more amber in the light of the fire. The warm glow lit the room, dancing over her brown hair that she'd pulled back in two braids. Loose strands framed her face as she brought the cup to her lips.

I rested my elbows on the table. "Your drawings," I replied. "You said they were trees. Don't you see enough of those? I mean, as soon as you walk outside, there are about a dozen to choose from."

Verena blinked, her eyes wide as she tilted her head. "My drawings are of the Waldwood."

Somehow, I knew that was the case even before she'd confirmed it.

I cleared my throat, somewhat uncomfortable. She'd been talking about leaving for the Waldwood since that first day. I assumed it made sense, being a witch, but I hardly believed she'd make it all that way. The woman had been near death when I had carried her back here. Three weeks wasn't enough to erase months of damage the dungeons had done. Three weeks wouldn't be enough to get her to the Waldwood. Not alive, at least.

"Right," I said.

"I *will* be leaving." Verena turned her head, casting her gaze to the flickering flames in the hearth, her tea held close as her voice lowered—barely a whisper when she added, "Eventually."

My stomach twisted uncomfortably. I didn't know the woman—hardly knew her history after what had happened. Her time in the cabin consisted of only necessary conversations. In the beginning, she had been a shell of a human. It was as if she had accepted death—given up on living save for the spark that entered her gaze whenever she mentioned the forest to the north.

What the Waldwood held beyond magic and murder, I didn't know. But that was none of my business, just as Verena was none of my business.

"You're free to leave whenever you feel strong enough to go." I stood up, draining the tea in a few quick gulps and relishing the burn on the way down.

"You don't think I can make it," she whispered, so low I could barely hear her.

When I looked up, Verena's gaze had intensified, the reflection of the fire dancing in her amber irises as she dared me to answer.

It was good. The fact that she no longer walked around like a ghost—the drawings of the Waldwood. It was all good beyond the reality that she'd never make it that far—especially not alone.

I couldn't imagine why someone, especially a witch, would want to return to the Waldwood after all that had happened there.

King Wineslowe had ordered witch hunts where soldiers pillaged the covens they couldn't burn—made victims out of many—orphans out of most.

I set my cup near the wash bin, a pinch forming in my gut. "I never said that."

"But you thought it."

I chuckled, glancing at her and noting the delicate curve of her neck—the gentle angle of her jaw when she turned, those wispy strands of hair framing her face. "You couldn't possibly know that."

"I could." Her gaze cut to mine, and my smile fell.

"So," I said, "that's the type of witch you are. I'd been wondering when you would tell us."

Verena looked away, running a finger along one of the teacups in front of her. "And what kind of witch is that?" she asked.

"A dreamwalker."

Her silence felt heavy—weighted with something like fear. I hated the way she wore her scars—the way, whenever we'd talk about her being a witch, she would stiffen as if preparing for the worst.

"Does that scare you?" she asked, and I slowly rounded the table, placing my palms on its wooden surface as my eyes became level with hers.

"We aren't scared of witches here, Verena. Not even the ones privy to our thoughts when we sleep."

She took a sip of tea, breaking eye contact with a soft nod.

"I'll be leaving in an hour," I announced. "There are hot springs about three miles to the west."

"What are the hot springs for?" she asked.

I pushed in the chair I had occupied at the table, returning to my empty teacup to wash it in the basin before replacing it in the hutch. "To bathe," I answered. "Sponge baths only get you so far, and it's only a matter of time before it snows again. The walk will be easier this way."

"I want to go."

The air felt stagnant—as if even the wind paused to listen and wonder if the witch had really said what it thought.

"Go where?"

"The springs. I won't—" Verena grimaced. "I won't interrupt you, but I'd like a bath. I'd like to get out of the cabin, and I'd very much like to test my strength."

"The walk is long," I said by way of answer. "You may get tired, and—"

"I'd like to go," she snapped, determination shining in her eyes. Those haunting eyes.

"Okay," I conceded, nodding once. "Okay. You can come with me."

Chapter Twelve

Verena

The frigid air burned my lungs as I begged the muscles in my legs to move. All of it reminded me of the way my body failed three weeks ago, the way I'd given up.

I clung to the hope of what The Waldwood had to offer. I'd known there were witches lurking between the trees for some time. As it was, the kingdom had tried to burn the forest down nearly three decades ago at the beginning of King Wineslowe's reign. Soldiers, hundreds of them, were sent to the southernmost border of the forest to throw torches at the trees. Sneering men with inflated egos did all they could to snuff out the magic of the land with the one thing they knew best—destruction.

Despite their efforts, the Waldwood held firm. In the stories, it was said that the flames danced between the trees, flickering vibrant shades of red and orange before shifting to an icy blue, the trees unwavering and unchanging. The blue light remained until the flames died, the forest appearing exactly as it had when they started. When the soldiers realized the trees weren't burning, noticed the colors of the flames and the scent of magic in the air, they ran. Most retreated all the way back to Marmere, where little could protect them from the oncoming winter, but a few remained, eager to purge the witches from the land.

Those few found the queen over the covens, taken her into Marmere and tortured her before throwing her on a pyre.

Without a leader, the witches dispersed from the forest—fleeing in an attempt to preserve their lives.

Queens of the Waldwood had always been chosen by the gods, though I didn't know how that happened. Without a clear sign, hope had been lost, the forest enacting her vengeance.

Maybe the gods had forsaken us—or maybe they had never existed to begin with.

Frigid and constant, the cold settled over the kingdom as retribution for King Wineslowe's attack. While the weather does warm enough in some areas for hearty crops, Alphaird was hardly equipped to handle such a drastic shift in climate. The first years brought famine, and scathing discussions revolving around the king's competency. Of course, this enraged Wineslowe, fueling his desire for power even more.

Five years after they tried to burn the Waldwood, King Wineslowe began executing the witches. It was slow at first, a few women accused of using their power to harm well-to-do merchants in the square, but the rumors quickly spread until high-ranking officials became the victims. The retaliation became fierce over the years, resulting in weekly burnings and a fanatic obsession with getting rid of all magic.

Twenty-seven years of endless winter, twenty-eight years of King Wineslowe's reign, and ten years of public executions led by whichever executioner had been employed at the time.

The public burnings were a warning—one I should have heeded when I'd chosen to use my magic months ago.

"How much further?" I rasped.

Caius glanced back, his brow lowered. "About a mile still. Do you need to rest?"

The question brought heat to my cheeks despite the cold. I'd once been strong—stronger than this, at least. Now, a three-mile walk at a pace I knew was slower than his usual trek sent my muscles aching and my stomach feeling hollow and pained.

If he were angry with me, Caius didn't show it.

"No," I said, my voice lower now. "I'm fine."

I didn't miss the way he slowed his pace, especially as I fixed my eyes to the pack he carried, attempting to empty my mind and dissociate from any protest in my limbs.

How I'd make it back to the cottage, I didn't know.

Caius slowed, dropping the pack into the snow.

By the cabin, much of the snow had melted away, leaving mud on the forest floor, but the ground had slowly solidified again—frosted over this morning when I'd awoken. Here, though, as the ground sloped upward at the base of the mountain, the snow stayed. It was as if it hadn't fully melted in years—probably since the initial burning of The Waldwood, if I had to guess.

Or maybe I was just cold and frustrated.

Caius looked at me, his dark eyes knowing. "I'm starving," he proclaimed, and I didn't miss the way one corner of his mouth turned up at his declaration.

He sat in the snow, opening the pack and pulling out the dried meat sticks from his hunting trip earlier in the week. My brows lowered.

"I'm fine," I asserted, the shame making anger take root in the pit of my belly. It wasn't directed at him, of course, but there, all the same.

"Verena," he said, and the way my name rolled off his tongue sent a shiver down my spine. "Sit," he commanded.

I obeyed, begrudgingly placing myself next to him in the snow, and accepting the food he offered. Though the sustenance did little to soothe the deep ache in my stomach, the rest helped me catch my breath. I'd never admit how weak I'd become to Caius. I'd long since decided he and his grandmother had no desire to hurt me, but it was still painful to know how vulnerable I was. I didn't need to admit it, too.

"What does Ahvi plan to get from town?" I asked, wiping snow from the skirts of my dress beneath my heavy cloak.

"Restocking food," he answered after chewing and swallowing. "Mostly staples. Fruit is expensive and saved for those in the palace. Most of it only grows at the southern border anyway, so don't get your hopes up."

"I'm aware of our kingdom's climate," I said, my tone soft.

Caius pulled at the strings of his boots, untying the knot and then re-forming it as he spoke. "I'm assuming she may pick up a few more clothing pieces for you. Pants, should you want them."

"That is—" I ran my fingers over the fabric of my dress, stiff and cold in light of our excursion. Caius and Ahvi had done too much for me—provided too much. And while I needed everything they offered, I couldn't help the guilt that swirled deep in the pit of my stomach. I could never repay them—not in a way that mattered.

"That is very kind," I finished, wondering what I could do to return the favor. A drawing, I supposed. Though those hardly seemed like a fair trade.

"Verena," he said, leaning in so that his eyes met mine, honest and warm against the chill of winter around us. Caius proved to be more stoic, but it didn't take away from the kindness that was there—always there and ready for anyone who needed it. I'd seen it last week when their neighbors had joined us for dinner. I'd seen it outside the cabin window as his broad form had bent over the deer he'd gotten, his head lowered as he gave thanks to the gods for their provision.

I didn't know much about what Caius believed—or what his story was, but I didn't need to. His kindness was evident. Even in the way he'd feigned hunger to give me rest without drawing shameful attention to the way I was slowing him down.

"We are happy to help you," he added. "It is no trouble to see you well cared for, so do not feel that you are a burden on myself and my grandmother."

I nodded, looking back to my lap before taking a bite of food. The saltiness coated my tongue as I chewed, the hollowness in my stomach easing just a bit, but I didn't know if it was from the food or his words.

"Watch your step."

Caius offered his hand as I climbed the lip on the lower side of the mountain. His fingers were icy but held firm as he helped me up.

Once we had gotten to the steeper slope of the mountain, I'd struggled more than the entire journey. I knew Caius was moving painfully slow on my account, and I hated that I couldn't be a better companion. I'd been the one insisting on coming in the first place.

We were hardly to the peak of the mountain, but the snow-covered trees wrapped around us, tucking us into what felt like a more private area as I found the depression in the rock filled with clear, steaming water. The warmth could be felt from where we stood, and when I peered through the trees, I glimpsed the spectacular view.

"This," I breathed, still out of breath from the climb, "is beautiful."

Caius smiled then, a proud smile that lit up his face in a way I hadn't seen yet. He looked down at me, my chest tightening as a dimple appeared on his right cheek. "It's something, isn't it?"

I nodded.

"There are trees lining this pool there." He pointed, directing my attention to the dense snow-covered pines sprouting from the side of the mountain. "Another pool sits just beyond it. That's where I will be." His smile softened, and he cleared his throat, clearly uncomfortable. "For privacy, of course."

One corner of my mouth turned up at that. "I promise I will leave you alone," I said, trying to ease some of his embarrassment. "I will be perfectly respectful."

Caius chuckled before disappearing through the trees, leaving me with a small bar of soap he'd left and my racing thoughts.

Being alone in the forest felt different. It drew up memories of when I'd wandered away from Marmere, freezing and on the brink of death—barely alive.

The frown pulled at my lips as my heart raced in my chest. I had almost wished he'd stayed—offering to bathe clothed instead of leaving me beneath the vast overcast sky above. The blue water emanated steam as I looked around, anxious, but refusing to become more of a problem than I already was.

I untied my cloak, letting it fall into the snow, and slowly took off my boots—too big and still the same pair I'd stumbled into their yard with. I wondered how the witch hunter was doing—if she'd helped any others escape or if I had been an exception—something to assuage her guilt.

When the icy air kissed my naked body, I touched the water with my toes, relishing in the heat of it—the longing to finally be clean after weeks of sponge baths in the cabin.

I slowly descended until the water lapped around my waist, moving as I plunged deeper into the small pool overlooking the frozen valley below.

The warmth encased me, coating my skin until it flushed a brilliant pink. As my chest went under the water, I felt a tightening sensation there—like a heavy weight pressing down on me and making it harder to breathe.

Panic seized me, and my vision flashed red like the flames of the pyres that burned in the city center of Marmere.

I was supposed to die.

I was supposed to burn.

I screamed, pushing through the water to the edge of the pool as my vision tunneled, and I clawed at the pool's edge, the mud and dirt packing beneath my nails, the flames burning my flesh, the smell of scorched skin, and the sound of crackling logs filling my senses.

I screamed again, but the sound was muffled, the flames rising above my head, threatening to take the very magic from my blood—the life from inside my body.

I felt weak.

Afraid.

Strong hands gripped my biceps, hauling me out of the fire until I was sitting on the edge of the pool, dripping and naked and painfully aware of reality.

I wasn't burning at all.

Caius was there, panting, and wearing his undergarments, his strong thighs on display as he sat next to me, one hand still wrapped around my upper arm and keeping me steady.

The tears fell in fat drops, coating my lips and tongue with their salty-sweet kisses.

"I'm sorry," I breathed out, as my chest caved in on itself. I covered my face with my hands, the shame burrowing beneath my skin and burning hotter than the flames I'd imagined were consuming me.

I'm sorry. I'm sorry. I'm sorry.

The words echoed in my mind—possibly through the trees as I sobbed on the bank, naked and still weak—still taking from these people who had opened their home to me.

It was kindness I hadn't earned.

"Verena," Caius's voice was soft—grounding as his hands gently encircled my wrists, pulling until my face was uncovered—bare and tear-streaked as my gaze met his.

"You have nothing to apologize for," he said, and though I was naked, his eyes stayed fixed on mine as if it were no question where his focus held. "You were screaming about fire—" He stopped, shaking his head as he corrected himself. "It doesn't matter. Do you think you can get back into the pool?"

I shook my head, another tear leaking out—my shame written so plainly across my face.

"What if," he started. "What if I help you?"

I swallowed, clenching my fists until my nails dug into my palms. The stinging distracted from the tightness in my throat, slowing my tears as I held his stare.

When I nodded, small and uncertain, Caius plunged himself into the water, holding a hand out to me as he encouraged me to join him.

My heart pounded, my limbs protesting as I screamed internally for them to push forward.

Get in the damn pool.

I lowered myself into the water, careful to keep it at my waist this time.

We stood close, though not touching, as Caius kept his grip firmly on my hand, steadying me. "Do you trust me?" he whispered, and I found myself nodding once more.

"Okay." He leaned around me, his bare chest brushing my arm as he reached for the soap, gripping it in one hand, his other still grounding me where we stood. "Turn around, Verena."

I slowly turned, trying to calm the racing thoughts—the breaths that rattled deep within my chest.

Warmth ran down my head and my back as he cupped his palm, pouring the little water over me and wetting the dirty strands.

Caius ran gentle fingers through my hair, using the soap as he slowly began washing weeks of grime from my head.

His chest rumbled when he spoke. So close to my back, I could almost feel it.

"A long time ago," he began, "there was a beautiful witch who lived in the Waldwood."

I turned my head to the side, keeping my gaze down as my heart steadied in my chest, my nerves easing with every gentle stroke of his fingers. "Are you telling me a story?" I inquired.

I could hear the smile touch his lips—just briefly. "Maybe, but you're interrupting."

"Okay, I won't interrupt."

Caius allowed his fingers to massage my scalp, my eyes closing as his deep voice continued.

"This is a sad story, I fear."

"The ones about witches usually are," I answered.

He leaned in, his breath tickling my ear as he paused washing my hair, just briefly. "I said no interrupting."

I chuckled.

"This beautiful witch lived in The Waldwood Forest, surrounded by her coven and practicing her magic. She was a mender, able to manipulate matter, but of course, it always came at a cost. Nature demanded balance.

"The witch was young, mid-twenties, and shared a home in the hollow of a Waldwood tree with her son, no older than three.

"The boy's father lived there, too. Kindhearted and adventurous, they both taught the boy about the forest and magic and everything beautiful that the realm had to offer. He, of course, wouldn't remember this because that same year, when the boy turned three, a soldier appeared in the coven's village, vicious and hateful in his quest to leave the woods.

"His king had ordered the forest burned, and when it hadn't worked, this man had entered through the towering limbs, cold with the oncoming winter, and found himself quickly lost. When the beautiful woman, the witch, attempted to help the man, he admonished her. Hatred leaked from his pores as he unleashed his wrath on the coven.

"The boy's father gave him up to the boy's grandmother, demanding she take leave and avoid slaughter as more soldiers had descended on the village, and even with magic coursing through their veins, the element of surprise had led to deaths. The boy's parents, being among the dead. And of course, magic doesn't pass to the men, so the boy would be safe."

I listened as my chest cracked open, his story pouring into me and creating a deep sorrow that seemed to touch on everything I'd known—everything I'd experienced in the Alphaird.

"He survived?" I asked as Caius ran his hands over my shoulders, my back, after handing me the soap and allowing me to wash myself, too. His touch remained in my hair after I was finished, still playing with the strands as his voice echoed through the trees.

"He did."

I turned, the steam rising between us as I was careful not to touch him, his eyes lined with tears as he looked at me.

Caius smiled—a sorrowful one loaded with the truth of his story, and I felt it heavy like the weight he seemed to carry—so obvious now.

"It's just a story," he said, but I didn't believe him.

"Then why does it feel like truth?"

Caius cleared his throat. "I suppose all stories are riddled with some truth, now, aren't they?"

I nodded, resisting the urge to reach out and take his fingers in mine. It made me want to offer him something—a small piece of myself in exchange for the small piece he'd offered me.

"I haven't used my magic in months," I admitted. "I've been afraid. And it's not like I'm willing to use it on you or Ahvi. You've taken me in—cared for me. I couldn't violate you like that, but still. It feels as if a part of me is missing." My brows furrowed as I looked at the blue water's edge and up to where the snow began. "I suppose something will always be missing. It's the part the kingdom took from me."

Caius reached out, tucking a wet strand of hair behind my ear when he spoke. "That may be true," he murmured, "but you're here, and you're growing stronger every day. I'm sure you could make it to the Waldwood with help if you left in another month or two."

My eyes flicked to his. "Are you offering to go with me?" I asked.

"I might be willing."

The silence hung between us, filled with unspoken words. If his story were true, if he'd lost his parents in The Waldwood, I couldn't imagine how painful a return would be. Why he'd be willing to escort me was beyond my comprehension. Though I assumed it was his kindness that drove him. It was the thing that had him cleaning my vomit from the floor of the cabin three weeks ago—the thing that followed him around like a dear friend.

"And as for your magic," he began, "if you need to use it—to practice and feel strong enough to do so, I'd be happy to let you enter my dreams."

My body warmed—more than even the hot spring would do on its own.

"You'd let me enter your dreams?" I asked.

Caius's full lips stretched into another smile. "Of course."

Chapter Thirteen

Theron

As it seemed, my predisposition to tardiness would not go away even if I promised my father punctuality during the last burning I'd attended.

Walking through the grand halls of the palace, I hurried my steps, anxiousness tying a knot in my stomach. There was no doubt my unreliability would be scolded if not punished, and it was important to me that I remained able-bodied in the weeks to come. Not only for my duties to the kingdom, but for my prospects of finding a wife.

Right.

My future courtship might be the only thing to keep my father's retribution at bay after this unfortunate mistake.

My boots touched the dark marbled floors of the west wing of the palace, that knot in my stomach tightening as I approached the ornate door to my father's study. Large black pillars lined either side of the hall, illuminated by flickering candlelight and the flashy gold accents my father had commissioned to decorate the ceiling, the tops of the pillars, and the space surrounding the black door in front of me. My eyes lingered on the ostentatious, stone statue to the left of the door, a replica of my father—one more purchase resulting from his inflated ego and lust for power.

I kept my face stoic as I nodded toward the guard stationed to the right of the door. He quickly opened it with a loud creak, revealing a room congested with cigar smoke, and the gathering of Alphaird's most prominent lords. The four men sat around the study sipping whiskey from their velvet chairs, red like the blood on my father's hands—mine too. When King Wineslowe's gaze found mine, he sneered.

"Late again, Theron."

I adjusted the sleeves of my tailored jacket, the golden buttons matching the shade of the accents in the hallway. It felt stiff and uncomfortable as I lowered myself into an open chair, muttering my apologies. King Wineslowe seemed to accept them, but by the blazing look in his eyes, I knew they were not well-received—not truly.

"Now that our prince has arrived, we can begin our discussion." He swirled the brown liquid in his glass before taking a sip. "As you all know, you've been invited to the palace because Theron wishes to find a wife. You each have daughters who should attend tomorrow evening to present themselves."

Renwick, with his dark, wispy hair, thin from age, leaned forward. Interest lit his eyes, souring my stomach. A vulture, he'd begun circling before the conversations had even started. "As you know, Your Majesty, Theron and my daughter have already been acquainted, being that we live in Marmere, and he frequents my home for the weekly burnings."

I fought the urge to scoff. My attendance was never a choice.

"Yes, of course, Renwick." My father smiled at him, a vicious and self-serving kind of grin that made me nauseous. "I'm sure Theron and Esper are *well* acquainted. We look forward to hosting your family during our celebration."

Lord Vespahr grimaced, shifting in his chair. Vespahr was lord of the neighboring city to the west, though he spent far less time appeasing my father. Vile and snake-like, he was the sort of man to get what he wanted, no matter the cost or morality of it.

"Of course," Vespahr began, "It would only be fair that Esper be the last on Theron's list of women to dance with at the ball." He gave me a pointed look, daring me to challenge him. "Especially seeing as they've already shared a bed. It is important Theron takes all his options into account."

I stared blankly at him, my tone flat. "Are you suggesting I bed your daughter?" Lord Bloodbane coughed in the corner, hiding a smirk by taking a long drag of his cigar. My father's anger radiated from across the room, but I kept my eyes pinned on Vespahr, one corner of my mouth turning up. The conversations surrounding my *activities* were insulting and inaccurate, though I'd done nothing to correct the kingdom's assumptions of me. It was easier for them to believe I spent my time hosting my fair share of women.

Renwick's daughter, Esper, though kind enough, had turned eighteen this past year. That, in and of itself, was enough to deter me.

Vespahr chuckled, tapping a finger against the glass held between his slim fingers. "If that is what it takes," he said, smiling.

I didn't respond as my smirk dropped. I returned my attention to my father as he began speaking.

"I believe Theron will be fair and cautious. And since I have you," he started, "I'd like to discuss the reports Lord Cask brought with him from further north." My father stood and walked to the large bookshelves lining the back wall. Rolled maps sat behind the glass case he opened. He carefully selected one, pulled it from its spot, and brought it to the desk at the head of the room. He unfurled it, studying it with great interest. "Lord Cask," he said, gesturing for the stout man to share his report.

Cask's gruff appearance was accentuated by his long graying beard, though his height diminished much of his threatening and barbaric demeanor. "We've found witches coming through Stromadale. Limping and weak and searching for the Waldwood."

"What have you done with them?" Renwick interrupted.

"Exactly what we ought. Burned them should they be captured, but the problem lies in their travels. How many have we missed? I believe the witches are using The Waldwood as a safe haven again. Perhaps they never stopped. It's been years since we entered the forest to assert power over them, and it is my belief that we've done the kingdom a disservice in allowing such. We already know the kingdom holds traitors who harbor anger for our king. They've never had a chance to truly organize, but should they find the witches...we'd have much more to worry about."

"What are you implying?" Vespahr asked. "That they're planning to attack their own kingdom? That there could be an uprising among rebels?"

My father grunted. "This kingdom belongs to no witch," he asserted. "And it certainly doesn't belong to traitors and cowards. As far as I know, they're disorganized. I do, however, believe Cask's worries hold true. I think it's time we sent forces to the Waldwood, take the witch hunts to their safe haven. Especially if we long to eradicate the vermin altogether."

Bile rose in my throat as I watched the men speak of their next move—the plan to spill more blood over the snow-covered ground of Alphaird.

I sat silently through the discussions, contributing little to their plans. Such detachment earned me the critical gaze of Vasphar. It was as if I could hear his thoughts—the wheels turning as he assessed me.

When the meeting concluded, plans made to send soldiers north, I took my leave. Striding down the dark hallway, I attempted to flee to the stables. A ride through the gardens might ease some of the tension pulling at my shoulders.

"Prince Theron."

Vespahr's cold voice had me halting as he caught up behind me, rounding me until we stood face-to-face and alone.

"Lord Vespahr," I greeted, dipping my chin.

His green eyes narrowed, making my skin itch beneath the collar of my jacket. I fought the urge to tug at the expensive fabric.

"My daughter," he began, "Odessa, plans to visit the palace library this afternoon." He paused, and I thought back to his comment in the study. I had goaded him, surely, but Vespahr hadn't been bluffing. He would sacrifice his daughter for power.

"Thank you for informing me," I said, my tone dry. "I plan on going for a ride this afternoon to clear my head before the ball."

Vespahr frowned. "She enjoys riding, should you wish to have company."

"I do not."

He crowded my space, his face inches from mine. The smell of stale liquor and smoke wafted from him, making my stomach clench. "What is it you desire, Prince Theron." He'd lowered his voice, menacing in his approach, and while I hated myself for it, I stepped back slightly.

"I don't know what you mean," I gritted out, though I knew full well where this conversation was going.

"I've seen you at the burnings," he started. "The way you look away when the witch gets thrown onto the fire. Why is that, Your *Highness?*" The title sounded like a slur.

I glanced at the wall behind him, cursing my weakness.

"I can offer you armies." His voice was hushed, and spit spewed from his mouth as he spoke. "Take my daughter for a wife, and I can offer my city's forces for whatever you desire. Nearly thirty, I'm sure you're tired of waiting for your father's reign to end. All young men crave power."

My gaze met his head-on, and I stepped closer. An inch taller, I used it to my advantage as my gaze hardened. "Are you suggesting treason?" I asked, my voice cold and calculating.

Vespahr cocked a brow. "I'm suggesting serving our kingdom's future," he said by way of explanation. "It is noble."

"You'd sell your daughter off like cattle for favor and power?" I asked, unrelenting in my questioning.

Vespahr's eyes narrowed briefly before he took a step back, his voice louder and his demeanor shifting to that of a lord—calloused and official in his presentation. "Odessa looks forward to getting to know you at to-morrow's ball," he said. "And I greatly look forward to learning about our future king—his interests—his *beliefs*." The threat was clear, but I didn't take the bait.

Nodding once, I ground my teeth together before speaking. "I look forward to that as well. Good day."

I turned on my heel, exiting back toward the way I'd come, veering down another hallway that led to the southern part of the palace. I'd stop by the kitchens and grab food before heading to the stable. In fact, I'd go anywhere if it meant I could get away from that vile man.

When I finally made it to the stables, I couldn't help but feel as though I wasn't alone, but I shrugged off the feeling, knowing it was silly. Of course, I wasn't alone. I was Alphaird's prince—a position that didn't promise privacy.

Chapter Fourteen

Rialey

My stomach fluttered as I trekked through the hallway to the ballroom near the center of the palace. In two years, I hadn't attended an official ball. Being left alone allowed me to keep a low profile and gave me the opportunity to leave at night without anyone becoming suspicious.

I was closest to Visha, and even she didn't know the truth of my identity. She didn't know the power I held—that my family had come from Abellona, one of the covens in the Waldwood.

My job as executioner afforded me options, but it also came at a cost. I'd still participated in executions—been given the task of those who'd come before me because of Wineslowe's orders.

Public executions started ten years ago, King Wineslowe's original executioner being a burly man—brutal and filled with all the bitterness that comes from being scorned. No one in the kingdom knew where the man had come from, but a witch had murdered him during a visit to one of Marmere's brothels. King Wineslowe had then taken it upon himself to kill the witch by his own hand.

That public execution—

I shook my head, knowing it wasn't worth remembering. I'd been desperate, cleaning for a prominent man with a home far too large for his small-minded opinions. The job offered me little coin, plenty of work, and most importantly, a place to stay.

When the call came that the king would need a new executioner, I saw the opportunity for what it was, and I was willing to use my magic to secure the position. While being away from the Waldwood had weakened me—weakened all of us, I still had what it took.

I took another step. The gown Prince Theron had sent to my rooms left my arms bare save for the thin straps, allowing the chill of the palace to bite at my skin. When I found myself closer to the ballroom, the bodies of nobles helped warm the space, leaving me missing the chill.

A tall woman, no older than twenty-three, cast her gaze in my direction as my heels clicked on the marbled floors common in the nicer parts of the castle. Her red hair hung to her waist, two twists pulled away from her face and pinned at the back, where a littering of crystal and diamond decorated the wavy locks. Her harsh eyes pierced, nose turned up upon my arrival.

Without a word, I moved past her, walking through the open doors with a small curtsy. I greeted the guards stationed on either side of the ornate entryway and descended the vast staircase leading to the mingling bodies below.

Music poured over the room from a balcony overhead, and upon the dais stationed at the center of the ballroom, sat the king, cold and menacing on his golden throne amidst a sea of black marbled floors, black walls, and golden accented ceilings.

When I reached the bottom of the steps, fisting my hands in the skirts of my gown, the king's eyes met mine as he nodded, his lips thin and pursed as if he regretted extending the invitation at all.

I sucked in a breath, trying to calm the nerves swirling in my stomach. I pushed my way to the table against the long wall. Food spread out atop the lavish golden tablecloth, with small pastries filled with fruit jams; expensive considering the kingdom struggled to obtain such things with the constant winter. Grapes had been laid out around large decorative candles. More a tablescape than an offering, it spoke of the wealth of the palace. Wineslowe gained power and riches while he killed anyone who threatened his position—burned the witches and starved the commoner.

Such was the way of kings.

I plucked a small pastry from the plate. The savory cream cheese center soured in my stomach, reminding me I didn't belong in this ballroom.

"Prince Theron."

The sound of his name drew me into a hushed conversation nearby as one of the lords spoke with a guard. Based on the symbol stitched into the guard's uniform, he hailed from the city closest to Marmere, working for the lord, no doubt.

The lithe man was practically skeletal compared to the burly guard, his green eyes cunning and lifeless in the way evil men's eyes seemed to appear.

"I would like to know as much about him as possible," the lord continued. "His whereabouts, what he does in his free time. My daughter plans to catch his eye tonight, but I believe information on the prince will prove beneficial in my endeavors. Especially if he should accept bribes."

I scoffed, turning on my heel and heading for the other end of the ballroom. The less I knew about Prince Theron, the better. I had no desire to see the prince, and I certainly had no desire to know him.

Born during Wineslowe's first year as king, the prince had grown up during the conflict against the witches. He had even taken part in the hunts around his eighteenth birthday, nearly ten years ago. I loathed the man and did not need to learn anything else.

"Should you be here?"

A woman's voice pulled my attention, causing me to halt and find the redheaded woman waiting, a sneer still plastered to her pale face.

"Excuse me?" I said, my tone cool.

She scoffed, adjusting the tulle skirt of her blue gown as if perfecting the way it hung from her lean figure. "The king's executioner isn't exactly in the running for the prince's hand," she said. "So, I'm not entirely sure why you are here, in such an ornate gown."

I lifted my chin, feeling the loose strands of black hair ghosting against my shoulders. Visha had added soft waves, spraying them with some concoction she believed would help them hold. "I am here because of my position," I started, keeping my posture tall and professional. I would be respectful, but I would not appear weak. "It was a courtesy to extend the invitation and nothing more."

She chuckled then, the sound grating against my skin. "Clearly." Her green eyes took in every inch of me, judging and fiery like everything about her. "The prince needs someone refined—not street scum who forced their way into the palace by murdering half the kingdom. Though," she mused, "I can't say I disagree with King Wineslowe's goals." Her tongue darted out over her red lips as if she could taste the blood of my people, and it pleased her. "The witches are certainly a disease upon our land."

My glare intensified as I scrutinized her. Rich, prominent, and entirely selfish, this woman was nothing if not everything I hated about court politics. "I earned my position through hard work and dedication," I said, and my words were greeted with an evil cackle pulled deep from the woman's belly. It ignited anger within me. Her eyes were familiar, her features sharp and like that of the man I'd overheard talking previously. I took my chances.

"I, unlike you, do not have a father willing to stalk the prince to secure his hand. But having met Prince Theron once, I'm sure you two will make a lovely couple. Conniving and cruel just as—"

She stepped forward, her lip peeled back in disgust. "You should watch your tongue, you filthy bitch."

"Miss Dagon."

The voice caused my back to stiffen, so familiar save for the formality. When I looked to my right, my eyes widened. Prince Theron stood with his black jacket, the golden buttons and thread contrasting against the dark fabric. His neatly styled blond hair left nothing out of place as his wide smile greeted me. It sent my stomach lurching and my heart pounding a rapid rhythm.

I curtsied, bowing my head and noting the way the redheaded woman did the same, her demeanor shifting in the presence of her sought-after husband.

"Your Highness," I said while rising.

Prince Theron looked at the other woman. "You must be Odessa," he said, offering a hand. She took it, and he pulled her delicate fingers upward, planting a stiff kiss on her knuckles before releasing her. "Lord Vespahr spoke highly of you at our meeting yesterday. Your father is…" he paused, thinking of what word he would use. "*Motivated*," he finished.

Odessa's eyelashes fluttered as she smiled, her teeth white and straight. "How kind of him," she said, her tone sickly sweet.

Theron's eyes turned to me once more, and I felt a chill run down my spine. It was as if the iciness of the palace returned, my flesh pebbling beneath his blue gaze. "Rialey Dagon," he said, tasting my name in his mouth. "I'm glad to see you are in attendance."

I cleared my throat, hoping to keep my fluttering heart under control. "Of course," I said, my lips pulling into a forced smile. "And thank you for the gown. It was a lovely gift."

Odessa gasped, and I fought the urge to chuckle.

Theron's eyes dipped to the swell of my breasts, down to where the plunging neckline stopped, and then lower still before slowly dragging back up to my face. "Beautiful," he said, and my cheeks flushed.

"And entirely unnecessary. I told you in town that I had gowns to use for this occasion."

He didn't respond, his eyes crinkling at the corners when his smile widened. Theron offered me a gloved hand as a new song began from the balcony over the ballroom. "Would you do me the honor of a dance, Miss Dagon?"

I blinked, my face paling. Despite the rage simmering in my chest, I could not refuse him. Offending the prince would draw attention to myself—attention I could not afford.

"Of course," I answered, placing my hand in his as he escorted me to the center of the dance floor.

Eyes, hundreds of them, lingered on us and made my skin prickle. It seemed I was destined for attention no matter what.

My body warmed as Theron guided me into position, careful to keep a respectful distance between us as one hand found my waist, scalding where it rested like a heavy weight.

I forced my feet to move, following his lead and doing a terrible job of it. When my heel pressed into his toe, he chuckled, and I hated how amused he seemed.

"You don't dance often, do you, Miss Dagon?"

I kept my eyes out on the crowd, noting every person who stared in our direction, clearly confused as to why the prince would be dancing with the king's executioner. "This is the first ball I have attended."

"Pity," Prince Theron said, his grip tightening around me as if scared I'd slip away.

I wanted to.

"I'm glad I ran into you the other day," he said as the hand at my waist held firm. We were standing closer now, my chest nearly flush with his as he directed my movements.

When I spoke, my voice was breathless. "You did not *run* into me. For which I am thankful, as you were on a horse, and I was not."

He chuckled, his face closer now. When I looked up into his blue eyes, I tilted my head to the side. There was a warmth there I hadn't noticed—something entirely contrary to everything I knew about the prince. However, I told myself not to be fooled.

"I like the dry humor," he said.

I grimaced, looking out to the crowd surrounding us, the curious eyes tracking every movement. "You are not supposed to *like* anything about me."

Odessa stood with a glass of wine in her hand, eyeing me from over the rim. In her gaze, I felt every ounce of disdain she had for me, especially as Prince Theron stepped away, guiding me to spin before meeting me back in our starting position.

He leaned in, placing his lips near my ear as his breath fanned out over my neck. "I've liked a lot of things about you for some time now."

I sucked in a breath, clearing my throat to hide the way his words had startled me. His hand at my waist felt near scalding, now. "We just met," I supplied, hoping to deter his interest.

"I see you weekly."

I pulled back, my brows lowering as I tilted my chin upward. "So, you like that I murder witches." My challenge hung between us, suspended like one of the expensive chandeliers overhead. Except this one was far more threatening.

Theron's smirk dropped, his expression hard as stone. "That's not what I said."

I cleared my throat, looking away again as he directed my steps further left. We turned, and I watched more eyes, more judgment wafting off the attendees. "Then I'm confused," I admitted.

My nerves spiked when I caught a glimpse of Odessa's father, I assumed. My stomach churned, and I looked back toward the prince, more comfortable with his attention than that of the entire room—which surprised me.

"I like your eyes," he said, leaning in just slightly. It felt as if we moved in slow motion, spinning around the dance floor where other couples gave us a wide berth, clearly consumed with the prince's activities for the night.

He continued. "You can tell a lot from the eyes. Typically, someone who relishes in murder holds no kindness in their gaze. One would have a stare empty and hardened, much like my father's." I raised a brow as he tilted his head to the side, studying me. My pulse picked up. "But not you," he said, his words softer. "Why is that, Rialey?"

Not *Miss Dagon*, but *Rialey*. He wet his lips as if he were tasting it, and whatever he found there seemed to please him.

"I—" My breathless voice betrayed me, same as the quick intake of breath when he pulled me closer, forcing me to keep looking at him until it was almost painful.

"How," he said, taking in the sharp angle of my nose, the kohl lining my eyes, the vibrant red Visha had painted on my lips. "How is there still kindness in you?"

When his eyes flicked to my lips, the tension between us pulled taut, and I hated the way my skin flushed—the way his compliments went to my head, making me feel dizzy.

Prince Theron had participated in the witch hunts to the north when he was eighteen. He had killed my kind and hated us as much as his father had. There was no mercy in him, even if his demeanor—everything about him said otherwise. Clearly, I couldn't trust my judgment.

"I'm not sure," I answered, pushing distance between us, cutting that tension with a knife. But instead of snapping and pulling us together, each end of the rope hung there, limp and lifeless as I gathered my senses. "It's strange you see kindness when I so clearly loathe you."

My brazen insult seemed to do very little, especially as the song continued to play around us, the stares of the court making me all too aware of how it appeared. Pulling my lips into a demure smile, I tried to make it seem as if nothing were amiss.

Prince Theron's hand flexed around mine just before he guided me into another spin. This time, when we came back together, he didn't pull me as close.

"And here I thought I was winning you over with my charming personality," he mused. One side of his mouth tugged upward, but the expression didn't match his eyes. I had unsettled him.

Good.

"You are arrogant," I said, gently pushing myself closer so that I would no longer look at him. His chest brushed mine, and I held him tighter, the scent of cardamom and juniper berries filling my nose. Looking away, I finally added, "And foolish."

The music slowed to a halt, and I pried myself from his grasp, doing my best not to view whatever expression he held. I didn't need to know how he felt or anything about him.

"You have about a million court ladies waiting for your attention," I commented, noting a woman donning a deep crimson gown, her long braids hanging to her waist as she glanced at the prince before glancing away. Her warm, brown skin glowed under the ballroom light.

The prince stepped forward, looking down at me with his voice low, intimate, like we were in a much more private location within the palace. "Then they will be waiting a long time."

A brief pause brought the sound of hushed whispers and murmuring from the crowd before a new song began. It sent my nerves on edge.

"Another dance?" he asked, using the same tone as before.

"And how will that look?" I questioned.

Prince Theron cracked a wide smile, charming and dangerous. "Romantic."

When I didn't respond, he put more distance between us, looking around the room before speaking again. "I will entertain one dance with one woman of *your* choosing, Miss Rialey Dagon. If only to not enrage my father or the beautiful woman standing before me. Then, when it is finished, we shall dance again."

I glanced back at the woman in the crimson dress, now staring fully. For a moment, I pondered what the prince had said—something about the eyes and kindness. I might have been able to see it in her—understand.

I nodded in her direction. "That one."

Prince Theron's brows rose before he bowed. "Let it be so," he said before departing from the dance floor.

Walking away had me finally catching my breath, replaying every lingering touch, and the soothing way the prince spoke—so contrary to the picture I'd had of him previously.

"Miss Dagon," a hand gripped my bicep, and I turned to see a palace guard speaking. "The king requests your presence at the throne."

I swallowed, nodding before making my way to the center of the room. My stomach twisted in knots, and whatever breath I thought I had captured was once again stolen from my lungs.

Before the throne, King Wineslowe sat stoic, cold like the carved statues he had commissioned around the palace. When he looked at me, I felt as if my skin would peel right off, exposing every inch of me to be plucked apart and thrown into the fires that burned each week at the center of Marmere.

"My executioner," he greeted. "I am glad you found time to attend this party."

I curtsied, dipping my head low in submission. One thing I knew for certain, powerful men loved to feel as if you would bend to their will, and in order for my betrayal of the kingdom to work, I had to continue to do just that. "I am grateful for the invitation, Your Majesty."

King Wineslowe scoffed, tapping a ringed finger on the arm of his throne. "I am glad, though I fear the invitation was a mistake."

I blinked; my hands balled in my skirts as I fought the urge to run.

"It seems," he started again, running that same ringed finger along the arm of the golden throne, his brows raised. "You are quite a distraction for my son."

"Forgive me," I responded. "I'm not sure what you mean."

His eyes flicked to mine, calculating and empty. A shiver worked its way down my spine. "Dancing with the prince when he is here to find a wife." One brow cocked in question. "As I said, a distraction."

"I believed it a courtesy for which—"

"I recommend keeping to the servant's wing. The stone is far more fitting than the ornate decor of the rest of the palace, wouldn't you say?"

I nodded.

"I've done an awful lot for you, Miss Dagon. I know your former master quite well. I'm sure you find your time here far more pleasing. No one bothers you. You execute the witches and aid the kingdom in fulfilling its greater calling. Of course, that would be payment enough. The gown you wear, the food you eat, that is all extra, really." He held my stare, and I fought the stinging in my lungs as I struggled to breathe. "Do not respond," he said, his tone cutting. "You will not be around the prince again. Take your leave."

I curtsied once more. "Yes, Your Majesty."

Turning on my heel, I rushed up the steps, through the entryway, and down the hall. I walked until the ornate marble floors turned to stone, until the smell of musk and baking bread replaced that of incense and expensive wine. I walked until my feet ached in my heels, and I found my way to my door. I quickly turned the handle, pushed the groaning wood open, and slammed the thing shut behind me.

Upon entering my rooms, I saw a bottle of that same expensive wine from the party placed on my nightstand. Thumbing the tag wrapped around the bottle's neck, I read the script, noting it was yet another gift from the prince—something he'd planned to have waiting for me after the ball.

I picked up the bottle, rage burning in my chest. Powerlessness in the presence of the king had my anger brewing. Aside from bowing down and lying low, there was nothing I could do to fight back against his cruel words.

When the bottle slammed against the wall, shattering and spewing deep crimson liquid over the paint and the stone floor beneath, I found myself panting. The dress, the wine, it was all too much.

Throwing myself on the mattress, I allowed my breaths to slow, that rage simmering just beneath the surface—just enough for me to muster up the courage to return to my job—the one I so carefully used to my advantage.

It, so it seemed, was my only use.

And my only way to fight back against a wicked king.

Chapter Fifteen

Rialey

"What an absolute waste of good wine."

I startled, shooting up from my place on the bed and cursing my bulky dress as I crawled backward. The simple wooden headboard dug into my back as my heart rose in my throat.

"Sorry," Eryx said, his mask carefully pulled across his face, black covering the rest of him from head to toe. "I didn't mean to frighten you."

"Shit," I muttered, pressing my hand to my sternum as if it could stop the hammering.

Eryx chuckled, rounding the end of the bed to sit next to me. The mattress sank under his weight, heat emanating from him. "Why are there glass shards covering your floor, Rialey?"

My eyes flicked to the wall. Red stains dripped down like blood, now dried and most likely difficult to remove. I felt a pang of guilt. "I was upset," I murmured before looking back to Eryx. His blue eyes looked darker in the low light of the fire. The other light had been snuffed out before I fell asleep atop my comforter, still wearing my dress and far too bitter to care.

He tilted his head, just slightly. "What upset you? Was it the wine itself?"

"No."

"The prince?" One brow quirked upward, and I swallowed.

Looking away, I brought my knees to my chest, wrapping my arms around the bulky skirts of my gown. Burying my chin there, I avoided his gaze. "Why would the prince upset me?"

"Because you danced with him tonight, did you not?"

My gut twisted, remembering the feel of his hand gently pressed against my waist. I had enjoyed it—the dance, and that realization had me hoping he'd moved on. Whatever strange interest he'd taken in me had surely vanished—shattered like the bottle of his gift on the floor.

"How do you know that?"

Eryx leaned in, his voice taking on a lower cadence. "I have my ways."

I stared at him, wondering how the one man in the kingdom who knew me better than anyone else—the one man who knew my deepest secret—could hide so much from me.

It wasn't as if he knew my past. Eryx didn't know about my family, or lack thereof. He didn't know where I'd come from or my favorite color. He did, however, know that magic swirled in my blood. He knew I could bend the world to my will by manipulating what those around me perceived. And while many pieces of myself were missing in the picture he'd painted of me, the most important piece remained. He knew my deep desire to free my people, and he knew what I was behind the evil I committed.

It had to count for something.

And yet—

"How is it that you know so much of me, but I have no concept of what your life looks like in the daylight?" I asked, knowing full well I was broaching a subject we never touched.

Eryx and I stuck to our work and flirtatious banter, but I longed for more.

He looked at me, eyes so familiar they gave me pause.

"My life in the daylight?" he questioned.

I buried my chin in the skirt of my gown, squeezing my legs tighter to my chest. "I know nothing about you, and you, Eryx, know my deepest secret. In fact, you're the only one who knows it, save for the witches we've unleashed beyond the city walls." I bit my lip, chewing on my next words. "Tell me one thing. Tell me a secret of yours that I may have. One thing I can keep for myself."

His gloved hand thumbed the hem of my dress as he watched, pondering what I'd just asked of him. It was as if I could feel that touch on my skin, the way it burned right through me. "We could have had that wine together, you know?" His thick lashes kissed the tops of his cheeks when he blinked, and then the corners of his eyes crinkled. "I would have told you a thousand secrets. Based on the note I found amid the glass, the prince sent you that bottle. And after dancing with you, too? He must have found you lovely."

My stomach flipped. "Were you there?" I prodded. "In the ballroom, I mean. Were you there among the guests?"

His eyes met mine, simmering with something I couldn't quite place. "I was."

"Why can't I see your face?" I asked.

Eryx chuckled, his gloved hand moving away from the hem of my gown to grip his knee. I missed the touch. "It's not that I can trust I'm seeing yours," he said before gesturing in my direction. "Not truly, that is."

I sat up straighter, my arms still wrapped around my legs. "You cannot be serious?" Frustration burned in my chest. "You're the only person in this gods-forsaken kingdom who knows what I am. And yes, this is my real face. Magic is finite; I cannot conjure as many illusions as I wish." The broken glass sat scattered on the stone floors. I made a note to clean it before Visha arrived in the morning. "Besides," I continued, "I wouldn't leave this scar along my cheek if I had the choice."

Eryx glanced at the raised skin—the mark left from my parents' death all those years ago. It was a reminder of all they'd sacrificed for me.

"I believed, Miss Dagon, that if given the opportunity to have *any* appearance, you would choose something extraordinarily beautiful. And seeing as you are, in fact, extraordinarily beautiful, I assumed that the face you now wear had been carefully crafted by someone with a keen eye."

I scoffed, but my cheeks heated anyway. "I don't know whether to be offended or flattered."

Eryx shifted where he sat, the hood of his cloak casting what I could see of his face in shadows. "It seems my flirting could use some polishing."

The smile threatened to split across my face, the corners of my mouth turning up against my better judgement. "Is that what this is?"

"Possibly."

Silence hung between us, the air thick with something new—something that hadn't been there at the start of our—whatever one would call it.

I uncurled myself and turned away from him, standing from the mattress on the opposite side to walk toward the corner of the room where a small hand broom sat with a dustpan. I gathered them before moving to the glass on the floor, slowly working to clean the area. I needed something to do with my hands—if only to rid my body of the buzzing energy that had worked its way under my skin.

"Where have you been?" I asked, listening as the glass shards clinked beneath the broom bristles.

"On business."

"Business I cannot know about?" I challenged.

"It's..." He winced from where he still sat on my bed. "Complicated."

Nodding, I gathered more glass, slowly walking it to the wastebin before setting to work again. I couldn't let Visha walk in and unknowingly cut herself. I also felt guilty for the stains coating the wall. I could offer to paint over it, but I'm sure it would be shot down. All I'd done was create more work for the staff in my frustration.

"Did you kiss him?"

I paused my movements; the broom hovering over the stone floor as I looked up at Eryx, his eyes glittering in the firelight. Was he jealous? *No.* The mischievous glint told me he already knew the answer. Maybe he was just toying with me.

"The prince," he added. "He seemed rather fond of you while you were dancing. I just assumed—"

"Of course, I didn't kiss him." I shot to my feet, brows furrowing in equal parts confusion and annoyance. "He's a vile, loathsome thing. Complacent as his father burns my people to ash. You really believe I would kiss such a man?"

"Rather harsh," he mused.

"Is it?" I asked.

Eryx stood up, his gloved hand brushing mine as he took the broom and dustpan from my grasp. Kneeling, he began cleaning the glass from the floor, sweeping up the last of the shards and dumping them in the wastebin for me. "I suppose not," he finally answered, setting the broom back in the corner. "Is it just that you have another lover?"

I tilted my head to the side. Maybe it *was* jealousy. "It is not."

"I see."

The silence hung between us as we stared at one another. Eryx kept a decent amount of distance, and I wished it had been him at the ball dancing with me. I could picture it, his hand around my waist, guiding my every move. Maybe then I wouldn't have had to feel guilty for enjoying the presence of my partner.

His eyes trailed down, dipping to the deep V of my gown, over the skirts, down to the floor, and back. "Your gown is beautiful, by the way." His voice lowered, taking on a rasp that sent goosebumps over my skin. "I don't know if you knew that."

With reddening cheeks and a flushed chest, I looked toward the fire. "Another gift from the prince," I answered honestly before scoffing. "I'm anxious to get the thing off."

Eryx cleared his throat, and I realized how my words sounded—what I'd said. My blush deepened. "Right," I began, trying to change the subject. "So, next week? I assume we will continue our work?"

"Of course," he answered, his hands now clasped behind his back. "I should go."

My chest tightened, a heaviness resting there like a permanent weight. "How is it you are getting in and out of this room undetected?" I pressed, somehow knowing he wouldn't answer.

"A secret." He stepped forward, mere feet away from me. "And I wish it would remain so." His head tilted to the side as he studied me. "Close your eyes, Rialey."

I shuddered. "What?"

"Close your eyes."

Obeying, I did just that, listening to the fabric of his clothes rustling just before the heat of him came nearer. I could feel him there—his presence—even though he wasn't touching me.

"Don't open them," he murmured, and my stomach curled and twisted, the goosebumps rising on my arms.

Fingers, ungloved, brushed the side of my cheek, sending heat everywhere they went. They trailed over my jaw before tracing the line of my neck until his palm rested where it met my shoulder. I couldn't think beyond that one touch, wanting desperately to open my eyes.

"Keep them closed," he whispered, his breath fanning over my lips, so close I could almost taste him on my tongue. Had he taken his mask off?

It had been a long time since I'd even considered getting close to a man. With my job at the palace, I knew there were pieces of me I could not risk exposing, but those very pieces were the ones Eryx already knew about. And here in my room, I could feel the need everywhere.

"I don't want you knowing all my secrets," he said as I fought the urge to lean in, touch my lips to his if only for a moment.

"Your secrets?" I asked, breathless. "As I said before, you already know mine." I licked my lips anxiously. "And you still didn't tell me something true about yourself."

His thumb moved, tracing a line from near my ear, down my jaw, and beneath my chin. "I know," he whispered. "I don't want you to know my secrets just yet."

His hand disappeared, but he still stood close. The temptation to open my eyes grew with every passing second.

I sucked in a breath just as the cold hit me. Cursing myself, I squeezed my eyes tighter, and when I opened them, Eryx was gone.

Chapter Sixteen

Verena

"Verena, Dear, could you hang the kettle over the fire?"

"Of course."

I dropped my quill, gathering the parchment littering the table in the cabin—the one we sat at for meals. At this point, I'd drawn the entire Waldwood, though Ahvi and Caius never judged me for it.

Each rendition of trees and snow lacked the magic of the forest, but sketching my memories gave me some hope that I'd return and find something there worth saving.

I knew separating a witch from the forest would weaken her magic, and I longed to know what it would feel like to have her thrum through my blood again with an intensity I'd forgotten. It was something I clung to—longed for. At a time when my entire being felt weak, I longed to renew a part of my strength.

Shoving the papers into the box beneath the bed, I stood up, dusting off my apron and padding to the hutch in the kitchen. I grabbed the kettle, poured water into it, and hung it over the fire.

Caius collected the water each day either from the fallen snow outside or the creek that cut through the woods a few miles east. This far into the forest around Marmere, we did not have the luxuries of the city, but I enjoyed the quiet life they lived, so uncomplicated and peaceful.

When I returned to the hutch to find the various herbal blends Ahvi kept there, I tapped my finger on my bottom lip, wondering which blend to select. Ahvi and Caius had more knowledge of their medicinal properties than I did. In fact, some of the names scrawled across the jars, I did not even know.

"Any preference?" I asked.

Ahvi chuckled as she gathered items from the worn wooden dresser near the foot of the bed and folded them into a satchel. She often left on trips, whether to town or to various neighbors' homes, from what Caius told me. He'd normally go with her, but opted to stay—just in case I needed anything.

Though her frequent trips had me believing the woman either loved a good hike in the snow or couldn't stand a third person occupying their small cabin.

The latter caused guilt to weigh heavy in my stomach, and so I preferred not to think of it.

"Your choice," Ahvi said before closing her bag and placing it on the now-empty table. "I plan to visit a friend today. I probably won't be back until morning."

I smiled, plucking the jar of dried calendula flowers, chamomile flowers, and a few other herbs that Ahvi had mixed together. Leaning against the long table where Ahvi and Caius prepared meals, I stared at her, folding my arms across my chest. "Who are you visiting this time? The Barbrooke's who own those horses you and Caius talk about?"

Ahvi waved a hand. "No, no. This is a dear friend who lives in the opposite direction. Another isolated cabin, I suppose. Not all of us prefer the city life Marmere holds."

I frowned. "You mean the burnings?"

Ahvi had been fairly vocal about her opinions as it pertained to our kingdom's treatment of witches, and while Caius and I hadn't discussed it since the hot springs, I couldn't help but wonder if the story he told me might have been the reason why. Maybe Ahvi had lost her son in the same way Caius lost his father—his mother, too.

But that was just speculation. I didn't feel I had a right to his stories. If he wanted me to know the deep pains of his past, he'd tell me.

Still, I couldn't help feeling as if I were missing an important segment of their lives—a puzzle missing the final piece right at the very center.

The door opened, bringing the cold winter air with it and Caius's comforting presence. The memory of his fingers running through my hair, the way he'd soothed me, were burned into my mind.

He glanced to the woodpile by the fire as the kettle sounded. "I'll need to chop more before this afternoon, I take it."

Ahvi kissed him on the cheek, her full lips pressing to his skin with a loud smack before she patted him there. "That's my boy."

I got a towel and used it to lift the kettle, carefully preparing three cups of tea. Ahvi gulped hers, long before the liquid had cooled enough for such a thing. I placed the other two cups on the table, listening to the fire crackling in the hearth and the tune Caius hummed as he folded a blanket over the sofa. His deep voice sounded through the air, the tune touching something in my chest as I pulled a chair out and sipped the steaming liquid I'd prepared.

"I'll be back by morning," Ahvi announced, slinging the bag over her shoulder and grabbing her cloak from a hook near the door.

Caius turned to her, his boots scuffing over the hardwood with the movement. "So, I get the couch tonight?" he teased.

I raised a brow, holding the cup close to my nose. "I'd be happy to take the couch," I announced, earning a scolding finger from Ahvi.

"You will do no such thing. I've raised this boy to be a gentleman." She tied the cloak around her neck, raising the hood carefully before offering us both a small smile. "Off I go."

"Love you, Ma," Caius voiced, Ahvi returning the sentiment before exiting the cabin.

When Caius joined me at the table, he took up his tea and stared at me over the rim of the cup.

At first, I ignored him, waiting for him to say something first instead of giving in and asking what he so clearly wanted me to ask.

In the end, I failed.

"What?" I questioned, noting the mirth in his brown eyes.

Caius took a sip of tea, his throat bobbing as he swallowed. "How would you like to help me chop wood when we are finished here?"

I set my cup on the table with a soft sound. "That would be fine," I replied. After all, I had spent five weeks in the cabin. This past week, I'd felt stronger and found myself helping more. I'd swept the floors, made meals, and washed clothes for Ahvi. And despite my guilt at using their resources, I felt confident that I'd contributed something worthwhile. While Ahvi chose to leave frequently, I didn't think she loathed my company entirely. Often, she'd tell stories made up from books she'd read previously as I listened with rapt attention. In the evenings, she'd knit by the fire, humming a tune and enjoying the quiet evening.

It was peaceful here—a true place to heal.

"I've never chopped wood before, but I assume you just slam the axe down as hard as possible and pray the wood splits. Will my lack of muscle be a problem?"

Caius laughed then, a real hearty sound. "No," he said. "It's all technique, and I'm happy to show you." Standing, he drained the last of his tea before turning to pluck the two cloaks from the corner hooks. "Come along," he encouraged.

Standing, I made my way to the door, where he instructed me to turn around. His gentle fingers brushed my hair to the side before draping the cloak around my shoulders. When I turned, Caius tied the front before repositioning my brunette strands over each side, hanging loosely in waves.

His gaze trailed over his handiwork, making my skin burn hot. "You may tie your hair back," he suggested. "That way it's out of your eyes."

I smiled. "Wouldn't want to swing an axe and miss, of course."

His grin warmed my skin even more. "Of course."

We walked out into the snow, the gentle flakes falling from the overcast sky above the kingdom. The winter was all I'd known of Alphaird, but I'd heard stories growing up of warm sunshine and swimming holes tucked in the forest where children used to play and dance beneath waterfalls. The covens also spoke of mossy forests and misty mornings—the beauty of each goddess's temple and how nature seemed to proclaim her power. Cyra's temple, the goddess of the sun, stood bright and in the direct path of the sunlight. Araxie's temple, the goddess of water, sat beside a bubbling brook—flowing and not frozen.

It seemed that image of our world had long since disappeared.

I'd grown up in Cyra and never seen the sunlight strike anything but frozen ground.

At twenty-one, snow and frosty air had raised me within the confines of the Waldwood until my mother had become ill, forcing me to look for life outside the forest. Finding myself in Marmere, I worked at the tavern until the day the guard caught me—had me thrown in the useless dungeons to be hunted by the king's executioner.

As the wind whipped around us, I thought of *her*—wondered how many deaths had been real and how many had been mere illusions. I'd thought her evil—in line with the kingdom and all its desolation, but that was so far removed from the truth.

How many others were working to undermine the commands of the king? Were they all witches?

"Here," Caius grabbed the axe from where it leaned against a tree near a pile of logs, presumably cut from the tree he downed a few days ago.

My fingers brushed his when I took the axe, its weight heavy against my limbs, threatening to pull me to the snow at my feet. Memories of the chilling wind and my failing body filled my mind as I stared at the glittering blanket on the forest floor. Biting my tongue, I tried to keep myself present—here. If I were to leave for the Waldwood, I needed to prove I was improving. I needed to know I'd become stronger in the weeks since Caius found me, and that I wouldn't be consumed by my fear in the same way I'd been at the hot springs.

A warm hand found my shoulder, and I looked up, my gaze finding Caius.

"Are you alright?" he asked, and I nodded.

"Yes," I said, forcing a smile to my lips, testing the weight of the axe against my growing muscles. "Just getting used to it."

One corner of his mouth turned up. "Good."

Caius grabbed a log from the pile, setting it atop a tree stump with a heavy thud. His muscles shifted when he stood, his cloak discarded on a nearby branch, leaving the black sweater and the stretch of its fabric around his toned chest and biceps.

"So, I just swing?" I asked, doing my best to look anywhere but him and fighting the reddening of my cheeks.

Caius chuckled, and the sound rumbled beneath my skin, vibrating the very bones that kept me standing. "Hardly," he said. "Here." He stepped closer, the snow crunching beneath his boots as he gently wrapped his fingers around my wrists, the touch near burning. He guided my right hand to the base of the axe, and my left toward the top. "You'll hold it like this, assuming this is your dominant hand." He tapped my wrist near the bottom of the axe. "When you swing, try to work with the weight of the tool. Don't overexert yourself." He stood, his feet shoulder-width apart as he held a pretend axe in his hand to demonstrate. "Your guide hand will come down as you lower the axe, aiming for the center of the log to split it in two."

I changed my stance, turning and planting myself in front of the wood he'd placed for me. When his hands found their way to the front of my cloak, I sucked in a breath.

"You should take this off," he said, his voice a low rasp. "So, it doesn't get in the way."

"Right," I muttered, feeling the way my entire body felt flushed. I did as he instructed, raising the axe above my head and sliding my guiding hand down as the weight fell into the log before me. Surprisingly, I'd made it to the center, but the log hadn't split.

The metal of the axe had buried itself in the wood, leaving a log completely useless for the hearth in the cottage.

I tried to pry it away, going so far as to shove my foot atop it, but the axe wouldn't budge.

"Don't do that," Caius said, chuckling. "Just lift it as if the wood isn't attached and do it again. It should split."

Again, I raised the axe overhead, now heavier than before. My muscles strained with the effort, but something buzzed in my veins. I felt strong—powerful. When the axe fell heavily on the stump, the wood split with a loud crack, either side falling away and leaving me there with the wooden handle in both of my palms.

"I did it," I beamed, noting the way Caius's eyes had brightened as if he were proud of the progress I'd made.

"Perfect," he said before lifting another log from the pile, this one larger than the last. "Now, only about one hundred more."

His smile was devastating. A flash of white teeth and the smooth skin of his sharp jawline. He must have shaved this morning, because I could have sworn stubble had dusted that same jaw the night before—not that I'd noticed.

When I swung again, something bloomed in my chest. Maybe I was closer to the Waldwood than I thought, and that thought alone felt like hope.

Most nights, I drifted off to sleep rather quickly. The exhaustion overtook me, and I gave little thought to Caius and Ahvi sleeping in the cabin with me.

Now, as I lie awake in bed, the sheets pulled up to my chest, my attention fixated on the steady breathing from the couch across the room.

As if summoned by my thoughts, Caius spoke. "Have you thought any more about using your magic?"

My heart pounded in my chest, and I tugged the blankets closer, as if they could protect me from the fears I now carried. "Thought about it?" I parroted. "Yes. Though, it's not as strong as it would be if I were in the Waldwood."

My eyes fixed on the ceiling, and I counted the wooden beams above, waiting for what would come next.

With sore arms and an aching back, I felt revived. Functioning as if I had something to offer the world instead of sucking the resources from everyone around me. It had felt good—chopping firewood in the forest. The last piece of the puzzle, the one thing that remained, was my ability to tap into my magic. If I could do it, my journey to the Waldwood could begin.

"I want to..." Caius cleared his throat, his toned body shifting on the worn leather of the sofa. "I want to give you permission to try it."

The beating of my heart quickened. I could feel the magic humming in my chest, begging me to call on the power I'd been so afraid of since my capture.

"Okay," I whispered.

A log shifted, the fire crackling in response.

"Don't kill me," Caius muttered from across the room, dragging a soft laugh from between my lips.

My magic didn't work that way. I'm sure if I wanted to, I could trick the mind into something. In fact, I'd heard of such stories—dreamwalkers lulling their victims into a state of comatose until finally, they accepted all that death had to offer and simply gave their life up as if it were nothing more than a mere thought.

The power was dangerous, certainly, but dreamwalkers were so rare among witches. So rare that my mother had been the only one I'd known growing up, and even as I traveled beyond my home, I still hadn't encountered that familiar magic. Though, it wasn't as though witches flaunted their power. Not in Alphaird. Not when Wineslowe thirsted for blood and charred flesh.

"How do we start?" Caius asked, the nerves clear in the wavering of his deep voice. "Or what does this entail, I mean?"

"Well," I began, my voice a near whisper. "You should start by falling asleep, but judging how fearful you sound, I'm not sure that is likely."

Another shifting sound came from where he lay. I risked looking over at him, tracing the gentle slope of his nose, wide at the base where another dip led to plush lips—soft despite the constant cold weather we endured.

"If I can get myself asleep, then what will happen?" he asked, staring at the ceiling as if the answers were just beyond the roof, written somewhere in the stars.

I smiled, letting my eyes linger on his smooth skin—the dusting of stubble that had formed on his jaw since this morning. "I will enter your dreams," I told him, my tone soothing. "It will be like... well... a dream. But I will be in whatever world your mind created. Then I can add things—change things. I can appear as myself."

He turned then, his eyes meeting mine from across the room. Even across the cabin, I could see the intensity—something raw and unflinching. I couldn't look away as he spoke. "How will I know it's truly you and not just something I've conjured?"

"I could promise to do something unexpected, like chopping wood without burying the axe into a log and struggling to remove it." He laughed then. "Or," I continue, "maybe I'll offer to fight you, though I've never been very good at throwing punches."

Caius smirked before turning away, and for a while, I thought the conversation had ended there—unfinished—but he eventually spoke again.

"You said you can change things in my dream? Like where I am?"

"Yes," I answered.

"Show me the Waldwood."

I sucked in a breath, thinking back on the hundreds of charcoal sketches tucked beneath the bed, the images I'd tried desperately to capture. I clung to the magic of the forest as if my soul were a part of it—and maybe it was. The Waldwood had long since been a safe haven for the witches, the one place untouched by King Wineslowe's fire.

When the name had left the witch hunter's lips, it had gently coaxed me out of my state of shock—the hardened shell of a person I'd become in the palace dungeons.

"Why?" I finally asked, not sure if he'd deem me worthy of an answer.

"I'm assuming you wish to leave soon. You're growing stronger, and I promised I'd escort you. Don't think I forgot." Caius cleared his throat as if he were trying to clear the emotion from his voice, but failed. "It's been over a month in this cabin, Verena. Show me the Waldwood the way you remember it. I want to be prepared for our arrival."

My brows furrowed, but I didn't look at him. It felt private—whatever he was battling. I didn't want to intrude. "The forest isn't scary," I assured.

"I know."

I thought back to the hot spring on the mountain—the story of a little boy saved by his grandmother. He hadn't confirmed it, but somehow, I knew it had been about him. And if that were true, Caius had lost his parents to the soldiers. Still, I wanted to hear it from him. Maybe it was selfish, but I wanted the truth from his lips—not a sad pieced together version of it I had conjured based on what small offerings he'd given me. "Then why would you need to be prepared to see it?" I pressed.

Caius sighed. "It brings back painful memories. Show me the Waldwood, and when I fall asleep, you can turn my dreams something good—give me something to look forward to."

My chest tightened at his words. "Okay," I whispered.

"Okay."

CHAPTER SEVENTEEN

CAIUS

Glittering snow capped the mountains in the distance as I looked toward the horizon. It had been so long since my skin felt the warmth of a summer sun, but the winter had become a companion of sorts. Beauty could be found in the gray skies and creaking limbs of giant trees coated in ice, though I'd hardly stopped to notice recently.

Life had become a constant routine of chopping wood, hunting, taking care of Ma, and watching as the strange girl in our cabin slowly came back to herself.

Glancing down, I looked at the hot spring emanating steam and felt the warmth kiss my skin. When I lowered myself into the water, my clothes sopping and heavy, I breathed deeply. Closing my eyes, memories of summertime in the Waldwood became as clear as if I'd been back in that place, a small child running on moss-covered ground dappled with the light from the sun.

As I ran, the water disappeared. When I came to a halt, I stood in the middle of that forest, looking on as my mother ducked beneath the entrance to the hollow tree where we lived. The base of the pine matched its massive height. Our home stretched as if reaching for the sun—as if the sun were the source of its magic.

The Waldwood had always been like this, housing families and witches within the trees that carried its magic—a safe haven for those who respected the very soil beneath their feet.

My mother stood as I remembered her, with smooth sienna skin, a shade lighter than my own, and deep brown eyes that warmed like fire in the hearth.

"Caius," she called, her eyes meeting mine as a wide smile split her face. "There you are."

My chest ached with the memory of it—the feeling of home that had long since left me. While I'd found a home with my grandmother, it did not replace the ache of what was—what could have been.

"She's beautiful."

I turned to find Verena there, a similar warmth shining in her eyes as they fixed to my mother. The dusting of freckles across her cheeks had become more prominent, her skin kissed by the sun as it shone through the trees. Her mouth parted to reveal the small gap between her teeth, her soft lower lip hanging in awe of the image before her.

"She was," I answered, offering the ghost of a smile—one faded like the memory of my parents.

Verena closed her eyes, dropping her chin as she let out a breathy laugh. When she looked at me again with new understanding, she smiled softly. Her presence felt so real—more tangible than the trees, and the sun, and my childhood home.

"I'm not sure why you asked me for a happy memory of the Waldwood," Verena observed. "It seems you have happy memories of your own."

I straightened, discomfort stirring in the pit of my stomach. This dream wasn't new, and soon, Verena would learn the horrors of my childhood. I winced. "Then I suggest you do not stick around for the next part."

Metal clanged, and a scream echoed through the trees right on time. The terror stood in contrast to the peaceful scene around us. I'd always thought it odd that such horrendous crimes could occur on the loveliest of days. Surely the skies should know when to cry.

A small child, so familiar it hurt, rushed past me, burying his face in my mother's skirts. Her expression shifted as she looked out between the trees, placing a protective arm around the little boy—around me.

Verena and I watched as she rushed inside, practically dragging the boy with her. I could still feel the bruising pressure on my arm—one of my earliest memories.

The ground shook, images twisting until summer faded into fall and then winter. Verena now stood next to me at the edge of a frozen pool tucked between the winter trees. The ice reflected a gray light from the overcast sky, but there was still a soft and settling energy in the air.

"Do you relive that memory often?" Verena asked as my throat tightened. Barely there, her soft fingers brushed mine from where she stood next to me—the touch disappearing just as the image of my childhood home disappeared moments before.

"I do," I answered honestly. Understanding wrapped around me as I realized Verena was here—in my head—my dream. "This isn't what I thought it would be." My brow furrowed. "You being here," I clarified. "It's so seamless. I can only tell because you appear more..." I shook my head, trying to find the words before I allowed my gaze to settle on her, soaking in the flowing tunic and brown pants she wore. Had she chosen this outfit? Even in such simple clothing, there was still a vibrancy to everything about her. "Real," I finished.

"That's the danger, really." Verena smiled. "I'm sure I scared the guard when I entered his mind. Anyone would be fearful." She sighed. "It's no wonder he caught me and sought revenge."

I nodded, refusing to pressure her into talking, but thankful that she trusted me as much as she did. "So," I started, gesturing to the frozen pool before us. "What is this memory meant to be? If it's a memory at all, that is."

Verena's smile stretched across her face, her wide eyes glittering in the reflecting snow. "It seems I'm a bit younger than you, as my memory of the Waldwood has always been in winter. My mother used to take me out on the ice. We'd slide around and see who could go faster on the pond near our coven." Her head tilted to one side, soft strands of hair kissing her face in the cold breeze. "Have you ever done something like that?"

"I can't say I have."

Shifting nervously on my feet, I watched as Verena held out a hand. Accepting it, I followed her as she led me onto the ice, where, as soon as my feet touched the surface, a loud crack sounded. Jolting, I looked up with wide eyes, somewhat shameful of my fear. This was only a dream, after all.

"It's okay," she assured. "You won't fall." Her breathy laugh warmed like the dappled sun through the trees—like the summertime long since forgotten in a kingdom of darkness and death.

I settled and slid my foot across the ice, slowly finding my bearings and becoming more confident. Verena never let go of my hands, clasping them gently as she slowly slid backward. Snowflakes descended from the clouds, decorating her brown, wavy strands. I smiled, then.

"You're actually very good at this," she said, watching my feet as if she needed to be sure I wouldn't slip and fall.

I kept my eyes on her face, drinking in her features. She was beautiful—truly. Even more so now that we'd spent weeks together in close quarters. I didn't know if the dream made her more vibrant, or if Verena just was.

Every time I'd watched her these past weeks, I'd found her humming softly to herself, drawing picture after picture of the forest she called home. With each passing day, she grew stronger—fiercer.

Unbreakable.

That's what she was.

"I would think, this being a dream world, that I could manifest more skill in learning this." I chuckled. "In fact, I would think I'd have full control over this entire experience."

Verena's eyes met mine, wide and blazing. "You would not have full control with me here." Clearing her throat, she looked away, the intensity of her gaze disappearing. "Unless I allowed you to have that control, that is."

"Is there not a way for me to overcome the power of a dreamwalker?" I asked, genuinely curious.

We continued to move around the ice, Verena releasing my hands and trusting me to glide on my own. She moved next to me as if sliding across a frozen pond were the most natural thing in the universe.

"There are ways to overcome a dreamwalker, but they're not easy. You would need to be very well practiced in remaining in the space between waking and sleeping. Trap a dreamwalker there, overpower their persuasion with your own awareness. Though most would kill you before they allowed that to happen. Inflict so much pain, your body would give up on itself just to protect your mind."

I nodded, recognizing the power she held. The kingdom had long feared the witches, and Verena was the most powerful among them. I could see the threat there, but somehow, I trusted her. "You wouldn't do something like that," I stated, sure of my belief.

"Maybe," she offered, her voice barely a whisper. "Maybe not."

I lurched forward, barely catching myself with my hands. As soon as I was on the ground, another shove came at my back, rougher this time.

Verena looked around, panic overtaking her soft features. "Caius," she whispered. "You have to wake up."

I turned, her vibrancy diminishing until the very image of her disappeared on the frigid winter wind. "Caius!"

I sat up on the couch, Ma's features tight as she stared at me, her hands firmly planted on my shoulders. She shouldn't be here, not in the middle of the night. Ma never traveled in the dark, by foot or on horseback.

"What?" I answered, my heart flipping inside my chest. Something was wrong—very wrong.

"Soldiers," she said, the pain in her gaze evident.

Shuffling sounds from the bed drew my attention before Verena found her place next to us. "Soldiers?" she asked, the remaining embers of the fire casting orange highlights across her mussed hair. She blinked, her skin a shade paler as realization washed over her—over us.

"I came as soon as I could," Ma whispered, her tone harsh and biting. "Soldiers are being sent north. I left once we saw them traveling past in the snow. Questioned me before I could really get going. You both have to leave, Caius. Take her somewhere. If they find Verena—" Her jaw hardened, eyes burning with an intensity I'd never seen before. "If they discover what we stand for—who we *are*—

She didn't need to finish the sentence. My chest tightened when I stood, grabbing a pack from beneath the bed and stuffing all I could in it—herbs, clothing, dried meat, and several tinctures Ma had stored in the hutch for emergencies.

With hurried movements, I rounded the cabin. My tongue stuck to the roof of my dry mouth, panic slowly taking hold as my mind turned over every possible horror that could befall us. It brought back memories of my dream—my parents' deaths.

A twinge of regret pinched in my chest. While we'd done our best to be honest with Verena, there were...omissions.

There were reasons Ma traveled—reasons I'd traveled with her in the past. Something was brewing in Alphaird, and in her state of weakness, we'd wanted to help.

If Verena wanted to join a rebellion, she would need a clear mind to do so.

Ma spoke to her as she gathered clothes and necessities. The moonlight shone through the window, blue light mingling with the dying embers. The clear skies were so contrary to the fear that wound its way around my heart, tightening until it felt difficult to breathe.

I would be leaving Ma while soldiers prowled through the forest, looking for—something. While we knew how to fight, leaving her alone didn't sit right with me.

"You'll need to be careful. I overheard them mention the Waldwood," Ma warned. "I'm wondering if King Wineslowe is sending them there. To do what, I haven't a clue, but it wouldn't be the first time he sent troops out to the forest. For twenty-seven years, they've kept away from the tree line that wouldn't burn. I can't imagine what's possessed him to try again. As if murdering the queen of the covens, and setting our world into a constant winter weren't enough punishment."

Verena nodded as she shoved her legs into a pair of fleece-lined pants, buttoning them and adding a thick tunic and sweater. She quickly braided her hair over one shoulder, tying it off with a piece of leather, her eyes hollow and void of feeling. The Verena from my dreams had disappeared, replaced by the shell I'd found lying in the snow weeks ago.

I hated to see her like that.

Especially because I didn't want to admit I was afraid. Verena had grown in strength, but the truth of the matter was she hadn't healed fully. The trip to the Waldwood would be dangerous, and soldiers lurked mere miles from our door.

She'd need the protection. Hell, she'd need more than that.

Ma gripped Verena's shoulders. "The Barbrooke's gave us a horse," she stated, every muscle on her face tense. "You will take that, and you will both go north."

"But what about—"

Ma cut her off as I shoved a few quills and pieces of parchment into the pack.

"Don't," Ma scolded. "I will be fine, and Caius will protect you." Her eyes blazed when they met mine, the charge clear in her swirling amber gaze. I knew what she expected of me. Just as she had protected me all those years ago, it was time to pass it on. We couldn't save my parents, but Verena?

"I'll do what I can," I promised. Ma walked to me quickly, wrapping her arms around my torso, the squeeze almost painful. I breathed in the scent of fresh thyme and sweet soil.

"Go west first," she advised, voice muffled as she buried her head in my chest. "When you feel safe, move north, but try to put distance between the soldiers and Verena—between the soldiers and *you*."

I nodded, holding her tighter as pain lashed through me.

Verena's glassy eyes flitted to the window where she gazed at the moonlight. Guilt and fear shone there, but I vowed I would do what I said—protect her in the ways I wasn't able to protect my own family.

"We should go," I said, shoving the emotion down.

Verena nodded, somber as she slowly walked to the door. Outside, a large black horse stood saddled and ready.

When I got to the threshold of the cabin, I allowed myself to look back once, but when we rode into the darkness, I didn't allow myself to think on the fear and worry I'd seen etched into every crease of my grandmother's face.

Chapter Eighteen

Theron

The palace libraries held images of the gardens from before winter descended upon the kingdom of Alphaird. Lush grasses and vibrant flowers decorated the garden beds, attracting butterflies and other insects that flitted around during the day.

It was said that my grandmother enjoyed wildflowers most. The back section of the gardens, the area closest to the forest, had been reserved for wild daisies, lavender, and other flowers selected by her during her time as queen. Her husband, my grandfather, had found it improper and ensured that the rest of the gardens were trimmed, organized, and neat.

I much preferred the paintings of the back parts of the garden, and as I rode over the dirt paths dusted with snow, I could almost imagine what it would have looked like then.

Shifting in the saddle, I stretched my heels downward and looked out at the barren gardens. Hearty plants, along with a large amount of cold dirt, had replaced all that was once here.

Still, the glittering snow and the quiet gave me space to clear my head.

Two weeks since the ball, and my father stayed an incessant thorn in my side, pressuring me to select from any of the lord's daughters I'd danced with.

Aside from Bloodbane's daughter, I found most of the women rather unpleasant. Odessa's persistence matched that of her father's, and I found her advances unwelcome. Vespahr hadn't left, claiming he had business here in Marmere and would return to his city at its conclusion.

I was starting to believe his *business* had to do with the offer of marriage that would never come.

I sniffed as the cold air bit at my cheeks, thinking of the way Rialey Dagon had called me arrogant and foolish, and made clear that she loathed me entirely. I wondered what she'd say if she knew that wasn't true at all. I noted the quick intake of breath, the warmth of her as she pressed in closer. Rialey Dagon did not hate me, no matter what lies she told herself—even if she vanished after that first dance.

Wraith's hooves cut into the thin snow on the path, her muscles shifting as I rode until standing before the two large greenhouses looming over the east end of the gardens. Their glass windows frosted and obscuring the rows of plants within.

"Easy," I muttered, patting Wraith's neck before dismounting and heading into the greenhouse I frequented.

The long rows of boxes stretched to the back, where a pale woman, no older than twenty, tended to the herb garden with the utmost care. Her blonde hair fell over one shoulder while she hummed and dug her fingers into the soil near the ground. With her soft voice drowning out my footsteps, she hardly registered my approach or the few other palace staff tending to the other boxes.

"Aurelia," I said, watching as she stood up, her cheeks already flushed from the cold.

She wiped her hands on her apron with rushed movements. "Your Highness," she answered quickly, lowering herself before standing straight again. Whispering, Aurelia leaned in. "I take it you've come for your monthly supply."

A smile stretched across my face before I turned, gazing at the raised bed behind where she'd been standing, the fragrant scent mingling with that of the cold soil. "You are doing a fine job here," I observed. "And yes."

Aurelia's blue eyes widened and scanned the greenhouse. Once she found all other servants were busy with their own work, she reached into her pocket to grab a small canvas bag tied closed with twine. I quickly grabbed it from her, shoving it in my pocket and finally looking away from the plants.

The door to the greenhouse opened, and a tall man with a curling mustache walked in, gripping a cane in his hand. He ambled through the pathways, glancing at the vegetables and the flowers—clearly taking a daily stroll.

"Strange for Mr. Rackwell to be going for a walk in the palace greenhouses," I mused. "Does he come here often?"

Aurelia didn't respond, and after a moment of silence, I turned to her. Her face had gone ashen, her features tight as her lips pressed together, and her jaw ticked. My brows furrowed when I noticed she was staring at Mr. Rackwell, one of the rich men who lived in Marmere.

His gaze fell to her, predatory and intense as his head tilted to the side, one brow quirked upward.

"Aurelia," I said, the air turning bitter and cold. I knew that gaze—had seen it on many men in our kingdom.

She still didn't look at me. "Aurelia, has he done something?" I kept my voice low, stepping in front of her and blocking her vision of the man with my own hands clasped behind my back. Staring down at her, I noted the way her eyes flicked around the room nervously.

"I—" She finally looked to me; her mouth pulled into a slight frown. "What?"

"I said, has he done something?" My eyes narrowed in question, but somehow, I knew the answer. I'd heard rumors about the man. Known for bribery and frequenting Marmere's brothel, Mr. Rackwell had created quite a name for himself. My father seemed to enjoy turning a blind eye to the man, but as I stood there, I felt the deep desire to push back against my father's cruelty. I was the prince, after all. I was not completely helpless.

"I'd rather not say," she whispered, watching as he came closer to where we stood. When she caught sight of him again, Aurelia flinched.

"I am not asking as a friend, Aurelia." I stood taller, keeping my tone sharp as the blade of the sword hanging on my hip. "I am asking you as your prince. Now tell me, has something happened?"

"There has been…" She raised her chin, her eyes glassy but determined. "An incident," she finished.

Anger burned in my chest as I clenched my fists. That anger had always been there, but recently, it had taken a different shape. I spent the majority of my time placating my father, dancing with important women, and participating in the witch hunts at such a young age to obtain his approval. I no longer desired the approval of evil men—in fact, I longed for something far more useful.

Their fear.

"Consider it dealt with," I stated, nodding once before exiting the greenhouse. My eyes tracked Mr. Rackwell as I walked to the end of the greenhouse.

Returning Wraith to the palace stables, my hand flexed around the sword at my hip—the herbs I'd collected burning a hole in my pocket.

It seemed my afternoon schedule had become rather full.

My hands felt raw after vigorously scrubbing them upon my return to the palace. My boots tapped the stone floors of the servants' wing, my jaw tight and muscles sore.

Sconces lit the darker halls of this part of the palace, mustier and sparsely decorated. This end of the castle contrasted the ornate designs where my rooms were. Thankfully, my father hadn't commissioned any statues of himself for this area. I found the absence of his likeness to be immeasurably pleasing.

Stretching my back muscles beneath my jacket, I kept walking until I saw her. With black hair hanging at her waist, a maroon-colored tunic, and dark, fitted pants, Rialey Dagon's steps hurried as she turned down the hall.

By the looks of it, she had been headed toward the servants' dining hall. I stopped, turned around, and rushed down a separate hallway, knowing that if I jogged, I'd be able to catch up to her.

One woman pressed her back against the wall when I rushed by, quickly bowing and muttering something that I didn't quite catch. When I finally rounded the corner, I saw Rialey just as she was about to open the doors to the dining hall. I rushed, grabbing the handle, my fingers brushing hers as I worked to keep my breathing steady.

"Allow me," I said, pulling the door open, murmuring and the clinking of dishes following.

Rialey stared at me, eyes wide and feet frozen in place. After a moment, she seemed to gather herself, curtseying and fumbling over her words. "Prince Ther—Your Highness." She winced, slowly rising to her full height, her eyes level with my chest. "Forgive me," she muttered.

"For?" I asked, raising a brow. I fought the smile threatening to pull at my mouth and failed.

Rialey cleared her throat, lifting her chin just slightly, and I wondered how she spent her time in the palace when she wasn't dragging prisoners to their death. She didn't frequent town, opting to stay in the palace during the week. I hardly saw her, though. The possibility that she'd been instructed to stay away from the other parts of the castle was high, certainly, but I'm sure my father could be convinced. He'd allowed her to attend the ball, anyway.

"Why are you here?" she asked. I gestured for her to enter the dining hall, but she glanced at my hand on the door and took a step back. "I'd rather not be a spectacle."

Allowing the door to close, I stepped in front of her, clasping my hands behind my back. "Alright." I smiled, noting the way she refused to look at my face. "As for your question, I was trying to run into you." In fact, there had been no other reason for me to end up on this side of the palace. I'd spent the morning in the gardens pondering the time I'd been around the woman, and after an early afternoon of business, I found I needed time to clear my head. A pleasant conversation, perhaps.

Though I hardly thought Rialey would offer pleasant conversation—not as I stood in front of her as a prince, and certainly not when she loathed me so entirely.

"Do you have any plans for tonight?" I asked. "Maybe you could accompany me to the palace libraries. I'd be happy to bring a bottle of wine since the last one I'd had delivered befell an unfortunate accident."

Rialey shifted uncomfortably, looking somewhat ashamed.

"How unfortunate you hadn't had the chance to taste it. Very expensive." When her eyes met mine, I licked my bottom lip, the smirk remaining on my face. Something about toying with her—flirting. There was nothing else I'd rather be doing.

I felt more comfortable around her—as if my duties as prince seemed to fall away. There were no meetings to worry about—no pressure to be anything other than myself.

"Unfortunately," she began, "The witching is tomorrow. I would need to prepare, of course."

I arched a brow. "Of course." I leaned in, just slightly. "You did promise me a dance."

Her cheeks flushed, and she tapped her boot impatiently on the stone floors. "Well, I had hoped you'd moved on. Possibly found a wife?"

My eyes traced her features before dipping down to her tunic, the dagger strapped to her belt, her boots—now more worn than the first time I'd seen them. I looked back up, her gray eyes swirling like storm clouds. "I have not moved on, nor have I found a wife."

"Well," she started, her tone tight. "You should."

Rialey grabbed the handle to the door, tugged it open, and walked into the dining hall—slamming the door in my face.

I couldn't help but feel that my trip to this side of the palace had been worth it. I quite enjoyed doors slamming in my face.

Chapter Nineteen

Rialey

Something settled in me the moment I set foot in the sewers with this week's witching victim trailing behind me.

I'd been on edge since running into Prince Wineslowe in the palace earlier. Every small pull of his mouth, every slight glimmer to his blue gaze had me replaying the entire interaction and desperately trying to pick apart what it had all meant. But slinking through the sewers beneath the streets of Marmere gave my mind a focused task—some reprieve from my own memories.

Or so I thought.

For two years, Prince Theron Wineslowe had stayed exactly where he belonged on the other side of the palace. I had assumed he'd been preoccupied with meetings, women, and whatever it was princes did during the day. I'd heard from servants that he frequented the gardens, riding his horse through the desolate palace grounds. With constant winter, I couldn't imagine why he'd enjoy such a thing.

My time was typically spent sneaking out at night to find someone worthy of dying in the witching, sneaking out at night to prevent innocents from dying in the witching, or lounging around the palace during the daytime to make up for my nightly activities.

I *had* been to the palace libraries before, though, and since I'd never seen Prince Theron there, I'd assumed he didn't enjoy them. The extensive collection of important texts distracted my mind from the guilt that had become my constant companion. Maybe I would have enjoyed spending time with him instead of dirtying my boots in the sewers. Maybe I would have sat across from Prince Theron, his juniper and cardamom scent mingling with ink and old leather as we read stories.

Did he read stories? Maybe he only read historical texts about war or the art of dancing in a palace ballroom.

I shook my head, my boots hitting the shallow water as we finally made it to the grate. I turned back, looking over the blonde woman, who had remained quiet since I found her. She was tall, lanky in build, with sharp features and an even sharper mind. Most of the women we pulled from the dungeons had lost themselves in one way or another—not this one.

"We will meet Eryx above, and he can help you out of the city," I whispered.

She lifted her chin, staring down at me. "And he will leave me to die on the outskirts of the city, I suppose?"

I pressed my lips together, my eyes narrowing. The sconces along the end of the sewer wall were sparse and let in very little light, but I could still make out the hardness in her expression. "You can also turn around and go back to your cell. I can come pick you up tomorrow morning, throw you in a covered carriage, and toss you into the flame from the city center's platform if you'd prefer." My head tilted to the side as I studied her. "Likely death seems favorable to certain death, no?"

She scoffed, and I made quick work of removing the sewer grate, climbing out onto the snowy street, and pulling the witch up behind me.

Eryx stood ready, with snow dusting the hood of his cloak. Clothed in black, he blended in with the night surrounding us, his mask pulled up just below his blue eyes. Eyes that stared through me as if they saw everything.

It sent a shiver down my spine.

"I brought you someone," he said, stepping forward with his arms folded across his chest. "Thought you could use a break from hunting true evil to use for the witching."

My stomach churned. Despite my abilities, I could not create the illusion of charred flesh, nor could I replicate the sounds that would echo during a burning. With my limits, someone always had to die. I just preferred it to be someone who wasn't innocent. Eryx knew this, of course. In fact, more often than not, he'd provided a target and the herbs necessary to make them docile—more easily persuaded to jump to their deaths.

"Did you use the dormiroot?" I asked.

"Of course." Eryx's eyes flicked to the witch briefly before returning to mine. "He should be unconscious in the wagon until morning." Reaching for the small pouch tied at his waist, Eryx fumbled with gloved fingers as he untied it before handing the herbs over. "This should help keep him a willing participant as usual." Clearing his throat, Eryx shifted where he stood. "He *is* injured, though."

My brows furrowed. "Who is he?" I asked, carefully tying the pouch to my belt beneath my cloak.

"A wealthy man."

I paused, slowly looking up, the bile threatening to rise in my throat. "So," I began, "his absence will be noticed." It was risky to take more prominent figures. While my illusion would mask them during the witching, and I was confident in my abilities, there was always a risk of discovery. Seeing as I prepared the carriage myself, that risk had been lowered—but still. Should some stray stable hand get curious, and instead of finding a drunk rapist passed out in the barn, they found a prominent man from the city, things could get bad quickly.

Everything was a risk—always.

"His absence may be noticed, but not missed."

I worried my lip, looking down to finish tying the pouch to my belt. "What did he do?" I finally asked, our voices still lowered.

"Earned himself the right to burn." Another chill went down my spine at the intensity of his words—the sheer hatred dripping from them.

"This is Rona," I offered, gesturing to the witch standing beside me in the cloak I'd brought.

Eryx glanced at her and nodded once. "We will keep to the alleyways," he started. "It will be easier—"

A sound echoed from the far end of the street where we stood as some-one rounded the corner. I quickly grabbed Rona's wrist, pulling her to the nearest building with Eryx following suit. We pressed our backs into the wall as gold flashed in my vision, my magic becoming clear to me as I molded shadows around us.

A palace guard ambled through the snow, the sword at his hip moving with every slow and measured step. He didn't look in our direction, but my heart raced so quickly, I became certain it would push itself right out of my chest.

What is a guard doing out patrolling this street?

When I glanced near his breast, the embroidered symbol on his uniform looked unfamiliar. This was not a palace guard. In fact, this guard was not even from Marmere. Instead, he hailed from one of the neighboring cities—making his movements even more questionable.

He passed, turned a corner at the end of the street, and my body re-laxed—just slightly. Stepping away from the wall, I was careful to hold my magic close, making the shadows linger around us and keeping my voice low. "Be careful," I whispered, my eyes holding firm to Eryx's blue gaze. At that moment, I realized exactly how much I meant it.

Eryx nodded, pulling a key from his pocket to undo Rona's bone cuffs. When she was freed of them, he nodded, urging her on as they disappeared for the night.

I hesitated, waiting until they were out of view before moving to the sewer grate and lowering myself into the opening.

My gloved hands gripped the cool metal, my muscles straining as I worked to cover the hole.

Before I'd finished, a scream ripped through the night, striking fear in the deepest parts of my being.

Pushing the grate aside, I lifted myself from the sewer, my boots crunching through snow with every hurried step. My mind flashed images of that first attempt at helping a witch escape the city—the night I'd met Eryx.

Blood had stained the snow beneath the witch's body—an arrow protruding from her chest as I fled the scene—desperate and fueled by my own self-preservation.

This time, I wouldn't allow myself that luxury. I gripped the hilt of my dagger and pulled it from its sheath as the hood of my cloak fell. The wind whipped through my hair, biting my cheeks and frigid against the heat now coursing through my veins.

I turned a corner, the moon now visible and peeking through lacy clouds overhead. It illuminated the snow-covered streets until the clouds shielded its light once more, plunging me into more darkness. The sound of metal drew my attention, and I raced ahead, desperate to find them—help them.

When a hand gripped my bicep painfully, I was pulled back into a hard chest. The man wrapped a strong arm across my chest—a sword gripped in his hand as his other covered my mouth.

"Where do you think you're going, Witch Hunter?" he asked, his nose trailing up the side of my neck until his lips were at my ear. Every nerve in my body screamed—begging me to run—to fight. "Or should I even call you that?" he spat, shoving me to the ground.

I turned around, crawling backward as he prowled closer, his sword pointed in my direction and so close—too close. I'd dropped my dagger when falling, leaving me defenseless and staring up the blade of this man's weapon. He wore the same crest on his uniform, clearly not from Marmere or the palace.

He pointed the sword at my cheek, his onyx eyes tracing the scar there. "How pretty," he crooned before moving the tip of his blade near the other cheek. "I should make one to match."

Frantically, I continued backing away. "Stop!" I begged, cursing myself for my fear—my weakness.

He chuckled, still moving closer as the snow seeped through my clothes. When my cloak tangled around my legs, my heart lurched.

"Stop?" he questioned, keeping his sword poised. "How pitiful," he snarled. "I believed you to be much stronger than that, Witch Hunter."

My limbs trembled, every part of me screaming in protest, as I stopped crawling away from him, grinding my teeth together just before kicking up at his hand. Surprised, the guard lost his grip on the sword, its blade grazing my calf before falling to the ground.

I kicked it again, desperate to push it further away from my assailant. Angered, the guard lunged, his hand at my throat before I had a chance to move.

With his heavy body pressing me further into the snow, I felt empty—my lungs void of air when his grip tightened. "Fucking bitch," he seethed. One arm shoved against my chest with bruising force.

His hand left my throat, reaching somewhere behind me, and I tried to suck in a lungful of air—unsuccessful with his weight still pressed against me.

My dagger appeared in his hand, the cool metal tracing a line at the side of my throat. Warm blood dripped down into the snow, marking the ground with my imminent death. "You're going to die," he warned. "You're going to die, and I am going to watch."

Tears stung my eyes. My body remained pinned beneath him. I could use illusion—use my magic somehow to distract him.

Gold flashed, but before I had the chance to do anything, the man screamed, his hand contorted painfully, dropping the dagger long enough for me to grab it as he reeled back, allowing me to plunge it into his stomach. I arched the blade upward to hit as many organs as possible.

He slumped, his eyes glazing over as the light left them.

I shoved, gasping when I finally took a full lungful of air. Rona stood a few feet away; her fingers painfully twisted at odd angles. "They have him," she said, hiding her hand beneath her cloak.

My chest ached, and my muscles protested when I stood up, grabbing my dagger, and tossing Rona the guard's sword before she turned, taking off down a nearby alley.

I followed her, feeling at my neck before pulling a wet glove away. The cut stung, but it wouldn't scar. It hadn't been nearly as deep as the cut across my cheek when I'd first gotten it.

"Your hand," I gasped, keeping pace with the witch in front of me.

"Will heal," she answered.

Metal sounded as we got closer, ducking and sprinting through the darkened streets of Marmere.

When we rounded the final corner onto the main road, Eryx stood with his back to us, his sword drawn, and body heaving with exertion.

The guard—the original one who had passed us near the sewer entrance, brought his blade down, slicing across Eryx's shoulder as he cried out.

"Eryx, no!" I screamed, fear crawling up my throat as another guard appeared, lunging toward Rona where she met him with her sword.

Eryx turned, and the guard shoved a boot at his chest, knocking him to the ground. He looked weak—exhausted.

Gods.

"Is that what he calls himself while parading around the streets like a common rebel?" the guard chuckled, pointing the tip of his sword at Eryx's chest.

My brow furrowed as I tightened my grip on the hilt of my dagger.

"I'll admit," the guard started. "I was surprised when Lord Vespahr asked us to follow you, but now I see he was right. You really are a traitorous prince." The guard shoved his foot harder against Eryx's chest, my mind struggling to keep up with his words.

Traitorous prince?

Pointing his sword in my direction, the guard smiled to reveal crooked teeth. "He really had you fooled, didn't he?"

Reaching down, the guard grabbed Eryx by the neck, dragging him upward, and turning him to face me, his eyes shining with fear and something like regret. Gone was his sword, replaced by a clenched fist.

"Don't worry, dear," the guard taunted, still looking at me over Eryx's shoulder. "We don't plan on killing him." The guard yanked back his hood, revealing sweaty blonde hair, and something like dread washed over me.

When his mask was pulled down, I stood in the snow, my dagger still clutched in my hand, my mouth agape as I stared at Prince Theron Wineslowe of the Kingdom of Alphaird.

"Rialey," Theron mouthed—an apology. "Don't."

I hesitated—stalling just long enough for the guard to drag him away and another guard to seize my forearm and twist it behind me, forcing me to drop my dagger.

Anger swirling, I dug for my magic, drawing up an image of myself and projecting it in front of us. In his confusion, the guard looked around, seeing another image—another. I surrounded him, distracting him enough to spin, swinging my leg out to sweep his own from beneath him.

When he fell to the ground, I grabbed my dagger from the snow and stabbed him, my hand sure.

He crumpled, blood coating the snow beneath his dead body.

Rona had disappeared, the street now empty save for the body of the guard she must have been fighting.

Panting, I gathered myself before I could attract more danger.

When I ran through the streets, I tried to keep my racing thoughts at bay, my muscles burning until I found my way to the sewer. Lowering myself in, I quickly found my way to the tunnel, stopping before I got to the dungeon entrance.

If the guard saw me—if he took Eryx, no—*Theron*, back to the palace, there was no way they wouldn't come for me.

With my betrayal, I'd certainly be put to death.

I sat in the dirt; the tears came quickly as I tried to conjure up a plan. Where would they take him? The dungeons?

Would they throw Theron somewhere else?

I had no clue.

All I knew was that I couldn't let him die—not when I was so certain his punishment would be as harsh as any. King Wineslowe would kill his own son for treason.

That is—unless I did something about it.

Chapter Twenty

Theron

Dirt marred my face—my *uncovered* face—as the hand on my bicep tightened. With my hands shackled behind my back and my sword left behind, I had nothing and no one to help me.

At eighteen, my father had sent me around all of Alphaird for the witch hunts. For seven years, the kingdom's armies spent their time searching for magic wielders with the explicit instruction to burn them alive in the town squares. My father had wanted to make an example of anyone he felt held more power than himself. It had been a constant theme ever since he'd come to power at only eighteen himself.

Guilt became my constant companion upon my return; the nightmares never ceased. Originally, I'd taken to the streets to clear my mind—outrun the memories that haunted me. But then two years ago, I'd watched a witch, much like the many I'd killed, fall with an arrow through her chest.

When Rialey Dagon, the newly hired executioner, had looked up, her eyes meeting mine, I'd seen the kindness in them and realized what she had really been doing in the palace. Helping her had come easily. At first, it helped with the nightmares, and after a while, I believed that my nights with Rialey had somehow cleaned the blood on my hands.

I'd purposefully avoided her during the day. It had been too risky, but lately, I'd found myself unable to resist.

Showing up in her room had been foolish.

The boots.

The dress.

The wine.

The dance.

All of it had been foolish.

My limbs felt heavy—sore—and the wound on my shoulder burned. When the guard had jerked on my arm, the fabric of my black tunic had pulled away with the dried blood. I bit my cheek painfully to avoid making a sound. It would only fuel their fire.

The onyx doors opened to reveal my father perched atop his throne, hot anger burning in his eyes. The crown on his head sat crooked, but it did nothing to ease the fear spiking within me.

My father had always hated anything and anyone who threatened his power. That sentiment remained with me. I'd long since become accustomed to King Wineslowe's methods of torture.

"The Traitor Prince," he spoke, lifting his chin as the guard shoved me toward the dais. My knees cracked when they hit the floor, and I ground my teeth together.

"Father." A dirty strand of hair hung over my brow, but it did nothing to obstruct my vision of the evil king.

"All this time, Theron. All this time, I had thought you spent your nights warming many beds." He tapped a ringed finger on his knee, and I fixed my eyes there, refusing to look at his face. "Then Vespahr came to me after our meeting with an... interesting theory. I gave him permission to remain in the city with his guards, and look what they brought me." He paused, and I felt a presence move to stand nearer to me. When I risked a glance, I saw Vespahr there, a smug smirk dancing on his lips.

"His guards brought me my own son," he continued.

My father stood, each step measured as he descended the steps of the dais. I stayed in place on my knees, refusing to move. I'd spent most of my life moving for my father, but now—

"I'm going to give you one opportunity to explain what you were doing in the streets of Marmere at such a late hour." He stopped a few feet in front of me, his posture stiff and straight as if I were a mere commoner kneeling at his feet, begging for forgiveness.

I supposed to him; I was.

"One opportunity, Theron, to explain why you were found with tomorrow's witch attempting to flee the city." King Wineslowe waited, patient as ever.

There was nothing I could say—no way I could spin it to protect myself, and thus far, he hadn't brought up Rialey. It was important I kept the focus on myself and my crimes.

I straightened a bit, lifting my chin in defiance. "I was helping her escape."

King Wineslowe stood still—so still, I could have mistaken him for one of the statues decorating the palace halls.

"Is that all?" he pressed.

I didn't answer.

My father nodded to Vespahr. "You'll be treated favorably, Lord Vespahr. I can assure you of that." He turned to the guards. "As for my son, he can be thrown in the dungeons with the lot of them. Since we no longer have a witch to burn tomorrow..." His eyes pinned on me, predatory and commanding. "We can offer my son to the pyre. You are dismissed."

My father turned, and Vespahr's guards hauled me to my feet, dragging me through the throne room and back to the onyx doors.

Rage swirled in my gut, all the fury I'd kept bottled within finally bubbling to the surface. I turned, fighting against their hold as they scrambled to keep me in place. I found Vespahr from across the room, now talking to my father, who had found his seat once more on the throne.

"Fuck you!" I yelled just before one of the guards slammed me against the wall, but I didn't stop fighting. "You're a fucking snake, Vespahr!"

They dragged me away, but I hadn't missed the slight curl of his lip, the briefest expression that showed I'd upset him.

I clung to the satisfaction of that even as they threw me in a cell, leaving me to rot like all of those I'd led through the dark streets of the city. Leaving me to rot like all those I'd captured all those years ago.

I'd awoken to a small hand on my arm, jerking me awake. The guard, tall and broad-shouldered, knelt near me, a scar marring his cheek. I blinked up at him, noting that my cell had been opened.

"We have to leave, Prince Theron."

I blinked again. That voice—

"Rialey?" I questioned, my voice hoarse. Dirt streaked my clothes and my face. The burning in my shoulder had dulled to a painful ache, deep and hot to the touch.

"You have to shut up," she seethed. It was so strange. Typically, when she wore the face of another, it wasn't this contrary to her typical appearance. Her voice exiting the lips of the large man before me had me questioning my sanity. "For the record," she continued, "I have not forgiven you for lying to me and playing me for a fool." The face she wore looked away, glancing backward as if checking if someone else was coming. "I don't know what I'm doing," she admitted. "I killed this guard, donned his face, and took his shift. They have you on lockdown, Eryx—" She shook her head. "*Your Highness.*"

"Theron," I interrupted, one corner of my mouth turning upward, though the expression was weak, just like everything about me.

"Your Fucking Highness," she said. "As I was saying, I don't know what I'm doing, but I can't let you die. Now, get up."

I pulled myself to stand, somewhat wobbly. Rialey looked around frantically, as if she were checking every corner at once.

When I took a step forward, my limp was apparent.

"You have to stop that," she said. "I'm going to disguise you as a guard, and I can't fix a limp."

My ankle screamed at me as I stepped forward, following her through the aisle. When we went deeper into the dungeons, my brow furrowed. "I've never seen the way to get out of here," I admitted.

Rialey didn't speak until we had cleared the dirt tunnel, finding ourselves in the sewers below Marmere. It was there she released her illusion and donned her own face, the one I'd spent two years learning.

"Visha, the servant assigned to me, should have your horse and one other waiting when we exit," she finally said, breaking the silence.

"Visha?" I questioned.

"She didn't know anything. I had to confess quite a lot, but she was willing to help. She's risking her life for you." She sounded angry, and rightfully so.

I cleared my throat, still raw. "They saw you, too, Rialey. You're at risk, too."

"Do you think I don't know that!" She stopped, turning to face me with her gray eyes blazing.

When we crawled out of the sewers, a cloaked woman stood with Wraith, and Rift, the gelding with the stall next to Wraith's. I winced upon seeing him.

I gripped Rialey's arm, forcing her to look at me. Despite my dire state, I still stood taller than her. "Are you a skilled rider?" I asked, and she huffed.

"I'm decent," she answered.

"Then you should ride Wraith. Rift is barely three and very green."

She eyed me then, taking in the state I was in. "Forgive me, Your Highness, but I don't care how spectacular a rider you may be; you are in no position to be taking the more difficult mount." Her gaze met mine then, determined. "I'll be fine."

Visha, I assumed, handed me a pack with clean clothes and a new cloak. I pulled the cloak over my shoulders and struggled onto Wraith, cursing myself for my sore ankle, the wound at my shoulder, and the weakness I suddenly felt.

"Thank you," I said, looking down at the woman. In the darkness, I couldn't make out her features, but she nodded, whispering something to Rialey before sending us off.

Leaving us to exit the city of Marmere.

Leaving us to flee like all the witches before us.

Part Two

She shook with the burning rage of the old gods.
Brimming with magic, the Waldwood sat watching.
Waiting.
Nature demanded balance, and the time would come when she
would take what was owed.

Chapter Twenty-One

Verena

Dawn crept up the horizon, but the gray skies remained.

Caius sat behind me, his strong arms bracketing either side of my body as he steered our mount northward. Snow crunched beneath hooves as the rocking made my eyes feel heavy. It had been a long while since I'd been on a horse, and not nearly long enough since my stay in the palace dungeons. My legs ached, body begging to dismount and rest—to sleep.

Caius gripped the reins tighter and shifted behind me. "We should be in Branwood soon."

A heavy weight pressed on my chest. "Branwood?" I questioned. "That's northwest. I thought we were headed toward The Waldwood. Why would we stop in a neighboring city?"

Snow floated from a limb overhead as the wind whipped through the trees, biting my already cold cheeks.

Caius shook his head, his voice a deep rumbling behind me. I could feel it where his chest touched my back. "We can't risk getting caught by the soldiers. Ma said they were moving north, and so I'm hoping to put some distance between us." His gloved fingers stroked the mare's mane, his voice softening. "Besides, you're exhausted."

I straightened, hating the way my back protested the movement, causing me to wince. "I'm fine."

"Verena." Caius leaned in just slightly, his warmth seeping through my cloak, heating my skin like the hot cup of tea I'd been craving. "You won't make it if we do not stop. We will rest in Branwood tonight—stay in an inn. We can then continue to the northwestern side of the forest and enter there."

I'd never considered myself weak—especially considering the power that flooded my veins and allowed me to enter the minds of those around me. But the past few weeks forced me to come to terms with the limits of my power and body. Guilt churned in my gut. If it weren't for me, Caius could have stayed at the cabin. If it weren't for my weakness, he wouldn't be risking his life to take me home.

If I could even call it that.

"I'm fine," I asserted.

Caius hummed, and I could almost hear the upward tilt of his full mouth embedded in the sound. "Yes, of course," he said. "You're fine."

We rode in silence, the tall pines surrounding us with their blankets of snow. I wondered if the forest tired of the winter—if the Waldwood longed for days like what I'd seen in Caius's dream.

Still—if the stories were true, if the forest's magic made the sky stretch gray and the clouds cry frozen tears, I couldn't be sure of the reasoning.

Many of the witches tucked in the safety of the Waldwood still believed in the old gods—worshipped them, even, as they had been the ones to pour magic into the soil. I'd long since stopped worshipping. Especially since it seemed the gods had turned against us and were punishing us all.

From Cyra, I'd never connected with the goddess of the sun—not the way others in the coven had. It seemed to me, the gods were dead and buried—the forest's rage all that was left.

The cracking of a limb pulled my gaze upward in time to see an owl swoop from a nearby tree. With cream-colored feathers and black eyes, the creature plunged me back into the memory of tripping over logs, lying in the snow until I had been sure the forest would take me.

"Did you see that?" I whispered, voice breathless. My heart fluttered in my chest, and I sat up, squinting to track her movements.

"What?" Caius asked.

I scanned the pines up ahead. "In the trees," I insisted, spotting her dark eyes peering down from her perch. "There." Pointing, I kept my sights fixed to the creature, hoping she wouldn't fly away.

Caius shifted slightly to get a better look, his thigh brushing mine from behind me. "An owl?" he questioned.

Her gaze held, black eyes absorbing the dim light of the morning. "She followed us."

Caius cleared his throat, and I realized how it sounded. He would deem me unstable—use the comment to assert his opinion that I need rest before we continue to the forest. Deep down, I knew I'd need what he offered. I hadn't asked him to change course; I merely kept silent on our journey toward Branwood.

I *was* exhausted—and sore—but I meant what I said.

I'd seen this owl before.

"She?" he inquired as we passed the creature, watching as she took us in with careful consideration.

My heart slowed, the excitement dissolving to be replaced with my need for sleep and a hot meal. "I think—" I shook my head. "Never mind."

Caius hummed, and we traveled in silence once more. This time, the gentle rocking of the horse below us became too much to bear. I felt my eyelids close with every step, my chin dropping, and my mind succumbing to rest before a powerful arm caught me around the waist. I came to, realizing I'd fallen asleep and subsequently tilted forward.

Caius held me there, one gloved hand still on the reins. His fingers flexed, and I righted myself, shame creeping up my neck to paint my cheeks a burning pink.

"I'm sorry," I said. "I'm—"

"Fine?" he interrupted, and I could feel his smile where his face stayed close by my ear. His other hand gripped the reins as he leaned forward, his breath hot in the hair near my neck. "If you wish to sleep, all I ask is that you lean back instead of forward." Caius cleared his throat. "I cannot hold you the entire ride while also steering our mount."

Hesitantly, I shifted my hips in order to lean back, my head tucked beneath his chin and resting against his firm chest. His steady heartbeat brought comfort as I continued to drift in and out of sleep.

"You're quite comfortable, actually," I murmured, and Caius chuckled softly, his body vibrating against mine.

My eyes closed out the forest, the snow—the owl—and I felt myself relax.

Caius leaned down, his lips so close to my ear, I could smell the lingering scent of mint leaves on his breath. "Sleep if you can, Verena," he whispered. "We'll be out of the cold, soon."

The sound of voices startled me awake, and my heart lodged itself in my throat. My eyes snapped open to find a horse-drawn carriage up ahead—two men laughing from the seat at the front.

"Relax." Caius leaned forward, his chest brushing against me and reminding me of the last—how long had it been?

His breath fanned over my neck, warm as his lips came near my ear. My stomach swooped, blood warming against the cold. "We're near the road to Branwood," he murmured. "Don't look so startled."

I blinked away the odd warmth blooming in my belly, sobered by the nearing city walls. "How are we supposed to enter?" I whispered, my breath coming out faster. "I have no papers."

Caius stayed close, keeping his voice down. "Ma keeps a collection of falsified documents for emergencies." The carriage moved ahead of us as our horse stepped onto the dirty road—snow mixed with mud and gravel. "You have papers," he assured. "We should get through without incident."

My brows furrowed, as if I'd uncovered something I shouldn't have known.

Memories of our departure flashed across my vision, and I cleared my throat.

"Caius," I said, hesitantly, "back at the cabin, Ahvi had said some things." I paused, gathering my thoughts. "Why do you keep falsified documents?"

He stiffened, gloved fingers tightening around the reins. "We have friends," he started. "Friends who do not...align with the beliefs King Wineslowe holds."

Somehow I knew this. I knew there were those in the kingdom who believed witches shouldn't be burned—believed the Waldwood should have independence. Something nagged at me as we rode, an undercurrent of *knowing*.

"Your friends," I began, treading lightly, "are there many of them?"

Caius leaned in closer, his voice a low hum that sent goosebumps over my arms. "There are," he answered. "All across Alphaird—all training for the day Alphaird becomes something different—better."

"A rebellion?" I whispered.

Caius did not answer, merely wrapped his arms tighter around me, letting the realization marinate.

There was a rebellion brewing in Alphaird, and I knew next to nothing about it, but Ahvi and Caius? They knew—were part of it.

As the city neared, my nerves sent my teeth chattering. Two women walked behind us, young and busying themselves with gossip about the prince and his ball that had taken place in the palace at Marmere.

"He danced with the king's executioner," one said, holding her cloak tight around her body.

The blonde one, much shorter in stature, giggled. "I'm sure it was just out of courtesy. Her position is valued among the royals."

"Not so," the first informed. "I heard it was rather... tense."

The carriage stopped in front of us, two guards appearing at the gate for questioning.

The roaring in my ears drowned out the conversations surrounding us. When Caius urged the horse forward and dismounted, handing one guard two pieces of parchment, every hair on my body stood on end.

Looking up, the guard's blue eyes pierced like a blade. "Farmers from the south?"

"We're on business," Caius started, stepping between us. "Transportation can be tricky, as you know. We are working on finding a more efficient way to—"

"Enough." The guard shoved the papers into Caius's chest, his nose wrinkling with distaste. "I don't much care so long as you're legal. Take your wife and be done with it."

Caius nodded before putting his foot in the stirrup, his warm body returning to its former position.

As we passed through the gate, I watched King Wineslowe's soldiers on the wall, poised with arrows and ready to strike down anyone who dared sneak into the city.

I swallowed, noting what the guard had said. "Your wife?" I whispered.

Metal clanked in the distance, and the sounds of the city square rushed toward us. A small child stood before a stall in a thick cloak, buying a loaf of bread.

"Ma's doing, of course," Caius muttered. "We'll do our best to be convincing, but I hardly suspect anyone will pay much attention."

My stomach growled as the scent of that bread hit my nostrils, dragging something primal from the depths of my hollow belly.

Caius breathed a laugh. "For now," he spoke softly, "let's worry about getting you some food."

CHAPTER TWENTY-TWO

RIALEY

I watched the fire crackle yards away, where Eryx—*no*—Prince Theron Wineslowe sat near our horses. Shirtless despite the cold, he worked to place a new bandage over the wound at his shoulder. Shadows cut across each rigid muscle, and I hated that I could not tell if his strength came from his training as a prince, or the nights he spent rescuing witches from his father's control.

Every memory seemed to sour at the sight of him as I struggled to marry the two versions of the man I knew. My attempts were unsuccessful.

The trees cast their ominous shadows over the forest floor, our fire tucked away where we'd cleared some of the snow. The whistling wind brought a bitter cold I hadn't felt in ages, and I wondered how the prince had made the journey this far to begin with. We'd traveled east at his request, and I watched him slumped over his horse's mane—half alive and weary.

He'd been correct about the mount I chose being more difficult to control, but incorrect in the thought that he should be the one to endure it. He certainly didn't have the strength to deal with the incessant protests of a horse that longed to select a pace of its own choosing. The man had been completely useless on his own horse.

Aside from the goal of keeping him alive, I found myself direction-less—betrayed and hurt; I didn't know what would come next, but I certainly couldn't return to the palace. They'd gotten a look at me, too.

"Here." I tossed the dead rabbit at his feet, and he looked up—his blue eyes all at once familiar and foreign.

Prince Theron's gaze hopped from the rabbit to me before he carefully pulled a thick shirt over his head and pushed his arms through the long sleeves. He gestured to the rabbit. "Where did you get this?" he asked, wincing.

Rage simmered in my blood at the sight of him—at the sound of his voice and the memories it dug up. I fought to keep the heat of that rage contained—the memories buried. "The forest," I ground out.

The prince huffed, grabbing the creature by its hind legs and holding it aloft.

I blinked. "A bit of illusion and a good knife." When I stepped around him, he didn't so much as move. I supposed that was for the best.

The memory of his warm breath—his nearness—flooded my mind. I'd wanted him to kiss me in my quarters, but now the mystery of how he'd ended up in my room made much more sense. The lies stung. "If you could start working on cooking it, that would be nice." I tossed over my shoulder, moving to our supplies. "Please," I added. "I'm going to set up the tent and look for the healing salve Visha packed somewhere. You'll need it."

The softness in his voice had me halting. "Thank you," he murmured.

I risked glancing back, noting the rigid lines of his tense shoulders, the dirt and blood streaked through his hair and across his face. He looked pained. If he regretted playing me for a fool, he didn't show it.

"Sure," I answered before busying myself with the tent. If it weren't for the methodical tasks of surviving and helping the prince survive, I would break. As it was, I had enough to keep my mind from wandering too far into the darkness. All I needed to do was focus on the next step—one at a time.

When I sat near the fire, my aching muscles thanked me as warmth seeped its way into my bones.

The orange glow sat as a beacon of hope in the winter forest, and I watched as the flames danced between the logs we'd collected.

"Eat," Prince Wineslowe said as he moved to sit next to me, handing cooked rabbit meat over. "It's pretty gamey," he added.

I didn't speak, merely gnawing on the tough, cooked meat and staring at the flames. The silence felt heavy, and despite my clear disinterest, Prince Wineslowe refused to leave.

"Why east?" I finally asked. "You never gave me a reason."

Prince Wineslowe cleared his throat, shifting where he sat in the snow. "I'm hoping Lord Bloodbane will have mercy on us."

I stopped chewing.

Every bone in my body vibrated with fiery rage and disbelief, but I kept my tone even. "You're going to get us both killed with all that hope, *Your Highness*." The last words carried a bite to them, and I swore he flinched.

"Would you stop calling me that?" he pleaded.

My patience snapped, hurt seeping out of my pores. "It is who you are!"

I blinked back tears, hoping he couldn't see them. I would not cry—not here.

"I..." He shook his head before his chin dipped subtly. "I know." The prince blew out a breath. "If you have a better option, then I'm willing to discuss it, but we won't make it far north. My father sent soldiers to The Waldwood, and they'll be sure to look for me."

My stomach twisted at the thought of King Wineslowe taking his soldiers to the forest I'd once called home. "And why is your father sending his army to The Waldwood?"

Prince Theron's gaze found me, burning with the same rage that had become my closest friend. It eased some of my frustration with him, but only slightly. "Why do you think?" He paused. The anticipation of his answer hung in the air. He was the *prince*. If anyone were to know his father's reasoning, it would be him. "Witches have been showing up across the kingdom. They've been caught fleeing to the north, and my father would like to investigate that matter."

Fleeing north. No doubt some of those witches were set on their course with our aid. I scoffed. "Investigate."

Pain twisted like a knife in my chest. It had been so long since I'd remembered my home. All I'd ever known was the endless winter spurred on by the king. He loathed magic—my people.

Staring at the fire, I thought of all the witches who'd died because of Prince Theron's father.

"The forest cannot be burned," he said, quieter now. Prince Theron leaned toward me as if his presence would bring me comfort, and at one time, it might have.

"Yes," I seethed, looking in his direction. "But her people can."

He reeled back, just slightly, and I went back to eating, letting my mind wander before continuing. "I haven't thought of my past," I confessed. "Not in a long while. Witches still live in The Waldwood, but they're difficult to find." I lowered the meat, gazing out into the darkened forest. "That's the only reason so many of us haven't returned. Because of your father, there may be nothing for us to return to." I cleared my throat. "That and we are all outrunning your father, and the chance that he'd re-enter the forest to pillage our covens. He did that once, you know."

"I'm well aware," Prince Theron ground out.

I couldn't stop the way my lip peeled back in disgust. "Right," I said. "Because you participated in those witch hunts when you came of age."

I risked looking at him and only saw the same pained expression he'd worn earlier when I returned from hunting the rabbit. "It's not something I'm proud of, nor was it entirely my choice."

I leaned forward where I sat, my face now a single foot away from him. "You *always* have a choice," I said. "*Your Highness.*"

His head snapped in my direction; blue eyes ignited with passion. "The same choice you had each time you opted to throw the witches on the pyre?" he asked, and tears crawled up my throat. "The real ones—not the vile men subdued with herbs and cloaked in magic."

The pain slashed across my chest, making my lungs burn and guilt swirl in my stomach. I'd done what I could to help, but it hadn't been without cost. Desperation and the need to live—to survive—guided my actions. Though I'd never be able to excuse them.

I felt bare, flayed open in front of a man I somehow knew and did not know at all. He met me there, eyes as pained as mine in the dim light of the fire.

"Morality is not always binary, Miss Dagon." His tone had softened, and despite deserving his judgement, I found none in his words. "This world is filled with choices colored every shade. You cannot condemn me for doing what I felt necessary at the time. And if you do, you will have no choice but to condemn yourself as well."

My eyes stung, but I blinked the tears back. "Maybe I'm already doing that."

"You shouldn't." Theron shifted, rising slowly and wincing against the pain of his sore muscles—the wounds he acquired for his betrayal. "Many witches died at your hand," he said, staring down at me. "But without you, many more would not have escaped." He bent down, snatching the salve from the now melted patch of snow. "We are all filled with a bit of right and wrong. Most of us just hope the *right* weighs a bit heavier." He glanced once out at the forest, then back to me. "Learn to accept things as they are."

When he turned, he disappeared into the tent, leaving me staring after him with words that felt loaded—double in their meaning.

I knew him as Eryx—saw his kindness and compassion firsthand. I didn't feel those were traits one could fabricate so easily. I'd spent the last two days desperate to figure out which part of him—Theron or Eryx—was the truth, but maybe it wasn't so simple.

Morality is not always binary.

It was entirely possible that he was both, and that was the truth I would have to grow to accept.

Chapter Twenty-Three

Verena

Exhaustion weighed heavy on my bones by the time I settled into the firm mattress of the inn. Caius and I ate our fill of beef stew and bread before he charmed the owner with a conversation about different tea blends and their uses.

Somewhere between learning the benefits of reve flower petals on sleeping and the dangers of dormiroot because of its similar appearance, I decided to retreat to our room before I fell asleep mid-conversation and ruined our positive relations entirely.

I didn't like admitting what was so obvious when we entered the city. My time in the small cabin with Ahvi and Caius had come to an abrupt end—an end my body wasn't quite ready for.

Dusk crept into the room with purple light while I stared at the wooden walls, and despite my fatigue, I couldn't get my mind to quiet long enough for sleep to find me. It wasn't the steady chorus of laughter seeping through the cracks in the door, but the incessant thoughts that plagued me.

Caius was part of a rebellion—in some capacity—and I didn't know what that meant for our travels. Did he have something waiting for him in the Waldwood? And more importantly, why hadn't they trusted me?

Vaguely, I remembered wandering through the forest before Caius found me and hoping to reach the priestess in the heart of the forest.

Silly, now that I remembered, and certainly proof that my mind had been failing me, too. I wasn't anywhere near the temple, nor had I accomplished anything significant enough to warrant the favor of the old gods worshiped by the covens—if they even existed to begin with.

No wonder they hadn't trusted me.

The door creaked, drawing my attention to Caius's wide smile when he ambled into the room, tossing his cloak on the desk near the door. "You're awake," he observed, his pleased expression never wavering.

Sitting up, I crossed my legs and tucked the muddied strands of hair behind my ears. My cheeks flushed because of my appearance. We'd been traveling almost nonstop for a day, and rooms with bathing chambers cost more coin than we could afford.

"You look pleased," I noted, a wide smile splitting my face. "I didn't realize how much you loved herbal tea blends. I'm surprised you could discuss them that long."

Caius chuckled, the sound low and rich like the soil of the Waldwood—filled with the same magic that ran through my veins. "It's not the tea," he said. The mattress dipped when he sat toward the foot of the bed, his silhouette haloed by the glowing orange fire in the hearth behind him. "This inn houses one of the town's healers. Ma has taught me plenty in the way of herbal remedies, and I've offered to help for the next few days." His smile widened, one dimple popping in the center of his left cheek. "Should earn us some extra coin in addition to the rest of our stay. When one of the nicer rooms opens up tomorrow, we will move our things over."

I lifted a strand of hair from my shoulder, examining. "You mean to tell me you haven't enjoyed smelling the rancid scent of this while sharing our horse?"

He let out a soft chuckle when he shook his head. "Your hair hardly smells rancid." Caius licked his bottom lip, eyes narrowing in thought. "It's more akin to fresh rain seeping into the earth on a spring day. At least what I remember of that scent."

Something pulled in my chest, and I cleared my throat. Heat bloomed in the pit of my belly, but I quickly tamped it down. I must have been delirious. "Of course." Pulling my legs to my chest, I rested my chin on my knees, peering out the window that opened to the small city. "Is there something I can be doing to help?"

His smile fell as he observed me. "I'm no fool, Verena." A log cracked in the fireplace, the light flickering around him. "You'll need to rest. We left far sooner than we should have had to."

Worry curdled in my gut. "Are you worried about Ahvi?" I whispered and watched as his jaw ticked.

"I can't *not* worry. Once you've found your way to the Waldwood, I'll travel back. There's..." He cleared his throat. "There are rumbles of being needed in Keslow to the east. I'd like to go—and I would certainly hate to see Ma traveling alone."

Something like sadness wrapped around my heart, squeezing just slightly. It had been there for a while—making its home in my chest, but now it felt more potent. I would return to the Waldwood, hope to find a coven tucked between the trees, and Caius would leave me—my debt to him and his grandmother forever looming over my head. "Right," I whispered, returning my gaze to the window.

Worry crawled into the pit of my belly, making its home. If they were needed in the east, what did that mean for a rebellion?

Caius sighed, and the mattress shifted when he stood. "I can take the floor," he offered, turning away to unbutton his shirt.

Warmth, from what I guessed to be the fire, bloomed on my cheeks. "What difference would it make?" I asked, and he turned to look at me. "I mean, aside from leaving you sore and uncomfortable?"

Caius's brow furrowed. "And what about your comfort?" he questioned.

I scoffed, the memory of the hot springs still fresh. "You've already seen all there is to see," I whispered, avoiding his stare. "I hardly believe sharing this bed could be any more scandalous. Besides, we spent hours on the same horse, anyway."

Caius made quick work of shrugging on a clean shirt before finding his way to the other side of the bed. I opted to turn away from him, watching the colors of dusk bleed into a deep navy. For once, the clouds broke enough to get a view of the stars peeking through what remained of them.

When the mattress shifted, I closed my eyes, hoping that sleep would find me.

"What do you think we will find when we reach the Waldwood?" Caius asked, his tone soft as if he were trying not to wake me, should I already be sleeping.

I opened my eyes again, taking in the night sky. "I don't know," It came out as a whisper. I tried not to think about the soldiers marching to the north or what they were tasked with doing. "I'm sure the king would like nothing more than to kill us all."

Truth—one that had claws. Those claws sank into my flesh, tearing me apart from the inside out. I'd viewed the Waldwood as an escape, but what if—what if there was none?

Tears rolled down my temple, wetting the pillow beneath my head as I quickly wiped the back of my hand across my face. I hated crying. It wasn't productive.

Warm fingers wrapped around my wrist, gently pulling until I turned to face Caius, his expression pained. Silence hung heavy, drowning the sounds from the tavern below the inn. Caius brushed a thumb over my cheek—another—until the remnants of tears had disappeared completely.

"I'm sorry," he whispered, and the thought that he'd apologize made the sadness in me swell. He'd lost his parents, too. What did he have to apologize for?

"Don't be."

"For what it's worth," he began, "I'd like to be a part of fixing this world for you—for everyone."

I nodded, and when I turned again to face the window, I could feel him—closer than before but not touching me. The warmth of his body and the steady breath at my back helped ease the chaos within me. As I stared out the window, my mind finally quieting, I thought of a world where witches could thrive—where magic wasn't punished and the king didn't crave power above all else.

As my eyes grew heavy, I blinked slowly, and just before I fell asleep, I could have sworn I saw feathers flash across the sky.

CHAPTER TWENTY-FOUR

CAIUS

I startled awake, the gray morning light bathing our room in the somber return of winter skies. Sweat beaded on my neck as I sat panting, another night haunted by the memory of losing my mother to that plague of a king.

When I glanced at Verena's sleeping form, her lashes kissed the tops of her cheeks. With a face less sallow than when I first met her, she appeared stronger every day, but I didn't know what our hasty departure would do to stifle that progress.

I moved carefully, shifting on the mattress so as not to disturb her. The floors creaked when I padded to the other end of the room, dressing for my time with the inn's healer. Lupin, the owner of the inn and tavern, had given me directions, saying that their healer had struggled to keep up with the city's needs. I'd heard of the woman and knew she would allow me to help. Besides, we'd need supplies to make it to the Waldwood, and those supplies would cost money—money we did not currently have.

Rebellion had been in the air since the very first witch hunts during King Wineslowe's reign, but the Guild had hardly formed at that time.

It wasn't until one of the lords had come into the power that things had become more organized. Ma spent time attending meetings to train, and

I'd frequently gone with her—knowing war lurked beneath the surface of unrest and waiting for the final pieces to fall into place.

The Guild of Eirdis, what the rebels called themselves, met in secret, slowly acquiring more citizens who disagreed with the king's evil.

It had given me hope when I'd turned sixteen—when my parents' deaths began to weigh heavier and heavier. Ahvi had invited me along—hoping it would heal the angry parts of me that had surfaced, and to some extent, it had. It had healed the sorrow and given me a direction to point my ire.

I longed for a kingdom where none would experience the horrors we had—longed for the death of a mad king.

Verena did not stir when I opened the door, nor when it closed with a soft snick.

The dusty halls of the inn narrowed as I approached the old staircase toward the back of the building—away from the tavern entrance to the front.

My muscles were stiff after the long night on the cheap mattress upstairs. I assumed our long ride contributed as well, but I felt well rested.

Below the first floor of the inn, another long hallway led to the wooden door at the end, carved with intricate designs. I trailed my finger over the smooth ebony wood, flowers, vines, and other depictions of herbs etched into the surface. Someone had taken the time to make this space beautiful.

When the door opened, a wall lined with wooden shelves and carefully labeled bottles and glass containers greeted me. A true apothecary, the collection of remedies was extensive, ranging from simple salves to tinctures far more unique. I spun a few bottles to face me, reading the smudged labels and taking stock of what was here. Whoever this healer was, she must have years of experience.

One wooden table and chair sat toward the end of the room with scattered parchment and a slim window overhead, letting in the only natural light. Herbs hung from the ceiling, and I turned to see the two simple beds along another wall—unoccupied.

Observing more bottles, I found a container of dried dormiroot, a common enough yet dangerous plant that could make one practically catatonic.

"Snooping?"

I turned to find a small woman, no older than twenty, with stark white hair and icy gray eyes that reminded me of the cold skies over the kingdom. Somewhat embarrassed, I moved one of the bottles back to its original spot.

"Apologies. I was looking for the healer. Lupin should have sent word about—"

"What ails you?" she asked, cocking her head to the side and studying me carefully.

I shook my head. "Excuse me?"

Her gaze narrowed. "You were looking for a healer, and you've found one. I asked what ails you."

I reeled back, and she turned away, walking swiftly to the desk below the window to rifle through papers and organize the jars scattered over the wooden surface. Her loose tunic looked more like robes—something akin to a priestess.

"If it's the sore muscles, I can hand you some salts, but I must warn, Lupin is stingy with those rooms upstairs. Bathing chambers are a luxury that will cost you."

I took one step forward, brows furrowed. "I'm actually just here to help," I confessed. "Though I will take the salts. We should be moved to one of those rooms tonight, and my..." I paused. While I knew the healer was part of the Guild, I didn't know how free we were to speak in her apothecary. "wife—"

The healer turned, those cold eyes slicing through the lie. "She is not your wife."

I swallowed, my heart pounding in my chest.

"I—" I had clearly offended her.

The healer clucked her tongue. "Don't worry. I'm not here to reveal your secrets. All I ask is you do not lie to me. You may speak more freely here than most places, but caution should still be taken." She turned to the shelves, plucking a small canvas bag and tossing it in my direction. I caught it, reading the smudged label for the bath salts. "You can use those for your companion. And as for help, there's no need for the dormiroot unless you wish to poison my patients."

I cleared my throat, making ready to plead my case, but she held up a hand to stop me.

"Florence," she said. "That is my name, and I'd be happy for the assistance. I'm sure Lupin explained your payment, but I fear it will be dependent on our patients and their ability to give. I do not make them pay beyond their means. It is whatever they offer. We will split the coin." She gathered up the jars from the desk, carefully placing them on the shelves before eyeing dried lavender hanging overhead. "Now, please prop the door open. We are ready to begin."

I'd never worked so hard.

Florence held a vast array of knowledge when it came to remedies and ailments—something to rival Ma's. Each one had been useful because she was the only healer in the city.

We'd taken care of several minor scrapes, bruises, and the like. This was where I found myself most helpful, using salves and bandages along with recommendations about keeping the wounds clean.

When a boy from outside the city had been brought in following a carriage accident, I'd found it difficult to hold on to the lunch Lupin provided midday. The boy's arm had been hanging at an odd angle, his pained screams dragging up old memories—nightmares.

"You did fine," Florence said from where she knelt on the floor, scrubbing away blood stains from the stone. "I expect you here tomorrow."

I nodded, putting the last of the vials on the shelves lining the wall before carefully pulling dried petals from their stems to add to a jar. I didn't know what plant *this* was, nor did I have the courage to ask, though that didn't matter.

"You should take some of those," Florence offered as she stood, wiping her hands on her tunic. "You crush them, add a bit of water, and can use the paste on any kind of wound. Helps fight off infection and with pain."

My brow furrowed just as a knock drew my attention to the door.

"I'm sorry. I was just..." Verena halted, standing with her eyes wide and hopping from Florence to me. The dirt had been scrubbed from her skin, her hair falling in soft waves over her shoulders. "I was looking for my—"

"Husband?" Florence asked before pursing her lips. "That is the second time I've been told this lie."

Verena's eyes widened, taking a step backward.

I met her there, placing my hand at the small of her back and leaning in. "It's fine," I whispered as she stared at Florence. "I think."

It took a moment for Verena to snap out of it. She turned to me; her gaze pulled to the healer every so often as she whispered. "Lupin sent your dinner up to our new room—larger, but the tub is...open to the room." She cleared her throat. "I've already bathed, but I figured I could find somewhere to go while you—"

"Of course." I could feel the heat creep up my neck and bloom over my cheeks. I turned to Florence, nodding once. "Tomorrow then," I said.

The corners of her mouth turned up in what was the first smile I'd seen from the healer. It seemed as if she were measuring the distance between me and Verena. "Tomorrow, then."

I grabbed Verena's hand, guiding her to the hallway and up the first set of stairs before turning to face her. I grabbed the bag of coins from my pocket, dropping a few into her palm and gently closing her fingers around them. "For whatever you wish to do to busy yourself."

Verena clutched the coins close to her chest. "I may look for food that will keep while we travel. Our room is on the same floor. Two doors down, same side of the hall." She refused to meet my gaze, then gently tucked the coins in the pocket of her pants. "The healer is quite young."

"I was surprised by that," I said.

She untied the cloak around her shoulders, making quick work of tying it once more to tighten it. "Beautiful, too." Her words were quiet—barely there. Verena pulled the hood over her head, glancing to the door that would lead out of the inn and to the alley behind it.

I stared at her, observing the slight press of her lips, her lowered brow.

"Well," she said, pulling the sides of her cloak closed around her. "I'll be back soon."

Verena turned on her heel, exiting the door to the back of the inn and leaving me standing and confused.

"What an interesting thing to say," I muttered, plodding up the second staircase to wash the grime from my skin.

Chapter Twenty-Five

Verena

The city of Branwood looked dreary in the dusk light as I walked the cobble street of the main road.

When I came out of the alleyway near the inn, several drunk patrons stumbled down the two steps leading to the entrance. I pulled my cloak tighter around my body and dodged them before wandering aimlessly down the main road.

With a decent amount of time to waste, I figured I would walk until my mood was set right.

It had been surprising to discover how young—how *beautiful*—the healer had been. What was more surprising was the gnawing jealousy that crawled its way into my gut at the sight of Caius standing with her. When she revealed that he'd told her the truth about our connection, at least in part, I'd first felt fear followed by jealousy's sharp claws sinking deeper into my flesh.

It was an ugly and unwanted emotion I did not enjoy feeling, and so I walked while busying my mind with thoughts of what we would need to get to the Waldwood, where Caius would depart and return home to Ahvi.

Shops and carts littered the city center, most constructed of old wood and the constant dusting of snow that settled over Alphaird. With the sun setting in the distance, the dying light slowly blanketing the town in darkness, I found patrons were sparse—probably opting for local pubs or taverns instead of daily shopping.

I made for a stall boasting of dried meats and hard cheeses, checking for the coins tucked into my pockets.

Armor clinking halted me in my tracks, shouts drawing the attention of the few individuals still shopping at the city's center.

I paused, watching as guards, both on horseback and on foot, surrounded the ornate carriage moving down the street in my direction. The sight of the guard's uniforms had sweat beading on my neck and dread weighing me down—pinning me to where I stood.

I was a long way from the pyre of Marmere, but Branwood was certain to house its own nearby. Phantom flames licked my skin at the thought, and I squeezed my eyes shut for a moment.

"Vespahr's finally returned," a woman nearby commented. The hood of her cloak was pulled down to reveal graying hair and deeply etched wrinkles. She stood with a younger woman, a head taller and most certainly related, if the sharp curve of her chin or the deep brown of her eyes were anything to go by. Shadows from the passing caravan moved over her sepia skin as her gaze fixed to the carriage.

"Unfortunate," the younger woman whispered. "I heard he played a part in outing the Traitor Prince and the king's executioner." I swallowed, and the motion burned my throat. "They're on the run, I suppose. Would explain the palace guards traveling with them."

The older woman clucked her tongue. "Just what we need—more guards."

Adjusting my hood to shield more of my face, I migrated to the stall where a stout man glanced warily at the carriage entering the city.

It seemed the people of Branwood were not fond of their own lord. To be expected considering Vespahr had built up a reputation for himself.

"How much for the dried meat?" I asked, running my fingers along the coins in my pockets to count them.

The man blinked before looking at me—as if he were coming out of a trance. "How much do you need?" he asked.

"A good deal. My husband and I are traveling north."

He leaned in, dropping his voice to a whisper as he tracked the guards behind us. "Not much to the north, Miss. I recommend adjusting the direction you're headed—at least for conversation." He rummaged through a bin behind the cart, pulling out a canvas bag that he filled with various hard cheeses, apples, and dried meat. He added a bag of nuts and seeds to the mix, packaging it carefully.

"Oh," I said, realizing he meant to give the lot to me. "I don't think... I don't have enough coin for all of that."

He cocked a brow in my direction. "Just pay what you can, Dear. You'll need all of this for your trip. Where did you say you were headed? West."

He leveled me with a stare, and I swallowed, nodding in agreement. "Yes," I confirmed. "West."

After paying him the coins Caius had given me, I pulled the strap of the bag around my shoulder, letting the supplies hang at my hip.

When I turned, I nearly ran into one of the guards, the emblem on his uniform indicating he'd traveled from Marmere.

Fear curdled in my stomach, and I looked down, hoping my hood shielded my features. If a guard from the palace dungeons recognized me, I'd hardly know. I hadn't been in the best state of mind during my stay, and it was unlikely I'd remember the faces of those on duty.

"Excuse me," I muttered, stepping around him and quickening my steps back to the inn.

Caius was certain to be done with his bath, and the jealousy I'd felt earlier had long since disappeared—replaced by something far more unsettling.

When another drunk patron leered at me near the inn's entrance, I opted for the door I'd used earlier.

Tucking into the shadows, I kept my grip tight on our supplies, my heart pounding a rapid rhythm in my chest. The sun had fully disappeared, cloaking the city in darkness and a sense of danger.

Or maybe that was my own perception.

My fingers gripped the handle of the door, turning slowly when a firm hand gripped my bicep and pulled me around until I was facing the guard I'd nearly run into on the street.

The smile on his face, the glint in his eye, told me he wasn't here for a pleasant conversation. He yanked me to the side, my hood falling as he pinned me to the outer wall of the inn and brought a dagger up to my throat.

Tears pricked my eyes, and I could feel the sweat dripping down my spine—the winter long forgotten and replaced by terror.

"Where do you think you're going?" he spat, leaning in closer. I turned my head, squeezing my eyes shut. His grip tightened—bruising the skin on my arm. "Ah, she's afraid. Rightfully so, Little Witch."

With the tip of his dagger pressed to my neck, the sharp stinging sensation followed by blood sliding down my skin.

Roaring filled my ears as I looked at my attacker. The large scar across his eyebrow felt familiar, but there was no way to truly know if he'd seen me in the dungeons or if he was just guessing.

With the dagger at my throat, I longed to pull from his grasp, but knew he'd sink it into my skin with little thought. The kingdom had never been kind to witches, and if that is what he believed me to be, there was no stopping his hatred.

The door near us slammed, and I watched as his wrist snapped just before his neck, the man dropping silently at my feet, eyes open and glassy—vacant.

I turned to find the healer standing by the door, a dagger in her hand, and her shoulder twisted at an odd angle. A line appeared between her brow, and she gasped as if in pain.

Mender.

"You're—"

She stepped closer, the fierceness in her gaze never ceasing. "I would advise that you both leave Branwood." She looked down at the dead man, a pool of blood forming at the back of his skull, painting the snow-dusted street a deep crimson. "I will let them believe this was you." She nodded in his direction.

I sucked in shallow breaths, trying to calm my racing thoughts. "Why would you—"

"Because," she snapped. "I will lose all the ways I've been helping in this city. My work is important for people like us." Her gray eyes narrowed. "This is your fault," she accused, her voice cutting like the dagger she now picked up from the ground. She pulled a bag of coins from her waistband, shoved it into my hand, and pressed the guard's weapon into my other. "Now leave," she ordered.

Nodding, I shoved the coins into the bag I'd been given in the city center and held the dagger hidden in my cloak.

I scrambled up the steps, bursting into the inn's room to find Caius standing shirtless by the window.

He turned abruptly, rushing toward me when he saw my expression. "What's wrong?" he asked, gently gripping the sides of my arms. I winced as his hand gently held the spot where a bruise had now formed.

"The healer," I panted. "She just killed the guard who attacked me in the alleyway."

"Shit," he muttered, turning to grab his shirt from the floor and pulling it over his head.

I gasped for breath, trying to calm my wild thoughts. "We have to leave," I said. "She told us to leave."

"Yeah." Caius nodded, rushing to gather our things from around the room. "Yeah, okay. We will head to the stable to get our horse."

CHAPTER TWENTY-SIX

THERON

Every breath I took sent a sharp pain shooting behind my ribcage. By the time we got our sights on Bloodbane's city, I couldn't enjoy the sigh of relief. For starters, it added to the pain. There was also the unfortunate reality that my suspicions about Bloodbane's loyalty were entirely wrong.

It had been a week since our escape from Marmere. The salve Rialey's maid sent seemed to help, but not nearly enough. I'd felt weak and useless—fully reliant on a woman who had grown to hate me for my lies.

Even so, Rialey seemed intent on helping me survive, albeit begrudgingly. She'd hunted for food, reminded me to apply the salve, and kept our horses fed by paying those with homes and livestock nestled in the wilds with coin—probably more than she should have.

The city walls stretched toward the overcast sky, beige stones in various shades cobbled together to protect the city. I wasn't sure if they would welcome us here. I wasn't sure we'd make it through the city gates.

"How would you like to appear, Prince Wineslowe? I was thinking portly and balding—maybe even an unsightly growth on one side of your face. We will have to enter the city, and I'm sure that illusion will make for a decent disguise."

My head snapped to Rialey at the first words she'd spoken in hours. She sat astride the bay gelding; her cloak streaked with dirt and the scars of a weeks-long journey through the snow-covered landscape of Alphaird. Her black hair fell over one shoulder, braided with loose strands at the wind's mercy. What surprised me was the small tilt to the corner of her mouth. A joke or an insult—possibly both.

Something warm bloomed in my chest—the smallest flicker of hope. "Whatever helps you, Miss Dagon. I've noted your struggle to pull your gaze from my direction."

Her smile fell, the cold rushing in to remind me where we were—what we were doing.

"I will disguise both of us for our entrance into the city. I'll also be fabricating papers. Don't speak. You are mute."

My teeth clicked as I snapped my jaw shut, obeying despite the frustration stirring in my gut.

When we neared the gates, my skin warmed, tingling as I realized her magic was working. I didn't dare look down at my hands—didn't dare glance at what she'd done to my appearance. I did, however, lose the battle to look away from her.

Rialey had changed her hair color from black to a stark white. Her lips appeared redder against her pale skin. The scar on her cheek had vanished. Her eyes darkened to a deep amber—reminding me of tree sap and clay. While I found the new appearance strikingly beautiful, it didn't hold a candle to the woman I'd grown to know. Rialey, in her original form, was beautiful.

I'd always thought that.

"White hair may draw attention," I commented.

Her lip curled, eyes hardening as she stared toward the approaching gate. "Men are simple creatures. Beauty softens them to your will, so I've chosen what will serve us well with the guards. Our chances of getting through the gates are far higher, Your Highness."

My stomach roiled, disgust covering my features—but I suppose she could mask that too.

There was little I understood about the witches' power apart from what I'd seen of Rialey's. An abomination, my father had called it.

No being should possess that kind of influence without earning the right to do so.

His hatred often sounded like jealousy. Even in my youth, I'd found it to be so.

A guard stood straight at the entrance, asking for our papers. I obeyed Rialey's command to remain silent. My muscles ached, the pain still sharp behind my ribs with every intake of breath.

I'd done my best to mask whatever pain I'd felt thus far. Feeling useless, I didn't want to give her another reason to hate me. It was bad enough I'd put us into this position. I could not make it worse by becoming even more of a burden.

"Your brother," the guard said, eyeing me questioningly. "What business have you in the city?"

Rialey chimed in quickly, diverting his attention away. "He's mute, Sir. Returned that way from the witch hunts from years ago. We are here to visit friends. That is all."

His gaze flicked back to me, uncertain. The stiffness in Rialey's shoulders only exasperated my nerves and the way she clenched a fist at her left side, digging her nails into her palm until I was certain they'd leave crescent moon shaped marks on her skin.

I refocused on the guard, aware that I should do something, but not knowing what.

"You don't speak?" he questioned, his tone biting and full of disbelief. "How can that be so? Is it by choice?"

I watched the guards at his back shift where they stood, one resting a hand on the hilt of his sword. This was certainly not good.

How was I to respond to the bastard? If I didn't speak, I wouldn't be able to answer his questions now, would I?

"Show him," Rialey demanded, and my gaze snapped to hers, snagging on the amber irises. For a moment, I saw that color shift to her usual gray color—almost blue in the daylight.

Most of my time with Rialey Dagon had been in the darkness, tucked into the corners of the city or veiled in the shadows of her room late at night, most recently.

In the light, close up, her eyes became a kaleidoscope of color—far more interesting than something resembling the overcast sky that was a permanent fixture above Alphaird.

My heart pounded, stomach churning with nausea at the fear.

What would he find if I opened my mouth?

I knew Rialey had magic she could use—it was evident in the disguises we now donned. The question was, how good was her ability? Could she hold on to all of those details? How deep was the well of her magic, really? I knew little of her limits, and with the latest developments, my trust in her felt unsteady at best.

"Show him," she repeated, a bit quieter now.

I turned to face the guard, unhinging my jaw to reveal the tongue that was very much inside of my mouth.

To my surprise, his nose wrinkled in disgust right before he turned his attention back to the papers.

He looked them over once more, shoving them back into Rialey's hands before gesturing through the gates.

"Unfortunately, we've no healers to give you a tongue." The light in his eyes glinted with malice, matching the smirk he wore. "Might need a witch for something like that. Too bad King Wineslowe keeps killing them all."

Ice coated my veins, but I kept my mouth shut, guiding my horse through the gates and onto the cobbled streets of Keslow, Lord Bloodbane's city, where I was unsure if we were welcome or not.

Lord Bloodbane's large home did not sit on the edge overlooking the busy city square but was tucked away at the end of a quiet street, barren vines wrapping around the spiked iron fence surrounding the yard.

For a moment, I wondered what the fence would have looked like in a different season—during a time before winter fell over the kingdom.

"Shall I remain mute for this?" I asked as we dismounted, tying our horses to the post just outside the gate.

"That depends," Rialey said, her hair still the white color she'd used as her disguise. Her magic had become a dull hum, but I could still feel it—still knew she'd cloaked me in magic. "Are we arriving as ourselves, or as the brother and sister the guards welcomed into the city?"

I cleared my throat, doing my best to disguise the slight limp I still had from my previous injuries. "I can't say how this will go," I admitted. "If my hunch is correct, I say when we see Bloodbane or his daughter, I show my face."

One brow lifted when she glanced in my direction. "His daughter, huh?"

Irritation flared, and I clenched my fists. "Yes. The woman you instructed me to dance with at the ball. I've known her for a time. I believe her father may help us."

"Hm."

I didn't respond as we walked up the steps to the large blue door complete with golden accents. The golden knocker on the front door had been molded into the shape of an owl. With my heart pounding, a slight irritation crawling beneath my skin, I reached out to feel the cool metal and steeled my spine as I hit once, twice, three times before taking a step back.

"Nervous, Your Highness?" Rialey asked, our disguises still in place.

I released a few shallow breaths; my eyes fixed on the door. "Yes," I whispered.

Akari Bloodbane opened the door dressed in a long royal-blue gown, the color of Keslow.

"Hello," she smiled, her white teeth contrasting against smooth brown skin. Akari's hair had been braided last I saw her; now it had been pulled back tightly against her scalp and secured at the back, with her tight coils wild at her nape.

"Can I ask what you might be here—"

A prickling feeling started in my chest, slowly fanning out over my entire body until Rialey's magic released me, leaving a gaping Akari with brown eyes, hard and frantic.

"Get inside," she practically growled, her delicate hands surprisingly firm when they gripped my bicep. I winced, knowing the touch would be bruising. "Now."

The door slammed shut behind us, leaving us in the empty entrance to Bloodbane's manor. The walls were painted the same royal blue color found on Akari's gown. She turned on her heel, slippers slapping the pale wooden floors of their home. The intricate carvings on the crown molding matched the details of the home. A light brown color, those accents matched the frames on every decorative image, and even matched the shade of the vaulted ceiling and the exposed beams.

The home certainly belonged to someone wealthy, but not someone who longed to flaunt their wealth in the way my father had.

Rialey followed at my side, her steps keeping time with Akari's. Not only had she gotten rid of my disguise, but she'd gotten rid of her own as well.

"I thought you might end up here," Akari said in a low voice. "My father gave me specific instructions for this very moment. We are not to allow anyone to see—"

A scuff at the end of the hall halted her sentence.

"Shit," she muttered, looking left to the wooden door near us. Akari opened it with haste, shoving us in with urgency, and leaving us crowded in the dark with a harsh whisper of, "Do not speak."

The door slammed shut, and I stepped back, immediately bumping into a shelf. My boot knocked into Rialey's, sending her spinning until her back hit another shelf at our side.

A supply closet of sorts.

"Would you—"

My hand moved on instinct, eyes adjusting to the dark enough to see where she stood. The light from beneath the door illuminated the closet just enough for me to realize this was a confined space—a hurried attempt at hiding us.

I slapped my palm over Rialey's mouth, leaning down and close. "You need to stop talking," I whispered.

Anger flared in her eyes, but she didn't move my hand away. Her skin felt cool to the touch, a result of our long journey, no doubt.

Murmurs sounded outside as we listened. Akari spoke to a servant. While she was kind in her words, there was a finality laced into the tone when she told the servant they needed to stop immediately and tend to something elsewhere in the house.

"Miss," the woman's voice started. "Allow me to just put this away, and I'd be happy to—"

"I'll do it."

A soft tapping followed shuffling sounds on the floor, the servant fleeing. Shadows mingled in the light coming from the bottom of the door, indicating that Akari still stood watching—waiting.

I finally peeled my hand off of Rialey's lips, a sharp longing piercing my chest. I fought to shove it down.

"I'd ask that you not touch me again, Highness," she whispered, her tone biting.

My frustration returned—that same annoyance I'd felt earlier at her casual dismissals. Despite everything, she'd had no trouble descending into something more than indifference. Possibly bitterness—maybe even hatred.

"That's not how you felt two weeks ago," I seethed, my voice still quiet.

Rialey stood up straighter. "Bold of you to assume you know anything about my feelings, Your Highness."

"Bullshit," I spat. "I was there, Rialey. I was there in your room as your breath quickened, and you leaned toward me. You wanted me to kiss you that night."

She looked away. I had struck a nerve. "I don't know what you're talking about."

"You once had feelings for me. As Eryx, Theron, whoever. That does not matter. It was me, and you *saw* me. You really wish to stand here and behave as if those feelings are no longer there? Not even a little."

Rialey leaned forward, her eyes blazing again. I could feel the anger radiating off her—something to match my frustration. "I feel nothing for you."

The words felt like a blade slicing across my flesh. An uncomfortable silence punctuated the sensation before I spoke to break it.

"Why did you save me?" I asked. The question had been haunting me for the past week. The most logical answer was that Rialey still had feelings for me. I *knew* she had them, and I didn't think they would just disappear—my own certainly hadn't. "Why," I whispered once more—pleaded.

She did not back away, nor did she balk at the question. "Because I also had to run," she whispered. "When I leave you, the price for your head will be far higher than mine. It may give me a chance."

The door opened, with Akari looking more hurried than she had been before. "Come," she said. "We don't have much time."

Chapter Twenty-Seven

Rialey

I'd never been to Keslow, but the lord's home contrasted with that of the lord in Marmere.

There was a warmth to Bloodbane's office. Tapestries and paintings hung on the walls, the desk backed by a large, built-in bookshelf littered with tomes and trinkets.

My gaze fixed on the owl figurine carved of wood as Akari presented us to her father. My heart beat wildly in my chest. Lord Bloodbane was difficult to read as he stood behind the desk, his features echoing those of his daughter.

The same shade as Akari's, his brown eyes held Theron's gaze. If he were surprised, no one would know it.

"Theron," he said. He leaned forward over the desk, hands braced on its glossy surface. The brass buttons on his coat reflected the light of the fires in the sconces. "It is a significant risk to have you here," he began, "in my home." Bloodbane raised a dark brow, his jaw ticking before his gaze flicked to his daughter, and back to the prince. "Your father's men will be here within hours looking for you. What makes you think I would not hand you over?"

My fear—my dread—had my breaths coming quicker. I knew there was a risk in coming to Keslow—that the welcome might not be warm—but after a week-long journey, I had hoped that we'd find favor with someone.

Akari had shoved us into a supply closet, a memory I did not wish to relive. She wouldn't have done such a thing if they'd planned to turn us in, but then again, maybe she was simply hiding us from the staff, waiting to deliver us to King Wineslowe upon his men's arrival.

"There have been whispers about you at court," Theron said. He stood tall despite the dirt streaked in his hair and clothes. He clasped his hands behind his back beneath the cloak, straightening in a way that reminded me of Eryx perusing my room. I cursed myself for not having seen it sooner.

I'd realized Eryx had an important position in the palace based on his behavior, but I'd never assumed he'd be the prince.

Foolish.

I was foolish.

"There have been more than whispers about *you*, Highness." Bloodbane tapped a finger on the desk, leveling Theron with his gaze.

Theron, for what it was worth, did not back down.

"Do you wish to have our heads on a spike? Is that where your loyalty lies? If so, this is your chance, Lord Bloodbane. I'm aware of the risks of having me in your home. I was aware of the risks in coming here, as well. It is a chance I decided to take."

"Desperate men do not make skilled negotiators," Bloodbane stated.

I looked at Akari, who stood off to the side. When her eyes met mine, I held her gaze, looking for any sign that we were to be killed for our crimes.

The dagger at my thigh burned, taunting and yearning to be put to use. The likelihood of me making it out of this room with an injured prince was low, but if I left Theron to fend for himself, that increased my chances.

I couldn't do it, though.

And I didn't want to admit why that was.

In the closet, I'd asked him not to touch me, and I meant it. I couldn't withstand the litany of memories that flooded my mind at his touch. Anger easily replaced sadness, for it was the simpler emotion.

I found it easier to lie to him in that moment, and maybe that was my attempt at repaying him for the lies he told me.

My eyes had slid to Prince Theron at the thoughts, and I quickly removed them.

Bloodbane peeled his hands off the desk, standing before he rounded it and moved directly in front of Theron. He stood a head taller—intimidating. "I have hope in you, Prince Theron Wineslowe," Lord Bloodbane admitted. "Hope for our kingdom—our honor."

My mouth parted in surprise as I listened with rapt attention.

"I will keep your secrets," he continued. "I will keep *you* for a short time, so long as you're willing to keep mine. So long as you're willing to turn yourself into the leader you are meant to be."

Theron's jaw ticked before he tipped his chin upward infinitesimally. "What secrets do you speak of?"

"That of rebellion," Bloodbane confessed. "I'm willing to bargain for your safety as well." For the first time, Lord Bloodbane looked at me. "Miss Rialey Dagon," he said, his voice smooth—cunning. "The king's executioner. The infamous Witch Hunter." He cocked a brow. "Imagine my surprise in finding that you are, yourself, a witch. A witch willing to kill her own kind, no less."

Theron stepped forward, his shoulder brushing mine as he placed himself before me. His protection did nothing—meant nothing. Bloodbane spoke the truth. I had saved, and I had killed. This was the reality I had to face.

I was not *good.*

Before I could speak, Theron interrupted. "Do not bring her into this," Theron said. "She is to be afforded whatever protections you afford me."

Lord Bloodbane scanned Theron's features, taking in the intensity of them—the sharpness to his words.

"You will be king," he said. "When the time comes. And Akari will be queen at your side should she choose that future. That is my offer."

One corner of Theron's mouth pulled upward as if he were pleased at this offer. Maybe his dance with her had gone well at the palace. Maybe she was his choice to begin with.

Jealousy was an ugly beast, and it had snaked its way into my chest.

"Fine," Theron answered, and I fought the urge to gape at him. "You have a deal."

Lord Bloodbane smiled. "We will seal it in blood. I would not be a Bloodbane if it weren't so." He grabbed a dagger from the bookshelf behind him, sliced open the center of his palm, and offered the weapon to Theron.

Theron hesitated for a moment, eyes sliding to Akari, who nodded once in encouragement.

With a slow drag across his palm, Theron's blood welled up, oozing out of the wound before he clasped Bloodbane's hand, sealing the promise with old witch magic.

I ground my teeth together. It was insulting—the use of magic within the kingdom. Magic existed within the witches but was also laced through the very fabric of the soil—most poignant in the Waldwood.

I'd never grown used to seeing it while the kingdom did so much to eviscerate my people.

All I knew was that Theron had just traded his life and his future for our safety. The blood magic would bind him to his promise. If it should be broken, his life would be forfeit.

"You should remain hidden," Bloodbane began, rounding the desk to grab a rag from the drawer. He wiped the blood off his palm before setting the soiled fabric onto the desk's surface. "I expect Rialey can handle an illusion or two. When you walk through my home, you will wear such an illusion. You cannot slip up." His eyes hardened as he stared at both of us. "One mistake, and my life's work will be ruined. It is important that you stay together for this purpose, but I recognize magic has its limits." He gripped the edge of the desk, smearing blood on its surface. "You will reside in the same room as a married couple from Keslow. Akari's friends. I give you one month, and no longer. Are we understood?"

Theron clenched his fist at his side, and I watched as a small drop of blood gathered, dangled above the hardwood floors before dropping to the ground.

"Understood," Theron answered.

When Bloodbane turned to me, expectant, I longed to scream. He'd just sold his daughter like cattle to the prince—crawled his way up to the top of the ladder like the rest of the lords fought to do. What was worse, Theron *agreed* to it. He didn't so much as bargain with the man.

Either we were well and truly desperate for survival, or he had wanted to propose to Akari, anyway.

It felt like betrayal, though I wasn't sure why.

Despite myself, I opened my mouth, my throat dry as if filled with ash and sand. "I understand," I ground out, noting the way Bloodbane cocked his head curiously.

When we exited the room, following behind Akari, my blood boiled with every step through the castle. She led us back to the front entryway, up a grand staircase that split in either direction.

Holding my magic close, I kept our features the same as they were upon entering the city. Theron's hair, now black, hung to his shoulders. The thick beard gave him a gruff appearance, along with the broader shoulders and the dark eyes. He looked nothing like a prince, though still attractive.

I, however, preferred his real features. In a world of lies, I'd learned to value the truth, especially when it pertained to who someone really was.

Maybe that's why his betrayal stung so much—even now.

On the third and final floor, we walked down a long hallway, our rooms at the very back of the house.

"You'll stay here," Akari said, more to Theron than to myself.

His future wife.

The queen.

"Thank you," Theron murmured. "I mean that."

Akari nodded once, her brown eyes hopping from me to Theron. "I expect you will hold to my father's bargain," she said, her voice smooth as silk. "The most important pieces, that is."

"I haven't a choice."

She hummed, digging in the pocket of her dress and pulling out a key that she placed into my hand. "Lock the doors at all times," she instructed. "When the servants come to run your baths in about twenty minutes, you should use your magic. We cannot risk being found out here. My father is an important man—not just for the kingdom, but for the kingdom's future. He loves Alphaird—Keslow, especially. One month is all we can offer you."

I gripped the key tighter, feeling the edges dig into my palm as I nodded my agreement.

When she walked away, I unlocked the door without a word, and we disappeared into the bedroom, where I dropped my magic.

One single bed sat at the center with blue linens to match the rest of the house. A seating area near the fireplace had two uncomfortable-looking chairs, and the tub was separated by a room divider that had my stomach sinking.

"I will sleep on the floor," I said as Theron closed the door behind us. The soft snick echoed far louder than it should, as if it were sounding the alarm regarding our situation.

"And why would you do that?" he questioned.

When I turned, his skin looked paler than usual, dirt-streaked and tired. We would need to find a healer to assess his injuries—one who could be trusted, if one of those even existed.

"Because you are now engaged."

His brow furrowed. "I am not engaged. Who am I engaged to?"

I scoffed. "Don't be dense. Look at your palm. You just sealed your fate in blood magic. You will die if you do not marry Akari. Are you so delirious from the journey that you do not realize what you agreed to?" My voice rose on the last sentence.

"That promise was that I should be king," he said, one corner of his mouth turning upward. "I know what I agreed to."

"And that Akari Bloodbane should be queen!"

"If she chooses." His smirk widened as my brow furrowed.

"Yes."

"Akari will marry me if that is something she should want. I can assure you, Rialey Dagon, she does not want that. Are you jealous?"

I reeled back. "What? No."

He unclasped his cloak, laying it delicately on the dresser near the door. He wasn't looking at me when he continued speaking. "Akari and I do not wish to relive the past, should we not have to. She is, quite frankly, in love with a man on her father's guard. There is no concern there."

My mind struggled to keep up, clouded by a flurry of emotions I did not wish to feel. I must have been exhausted after the journey. It was merely exhaustion.

"Relive the past?" I questioned.

Prince Theron turned to me then, his smile widening. "We have a... history. We were not a good match as lovers—more as friends. Akari despises horses—afraid of them, in fact. It would not have made sense."

Somehow, my jealousy did not disappear. In fact, it grew at the insinuation. Akari and Theron had been... together. I hated that it bothered me so much.

I hated *him*.

When the servant knocked on the door, I found that gold thread in my vision, tugging on the illusion and allowing it to cloak us in our disguises.

"You may bathe first," Theron said while striding to the door. He placed his hand on the knob. "I will not look."

"Won't you be stepping out?" I asked, my brows furrowing as nerves fluttered in my stomach.

He turned to look at me, his hand still resting on the knob. Another knock came. "I cannot," he answered. "I'm tied to your magic here." He frowned, a genuine expression. "I'm sorry, Rialey. It was the only option I thought we had. I will not bother you."

Without another word, he opened the door to let the woman in.

Dread filled me as I realized I would not be alone—not while we were here, anyway especially not with King Wineslowe's men on the way. We would be trapped in Keslow. Trapped in Lord Bloodbane's palace together.

Chapter Twenty-Eight

Verena

Three weeks of wandering the forest and relying on the kindness of the strangers we'd encountered left me yearning for a soft bed to call my own.

I found myself missing Ahvi's cabin, the medicinal tea blends, and even the hours I spent sketching the Waldwood from the old kitchen table. I'd longed for home—what I remembered of it and my childhood—and taken for granted the peace I'd found there.

Somehow, even amidst the deep ache in my chest at the loss of that quiet place, I felt I was missing something. The Waldwood called to me like a siren from the books I'd read growing up. Though I'd never been to the coast of Alphaird—never seen the sea—I couldn't help but wonder if such creatures existed amongst the trees, or maybe, possibly, it was the magic of the forest itself. The stories of the old gods who had created it—tended to it—angered at the destruction of the Waldwood's gifts.

Caius and I had decided it was best to travel north, avoiding the mountains so we could enter the Waldwood from the western side, and have an easier time navigating the terrain. The risk of the most direct route was too high. If we were to encounter soldiers from King Wineslowe's army, there was no telling what would happen.

"The sky is getting dark again." Caius shifted behind me on our horse, the familiar vibrations of his voice comforting after so long together. I'd avoided thinking about what happened *after*. He'd mentioned leaving—going back to his grandmother after I'd settled and returning to a rebellion I'd just learned existed, but there was no telling how long it would take to find what we were looking for.

Guilt had burrowed beneath my skin long ago, and now it penetrated deeper—engraving itself on my bones. I couldn't ask more of this man—I simply couldn't. And so, we would part ways, and he would live out the rest of his days with Ahvi—maybe meeting a kind woman—creating his own family.

"We should be to the Waldwood in the next day or so," I said. "If I'm remembering correctly. There's no telling how long it will take once we are within the trees." There was a question embedded in the words, one Caius picked up on easily enough.

"Verena," he murmured. "I've promised to see you home—no matter how long it should take to do so."

We found an area tucked between the pines, tying up our horse. I worked on the tent while Caius took off to find food; the moon shining down between the sleepy branches creaking overhead.

Once the fire was lit, I edged closer, watching the orange flames dance in the darkness as my limbs warmed from the cold.

"Rabbit again." Caius's voice came through the trees before I spotted him with two creatures hanging from his fist by the tail. When his nose wrinkled, I chuckled.

"I take it you're tired of that meal?"

He tossed the animals into the snow near the fire, unclasping his cloak to create a spot to sit on next to me. Deft fingers pulled a knife from his belt when he sat, getting to work on the carcasses.

"They're not my favorite," he admitted. "I would sell the clothes off my back for something less…" The words hung in the air.

"Gamey?" I finished.

When he turned to me, his full mouth had stretched into a closed-lip smile, small crinkles etching themselves into his warm, brown skin. A beard now hid the angles of his jaw, but my memory was strong. Each new thing I discovered about Caius stuck with me. His gentleness, the faded stretch mark across his back from puberty, I assumed, the dimple printed into his cheek, now hidden by facial hair. I remembered it all—tried to file it away for when he would leave me.

"It is rather gamey," he answered. "I'm sorry our feasts are so lacking."

One corner of my mouth turned up. "Your hunting skills are not, though."

Something unspoken hung between us, the knowledge that he'd hidden something from me. "Your skill with a blade?" I pressed, longing for more information.

"I am well practiced," he answered, his tone carrying a finality that kept me from pushing any further.

As we sat beneath the moonlight, the tough meat working to ease the gnawing ache in my stomach, Caius told me the stories he remembered of his mother—the stories she'd told him.

It seemed a fair swap. While he didn't speak much of rebellion, he told plenty of his life—his home before King Wineslowe had destroyed it. I suddenly saw his reasoning—why he'd hold something like his childhood so close. I saw why he'd long to bring a bit of that peace back—longed for it myself.

"I get frustrated for not remembering much," he admitted. "The most vivid details come in the night, but they're stained—tainted with the memory of their deaths."

A stiff wind blew through the trees, sending snow cascading from the branches.

My chest tightened at his words—the sadness in them. "I'm sorry," I whispered.

He shook his head. "You've no reason to be. It is not your fault."

I swallowed the burning in my throat. "It doesn't change that I am sorry for your situation—for the loss you experienced."

His eyes met mine, dark with the depths I longed to discover. "We've all experienced loss. I cannot pretend my sorrow is deeper than yours."

"It is still sorrow."

He blinked once, and I wished I knew what it was he saw when he looked at me. Did the memory of my near-death unearth itself? Was that what he saw? Did it bring back the haunting memories of the others he'd lost?

"It is," he whispered.

Another silence met us, but I did not mind it. Over the past three weeks, I'd grown more comfortable with that peaceful silence.

"My mom used to tell me the stories of the gods—the old ones worshipped by the covens."

I smiled softly, glancing at the crackling wood of the fire. "Seems fitting for a young child. Do you remember any of them? I know you said you were young when she died." I swallowed the lump in my throat. "I saw—"

"Do you know the story of Eirdis and the creation of the Waldwood?" Caius shifted closer, and I felt the warmth radiating off his body—more than that of the fire, it seemed.

"I do," I answered honestly, "but I think I'd like to hear it from you."

His breathy chuckle sent goosebumps over my skin, the warmth of him seeping beneath my skin. "And I would like to tell it to you."

His warm eyes found mine before we both looked to the fire, watching the orange embers glow beneath dancing flames.

"Long ago, where the sky met the sea, Araxie, the goddess of the deep, stayed in her waters watching the moon of our world rise above the horizon. The moon goddess, Onelia, was beautiful with her luminescent white hair, and deep skin—skin that spoke of the secrets of the night.

"Over time, Araxie fell in love with the goddess. She longed to reach her, and so during the night, her waves would bleed onto the shore.

"One day, Araxie watched as Caelus, the god of the sky, began flirting with Onelia during the night. The goddess of the moon slowly fell in love with Caelus, but Araxie, awake during the day, saw that Caelus had also courted the goddess of the sun, Cyra.

"Day after day, Araxie would look to the skies as Caelus whispered false promises to both the sun and the moon without the other's knowledge.

"Her sorrow shifted to rage, pushing Araxie to emerge from the water at high tide in an effort to reach Onelia—to tell her of the traitorous god. But Araxie was bound to the water as most gods and goddesses are bound to the nature they serve.

"Crying on the shore, Araxie lost herself to her sadness, unaware that Eirdis, the goddess of the wild things, emerged from the forest at the sounds of her sobbing.

"Eirdis had been so moved by the sorrow of the sea, she risked stepping out of the shadow.

"'Why are you crying?' Eirdis asked, laying her bow gently in the sand.

"'The lies of above,' Araxie answered.

"Upon further questioning, Eirdis had learned of Caelus's betrayal—his dishonesty. In her desire to please Araxie, whom she found stunningly beautiful, Eirdis set off into the wild to find the sky and hunt Caelus from the clouds.

"For weeks, Eirdis wandered the forests, until one day, she climbed the trunk of the tallest tree, where she found Caelus whispering his love to Cyra, the sun god.

"In her rage, Eirdis demanded he tell the truth, and so the first eclipse of our world occurred, but it didn't satiate Eirdis's growing rage.

"Eirdis shot Caelus with her arrow, piercing him through the heart and causing his descent from the sky. Without his beloved domain, Caelus lost his magic and was dragged to the shoreline at night.

"But when Eirdis presented the sky god to Araxie, it didn't change her sadness. For Onelia's heart did not change—she did not love Araxie, and Araxie did not love Eirdis.

"And so sorrow, contagious as it is, consumed Eirdis.

"She wandered into the wilds of the wood, lying in the grass until the forest swallowed her whole, consuming her magic right along with it.

"That magic is the very heartbeat of the Waldwood—the origin of it all. Eirdis, goddess of wild things, and mother of the witches."

When Caius finished the tale, full of strife and heartache, I looked to the sky, thinking of Caelus, and Eirdis, and the gods of the witches.

The night stretched on above us. The clouds breaking just enough to reveal the stars and the moon.

Caius nudged me with his shoulder, and my gaze landed on his.

"Do you believe?" he asked. "In the gods, that is?"

A half-hearted smile pulled at my mouth. "No," I answered, looking back out to the forest. Wings fluttered above, and I watched as an owl swooped between branches before landing on one to watch us intently.

"However," I began, "I sometimes hope that I am wrong."

Chapter Twenty-Nine

Caius

Bright light seeped in through the small gap at the entrance of our tent, guiding me awake.

I sat up, sore from another night on the frozen ground. Frost coated the inside of the tent fabric, and Verena turned over where she slept, unaware.

Freckles dusted the bridge of her nose, lighter on her cheeks but still present. Her steady breaths came from parted lips, bright pink and contrasting against her pale and dirt-streaked skin. I sat there, memorizing the gap between her teeth, the way her hair draped over her shoulder, and the brown eyelashes kissing those freckles at her cheeks.

I thought with the harsh travel conditions, she'd grow weaker, but despite all logic, Verena had grown stronger over the past few weeks. Far from the girl I'd found in the snow, her body had become softer, capable muscles forming beneath velvety skin.

Once we made it to the Waldwood, my task would be completed. Ma would expect me to return, and I *had* to. With the soldiers passing through our yard—the looming violence of the kingdom—I needed to make sure she was safe—to go with her and do what it was I'd set out to do in the beginning.

Still, a thread of sorrow pulled in my chest.

My worries occupied two spaces—my heart slowly dividing itself in two.

For one half, my grandmother was my only remaining family—all I had. We had a duty to the kingdom—to the rebellion. And for the other half of my heart? My feelings grew roots beneath the frosted snow—unseen and useless.

Verena longed for the Waldwood.

I was simply someone she passed along the way.

She stirred, one delicate hand releasing its grip on the cloak draped around her. Unknowingly, Verena shifted slightly nearer.

As if her magic called me closer, I was helpless to move my hand toward hers, my cool fingers slowly brushing the back of her hand.

Verena's eyes opened, and I pulled back, smiling despite the small twinge of guilt sitting in my gut.

"Good morning," I whispered. "It seems there is a bit of sunshine outside our tent. I have a good feeling about today. What do you say we find the Waldwood?"

Verena smiled, sitting up and clasping her cloak around her neck. She gently grabbed her hair, un-tucking it from the garment as I watched, thinking about that fleeting touch I'd stolen mere moments ago. My hand flexed of its own accord.

"Good morning, Caius." She smiled, soft lips curling up at either corner. "Let's go home."

"Do you feel that?"

Verena shifted in front of me, leaning forward to glance around one of the tall trees. In doing so, her bottom half pushed backward in the saddle.

I grunted, my grip tightening on the reins, arms wrapped around either side of her. "Feel what?" I questioned, my voice somewhat strained. For what it was worth, she didn't notice.

"Turn right," she said, her voice barely audible.

The trees pushed taller into the winter sky, now overcast with the descending sun. As snow floated from looming limbs, a strange sensation crawled up my spine.

"The Waldwood," I whispered, in awe.

The magic of the forest was almost tangible as we crossed over the invisible boundary. The trees appeared older, wider, and wiser than those of the forest we'd been traveling through previously.

Snow still painted the forest floor, but there was a hum of life buried beneath—something dying to be awoken.

Quiet surrounded us as our horse pushed forward through the snow—soft snorting breaths and the gentle movement of our mount mixed with the wind.

It was far quieter here than I imagined it would be.

"Now," Verena began. "We should only have to wander for days to find any hint of life—any coven to discover."

I grinned, leaning forward just slightly. The strands of her hair tickled my nose as I breathed in the scent of earth and magic. "The easy part," I whispered.

Verena shivered, and I tightened my arms around her to ward off the cold. Somehow, it seemed to make it worse as another ripple ran through her.

A crack sounded in front of us, and I drew back on the reins, shifting my weight backward. "Was—"

"No," Verena whispered, and I could hear the smile in her voice. "It seems we've found favor with Eirdis."

"You don't believe in the gods," I said through a chuckle.

"In this case," she responded, "I'm happy to be wrong."

I pushed our horse forward, following the sounds that seemed to increase as we moved through the trees. The cracking branch became metal clanking, and voices floated up toward the sky.

I caught sight of someone walking between the pines, with a sword hanging at their hip.

My stomach dropped, and I tightened my grip on the reins. "Verena," I warned, my voice laced with a deadly calm—as low as I can get it. "This discovery has nothing to do with the gods."

My heart hammered in my chest as she leaned back, her fearful breaths coming out faster, the whisper of them floating on a cloud through the air. "We should turn around."

We veered left, quietly retreating away from whomever lurked in the forest.

I urged our horse onward; the panic coating my veins in ice.

Silence descended around us, the magic of the woods still buzzing over my skin along with the awareness that we are not alone—and that might not be a good thing.

A flash of black through the trees.

The clank of metal.

Our horse reared up, leaving me vaguely aware of Verena's scream as my legs gave out. Weeks of riding had done nothing to strengthen the muscles there—if anything, it made me weaker.

"Caius!" she shouted just before we both hit the ground. Her body landed on top of mine, knocking the wind from my lungs as our horse took off in the opposite direction, carrying our things with it.

Thankfully, we still carried our daggers and coin—though I wasn't sure the latter would help us. I hadn't earned much back in Branwood—hardly enough to satiate the greedy.

Verena rolled off me, and my vision tunneled when we sat up.

More streaks.

More metal.

A towering figure appeared through the trees, sword drawn, face taut with rage.

"Look at that," he mused, his voice slithering through the trees like a snake. "A witch and her escort." The emblem on the soldier's uniform told me all I needed to know about his origins—that and the thick armor protecting all that was beneath.

I gripped my dagger, moving between the man and Verena. The scar slashed across his brow taunting me like a gruesome promise.

The likelihood of us making it out of this alive was not good. While Verena and I held the advantage of numbers, our weapons were far smaller, fit for close combat.

Beyond that, while I was confident in my ability to wield my knife efficiently, I wasn't sure of how my skill compared to that of a trained soldier.

Especially one from Marmere.

"Verena," I cautioned. There was one strong heartbeat between my words, one that pounded against the cage of my chest and shot worry out to every limb. I braced myself; my tone laced with command. "Run."

She took off just as the soldier lunged for me, his sword arcing sideways to slash toward my right arm.

Stumbling back, the awareness that I was in no position to be fighting slammed into me. My bones were weary—muscles sore from weeks of traveling.

Still, I had promised to protect her, and with everything inside me, I intended to keep that promise.

Again, the soldier stepped forward, his sword arcing downward as I dodged. My knife held between us, I tried to calculate the best method for getting closer.

I ducked, pushing forward and grabbing the soldier around the waist, sending us barreling to the ground.

My grip slipped on my knife and the grip on his sword, leaving us both weaponless.

Good. My chances like this were far better.

With harsh pants, I struggled to climb on top of him, taller and broader than myself. Still, I threw my weight behind the punch as I went for his face, the cracking of his nose sending bile crawling up my throat.

Relentless, I threw another punch, another, until blood painted the seam of his lips, and he gasped for breath.

"How many of you are there?" I asked through blows. There was no way he traveled alone in this forest unless he'd gotten lost, or better yet, deserted his men. Either option would be favorable to the alternative, and I found myself praying to Eirdis that it wouldn't be the truth.

The soldier smiled, his tongue flicking out to lick the blood off his lips. Red painted his teeth, his gums, as his smile stretched wider. "You're going to die today," he warned. "You and that whore of a witch."

Anger burned in my chest as I punched him again with enough force to send his head whipping sideways.

Again.

Again.

Until I couldn't see past my rage—my desperate desire to survive, to protect, to save.

The bloodcurdling scream that climbed skyward had me glancing left.

"Verena," I whispered, watching through the trees as flashes of another soldier came into my vision. He gripped her hair, pulling hard as she plummeted into the snow, another scream followed by my name.

I have to get to her. I have to—

Verena kicked upward, a flash of metal shining through the trees.

The soldier beneath me shifted, and I looked down just in time to watch his blade sink into my stomach, blood blooming from the wound and seeping into the fabric of my clothes.

A roaring filled my ears—the snow stained red beneath us.

I couldn't feel it.

I couldn't feel anything but the cold as I toppled to the side, the soldier limping away toward an approaching Verena.

Verena.

Her dagger dripped red, mirroring the blood gushing from my wound.

There was so much blood.

So much death.

"Caius!" she screamed, but the sound was muffled—as if she were underwater and crying out for me in the way she had at the springs.

She turned to the soldier stumbling toward her just before he fell to the snow. Wasting no time, Verena shoved her dagger into his back—his arm—across his neck with ruthless accuracy before she sprinted toward me.

Her cloak splattered with dirt and blood—damp from the snow.

"No." Her voice broke on the word, soft hands finding me as I closed my eyes, relishing the touch.

Pain found me, everything growing heavy as I grunted—coughing before caving to the sleep calling my name.

Chapter Thirty

Verena

In a kingdom riddled with strife, sorrow-filled screams had become the norm—hardly demanding a glance from passersby.

When my horror released from my lungs, the forest remained silent—quiet and watching—as if it had seen too many sorrows to pay heed to mine.

"Somebody help!" My voice cracked on the second word, the sound echoing through the trees as darkness befell the Waldwood.

If it weren't for the dagger sticking out of Caius's stomach, he would have looked to be sleeping.

Blood consumed the snow beneath where he lay, the image feeling like a blade slicing through my chest as the tears stained my cheeks.

With hesitant movements, I tried to come up with a plan, but my mind felt clouded. There was no plan that would help save the dying man before me. I gasped for air, my fingers ghosting over the knife before I thought better of it.

With so much blood pooling beneath him, he couldn't stand to lose any more. If I removed the knife before we got to someone—anyone—his death would come swiftly after.

My eyes darted around the forest, gaze catching on the other body lying in the snow—the man I'd murdered. There was no sorrow for that soldier, only the roaring in my ears, the horror of Caius's sacrifice, and the overwhelming realization that another soldier haunted the woods—the one that had escaped.

I touched the wound, warm blood coating my shaking fingers as another scream ripped through my throat. It sliced on its way out of my body. I fumbled with Caius's tunic; the buttons refused to cooperate, and my fingers slipped.

Stop the bleeding.

I have to stop the bleeding.

"Help!" I cried to the empty forest. Maybe the trees would listen. A swooping sound echoed back above me, and I looked up, watching as an owl dipped low to perch on the branch above. Its black eyes swallowed what remained of the daylight.

I'd never been one to pray to the gods, even in my desperation trapped beneath the palace in Marmere.

I could not pray for myself, but for the man who'd saved me?

"Eirdis," I whispered, closing my eyes as the tears painted my cheeks in sadness. Sobs racked my body, and I tasted salt, hoping for an answer as the owl blinked its beady eyes—unfeeling.

No answer came, and so I assumed the gods were the same. If they were real—the reason the Waldwood held magic—they certainly didn't care for the woes of my people, and especially not my own personal trials.

I swallowed my misery, standing on shaky legs before tucking my arm beneath Caius's torso. With every attempted pull, his body shifted, and I gasped for air. I was hurting him, but more than that, I was so weak and cold, and so, *so* foolish.

I couldn't move him—could not drag him through the Waldwood bleeding to his death.

Another sob racked my body, and I slumped on the ground, eyes closing before opening at the light crawling through the trees.

With a lantern clasped in one hand, a woman approached. Her dark eyes pinned to me. Wholly black, her eyes matched those of the owl still watching—waiting. Snow-colored hair woven in one thick braid fell over one shoulder. Her dark skin contrasted against the color of her hair and the dusty blue cloak she wore—decorated with golden embroidery.

With every graceful step in our direction, her cloak flowed out behind her.

When she stopped, strides away from us, those dark eyes took in Caius with cold calculation. Not a hint of sadness touched her features—as if she'd seen too much to care about it now.

"Onelia?" I whispered, for the woman looked like the goddess of the moon—at least what I'd heard of her in stories.

"Come now," the woman spoke, her hand stretched out to mine. "Let us find a mender."

The moment I walked away from Caius's body, things seemed to happen *to* me—*around* me—but I couldn't process them.

Roaring filled my ears as the woman I'd mistaken for a god guided me through the trees.

Snow crunched beneath my boots and numbed my toes. The cold seeped into every inch of my skin, chilling my bones until I could think of nothing—feel nothing.

I walked like a ghost, as if haunting the forest. Narela, the woman who'd retrieved me, guided my steps to the base of a stone archway. Remnants of ivy crawled up the sides, brown and cracking with a dusting of snow; they, too, had been taken by the endless winter of our kingdom.

Beyond the archway, an intimidating building watched over the forest, humming with power. I took in the worn gray stone and the intricately carved forest animals etched into every available surface.

"Watch your step." Narela turned back, an inscrutable expression on her face when she looked at me. "Eirdis temple," she informed. "I am a priestess, here. A mender arrived a week ago, and I believe she can help."

Help.

At the last word, I looked at her—really looked—and nodded. My fingers shook when I followed her into the temple—the concentration of magic almost enough to have me believing in the gods—almost.

"Wait here."

Narela disappeared down a narrow hallway to our left, leaving me at the temple's entryway to wait—to stare at the stone floor until she rejoined me with another at her side.

I barely looked at the woman—tall and thin with sharp features that could cut the ice off the trees. Her harsh expression did nothing to jar me from my strange state.

It felt as if I were underwater—floating with neither feeling nor thought.

"Rona," Narela said, and I nodded once. "She will help."

I kept my eyes low and followed them back through the trees, staring at the snow or Rona's hand peeking out from her cloak. Her fingers looked crooked—as if she'd broken them and they hadn't quite healed properly.

When Caius appeared, still lying in a pool of his own blood with a blade sticking from his gut, I closed my eyes, one tear tracing its way down my cheek.

Rona wasted no time in kneeling beside Caius, her hands placed on either side of his wound. When she closed her eyes, one line formed between her brows in concentration just before the warmth of magic licked at my skin.

I watched as my emotions slowly trickled in—pain and anger—regret.

If I hadn't led him here—had snuck away in the dead of night instead of allowing him to escort me to the Waldwood—

Rona snatched the knife, dragging it from Caius's torso with a brutality that had me stepping forward as if I could stop her. Blood gushed from the wound, thick and so red it was nearly black.

Rona tossed a warning glare in my direction, her blonde hair whipping across her face from the cool wind.

Every second seemed to make my heart pound harder.

When the witch finally stood, Caius shifted, his eyes cracking open before closing again. I almost rushed toward him until I saw the matching stain on Rona's abdomen—the red blood blooming in a near-perfect circle on her tunic.

I stood, froze, watching it spread outward. Where the mender was now bleeding, Caius's bleeding had ceased.

She looked down to where I was staring, touching the spot with one crooked finger. It came away crimson-stained and wet.

"Nature demands balance," she explained, the dark circles under her eyes more prominent against her paling skin. "But we will both survive."

And with that, Rona swayed and collapsed to the ground. Her body lay still next to Caius.

Narela placed a gentle hand on my shoulder, turning me away from the gruesome view.

"Come," she said, her voice smooth as silk. "Let's let someone else take this over."

Without another word, I let her usher me away.

CHAPTER THIRTY-ONE

RIALEY

Morning light poured through the window of our rooms, but I didn't shift for fear that I'd wake Theron.

The first night, three weeks prior, he'd insisted on sleeping on the floor. Slowly, as the days passed and boredom intensified to unbearable levels, I'd given up and offered the other half of the bed.

Even so, I'd been careful not to stir in the night—to keep a distance from him despite the way my heart began warming to his presence.

I carefully climbed out of the bed, my feet touching the cold hardwood floors of Lord Bloodbane's castle. The fire in the hearth did nothing to keep out the chill of the relentless winter beyond the walls. The blue curtains, almost sheer on account of the thin fabric, hung over the window. I walked forward, peeling them back slightly to gaze at the snow-covered mountains—the tall trees blanketing the landscape.

For the first time in a long time, a pain pinched in my chest. I longed for the Waldwood.

In our time prowling through the rooms of the palace, my magic a careful mask for us both, I had unearthed a plethora of emotions from my years as the king's executioner.

I found that rage is often a byproduct of sadness—a yearning to snatch some sort of power from the hopelessness of our circumstances.

"Do you wish to take breakfast here this morning, or would you like to dine with our hosts?"

I startled, the curtain falling back into place when I turned to see Theron already standing by the bed and adjusting the sleeves of his tunic.

The cream fabric parted beneath his collar, revealing a hint of skin at his chest—clean-shaven now that we'd had an opportunity to bathe properly.

My eyes fixed on his face, blue eyes hooded with the remnants of sleep, and the full bottom lip that led to a slight tilt to the corner of his mouth. There was a sadness that hadn't existed before.

Gone were the smug remarks and devious smirks he'd given me at the palace as Theron. The pieces of Eryx were missing, as well. There were no stories—no taunting jokes. In line with my request, Theron hadn't touched me since our arrival—even as we shared our rooms.

"I think we should dine with our hosts," I answered. "I can't be in this room any more than we have been already. It is no strain on my magic to wander the halls with illusions painting our features."

Theron nodded once before turning to the basin of water in the corner, splashing it on his face and running it through his hair. The blonde strands had a subtle wave—perfectly styled despite the sheer lack of time he took to tend to it.

I would not be so lucky.

"You look like a prince."

He turned to me, brow slightly lowered, lips still pulled downward at the corners. "That is what I am."

On instinct, I stepped forward. "I know. I—" My hand stretched out only to find its way back to my side.

If I were honest, his newfound sadness bothered me. There was nothing of *him* left—whatever he was. Combined with my own sorrow, I couldn't bear it. All we had was each other.

I'd seen him in the dungeons—the way they'd beaten him.

Theron was to be sent to his death by way of the pyre—burned with the witches as the traitor prince.

He had nothing to go back to aside from a throne that no longer belonged to him—something he'd have to fight for on account of the oath he swore.

"I'm just saying there is a difference." My tone lacked the harshness I'd grown accustomed to in his presence. "When you were... Eryx, you were more relaxed. When I think about it now, there was still a stiffness to your posture on occasion, but not always."

He watched me carefully, his blue eyes a kaleidoscope of color—like the waves of the sea reflecting all the shades of their depths.

"As Theron, there was always a stiffness to the way you spoke—how you behaved. I see that now—almost always." My fingers found the hem of my tunic and toyed with the fabric.

Theron spoke slowly. "I am... both things, I suppose." He walked to the wardrobe, pulling out a fresh pair of pants provided by Lord Bloodbane and his generosity. His hand gripped the brown fabric tightly when he turned to me. "Being a prince... there were certain expectations—pressures on account of my father. I was expected to present myself for official meetings and business—attend events as an heir to the crown. I'd spent so long preparing for my role as prince, those attitudes became a part of me." His brow lowered. "I am both things, Miss Dagon. I never lied to you."

My voice came out as a whisper—the ghost of a truth spoken between us. "I know."

Theron turned to the privacy screen set up in front of the bath. Akari had brought it up the second day as a gift since we were not to leave the rooms apart.

As he changed, I squeezed my eyes shut—cursing myself for such a ridiculous interaction. I needed to work on healing the sorrow in him—in myself, too. We could not be useful—could not go on without a goal or a task, and so I created a new one.

Find something worth living for and share it as much as possible.

When Theron finished changing, I grabbed a gown fit for breakfast out of the wardrobe. The pale blue gown fit snugly around my chest and waist, the skirt draping to the floor. The sleeves clung to my upper arms, bare at the shoulders, but flowing fabric draped from my elbow to the ground along with the skirt.

It was simple—not necessarily my style, but beautiful, nonetheless. And the color would look far better once I altered my appearance.

We'd opted for minimal servants in our quarters on account of giving my magic time to rest. As they believed we were a married couple, I could imagine why they thought we'd requested such privacy.

I tugged at the ribbon laced at my back and tied a knot. The awkward angle had me struggling, the corseted part of the dress loosening too much.

Again.

Again.

I closed my eyes, cursing myself for choosing the one dress in the wardrobe I couldn't seem to put on myself.

No servants were coming to help me, and as Theron shifted on the mattress, likely waiting to depart for breakfast, I hoped he'd forgive me for what I was about to ask.

"Highness?" I spoke, my voice coming out an octave higher than in-tended.

I could hear him sit up from his spot on the bed behind the privacy screen. "Yes?" he inquired.

"I... um..." I stepped out from behind the privacy screen, my hands still clasping the ribbons at my back. Heat warmed my cheeks as I looked everywhere but the prince sprawled out on the bed of my chambers.

He stood up abruptly, and I watched his boots as he strode in my direction.

Theron stopped two feet from me and stood stock still—the only sounds in the room were that of the crackling fire and our slow breathing.

"Yes?" he asked again, and I could hear the smirk in his voice—hear it the way I'd heard it behind Eryx's mask not so long ago. When I looked up, that devious tilt caused a dimple to pop in one of his cheeks—the same I'd seen on Prince Theron Wineslowe at the ball and in the halls of the palace.

He was... amused.

A small glimmer of warmth sparked in my chest, and I rolled my eyes.

"Now, don't look so smug," I said, failing to contain the small smile that pulled at my mouth. "I will not ask for your help if you do that."

He took a step forward, the warmth of his nearness licking my skin. "I fear Lord Bloodbane will not be pleased if you show up to his breakfast table with your dress..." He gestured to the garment, his smirk becoming infinitesimally more prominent. "Unfastened." He finished.

I sighed.

"Was there something you wanted to ask me, Miss Dagon?"

He waited expectantly, and I got the feeling he would not back down. I would be forced to ask or change out of this dress and into another—delaying our arrival to breakfast further. The worst part of that plan was that I couldn't bear to see the sadness return to his features.

The taunting was good—for both of us.

"Would you, *Your Royal Highness*, be so humble as to help me tie the corset of this dress so we could attend this morning's breakfast?" I asked, emphasizing his title in playful mockery.

His dimple deepened, the crooked smile causing my stomach to flutter. "Turn around, Rialey."

I did as he instructed; the air turning thick with anticipation as he stepped closer—closer still. I could almost feel his breath on the bare skin of my shoulders. My hair hung over one side, making his task easier.

As if in slow motion, Theron's fingers toyed with the ribbons, starting at the very top, and tightening them all the way down.

Every delicate brush of his fingers on my skin sent chills down my spine, although the room had become unbearably hot.

I'd have to ask the servants to put out the fire while we were gone.

Theron found his way to the bottom of the corset. When he pulled, my entire body shifted, and I sucked in a sharp breath.

"Too tight?" he asked, his voice dropping to depths I did not want to read into—could not believe.

It was my own flesh leading me astray. Theron, of course, would be unaffected.

"No," I whispered.

He pulled again, one more time, before tying the ribbon into a neat bow. Before he stepped away, Theron drew in a long, slow breath.

I turned, hardly able to look him in the eye on account of the awareness that my skin had certainly flushed red. I quickly grappled with my magic, pulling on that golden thread I saw in my mind's eye to cast my illusion.

My hair turned bright white at the shift, my disguise from the last three weeks fixing itself into place.

I didn't, however, change Theron's. Not yet, anyway.

"Ready?" he asked, his eyes now darker than they'd been before—pupils swallowing the light from the window.

"Yes," I answered, taking in his features one last time before masking them with that of the handsome stranger I'd invented upon our arrival to the city.

I knew logically that the illusion was made from features I'd seen on others. That was the key to my brand of magic.

However, I figured it didn't matter how I changed the prince's appearance.

I'd always prefer the truth of him—something I was just now learning I had known the entire time.

Chapter Thirty-Two

Theron

The wooden door to the dining room had been closed when we arrived for breakfast.

Normally, we'd find it propped open, Akari, Lord Bloodbane, and his wife seated around the table with whatever guests occupied their home, but a servant seemed to have been waiting for us, opening it just as Rialey and I arrived.

I'd been here before, of course. Even considered asking Akari to be my wife, as Bloodbane had mentioned that first day here.

If I had to choose someone, I'd hoped it would be a friend—someone with whom love could grow. Whether it was romantic or not did not matter. What mattered was that I would fulfill my duty as prince, become king, and walk the path laid out for me.

That changed when I'd been sent away for the witch hunts.

It is funny—what we care about before we walk with those who have not lived in the circle of our childhood. What I saw during my time away was too many men driven by fear, though they would have told you it was anger—morality. But I also saw families ripped apart for no reason aside from the magic coursing in their blood.

Stepping out into the world provides perspective. It is very hard to hate a man you've walked with—very hard to hate once you've sat at the same table, eaten the same food.

I'd been injured during the witch hunts and cared for by two menders who had welcomed me into their home. I'd spent the past month slaying witches by my blade because of their magic, but in the end, it had been their magic that saved me.

And thus began my title.

"The Traitor Prince," Bloodbane greeted as the door clicked shut. My blood ran cold, every fiber of my being on high alert as I took in the room.

Akari, Bloodbane, his wife, but no servants stood around the room as usual.

The only unfamiliar face I found was that of a young woman, hair white as Rialey's disguise, though her skin was far paler—near translucent. Icy gray eyes found mine, and I instinctively stepped in front of Rialey.

Her magic still buzzed along my skin, leaving me confused with my heart racing.

"Miss Dagon," Bloodbane introduced, with a hand gesturing to Rialey at my side. "You may drop the disguises if you wish. We are among friends here, are we not?" One brow quirked up, and Bloodbane gestured for us to sit. I did not move.

Rialey stiffened, inching closer as she whispered. "What would you have me do, Highness?"

I swallowed. No matter how much practice I'd had in making decisions, there would always be a small part of me that feared myself and any mistakes I would make.

"Lord Bloodbane is our host," I said, eyes fixed on his gaze full of challenge. "We should not be rude guests."

Her magic disappeared, and though I could feel its absence, I confirmed it by the strands of black hair that flashed in my peripherals.

We had walked into some sort of trap, certainly, though I still could not ascertain what that trap could be.

I did not know the white-haired woman in the seat next to Akari, nor did I know Lord Bloodbane—not truly. It seemed, though, despite the lack of a crown on my head, I would still be responsible for political negotiations.

I would be used, no doubt, but I hardly wanted Rialey dragged into that.

Pulling out her chair, I gestured for Rialey to sit and then took the spot next to her, leaning against the tall back of the chair. The phantom crown on my head felt heavy.

"An unconventional breakfast, to say the least," I observed, glancing briefly at the mysterious woman. "Do you plan on explaining yourself, or should I ask?"

Our food had been plated prior to our arrival, something that had not been done before. When Rialey reached for her fork, I gently placed my hand over hers, halting her. To poison the traitor prince and reap the reward of returning him to Marmere would be an honorable feat.

My trust of Bloodbane only went so far.

Bloodbane chuckled, leaning back in his chair and bringing a glass to his lips to drink. Water, it appeared.

Rialey's hand returned to her lap as her knee bounced beneath the table. Again, I reached for her, causing her to still.

Fear did not bode well in political bargains. I had been weak upon our arrival —desperate. My introduction to negotiations with Bloodbane showed he would hold the power in any arrangement. I'd sworn a blood oath to secure housing for a month. I would be king, or I would die—a fate already chosen for me at birth, there was no reason not to take the deal.

Akari would not marry me, either. Of that, I was certain. And while she'd always spoken positively about her father, family held a different level of compassion. One could love their family but negotiate with little empathy. My father, on the other hand, lacked empathy in all areas.

Bloodbane placed the glass back on the table. "Florence has traveled from Branwood. She works as a healer there. Her apothecary sits in the basement of one of their Inns."

I kept my expression blank as I waited for him to continue.

Florence lifted her chin, peering down her nose in our direction. "Tell me, Prince Theron, what do you know of Alphaird's rebellion?"

Instinctively, I took stock of each presence in the room. Akari nor her father appeared surprised at the brazen mention of those actively fighting against my father in his own kingdom. I'd heard whispers of dissenters within the kingdom and seen evidence of it during my nights in Marmere. Foolish as it was, I knew little of how large that presence was—how organized.

A brutal king, my father executed all who rallied against him. I'd assumed the dissatisfaction among our people had been kept hidden for that very reason—any true rebellion squashed before it got legs to stand on.

Best not to show my ignorance.

"Rebellion always exists where there are kings." I tapped my finger on the table, my food cold, no doubt.

Florence scoffed. "You do not know the destruction that awaits your own kingdom." Florence pursed her lips, small lines forming there. "Foolish, Traitorous, Prince."

Rialey shifted in her seat next to me, and I released her hand.

I tilted my head to the side, appearing bored. "I have actively gone against my father for years, as you probably now know."

Bloodbane leaned forward, his elbows on the table, causing the wood to creak. "You have sworn a blood oath to be king," he started.

I didn't move. "A destiny I was already familiar with."

"You will be *our* king, Prince Theron. I hope that you find the rebellion aligns with your own beliefs about the Waldwood and those born from her trees."

My lip peeled back, disgust flaming my skin. "I will be the king of my choosing, *Lord* Bloodbane."

He sat back again. "There will be a meeting tonight beneath my home. Florence here will be in attendance as she is a spy in Vespahr's city." Bloodbane licked his lips. "Rebellion is coming, Your Highness, and we need a leader."

A weakness presented, they were not as organized as I feared.

"And why not you?" Rialey asked from beside me, her features sharp as the blades she wielded. "As far as I'm concerned, you've lurked in the background since our arrival, attempting to pull strings and tilt the scale in your favor. You position Prince Theron as your king, but at what cost? Do you find him weak?" Her lip curled into a snarl. "Do you expect to rule *through* him, while escaping the risk. If Wineslowe found you were leading a rebellion, hosting it in your city, you'd be executed." Rialey leaned forward, her elbows pressing on the wooden surface of the table. When she cocked an eyebrow at Lord Bloodbane, I fought the urge to smirk. "I am *very* familiar with executions."

Bloodbane's slow smile sent chills down my spine, but he did not look away from Rialey nor her challenge. "An executioner with the makings of a queen," he observed, watching her intently as if noticing her for the first time. Rialey stiffened at his remark before he continued speaking. "I assure you, Miss Dagon, I have no intention of ruling. I do, however, intend to see the Waldwood free of King Wineslowe's clutches."

"And what motivates you to do that?" she questioned, refusing to let up in her interrogation. "Is it your honor? Is it through the kindness of your own heart that you wish to free my people?"

I picked up the knife next to my plate, moving the potatoes around as my smirk pulled at my lips. Rialey, it seemed, was made of steel. While I'd known this before, I quite enjoyed seeing it in this setting.

"Careful, Witch Hunter," Bloodbane warned. "How does one claim the very people she's killed?"

I dropped the knife; my tone laced with deadly poison. "Insults will get you nowhere, Amias."

Bloodbane's wife cut in, the spitting image of Akari, her brown eyes blazed like a hearth fire. "You as well." She spoke so calmly, but it did nothing to hide the warning in her words. "You will not refer to my husband by his first name."

Rialey didn't back down, straightening her spine and lifting her chin. "You did not answer my question. What is your motive for freeing the Waldwood if not power?"

Lord Bloodbane sat back, gesturing to his wife, who still sat at his side.

"I am his motive," Lady Bloodbane answered. "As is Akari."

Rialey's eyes narrowed, my own suspicions growing alongside hers.

"I belong to the forest," she offered.

Eyes flicking between Akari and Lady Bloodbane, Rialey kept her features schooled. If she was as surprised as I was, she didn't let it show.

Akari cast her gaze downward, busying herself with the food on her plate. I wanted her to look at me—show some sign of guilt for the lies she'd told about herself. It wasn't so much the lies that cut, but the knowledge that Akari hadn't trusted me with the information.

"You are witches," Rialey spoke low.

I ground my teeth together to expel some of the energy coursing through my blood.

"We are dreamwalkers," Akari answered. "So, yes. Witches."

A small twinge of pain pinched in my chest. While there were no romantic entanglements with Akari, I'd considered her a friend and believed she thought the same of me.

"It is funny, Miss Dagon," Bloodbane began, his words layered like folded paper—a hidden message tucked safely away, though I couldn't ascertain what the message was. "It is funny what we do for love."

Florence stood, striding around the table to pluck a potato from my plate, then from Rialey's. She popped them in her mouth one after the other in a rather obvious display.

"We expect to see you tonight, Traitor Prince," she said as she finished chewing. "War is coming, and I'd like to see it before the Waldwood burns."

"The Waldwood cannot burn," Rialey threw back, her expression icy.

"Everything burns, Miss Dagon," Florence answered—unfazed. "We are in the forest, and the forest is within us. We burn; she burns."

We.

It seemed Lord Bloodbane had been keeping a house of witches all along.

I picked up my fork as Florence walked out the door, dismissing herself. I stabbed a piece of meat on the plate, placing it in my mouth and chewing.

When I'd finished, I looked around the table, my mind made up.

Growing up, I always knew I was on track to become king. My childhood had been spent with tutors who spared no punishment in their pursuit of molding me to my father's will.

I assumed many men of noble blood would have defied their father's wishes. In fact, I'd known quite a few at court who had done just that. They'd spend their time filling their cups with spirits, drinking themselves into a stupor night after night while turning their sights on any beautiful woman that passed.

Such was a path I could have taken, especially since defiance ran through my veins.

Perhaps my desires were born of that same rebellion, anyway. I longed to be king—longed to make something of myself and the kingdom—fix the brokenness my father introduced.

Maybe in the process, I even thought I'd be able to fix myself.

There was no doubt where my goals resided, and so I would use the opportunity that had been given to me.

"We will attend tonight," I said, my voice taking on the confidence I'd been taught to display. "I will be your king."

Bloodbane tipped his cup toward me, a satisfied smile on his face. "Good," he answered before looking to his wife and daughter. There was a softness there when he beheld them—one that, despite my years of instruction informing me that anyone could betray you, planted a seed of trust in me.

Bloodbane's cup touched the table with a soft clink. "Very, very good."

CHAPTER THIRTY-THREE

RIALEY

I released my magic as soon as the door shut behind us, plopping on the bed and taking in the same monotonous decor we'd been subjected to for days.

The blue walls seemed to close in, pushing until the air fled not only from the room, but my lungs as well.

I sucked in one full breath before my jaw tensed, and I watched Theron throw himself into the chair across from me.

As requested, the fire had been put out, and I found our room a touch too cold now, but I would never say anything. We could busy ourselves in the library while we waited for whatever Lord Bloodbane had planned in the evening.

Amidst the chaos, I found I enjoyed Theron's constant company—his steadying presence.

"I'm growing tired of this room," I admitted, my fingers toying with the skirt of my dress.

Theron ran a hand down his face as he smiled. He didn't look like a prince, slouched in the chair with his knees spread apart, his hair mussed from running his fingers through it during our walk from breakfast. He was Eryx now—kindhearted and hopeful—one wouldn't know the political chess game that had taken place downstairs a mere hour ago.

"Don't worry," he mused. "I'm sure Bloodbane is planning an eventful lunch for this afternoon. It will be here before you know it." He sat up swiftly, leaning his elbows on his knees with his hands clasped between them. "I am certain there will be new terms we must agree to, but only after we find our way out of the mental labyrinth that is political conversation masked as harmless small talk."

I huffed a laugh, noting the lightness in his tone. I quite enjoyed this side of Theron far more than the shell of a human that had walked around earlier. "Ah, yes. More negotiating." I crinkled my nose. "Though I found Bloodbane far more obvious about his intentions than what you're suggesting."

Theron gestured to me. "This explains why you seemed so adept at handling political negotiations. A natural talent, I suppose." There was a pause filled with the slow stretch of a smile across his face. "What was it Bloodbane said?" He tapped his chin as if he were thinking. "Oh, I remember. An executioner with the makings of a queen. I can't say I do not agree. I enjoyed seeing this hidden aptitude."

My cheeks flushed at his praise, but more so at the implications of what Bloodbane had said. I rolled my eyes to hide its effect on me. When I cleared my throat, I allowed myself to make eye contact. Mirth and oceans, his eyes lighted like glittering blue waters of the sea beneath the sun. "Forgive me," I started playfully, "but you are shit at negotiations."

Theron tilted his head back, revealing the strong column of his throat. His laugh pulled a suppressed chuckle from my lips, and I smiled with him.

The more I saw life return to his gaze, the more I longed for it—yearned for his happiness as if it would heal the kingdom. And I supposed it would. Theron was to be king after all.

When his laughter subsided, he looked at me and leaned forward in the chair, eyes slightly hooded in a way that sent heat through my core. "If my shitty political negotiations give you room to dominate the discussion the way you had, then remind me to never improve."

Deep crimson stained my cheeks, burning right along with the fire ignited in my blood. I couldn't help the way my stomach flipped or the way I fought to look anywhere but the traitor prince sitting in my room—the room we shared.

I thumbed the pale blue fabric of my dress, the shade a number of degrees lighter than the blue wallpaper decorating most of Bloodbane's home. I found I liked the color of the dress better. It reminded me of the icy blue tint of the Waldwood just before dusk.

At the thought of the forest, of home, the conversations surrounding breakfast returned to the forefront of my mind.

Theron had agreed to Bloodbane's terms so easily. During the blood oath, and when propositioned with leading an entire rebellion. It made me question what he felt or thought about his future.

With his identity hidden, there'd never been time to talk about what he longed to do with his future. As Eryx, I knew he longed to make a difference. I just didn't realize how much power he'd possessed to do just that.

It was another piece of him I craved.

"Do you really want to do this?" I whispered, somewhat startled that I'd asked aloud. "Do you really want to lead a rebellion? To be king?"

Theron's smile fell along with his brows. "I was always positioned to be king," he answered. "It has been the plan since before my birth."

I smiled softly, knowing the expression didn't reach my eyes. It was a trained answer—one he'd been taught, no doubt. I didn't want to know who Prince Theron was *supposed* to be. I wanted to know who he was. "Yes," I answered, swallowing. "But is that what you truly want?"

Nerves fluttered in my belly. I didn't know if he'd trust me with the information—if he'd trust me at all anymore.

"An opportunity to right my wrongs?" Theron asked. "To right the wrongs of my father, and build something better?" There was a long pause. "Yes," he answered, conviction laced into the word. "Yes, Rialey. I want that very, *very* much."

"Are you nervous?" I asked, smoothing down the black pants and tunic Bloodbane's servants had dropped outside of the door earlier in the day. I grabbed my dagger from beneath the mattress and sheathed it at my thigh before looking at Theron.

Dusk seeped into the room, pouring over the floor and coloring his blue eyes with a subtle tint of purple. Theron offered a tight-lipped smile before pulling a leather glove over his fingers. His fitted tunic, black like the one I wore, stretched across the planes of his chest with careful precision—highlighting every toned muscle beneath.

The tension wove through his shoulders and climbed up to the tense set of his jaw when the smile dropped. "I've no clue what to expect," he answered before grabbing the other glove from the chair in our room. He tugged it on, flexing his fingers to check the fit. "When we arrived here, I had been weak. It wasn't ideal for the beginning of negotiations. I had been friends with Akari prior to all of this. At one point, I'd figured I'd marry her."

I swallowed hard, my hand flexing around the hilt of my dagger, testing the feel of it. There was a possibility that we would need to use weapons tonight.

Theron cleared his throat. "My life has been upended, and I am finding myself more a failure than anything. I have lost my title—my influence amongst my father's lords." He winced as if the confession pained him. "This could be a trap, you know."

Stepping forward, I placed a gentle hand on his arm on instinct, feeling the heat of him on my fingertips. "I know," I said. "And should it be, we will be prepared." My eyes scanned his, finding his voiced insecurities there. "Together."

Theron nodded once before I called on my magic. White strands of hair fell over my shoulders, the dagger I kept against my thigh hidden by the illusion I cast. I waited an extra moment before replacing Theron's blonde hair with black, hiding his blue eyes with something darker.

"I'll never get used to it," he breathed, still holding my gaze.

I cocked my head to the side. "Used to what?"

"The feel of your magic," he answered, one gloved hand coming up to touch the white hair at my shoulder. He observed the strands as if he were looking for the crack in my magic—the glimmer of black hair seeping out to reveal truth. "This is beautiful," he said, "But I think I prefer the other."

Theron turned to miss the flush of my cheeks as he turned the handle on our door and walked out into the hall.

I followed, walking in silence as we passed an ornate tapestry hanging on the wall. The blue and gold shades matched those of the rest of the home. I slowed my steps, turning to take in the intricately woven image of a forest—gold and stretching across the tapestry into a golden mountain range. An owl, gold like the trees, flew overhead, lending its watchful gaze to the land.

My brow furrowed, recalling long-forgotten stories my father used to tell me growing up. "This is the Waldwood," I whispered. Tears crawled their way up my throat, but I swallowed them down.

With every passing day in this castle, every moment I spent away from the palace where all I'd been focused on was surviving, I missed the Waldwood more and more.

I hadn't touched my pain.

Theron stopped, turning and walking closer until I felt the warmth of his presence at my side.

When I finally looked at him, he wore a pensive expression, his hands gently clasped behind his back. "I am not surprised," he said. "Lady Bloodbane is a witch, after all."

A beat of silence before a foot scuffed against the hardwood further down the hallway.

Akari wore a brown tunic, a black, fitted vest fastened over the top to cinch in her waist. Her hair had been slicked back against her head, a leather strap binding it at the base of her neck where her natural hair was left alone.

When I turned to her, Akari lifted her chin, dark eyes narrowed, and jaw tense.

"It's good to see you both," she remarked, glancing behind us to a servant moving through the halls behind us. "I dread your return to Keslow so soon."

Theron pressed his lips together briefly, biting back any truth about our identities. We were to pretend to be a married couple from another city—a ruse that had taken very little to keep up.

"Yes," he started. "We are, however, thankful for the hospitality of your mother and father, Lady Bloodbane."

When the servant vanished into one of the other rooms, the door shutting with a soft *snick*, Akari broke the mask. "We will go through the libraries." Her low voice had gravity when she spoke. "I take it you've brought your weapons despite my inability to see them."

My heart beat like a drum. We kept silent.

"Keep pace," she commanded before turning on her heel.

We followed Akari through the castle, down the steps, and to the main floor. Tucked at the front of the home sat a library with large windows stretching from floor to ceiling.

Thick flakes of snow fell through the darkness outside, some catching on the limbs of trees that swayed gently in the wind.

I clung to my magic as we wove through shelves lined with tomes of all shapes and sizes.

Theron and I had spent some time in the library during our stay and were familiar with the leather chairs positioned on either side of each window. Small with walls to match the rest of the home, the library boasted an extensive collection of books packed into the tiny space.

Tomes lined every bowed shelf—sometimes layered with more than one row of books.

As we walked along the back aisle, I took in the quiet. No sounds echoed along the floors save for our own footsteps.

It was hard to believe Bloodbane planned to meet in the library—not when it was this empty.

My fingers brushed the hilt of my dagger on instinct. While we'd had time to settle, Theron and I both knew that time was coming to an end.

With our approaching departure, I wondered where we would go next. The Waldwood, probably. Though I didn't know if I was ready to confront my past.

I longed for the forest—more and more with every passing day. The magic flowing through the roots of the trees called to my blood in the way it did all witches. It did not mean that all of my memories there were positive. I'd lost my parents, after all—a scar that haunted most of the witches in our kingdom.

Akari paused at a small gap between shelves at the back of the library, glancing at us over her shoulder. The dim lights danced over her smooth, brown skin as she placed a hand on the two feet of wall between the shelves. "Watch your step," she warned, and I tensed.

Theron's fingers brushed mine gently—so fleeting, I wasn't certain I'd felt it. Still, a comfort just the same.

With a smooth sliding sound, the wall gave way, opening as any door. Akari knelt to pick up a lantern that had been placed at the top of a stairwell, holding it aloft to slice through the shadows beyond the libraries. "Don't try to open it yourself," she said. "Old witch magic. It will not work for you."

We followed her down the steps until stone and dirt surrounded us to form long tunnels that reminded me of those built beneath the palace in Marmere. Sweat beaded on the back of my neck despite the way my blood cooled—sending a chill rippling down my spine.

Every slick step on the stone floor reminded me of the palace. I pinched my eyes shut for a moment, sucking in a deep breath as I confronted the memories that surfaced.

Two years I'd spent smuggling prisoners beneath the palace to a man I now knew as the Prince of Alphaird—the Traitor Prince, if I were to go by the new title.

There, in the deepest bowels of the palace, I'd shed blood—watched as women wasted away on account of their magic. I feasted on the small glimmer of hope that came with abandoning them at the edge of the city without guaranteeing their safe return to the Waldwood.

I could hear the guards snarling in the night, prowling the halls like beasts as they looked for women to torment.

My stomach roiled, and I stumbled a step, only to be met with Theron's gentle and steadying hand on my elbow.

His eyes slid to me, concerned. "Are you alright?" he asked.

For a brief moment, I wondered if the same memories that haunted me haunted him. Did he think about what would happen to the women when they crossed the city wall? Did the thought that he hadn't done enough gnaw at his chest until his heart ached with the pain of all he had failed to achieve?

"I'm fine," I answered, noting the way Akari's head turned to the side just enough to hear us better.

While Theron might have been friends with her at one time, and while she shared the same magic-rich blood that ran through my veins, I hadn't grown to trust her. I knew little of the woman who led us through the labyrinth of tunnels, and that realization was unnerving.

"You are sure?" he whispered, leaning closer until his scent of juniper berries wrapped around me.

I nodded once. "Yes."

The dripping of water echoed off the stone as we drove deeper—farther until I was certain we'd walked far past the Bloodbane's property and into the heart of the city.

"Might I ask what the expectations for this meeting are?" Theron interrupted when Akari slowed to a halt just outside of a tall metal door.

Lined with ancient carvings, I squinted at the symbols and tried to distinguish what they were. When Akari placed her hand on the metal frame, blue light seeped through the cracks of the carvings. Magic hummed in my blood as the runes locking the door worked one by one until the lock clicked into place—giving us access to wherever the Bloodbane's daughter was taking us.

My anxiety peaked, and I squeezed my fists together until crescent moons imprinted on my palms.

The old witch magic was one I'd seen used in the temples of the Waldwood, but not within Marmere's palace, though I'm sure King Wineslowe would have had use for such things if magic ran through his blood.

I could not decide whether he hated our power or longed for it.

Maybe both.

The metal door creaked open when Akari pushed it forward, warm light pooling on the tunnel floor from the small crack when she turned to face us, one hand still on the door. "Your father's soldiers have gone into the forest to raid the covens there," she informed. "We are planning to intercept their attacks, but we've been waiting to grow large enough in number—to have a figurehead who proves himself capable and willing to join our cause. Those in the rebellion value a good fighter."

Her full lips pulled into a smirk as my brows furrowed, my stomach dropping abruptly.

"What do you mean by that?" I asked.

Akari did not answer.

She nodded toward the crack in the door. "My father will have more information for you." She pushed the door fully open, the light illuminating the hallway—near blinding after our time in the tunnels.

A cavernous room sat beyond the door. Like an amphitheater underground, the center stage was surrounded on all sides with rows of people, thousands of them watching and waiting for our entrance—so it seemed.

In the center of the arena, Lord Bloodbane stood wearing fighting leathers. Two swords crossed at his back, and he wore a pin at his breast—golden, but far too small to make out its shape.

Theron walked stiffly toward the center, though he kept his chin raised and his back straight. In fact, if I hadn't spent so much time in close proximity with him, I would have hardly noticed the slight change in his gait—the way he stumbled a step once our eyes adjusted, and then every step following came as if he were forcing himself to take it.

"What is this?" I whispered, my stomach churning as I looked out at the crowd.

Men and women filled every seat, dressed in all different attire. I couldn't think with the noise roaring and echoing off the ceiling. Each stood shouting—cheering as we entered what could only be an arena. My pulse kicked up, and I looked toward Theron.

For none of these people were staring at me. They all wore a golden pin, one matching that of Lord Bloodbane's, on their chests, and they all kept their eyes fixed firmly on the man before me. Though still wearing my disguise—it seemed the crowd had been expecting us.

It seemed—they had been expecting Theron.

And I was willing to bet they'd been expecting him for quite some time.

Chapter Thirty-Four

Theron

Icy dread coated my entire body as I walked toward Lord Bloodbane at the center of the underground amphitheater.

Shouts and roars rose all around us, every eye fixed on me as I marched towards what felt like my death.

Rialey's magic hummed along my skin, and I clung to its comfort—steadied by her nearness as Akari fell away into the crowd.

When I was a child, my father had me practice negotiations. During my studies, he'd bring me to his office in the palace—maps pinned to the walls and an obsidian statue of himself looming in the corner.

At ten, I'd been intimidated by the relic, but then again, there'd always been a part of me that feared my father.

Time and time again, he would give me a goal—an objective. Sometimes it would be a piece of information I needed to discover, and sometimes an object I would need to steal from beneath his nose.

I'd often failed—convinced my negotiating powers were a true weakness—one that would tarnish my rights to the crown.

But as I grew older, as I entered court, I began to see through my father's strategies in negotiating with the lords in our land. His hand became so clear to me as I realized he'd been fueled by a lust for power and a true desire to conquer.

My father yearned to be the smartest man in the room—and as soon as he was not, brute force would make up for his shortcomings.

In all of this, I learned that flattery, trust, and deception were often the key to proper negotiations. Curate a situation where you held the power and maintain it. Give just enough to gain trust, but not enough to lose your control of the situation.

When I'd turned eighteen, just before I was sent off to the witch hunts, I'd outsmarted my father for the first time. He'd challenged me to steal a quill from his desk—one made of gold—easily accessible and easily seen from where he sat.

I'd conversed with my father—stroked his ego until he became suspicious of my intentions. At which point I confessed that I'd wanted the quill all along. I admitted my defeat and endured a lashing for such weakness.

As my father's confidence grew in the light of my failure, I used that moment to pluck the pen from his desk—just as he poured a celebratory glass of brown liquor.

My accomplishment only made him become harsher—firmer.

King Wineslowe did not take kindly to losing, and so I did not attempt to outsmart him again.

However, I honed the skill with others.

Ten paces away from Lord Bloodbane, I paused, my stomach churning until I swallowed hard—the rancid taste of vomit lingering in my throat, only to be tamped down by sheer will.

I had been the one outsmarted.

Easy agreements and negotiations made while I was desperate led me to my ultimate failure.

I'd been tricked into something far more nefarious, or at least, something I was not prepared for, nor did I fully understand.

In fact, it had all seemed too easy—had *been* too easy.

I'd failed, and those failures put Rialey at risk right along with me.

My hand flexed around the dagger at my side. There was no getting out of this—not for me—but for Rialey? She would escape no matter what it should cost.

"Miss Dagon," Bloodbane said, voice smooth like honey. I glanced out at the crowd, finding Akari seated on a small balcony cutting the seats midway. She and her mother sat side-by-side on ornate chairs overlooking the arena, with one empty chair to the right, saved for her father, I was certain.

I squeezed the hilt of the dagger, looking back at Bloodbane's hardened expression as he zeroed in on Rialey.

"I ask, Miss Dagon, that you release your magic at the end of my introduction. I feel it would help with the aesthetics." He winked, turning and stretching his arms wide, the crowd quieting in response.

"Tonight, I would like to address The Guild of Eirdis with important news for the work we are doing here in Alphaird."

Rialey stepped closer, the warmth of her brushing against my shoulder. I fought the urge to cling to her—to grab her hand and sprint for the rune-encrusted door.

Somehow, I didn't think we would make it far.

"It is only in the past few months we've become organized enough to hope for any kind of change in our kingdom," Bloodbane continued, "and now, I believe the answer to our long-awaited battle has arrived."

Bloodbane's sharp gaze fixed on Rialey, and he nodded. "Release your magic," he commanded, his voice quieter now as he addressed only us.

Rialey tossed me a wary glance, and I nodded. Until I could parse what Bloodbane wanted from me, I wouldn't be able to shift hands. I was at his mercy, and I prayed to the gods that it wouldn't be the death of me—of us.

The warmth of Rialey's magic left me, and I stood revealed to the crowd. Gasps echoed around the room, followed by distinct murmurs of my new name.

Traitor Prince.

"I present to you," Bloodbane announced, pausing for emphasis. "Alphaird's very own, Traitor Prince."

When he lifted his hands, the hushed whispers subsided.

In the silence hung the heavy weight of anticipation—swinging overhead like an anvil waiting to drop—threatening to crush me right where I stood.

"It is my belief," Bloodbane started, "That Prince Theron will rise to be king of a new kind of society—one that respects the Waldwood and embraces the magic within her. I have seen Prince Theron at court—watched him risk his life for those oppressed by his cruel father." Lord Bloodbane looked at me, a certain warmth to his gaze that had the hairs on my neck rising. These were compliments falling from the lips of a man who had been spinning pretty tales since we arrived. This was the flattery—this was where he would make me believe I had won before revealing his hand.

I stood taller, my heart pounding a quick pace in my chest.

"Bound by a blood oath, Prince Theron has committed himself to be king—committed himself to fighting alongside us in the coming war against King Wineslowe and his armies." Bloodbane gestured to Rialey, and my hackles rose. "And Miss Rialey Dagon, a witch, a skilled illusionist who acted as the king's executioner, only to aid her people in escaping right beneath his nose, will provide a perfect ally to win over the covens hidden within the Waldwood."

Rialey's sharp intake of breath told me all I needed to know. I reached for her on instinct, only stopping myself enough that my fingertips brushed hers.

"I believe we have found our answers here, with these two," Bloodbane continued. "It is now that their loyalties should be tested—their abilities displayed for our cause. For we look to strong leaders with compassion—not weak leaders with a desire to serve only themselves."

Bloodbane stepped back, lowering his voice to address only Rialey and me.

"I'm glad you brought your weapons," he said, a slow smile forming. He stepped back again, gesturing widely. "Bring out the beast!" he shouted, and my heart nearly stopped, everything slowing and narrowing in on the crawling, creaking of a cage door being opened.

At the edge of the arena, the heavy metal bars lifted to reveal shadows. I squinted to make out the beast he spoke of, but found nothing.

"You will represent an alliance between the Guild and the Covens," he said. "Fight together and survive. If you prove yourselves, I will step down from my leadership role within the Guild. I will hand the reins to you, Prince Theron, and I will not stand in your way during the coming war. My life will be to serve you."

Bloodbane plucked a dagger from his belt, making quick work of sliding it across his palm before offering his hand to me.

A blood oath.

He was swearing a blood oath—loyalty to me, should I defeat whatever beast prowled beyond the cage.

If I shook his hand, I would doom Rialey to the fate I'd brought upon us—the trap that we'd been ensnared in.

I looked at her, eyes pleading as I struggled to piece together what she was thinking.

"Do it," she demanded, her voice strong as the metal door hiding this underground arena from the world. "Get his loyalty," she said, "for it is owed."

I grabbed a knife, slashing my own palm and biting the inside of my cheek to distract from the stinging pain. In one moment, I sealed our fates, shaking hands with the lord.

Magic zapped through me before he released his grip, and scurried off to the edge of the arena, disappearing into the crowd until I turned back to the pitch black hiding whatever monster we were being forced to fight.

One heartbeat—two—until a guttural roar reverberated off the ceiling, swallowing all other sounds, leaving me with nothing but fear.

A large paw stepped out of the shadows, followed by the imposing figure of a bear—white like the snow with eyes burning red like embers of a fire.

I grabbed at my weapons, filling my hands with whatever blades I'd chosen to bring. It was not much.

"Rialey," I whispered, my breath shallow against the terror that iced my veins.

"Yeah?" she asked, and I swore I heard her swallow—hard.

I blinked once, watching as the entire creature came into view.

There were no choices here. Nothing but a need to prove myself and obtain Bloodbane's sworn loyalty—get an army I could use to fight my father—an army I could use to win a war.

One word hung on the tip of my tongue, squashed by the second roar from the bellowing beast as it rose on its hind legs.

When all four paws touched the ground, my knuckles turned white as its fur on account of my grip.

The last word came out low, but I knew Rialey had heard me—knew she would listen.

Or so I hoped.

I had swallowed my fear, readying my stance to battle the beast before giving that one command.

"Run."

CHAPTER THIRTY-FIVE

CAIUS

I didn't know what I was looking for. All I knew was that it was here and that it was important.

Taking every step descending into the basement of the inn with caution, I gripped the railing. My heart pounded in my chest as the clinking of glasses and bawdy shouts mingled with the laughter from the main tavern upstairs.

One minor slip, and I was certain to be caught.

At the bottom of the steps, I found my way to the healer's quarters, Florence luckily absent amid the filled jars and tins lining the shelves. Her desk, still littered with parchment and various tinctures, glowed beneath the faint light from the small window. A beacon of... something.

With silent steps, I held my breath, rounding the side of the desk and frantically opening the drawers.

"Letters, herbs, tinctures," I muttered, finding a mess of various healer remedies buried in the first and second drawers of the desk. The disorganization sent a frantic energy buzzing beneath my skin. I watched the door and strained my ears to listen for any presence that might be unwelcome—knowing I had to find it.

My fingers gripped the knob on the bottom drawer, and I tried to jerk it open, finding it stuck—no—locked.

"Come on," I whispered, my breathing becoming shallower with every passing second. I didn't know why I was racing against the clock, only that the matter was urgent.

I moved the papers on top of the desk; each scrawled with notes and ailments—their potential remedies. Florence kept notes as disorganized as her desk space, it appeared.

Gold winked from beneath a rather worn piece of parchment, and I snatched the paper up, hoping to find the key, but found only disappointment. A golden coin, one I'd seen tucked away in our cabin, taunted me from its hiding spot.

I grunted, dropping to my knees to search beneath the desk, to feel each wooden plank of the floor. Nothing seemed loose, and the pressure to tear her apothecary apart grew in my chest, straining at the barrier of my sternum.

"Where is it?" I whispered before looking up. There, fitted in a small gap between the top of the desk and the back panel, a glimmer of silver peeked out.

My fingers fumbled with the warm metal until I freed it from its prison.

Shoving the key in the drawer's lock, I turned it with a small click and yanked on the wood.

Pride washed over me as I found exactly what I had been looking for.

The golden pin had been placed in the center of the drawer, a symbol of... something. I cursed my failing memory, fingering the detailed symbol. On the black iron backing of the round pin, a golden owl perched on a branch at the center. At its back, two swords crossed over one another, their hilts engraved with the word "Eirdis" on either side.

I knew this symbol—had a duty to...

I couldn't remember.

"See something that interests you?" I looked up from my perch behind the desk, horror washing over me at the sight of the petite woman standing at the other end of the room. Gold embroidery decorated the edges of the blue robes she wore—icy like her scolding gaze.

I stood to my full height, mustering more courage than I thought I had. "Florence," I said, forcing my tone to even. "When is the Guild meeting? When is the war?"

"These things take time, Verena."

My eyes cracked open, vision blurry even with the dim lights of the room I was in. The pain in my stomach struck me first, followed by the pain in my skull. I wanted to speak—wanted to move, but the slicing in my abdomen kept my brows pinched and my mouth closed.

"It's been two days." A familiar voice—one that settled something within me, but I couldn't place it.

"And it will likely be more," the other woman snapped. I kept my eyes closed, fighting through the pain to *focus*—to *listen*. "Rona is still sleeping as well, and there is nothing we can do to speed up the process besides pray to the gods."

The familiar voice scoffed. "The gods," she said as if mocking their existence.

My temples pulsed, an ache forming around my entire head. My body tensed, a deep groan ripping through my dry throat and drawing a gasp from the other end of the room.

"He's awake."

I didn't know who said it; all I remembered was the warmth of a palm pressed to my forehead and the bitter liquid soon brought to my lips.

I coughed, my thoughts becoming fuzzy—the voices muffled as if under water.

"Start the fire," one said. "It's grown too cold in here, and he no longer has a fever."

I dipped into the blackness before hearing the crackling of a hearth; the warmth soothing to my bones until it felt scalding—too hot and suffocating.

"Bring the bitch here."

I opened my eyes to look out through the trees of the Black Forest. The darkness swallowed the light of the fire in front of us, melting the snow surrounding it.

Men I did not know sat around me wearing the uniform of the king's guard—his emblem stitched neatly at each of their breast pockets.

From between the trees, a man stepped forward, his wolf-like eyes lighted with sinister glee when he shoved a woman forward.

My heart clenched watching her kneel next to the fire. Torn clothes hung on her gaunt limbs. Her eyes were hollow and sunken in from clear starvation.

When the man fisted her matted black hair, he pulled her upwards, causing a harsh cry to reach past her chapped lips.

I stood up on instinct, anger burning in my chest. "Let her go," I commanded, but nobody responded.

The men surrounding the fire only leered at the woman, laughing at her pain with hate in their eyes. I turned to the man next to me, shoving his shoulder as he tossed out an obscene remark, only to find my hand went right through him.

They could not see me.

I was not...here.

The soldier, with his hand fisted in the woman's hair, bent down, his angular features twisting in disgust as he spat directly into her ear. "Tell me, Witch. What should your punishment be for killing a guard in the dungeons and then escaping?"

Another hollow cry, and I fought the urge to look away. My chest was squeezing until pain radiated down my limbs.

"Toss the bitch in the fire!" The soldier I'd attempted to shove shouted, garnering jeers from the other men.

The man holding her hair shoved her closer to the fire, keeping his grip firmly on the back of her scalp. "I heard the king's executioner turned out to be a traitor," he said. "Do you think I'm skilled enough to take her spot?"

The woman cried out, so close to the fire now, I worried the flames would begin licking at her skin.

"I'd be happy to burn the witches," the man taunted. "Happy to burn the little bitch witch who killed a guard."

Anger twisted his mouth as he pulled back, readying himself to shove her into the flames.

I wanted to close my eyes—wanted to disappear from this nightmare, but I couldn't.

Just when I fought for the chance to squeeze my eyes shut, I watched as the man fell to his knees behind the woman, giving her time to scramble away. An arrow protruded from the center of his chest, blood now blooming around the wound as his eyes turned glassy.

For a moment, his eyes locked on mine, and I swore he saw *me.*

In my rage, I stepped forward, noting the way men and women broke through the trees, surrounding the fire with weapons pointed at each of the remaining men. The witch stumbled away, finding her place behind one of the newcomers.

I fixed my gaze on the dying man, and he looked up at me. "You should have suffered," I seethed. "Death was not a high enough price for the darkness of your soul."

When he finally fell forward, releasing his last gargling breath, I backed up. Still invisible to those around me, I turned, watching the chaos as these people stormed the campsite and left no soldier remaining.

On each of their chests, a golden pin remained. I'd seen it before. I—

My eyes cracked open, the room becoming clearer with every blink.

Tapestries lined the walls of the small room. Stone walls surrounded me on all sides, only broken up by one glass window, and a hearth carved into the building itself, crackling with the fire.

Humming pulled my attention to the corner where Verena sat, a waterfall of blue fabric in her lap and pooling around her ankles. She worked to stitch something into it—the garment, I assumed, matching the robes she now wore.

I didn't speak, and she didn't look at me.

When Verena set her project down, she gazed out the window, her humming ceasing.

"I've joined the temple," she said, as if speaking to me. I tried to answer, but my throat felt filled with sand.

"I don't know what happened out there, but you're not dead." Verena's brows rose, her skin glowing beneath the firelight. "I suppose that is something, but more than that, the temple gives me a place to live." She glanced down at her hands, picking at her nails. "At least I know I'll be okay when you're gone, you know? When you go home to Ahvi."

I blinked, hearing the name again, but further away—from a different mouth.

My own.

"Ahvi, where did you get these?" I asked, shuffling through the documents tucked in the box beneath the bed. Each appeared to be official papers—those required by the kingdom to pass into different cities—to prove you were not a witch.

We didn't know any of the names on these—we had never met these people before.

"Boy," Ahvi warned, "You will not disrespect me by calling me by name."

I lifted the documents, turning to where she'd entered our cabin.

"What are these?" I asked again, my voice more assertive. Anger burned within me—more nagging as I found myself thinking about the past more and more.

Ma's footsteps scuffed when she stopped, staring in horror at the documents I held tightly gripped in my hand.

If she were caught with these—if we were caught—we'd be executed.

While we rarely got visitors this far away from town, there was always a chance of being discovered by one of King Wineslowe's men. Anything could happen—anything had happened—and I'd lost too many of those I love to justify keeping these.

Ma straightened, steeling her spine as if preparing for a fight. "There are things happening, Caius," she began, voice strong. "Things you may wish to be a part of."

My stomach roiled, worry gnawing at me from within. I couldn't lose Ma, too. I had so little—I had made peace with so little.

"My greatest accomplishment," she started, dark eyes softening. "My greatest accomplishment was raising you." My frown deepened as I fought the stinging in my eyes. "But now you are grown, and there is more out there for me. More for you, too, Caius." Her head tilted to the side—studying me. "Verena."

"What?" I asked.

"Verena."

I gasped, abruptly sitting up to see the chaos unfolding in my room. Verena stood over me, a cloth in her hand. "Narela!" she yelled.

The woman grunted, already four paces through the door. "I am right here, Verena. I've said your name at least three times."

"He's awake." When Verena turned back, she gasped, surprised I was sitting up on the small cot.

Narela, the woman now standing beside her, smiled. Her full lips stretched to reveal teeth as white as her hair. "So he is," she said. "I'll go get some tea."

When my eyes met Verena's, there was a fury there—something I had seen little of in her the past few months. "It's been a week," she scolded, and I fought the urge to chuckle. My stomach ached, as well as my head, but it was nothing compared to the stabbing pain I felt coming in and out of consciousness. "We had to pour water down your throat. You had a fever the first day, and I thought," Verena's voice caught, her eyes going glassy as her anger shifted to relief and then sadness. "You *died*," she finally said.

I cocked an eyebrow, settling back deeper into the nest of pillows around me. "Did I?" I questioned, my voice coming out scratchy and rough. My throat burned as I spoke, but that didn't deter me. "I can't seem to recall."

Verena frowned, one hand reaching out to slap me in the chest. I caught it, shifting against the dull aching in my bones.

I kept her warm hand gripped in mine as I shifted. "Don't do that," I said, and she seemed horrified she'd even thought it. "You'll hurt me."

Tears skated down her cheeks, over the freckles dotting her pale skin. Verena closed her eyes, shaking her head in disbelief.

"Verena," I said, drawing her attention to me once more.

I kept her hand close, holding it to my chest as if her closeness was the very thing that kept my heart beating.

I suppose it had been.

Memories crept in as I stared at her, remembering the attack—the knife to my stomach—the pain.

"Thank you, I whispered. "For saving me."

Another tear welled in the corner of her eye before releasing. Verena let out a shaky laugh, her hand now squeezing mine where I held it. She shook her head again as if refuting my claim. "No," she whispered. "You saved me first."

CHAPTER THIRTY-SIX

RIALEY

"Where are you going with that?"

I stomped in the snow, following my father as he wove through the trees away from our coven with a sword in one hand and the scruff of a fox held firmly in the other hand.

The creature squirmed and yelped despite being trapped, gnashing its teeth toward my father's leg and twisting its body at odd angles to escape.

"It's mad, Rialey." My father's pace never slowed, nor did he turn to face me. His broad back shifted with each step forward, sunlight glinting through the snow-covered limbs of the trees stretching tall above us. It was far too sunny for something so evil—so wrong.

"You can't kill it," I asserted, jogging to catch up before rounding on him. I planted my feet in front of my father, crossing my arms in protest. I'd grab the sword if I had to—shove him—knock him down. Though it seemed my father was made of iron. With an iron will and an iron glare, he didn't need magic to intimidate anyone. He was capable of doing that all on his own.

"You can't," I said. In my thirteen years of life, I'd never felt so strongly about saving a creature as I did in this moment. I didn't understand where my father had gotten the fox, or why it still attempted to wriggle out of his vice-like grip. All I knew was I saw him walk past our house with it, watched *as he grabbed the sword leaning against the nearest tree, and marched off with the thing held out so it wouldn't bite him. "I won't let you."*

My father growled in frustration, thrusting the small fox toward me abruptly.

I gasped, reeling back as its teeth snapped in my direction.

With eyes black as onyx, the fox screeched. A black substance coated its mouth, leaking out onto the tan fur of the creature.

My dad shoved it closer. "If you want it to live, you deal with it."

I stepped back again, shaking my head. Something was wrong with the an-imal—that was obvious. I'd never seen something so aggressive—so... wrong.

I looked up into my father's eyes, a mirror of my own. "What happened to it?" I asked.

His grip tightened on the hilt of his sword when he released a long sigh. "A mender," he answered. "Sometimes the young witches get it into their head that they can..." he paused, choosing his words carefully. "Experiment. I'm sure they want to use their skills, and it's not like they can go around breaking bones and moving blood around in just anyone. Especially considering they're not experienced. As you can see, this sometimes goes wrong. They're not sup-posed to—" His nose scrunched as if he smelled something foul. "Never mind. This creature is already lost, Rialey. I'm not doing anything that shouldn't be done."

My eyes watched as the fox stretched backward, its spine curving at a grotesque angle as it attempted to pull away. It yelped, clawed, fought without wavering. My eyes stung as I watched it—suffering through no fault of its own.

"You could release it," I said, discomfort winding its way around my stomach and squeezing. It almost made me feel nauseous.

My father scoffed, looking down his crooked nose at me. His black hair had turned gray this year, speckles of it appearing more and more with every passing day. "You still wish it to live?" he asked.

I didn't understand why he was still frustrated with me. "Who are you to decide it should die?"

My father leaned in more, holding the fox away from our faces as he dropped his voice low. It was what he did when he wanted to make a point—when he knew he had me ensnared. My will was strong, but my father's was stronger. At least for now.

"And who are you to decide it should live only to come back into the coven and harm someone, eh?" He cocked a dark eyebrow. "What if your little fox friend turns around and lunges at Lou? Then what?"

My stomach twisted in knots. Lou lived in the hollow tree next to ours, a mere two years old, she'd never survive if this... animal got ahold of her.

"Fine," I conceded.

My father stood up to his full height, walking past me until he stood behind one of the trees. "Close your eyes, Rialey. We will take its carcass to Abellona's temple—let the goddess of death decide what she should do with it."

I knew I shouldn't—knew it would bother me, but even then, I couldn't look away. I stepped to the side of the tree until I saw my father there, pinning the fox to the snow with a firm grip still on its neck. With his sword raised high, the metal glinted in the sunlight. I watched the fox fight until its last breath—watched as my father's sword swung, cutting the fox's head cleanly off its body.

I understood why he'd done it—understood that my father was not a harsh man, nor would he have wanted me to see such necessary brutality—even at thirteen. My throat burned at the sight, tears welling in the corners of my eyes.

When he turned to me, I quickly wiped them away, not wanting him to see.

His eyes softened when he looked at me. "I'm sorry, kid," he said, his deep voice soft, unlike the rest of him. "We cannot know the consequences of our actions or lack thereof." I hiccupped, hating the sign of weakness. "Sometimes there isn't a simple right and wrong—only the best we can do with what we know and have."

I wiped another tear furiously from my face, squeezing my fists together so hard until the pain distracted me from my sadness.

My father grabbed a large grain sack from his belt, placing the bloodied body and head into it with care before tying off the top.

"Walk with me to the temple?" he asked. "I hear the goddess of death is a good listener."

My father offered his hand, thinking better of it before pulling back to wipe blood on his tunic. He nodded toward the depths of the forest, gesturing for me to follow. "Come on," he said.

And despite my aching heart, I followed.

In the temple, I found that Abellona was a good listener. In fact, all the gods were. The older I got, the more I realized all they ever did was listen.

Maybe they were too irritated with mortals and witches to intervene.

Fear iced my veins as the bear rose on its hind legs, releasing another roar up to the ceiling of the amphitheater.

"Run!" Theron commanded, but my feet wouldn't move.

I was stuck in place, looking into the fathomless black eyes of the beast. Black coated its mouth, dribbling onto the white fur of its neck.

I'd seen this before—knew this ailment.

Though the bear was a far larger creature—larger than natural.

No doubt a mender had manipulated it, but this didn't seem like an accident. I was willing to bet this beast was intentionally created. What for, I had no clue. If it were only for this battle, we were thrown into at

Bloodbane's command, I'd consider that a waste of resources—a weakness I could point out in Bloodbane's leadership.

I couldn't help but wonder if it was something more—an experiment of sorts to increase their armies.

Gods. The rebellion.

We'd been so blind to what the bigger picture was here. Played for fools in our desperation. The betrayal cut deep. It wasn't Lord Bloodbane's decisions that stung, but those of Akari and her mother. They were witches—cursed in the same kingdom I was, and just trying to survive.

I supposed that was excuse enough. I'd committed heinous crimes against my people for survival—a guilt I'd carry for the rest of my life, maybe even into the afterlife if there was one.

"Rialey, run!" Theron's voice boomed in my ear just before he shoved me to the ground.

I landed hard in the dirt; the air stolen from my lungs as I gasped and watched the giant bear come down over top of Prince Theron.

My fear knocked me out of my frozen state, and I scrambled to my feet, clutching my dagger in one hand.

"Theron!" I screamed just as he kicked up at the bear's gut before digging his heels into the dry soil to push himself out from under the beast.

He stumbled when he stood, running away just as the beast lunged for him, black-coated teeth slicing through the air and snapping shut beneath the significant force of a massive jaw.

The bear took off after him, and I panicked, eyes locking onto the creature's back as I reached for my magic. Gold flashed in my vision, and I used my power to make Theron blend with the wall. The illusion was weak at best, made worse by Theron's constant movement and my inability to focus on just one thing.

The bear paused just briefly, sniffing the air before its black eyes fixed on where Theron now ran at the wall of the amphitheater.

Shouts rose all around us, and I realized my magic would be next to useless in the ring. The beast could smell—it could hear. We stood no chance.

"Hey!" I screamed, flailing my arms overhead to distract it.

I released my magic, choosing to focus on the distraction instead.

The bear turned, its massive paws hitting the ground when it descended onto all fours.

My heart leaped into my throat as I took a step back, my boots kicking up dirt.

With another roar, the creature sprinted toward me, every leap making the ground tremble beneath my feet.

I felt entirely useless with a measly knife—a short dagger used for close combat. I didn't want to get anywhere near the bear—not when it was like that.

I turned on my heel and ran, sprinting as fast as I could, though I was aware the creature chasing me was faster.

My pulse thundered, the sounds of the crowd growing louder with every heartbeat.

When Theron appeared in front of me, eyes fixed behind me and sword lifted at the ready, I shouted.

"It's mad!" I yelled. "The bear is not normal."

Theron looked at me for one distracted second, fear shining in his blue eyes. "What?" he questioned, keeping his stance solid.

I got within feet of Theron before he shoved me aside, swiping his sword across the bear's arm, black blood oozing from the wound.

"When I was a child," I shouted, my hands shaking around my dagger. "I learned that menders could manipulate animals—turn them mad."

The beast lifted onto its hind legs, and I turned to face it—face the creature right alongside the prince.

Theron grunted, shoving the sword upward, but the bear veered away just in time for Theron to strike the earth instead.

"What do you mean?" he said.

"I think this was done on purpose. I think a witch changed this animal."

Theron sprinted in the other direction, and I did too, following the wall of the amphitheater. The bear stuttered a step as if trying to decide who to chase before choosing me.

I could barely think over the constant noise—the loudest sound being the hammering of my pulse within my chest.

"All the more reason to kill it," I heard Theron shout across the arena. "Rialey, turn around!"

I obeyed, turning just before the beast shoved its massive face into my gut.

I flew through the air, weightless, until my back slammed against the stone wall at the base of the arena. The scrape against my skin didn't sting—as if my body were too shocked to register it—but I gasped for air, my breath leaving my lungs for the second time tonight.

I didn't dare look at Bloodbane—worried he was enjoying this far too much. This had to be some kind of sick game with him—a way to manipulate us and bend us to his will.

Though one piece of the puzzle didn't make sense. He swore a blood oath just before—swore his loyalty to Theron—swore he'd step down from his leadership role among the rebels.

The Guild of Eirdis, he'd called it.

A mockery of the goddess, to be certain.

I sat limp on the ground, catching my breath as I watched the bear make a sharp left turn away from me, charging toward Theron once again.

When the beast got close enough, Theron shoved his sword upward, cutting through the flesh of the bear's shoulder.

It stumbled a step, roaring out in pain when Theron took a step back.

I got up, frustrated at myself and my lack of ability in the arena. If we were to prove ourselves to the rebellion, so be it.

I ran at full speed, jumping into the air and throwing myself onto the creature's back. My legs hooked on either side of it, but I could barely find purchase. Its fur, slick with dirt and blood, made it difficult to hold on.

Still, I gripped the hilt of my dagger in both hands and shoved downward, hoping to find the bear's spine.

I'd missed by a few inches, frustrated when I was thrown off the creature, landing in the dirt with my dagger absent.

"Shit," I muttered, scrambling to my feet as the bear approached.

It was going to kill me. I had no weapons—my mind too frazzled to use my magic properly.

I had to try, though.

Gold flashed, and I crafted the image of Theron and myself running around the arena. There were now four of us, and the bear halted, looking around, confused at the new targets.

It shook with one giant movement and continued lunging my direction. My magic slipped, and I cursed myself for being so unpracticed. I hadn't had to use it in situations like this—in battle.

Instinctively, I squinted when the bear took one last mighty leap forward, opening my eyes quickly when I realized the blow had never come.

Theron jumped in front of me, blocking the attack as the bear's giant maw slammed shut around his upper arm, teeth digging into his flesh.

"No!" I screamed, just as he released a yell of his own.

The bear stood over him, his sword now discarded in the dirt, and I watched as the bear shook once, twice—Theron's body limp and helpless to its attack.

Pain and anger welled in my chest as I sprinted forward, gripping Theron's sword and charging at the beast.

I couldn't get beneath its belly—not while it still had Theron's arm in its mouth, but I would stab the thing—anywhere I could.

I shoved the sword forward; the hilt pressing into my stomach and bruising as I threw my entire weight into it.

The tip of the sword sliced cleanly through the bear's fur and skin at its side. I pushed deeper, screaming my fury when I felt the cracking of bones against my blade.

The beast's mouth had opened, releasing Theron, who stood now, dripping blood onto the soil beneath his feet.

With a swift movement, the bear turned its neck to the side, gnashing its teeth in my face, reminding me of the fox my father once killed.

I had no doubts about this animal—no feelings of regret for shoving my blade deep into its soon-to-be carcass.

It didn't relent, somehow thrashing as I struggled to hang on to the sword. I would not lose another weapon in the body of the bear.

Theron took a staggering step forward, a dagger he'd carried in his good hand as he used a split second of the bear's distraction to shove the weapon into its throat.

Blood spurted from the wound, and the bear slowed just enough for me to stop fighting against its movements.

I gripped the sword, now embedded so deeply I could not pull it out.

Theron, though, pulled the knife out and stabbed again, again, fury igniting his gaze and fueling his every movement until the bear finally slumped and fell to the earth beneath.

I panted, placing my foot on its side as I pulled at the sword, using my entire body to free it from the carcass on the arena floor.

Theron's arm hung limp at his side, dirt and sweat streaked across his brow as he climbed atop the bear, retrieved my knife, and found his way to my side.

"It seems you lost something, Miss Dagon," he teased, and I let out one breathy laugh in disbelief.

Blood coated his tunic, the sleeve completely wet with it. The sight sent my stomach dropping. He couldn't lose this much blood—couldn't.

Theron's eyes rolled, and he dropped to the floor unconscious.

Akari was there first, rushing to his side and calling for a mender from somewhere in the crowd.

Bloodbane appeared behind her, with a severe expression on his face.

Anger burned cold in my chest, fueling whatever hate I'd now developed for the man. I loathed him. "Was that good enough?" I spat.

To my surprise, Lord Bloodbane did not smile. He looked...concerned as he peered down at Prince Theron.

"It is quite enough," he said. "Our meeting is over. Get them to the healers' quarters," he commanded. I didn't feel any wounds on myself, but looking at the holes in my pants and shirt, I knew there had to be some—certainly something I'd feel by morning.

"Now!" Bloodbane's voice boomed in the amphitheater just before the woman we'd met at breakfast earlier knelt beside Theron, replacing Akari, who walked to me.

Akari grabbed my upper arm in the same place where Theron had nearly lost his, and I winced before pulling away.

"Get off me!" I yelled, and her features hardened, voice lowering.

"I understand your anger," she said, "But I do not care for it. We are on your side. Now stop being so bullheaded and come. We need to get you back to our house."

"I don't want to be in your fucking house," I seethed, and she leveled me with a hard stare.

"We are on your side," she asserted. "There's more at play here than you think. My father did the best with what he had, now go."

Theron coughed and sat up from where he lay in the dirt, Florence clearly working on him.

When blood bloomed on the sleeve of her arm, I knew she'd done what she could to help him.

Surprisingly, he stood, brow furrowed as he turned to me, not stopping but following close behind all the way back to the Bloodbane castle.

CHAPTER THIRTY-SEVEN

RIALEY

Anger stole the breath from my lungs, every intake of air growing shallower as I stormed through the door of our bedchamber.

Theron followed behind with a bandage wrapped around his arm over the place where his tunic had been sliced by the bear's teeth.

The beast had shaken him. Like a dog with a toy, the creature tossed him around by his arm until I was certain he'd bleed out on the arena floor. Emotion clogged my throat as the visual of it came to the forefront of my memory.

I squeezed my eyes shut to fight against the image to no avail. Anger burned in my chest, but I knew the truth of what was beneath—fear.

"What *was* that?" I seethed, turning to face him fully.

Dirt marred his face, his tunic tattered and dampened from sweat and blood. A hollowness had taken over his gaze—the exhaustion plain in the purple blooming below each of his eyes as if he were bruised.

I took in another sharp breath—another. My lungs stung, nausea souring the bile in my empty stomach. I would have my own bruises—ones that I was just now feeling.

The bear had shoved its head into my stomach, thrusting me into the arena wall. I would be sorer once my nerves settled.

"A test, I assume," Theron spoke plainly, his voice taking on a rasp from the strain of shouting.

I scoffed, folding my arms across my chest, but thought better of it when it sharpened the pain around my abdomen. I winced, and Theron cocked his head to the side to study me.

"You're hurt," he observed, taking one long step toward me. The hollowness disappeared only to be replaced with a blazing determination. "Show me."

I swatted him away, an ache forming around my midsection. We only had another week to recover before Bloodbane would send us off to the Waldwood. How were we supposed to travel in this condition?

Sure, Florence had taken the time to heal Theron's wound, but the bite mark was deep enough—severe enough—she'd had to leave some to heal on its own. I hadn't even had time to look at the wound, and here he was, demanding to see my bruises.

My cheeks heated, and I avoided his gaze, glancing at the white bandage tied around his upper arm. "You first," I dared, noting the crimson stain already leaking through the dressing. Instinctively, I reached for the tie, my fingers ghosting the fabric just before he flinched away.

"Don't."

Determination had me standing up straighter. "That bandage needs to be changed," I protested. "You've already bled through. The wound should be cleaned, too."

Theron shook his head, refusing to look at me. "You were not tended to by a mender, so you first." He nodded toward the privacy screen. "The bath's been filled. I can call up for another while you go first. We have that bell outside the door for a reason." When he looked at me again, his eyes softened into a pleading expression.

I looked down at my own tattered clothes, the dust and grime coating every inch of fabric—coloring the black tunic and pants a dark shade of rust red—just like the dirt of the arena.

Pressing a finger gently to my stomach, I tested the skin there where the bear had shoved its head into me. The wound was tender, a bruise already forming on either side of my torso.

"Rialey." Theron's voice came out strained as he reached for me, his hand falling away before he made contact. "Please," he whispered. "I need to know you're okay."

A smirk danced at the edge of my lips. "You seem very anxious to get me to remove my shirt, Your Highness."

I'd hoped he'd respond with a teasing tone, but he leveled me with a flat look.

Gingerly, I gripped the hem of my tunic, sliding it upward to reveal the planes of my stomach—stopping just beneath my breasts. Shades of blue and black painted my pale skin like a sash across my middle. I assumed my back looked more or less the same.

Theron stepped forward, his features hardened. "You should be seen by a healer, too." His finger ghosted along the bruise, his touch cold and sending goosebumps over my skin. "Are you in pain?" he asked, and I fought the urge to lie to him.

It would be so easy to minimize the damage of what had happened, but I wouldn't—not when we were now bound to a rebellion—not when he was the only one in all of Alphaird I could trust, even after the way he'd lied about his identity.

I trusted him.

If Bloodbane had given us time—introduced us to the Guild differently, we might have joined on our own. Frankly, the Guild supported the things I believed about our kingdom—about my people. If anything, his manipulation soured our relationship with the rebels.

"It's a bruise, Theron," I whispered, noting the way his finger still skated along my skin, tracing the edges of the mark. "Of course it hurts, but I will recover."

My blood heated at the way he was looking at me so intently—the worry creasing the center of his brows. I felt stripped bare under his gaze, a flush painting my cheeks pink as a clear sky with the sun dipping below the horizon.

I lowered my shirt and took one step away before reaching for his bandage again.

"Fair is fair," I said, and this time, he didn't stop me. I unwound the plain fabric to reveal angry red puncture wounds. Near some, the skin had been torn, likely from the bear's shaking. Blood still seeped from a few spots, and I turned to grab fresh linens from a drawer. With as much strength as I could muster, I tore the fabric right down the middle, tore it again until I had useful strips of fabric to work with.

Each forceful tear had my bruises aching—a sharp pinch at my back that made my brows pinch together despite my desire to hide the pain.

"Come on," I said, nodding to the bath behind the privacy screen. "Let's get you cleaned up."

Theron's mouth quirked up at one corner. "Now who's trying to see the other naked?"

I chuckled, shaking my head in response. More blood rushed to my cheeks at the implication. "I'm just cleaning your arm."

"Pity," he quipped with a crooked grin.

When he followed me to the tub, I was aware of every aching breath that passed through my lips. My body attuned itself to his nearness and the sound of his steps padding across the wooden floor. His gait was measured.

Steam from the tub rose around us when he leaned against the lip of the porcelain facing the privacy screen. I stepped forward, facing him and nearly between his legs, when Theron reached for the hem of his tunic.

Wincing, he lifted it over his head, slowly and cautiously pulling the tattered sleeve off his injured arm.

With my blood still heated, I plucked one of the scrap pieces of fabric from where I hung it over the tub, dampening the rag in the water. When I lifted the sodden fabric, Theron nodded in assurance.

He hissed when I pressed onto his arm, every muscle in his body tensing.

"I'm sorry," I whispered, adding more pressure. "We should clean it, too." I lessened the pressure, gently running the rag over each puncture wound and cleaning the dirt and blood from his arm. "Luckily, we only have soap and not alcohol."

One corner of my mouth turned up when he let out a breathy chuckle.

The events of the night played back repeatedly as I cleaned and then wrapped his arm with my makeshift bandages. My brows lowered.

"Why did you do it?" I asked.

Theron breathed deeply, and I worked to tie off the end of the bandage. "Do what?" he asked, causing my gaze to meet his.

My lips parted, body warmed by the intensity in his eyes. "Why did you jump in front of me?" I whispered. "Why risk death like that?"

His head tilted to the side, a pitying look on his face. "Rialey," he said, his voice rasping in a way I could feel across my skin.

When his thumb brushed along the heated skin at my cheek, I let out a stuttering breath. He traced a line from below my ear, down my jaw, to my neck. Shivers skated down my spine, goosebumps rising on my flesh.

His fingers were cool, but I could feel the warmth radiating off his body—especially with how near he was, every breath mingling as he inched closer.

My heart sped up, and without meaning to, I glanced at his full lips—ripe for the taking.

I'd dreamed of this—of kissing him. At one time, I'd thought he would follow through in the quiet of my room back in the palace, but he hadn't.

The longing to feel his lips on mine returned, but this? This felt like more.

"How could you not know?" he whispered, and I felt his breath on my mouth, longing to close the distance—taste him just to ensure he was real and alive.

Theron's fingers paused at my neck, his hand wrapping around my throat gently, thumb stroking up and down the side like a gentle caress.

I closed my eyes. So close now, his lips brushed mine when he spoke. "Please," he begged.

I nodded on instinct just before his mouth met mine with gentle pressure, a slow give and take that had my awareness heightened. I could feel every inch of my skin, every thump of my heart beating in my chest, reminding me I was alive.

Theron's hand stayed at my throat, his thumb stroking as my lips parted on invitation.

His hand finally migrated to the back of my head, fingers threading through my tangled strands of hair to pull me closer, angling his mouth to take the kiss deeper.

When his tongue traced my bottom lip, I sucked in a breath only to be met with a low groan—one pulled from his throat.

My hand found his torso, tracing the lines of his abdomen, careful as to not migrate higher to where he'd been injured.

Theron kissed me harder before pulling back, his forehead now resting on mine. "You'll be the death of me," he whispered.

I matched him, breath for breath, my body now buzzing with need. I needed him closer—longer, deeper. My want left me aching for a different reason when he pulled away, standing fully with his lips swollen and pink from our kiss.

"You should get cleaned up," he said, the darkness in his eyes contrasting against the way he stepped backward.

His mouth quirked as if he had more to say, but instead of telling me, Theron left me bereft behind the privacy screen.

We'd gotten used to bathing in one another's company—closed off only by the wooden panels separating the bath from the bed.

I wondered if Theron strained to listen—if he imagined watching as my tunic and pants hit the floor.

I stepped out of my clothes, sinking into the steaming bath with need winding tighter in my gut.

After drying off, I pulled on the fresh set of clothes laid out near the tub and stepped around the screen to find Theron asleep, his eyes tightly shut as if in pain.

I didn't care about his dirty appearance.

Without thinking, I crawled into the bed next to him, my exhaustion finally taking me under.

Chapter Thirty-Eight

Verena

I watched the fire flicker at the end of the match for a moment before holding it to the incense Narela had given me.

Most of the tasks I'd been given seemed pointless—meaningless items to check off a to-do list with the sole purpose of keeping my body busy and my mind from spiraling.

The worst part was that, for the most part, it worked. Narela had been successful in menial tasks as distractions, and I could not figure out if I was thankful or upset at that.

Most of the temple had been constructed of old stone, ancient and moss-covered like the forest before endless winter descended on Alphaird. I'd been told of the beauty of the Waldwood—the misty mornings amid homes built in and around the trees that breathed life into the forest. Every inch of Eirdis's temple made me think of what had been lost—what the Waldwood kept hidden in her rage against Wineslowe.

Sorrow clogged my throat, tightening my chest as I blew on the flame of the incense, the heady scent of pine wrapping around me like the smoke dancing above the stick. This temple was nothing like the temple where I'd grown up—I felt more at peace here, even amidst the turmoil.

I placed it in the holder, walking through the temple where the priestesses met every morning to pay respect to Eirdis.

I supposed I was one of them.

The dusty blue robes kissed the stone floors and the tops of my slippers as I walked a slow pace, meandering through the long benches facing the back of the temple room. Webs of dead ivy climbed their way to the ceiling, dried and brown with the smallest tint of green to remind us of what once was.

At the back, an owl statue sat perched on the branch of a golden tree, intricately carved and beautiful.

Growing up, I'd thought the stories of the gods to be just that—stories.

For a moment, when Caius had lain in the snow, blood pouring from his wound, I'd reached out to Eirdis, only to be answered by who I thought was Onelia, the goddess of the moon. Narela sure looked the part with her dark skin and vibrant white hair; she looked as if she'd been birthed from the moon itself. Dipped in the beauty of night and its silvery light.

I wasn't certain why she'd chosen to serve Eirdis, but I hadn't had time to ask. Between mopping the floors, cleansing the temple space, helping in the kitchens, and organizing long-forgotten storage closets, I'd been busy.

The door behind me creaked open, and I turned to find Narela standing with her arms folded across her chest. She leaned against the door frame with a closed-lipped smile on her face.

"You cannot merely walk through the temple with incense to cleanse the space," she said. "Intention matters. *Words* matter. You should be speaking your intent to the gods."

I cleared my throat, my gaze turning downward when I nodded.

"You do not believe," she observed, and I met her gaze. "You do not believe in the gods?"

Narela seemed nothing but amused with me. There was no anger there—no tension. I'd assumed that a head priestess in the temple would have strong opinions about a witch joining the temple for a god in whom she did not believe.

Discomfort churned in my stomach, making me feel nauseous. I wanted to run, but I did not. "I am thankful for the opportunity to serve in the temple," I said, the incense smoke burning between us just as the lies.

Narela scoffed, pushing off the doorframe to come closer. She smelled of cinnamon bark, vanilla, and smoke—ancient and wild like the goddess herself. "Follow me," she said, her blue robes flowing like water around her ankles as she rounded the owl statue, pushing against the stone wall behind it until it opened, sunlight pouring into the room until the statue sparkled beneath its rays.

I'd expected more clouds overhead, but we found ourselves in the center of a courtyard surrounded by sparkling snow and light through the pine trees.

Narela did not look at me or speak as we walked through the snow, the bottom of my robes collecting snowflakes as the incense smoke was lost in the wind.

I stuttered a step, looking back at the entrance to the temple.

"I should—" Words caught in my throat. "I'm meant to be cleansing the temple—this is a courtyard." Narela chuckled, and my brows furrowed in confusion. "We are outside."

"Fitting, isn't it?" she asked. "That the goddess of wild things should keep the most sacred part of the temple outdoors." Narela looked up at the sky, squinting at the sun. "It's almost always sunny here. I cannot explain it, nor do I try."

I nodded, letting the whistling wind fill the silence as we walked, the cold biting against the tips of my fingers—my nose.

"Where is the coven near the temple?" I asked, fearing I already knew the answer. "Each coven has a temple for its patron goddess. Where is this coven?"

A shadow passed over her face. "Gone," she said, her lips pulling down at the corners. "Exactly what you would imagine." She stopped to face me, and I matched her stance. "What coven did you grow up in? You said you'd once lived in the Waldwood."

"Cyra," I answered.

Narela's brows rose. "The sun goddess," she mused. "No wonder you do not believe in gods. I do not see her fingerprint on you."

Before I could stop it, my features twisted, and Narela laughed—a light sound that wrapped around the courtyard. "What fingerprints do you see then?" I asked, helpless in the way my skepticism showed.

Her features turned thoughtful when Narela's head tilted to the side. "You may not believe in Eirdis, but she follows you. A veritable god does not rely on belief for their power—they exist regardless of our thoughts or actions, but I see her near you—almost always."

I swallowed, unsure of how to take her words. My discomfort dissipated when a slow smile stretched across her lips.

"I also see the fingerprint of the man you saved. Caius, is it?"

I sucked in a breath, cheeks warming at my obvious reaction to her observation.

Narela's smile widened. "You care for one another, but there is a sorrow there, is there not?"

My chest tightened. "He's leaving," I answered.

"Ah." Narela nodded in understanding. "And so, you needed somewhere to stay within the Waldwood where you would not burden him or change his mind. So, you've dedicated your life to a goddess in whom you do not believe."

My flush deepened in embarrassment. "That sounds—"

"Terrible?" she answered with another light laugh. "I find it romantic. You do not wish to tether him to a fate he does not choose. Nor does he wish to pull you away from the Waldwood where you belong. Masters of your own fates."

I did not respond.

"A love story the goddess of the wild would certainly support. Untethered and free, but one day coming back together."

The door to the temple opened, and we turned, Caius stepping into the light with a fresh tunic and pants matching the color of the priestess's robes. "Verena?" he said just before his eyes locked with mine.

"I will leave you," Narela whispered, nodding once to Caius before disappearing into the temple.

"Quite beautiful," Caius remarked as he stepped further into the courtyard.

Despite my knowledge that he was talking about the general scenery, my face flushed. Luckily, the chill in the air could be blamed for my pinkened cheeks.

The incense stick in my hand had burned out, leaving me with nothing but a small stick pinched between my fingers and thumb. Caius's eyes looked there first, then back to me, drinking in my features as if he longed to memorize them. A sorrow shone in his eyes, and I fought against the lump in my throat. Without a word, I knew what he was here for—what he would say.

"You will be leaving," I remarked, freeing him from the burden of saying it himself. Maybe it was no burden for him at all.

"Ahvi—" The name was lost on a breath, carried away with the icy winter wind.

"You should go to her," I said, forcing a tight-lipped smile. It was the best I could do at hiding my true emotions. "You feel healed?" I asked.

"I feel well enough to travel."

To fight? I longed to question. I knew what else awaited him.

Silence hung between us, filled with all the words I longed to say but could not. I knew that Caius cared for me in some sense—he cared about everyone; it seemed. There was not a part of the man that did not care.

Even so, I did not believe it moved past that. While I had spent the past months watching him, caring for him in a way that I did not fully understand, I knew that we had been thrown together by circumstance. Caius had done what anyone kind would have when faced with a dying girl in the forest.

And I...

I wasn't quite sure what I felt. Maybe I'd been desperate for kindness, or maybe Narela was right. Caius had left his fingerprint on me, and I would carry that for the rest of my life.

Either way, regardless of what I believed, Narela was right about one thing. Caius should remain untethered. I had used up enough of his time as it was. He still had a family—a rebellion to be a part of.

"I hope she hasn't forgotten me," I joked, though it seemed to fall flat. Tears lined my eyes, but I blinked them away, wishing he'd stop looking at me so intently. These emotions were mine to keep—my burden to shoulder.

In a slow and unsure movement, Caius lifted a hand, warm fingers brushing a strand of my hair behind my ear. His gaze warmed me just as his touch had, and I fought the urge to close my eyes—to sink into him. He smelled of black tea, the kind Ahvi would brew back in the cabin, mixed with tonka bean and pine resin—like a warm forest—home.

"We could not forget you, Verena," he whispered. "You saved my life."

"As you did mine," I answered.

Caius leaned forward, his eyes closed as his forehead rested against mine. I drank in the moment, knowing this was our goodbye.

"My salvation," he whispered, his warm breath fanning over my face.

When he pressed a soft kiss to the top of my forehead before turning and walking back into the temple, I let the tears fall, looking up at the sunlight through the trees.

Overhead, an owl dipped into the courtyard, perching on one of the tall pines encased in the temple stone. The creature blinked at me as if it knew my sorrow—understood.

I stayed there like that for a moment before trudging through the snow, finding my way back into the temple to get a mop and bucket from a storage closet I'd organized days ago.

As I mopped the stone halls of the temple, my chest ached with his absence.

An ache I'd soon grow used to.

Chapter Thirty-Nine

Caius

I'd contemplated death far longer than I cared to admit.

After my parents died, I'd been forced to confront mortality head-on—learning that death claims and once she sets her sights on a target, there is no stopping her from striking.

My abdomen ached after the long hours in the saddle. My wound was mostly healed, but it was certain to leave a scar. It would be a reminder of death, the same as the nightmares that plagued me during the night.

They'd lessened as a result of what I assumed to be an exhausting journey. Each night when I pitched my tent, my body would be so worn, I would drift off into a black void of sleep almost immediately.

Only during the day would I be haunted by the scar that remained slashed across my stomach, the memories of my parents dying, and the worry that gnawed at my insides.

Soldiers had passed through the night Verena and I had left the cabin. There was no telling what we'd find. Had the searched the neighboring cabins? Had they taken members of the guild?

It had been weeks since our departure—a week since I'd left the Waldwood and its magic behind.

Verena's brown eyes flashed in my memories as the horse plodded along beneath me. The image of her standing in the courtyard was so vivid, it felt as if it had happened yesterday. I'd watched as her expression dipped to sorrow, her brown eyes leaning toward hazel in the rare sunlight shining through the trees. The sorrow I saw in her gaze made my chest tighten. I owed it to Ahvi to return—to protect her. I owed it to myself to finally put my training to use, but leaving Verena left me with a different sadness.

Her absence carved a hollow space in my chest, an empty cavern where my pulse should have been.

I gathered the reins in one gloved hand, using my free hand to hold my cloak closed when the wind whistled through the trees. With it, it brought a biting chill that numbed my limbs.

Unfortunately, the ache in my heart, the guilt churning my gut, and the remnants of my near-death remained.

When the clouds overhead turned a warmer color as the sun kissed the horizon behind them, I passed the ruins of an old graveyard that sent my heart skittering.

Home.

I was almost home.

The dusting of snow across the gravestones obscured the names of those buried. I did my best to steer my mount away from the graveyard in respect for those who had died. How they died, I didn't know, but most dates engraved on the stones were prior to King Wineslowe's rule.

Alphaird had remained what it was for so long, I couldn't imagine a world where people—my people—weren't burned for their existence. The only thing that had saved Ma was that her son was not a witch, though he married one. She did not possess magic, nor did I. The only reason *I* did not was because I was a man.

Verena had seen horrors I'd never have to endure. When I'd found her months ago in the forest, her skin had been sallow, her body all harsh angles and ghostly skin.

The memory made my stomach churn. Little did I know how close we'd become over the months—how much I'd grow to care.

My mind wandered as the horse's hooves crunched through the snow. Memories played themselves across my mind, distracting me from the dropping temperature that came with the evening.

The sight of the cabin through the trees had me sitting up straighter in the saddle, anticipation simmering in my blood when I urged the horse onward.

Upon approach, I noted the tattered curtains in the windows, the icy glass collected snow at the corners. Not a lantern had been lit inside our cabin, and my head tilted to the side. I couldn't stop the seed of dread that germinated at the sight—growing despite the cold.

I swung my leg behind me, dropping to the snow-covered ground with a slight stumble. Hours in the saddle had left me numb and wobbly.

My gloved hand brushed the knob on the door, and I sucked in a breath of anticipation. There was no telling what I'd find beyond.

Emptiness.

The cabin's near-empty appearance struck me first. Herbs, blankets, and the kettle over the fire were missing. Drawers had been raided, left haphazardly open and slanted as if whoever left had exited in haste. The other possibility felt like lead filled my stomach, weighing me down until it became suffocating.

I wandered the cabin, looking for any stains of crimson across the floor—on the furniture.

Had she left of her own accord?

I slowly walked along the creaking floors to the kitchen table, where Verena and I had drunk tea. I recalled the sketches of the Waldwood she did during her time in the cabin and glanced beneath the bed. The box sat empty, every drawing snatched except for one piece of paper, tattered on the edges and yellowing.

My boots scuffed the ground when I walked to the box, knelt, and plucked the scrap paper from beneath the bed.

Caius,

My jaw tightened at Ahvi's neatly scrawled words.

It's time we did something here. You're grown—finding your own way. You've worried about me for far too long. Should you return, I've left dried meat in the cupboard, but it is not much. I don't expect you to stay. In fact, you should not.

I've gone west to meet with the others. There are rumors of things happening in Keslow—whispers of what is to come.

Raising you has been the single joy of my life, Little Warrior. Step into your power.

Ahvi.

My breath came out shallow, every inhale stinging like the tears gathering at the corners of my eyes. How could she do this? Where had she gone?

The door creaked behind me, and I spun to find a lanky figure leaning against the door frame. Sullivan Barbrooke looked older than the last I'd seen him, still growing into his long limbs, it seemed—that or famine had touched his family in the way it had touched ours before.

When he pushed off the door frame, I swore I heard his bones creak like the wood beneath his boots. Dark circles shadowed his sunken eyes, framed by sharp cheekbones. "Branwood," he said. "She's gone to Branwood with a member of the Guild."

Sullivan tilted his head to the side, and for a moment, I could see the boyish expression hidden beneath—smothered by struggle.

"What happened?" I asked, and his jaw tensed.

"The soldiers came through the night you left," he answered. "And then they just kept coming." Sullivan stared at the window as snow started falling from the clouds overhead. Fat flakes floated from above, and I shivered.

"There's a haven in Branwood—an Inn with people who think like us."

"Like us." I parroted, and he stepped forward, one corner of his mouth turning upward.

"It's good to see you, Caius. We didn't know what you'd choose." His mouth broke into a true grin. "I thought maybe you'd stay with the girl. Ahvi talked about her during her visits. Said you seemed fond of her, and I hadn't seen you at the trainings."

Verena's chestnut hair and warm gaze made my heart squeeze. "I came back for her," I said. "She needs—"

"Caius." Sullivan's tone turned brittle. "You've spent your entire life with Ahvi. Helped my family by bringing in wood and food, watching me and my sisters. You're loyal, but it's time you make decisions for yourself."

I chuckled, a hollow, breathy sound. "She tell you to say that?"

His slowly unfurling grin answered my question enough.

"I'm going to Branwood," I asserted, and Sullivan nodded.

"She told me you'd say that," he said. "I've found a job in Marmere, so I won't be joining you, but she gave me this."

Sullivan reached into the pocket of his cloak, pulling out a piece of paper, a name and story scrawled across it—one of many Ahvi had kept hidden in the cabin.

"Be safe," he said, turning back through the open door to disappear through the trees.

I walked to the cabinet and found the dried meat waiting. I took the jar out with me, grabbed the sack of grain resting on the side of the cabin, and brought it to my horse.

We ate in silence, sitting in the snow until the darkness returned to the forest.

I lit a fire in the cabin and dusted off the mattress.

One night here. One night, and I'd be off in the morning to find Ahvi.

CHAPTER FORTY

RIALEY

For the second time during our stay at Bloodbane Castle, we were invited into Lord Bloodbane's office to discuss what would come next.

He'd left us for the past two days, and after our encounter with the bear, neither Theron nor I longed to seek him out. I hadn't decided if the man was a monster, and I didn't think I was in the right headspace to decide.

Theron and I hadn't kissed since after the arena, and I'd chalked it up to a heated moment following near death. That was all. Though the desire still lingered in my blood whenever I'd catch him looking at me from across the room, wondering if he was remembering the feel of my lips on the way I thought of his on mine.

"I apologize for how we've gotten here," Bloodbane said, tipping back in his leather chair. The shelves behind him looked the same as the day we'd arrived nearly a month ago—not a single artifact out of place.

My eyes locked with his, chin tipped downward, and brows lowered as I fought the anger bubbling up in my chest.

The man before us not only exploited Theron's weakness after leaving the palace of Marmere, but he'd locked the prince into a blood oath and thrown us into a rebellion we didn't know enough about to properly contribute to. Not only that, but losing autonomy in the decision eroded any trust that could have existed.

Theron lifted his head, looking bored, and I wondered what emotions lurked beneath the surface. Did he feel angry? Foolish, maybe? "You've sworn your loyalty to me by blood oath," he asserted. "Who is to say I couldn't have you killed once I step into power? You've postured me to become king amongst the Guild of Eirdis. Theoretically, I could have them turn on you."

One brow quirked up as Amias Bloodbane reached for a glass set out on his desk. He uncorked a bottle of wine and promptly filled his cup along with two more. "I've bared my neck," he said. "Regardless of what you think, I did what needed to be done for the kingdom. My position matters little if we can liberate the Waldwood."

"A noble cause, surely." Theron reached for the glass, lifting it to his nose to inhale before taking a sip. I followed suit. "I've known dissatisfaction has been brewing for years," Theron said, his glass touching the polished desk with a soft clink. "As far as my father's information went, which was, regardless of what we believe about his morality, very *good* information, the dissatisfaction had never risen to more than that."

Theron's eyes sharpened into blades, and I swore Bloodbane flinched. "At what point did you take it upon yourself to organize a cause. There were quite a few in the arena."

Shielding any further reaction, Bloodbane held his glass aloft, swirling the crimson liquid. "The recent invasion of the Waldwood has prompted more support, but the Guild of Eirdis has existed for years. We have recruiters in every city throughout the kingdom. Though I will say it is difficult to avoid those who would ruin any chance at reform." Bloodbane took a sip of his wine before setting his own glass down, elbows now resting on the dark, wooden surface. "As you know, emotions can get in the way of calculated moves designed to better our chances at winning."

"Winning what, is my question?" Theron's jaw tightened, and I knew he was holding back—dragging the answer out of Bloodbane despite knowing it for himself.

"A war, Prince Wineslowe. We wish to go to war."

"In our time since the...arena, I've thought about what could potentially come next. While the size of your rebellion is impressive, it's hardly enough to go against my father."

"Which is why we need the Waldwood," Bloodbane informed. "Without witches on our side, there will be no point."

My nose wrinkled when I glared at him. "Who is to say there are any witches left in the Waldwood who want to go to war?" I questioned. "We've been scattered across the kingdom, weakening our magic like an atrophying muscle. Not only that, but you are a lord in Alphaird. Theron is the *prince*. Traitor or not, you will have a difficult time convincing anyone in that forest for an alliance."

Bloodbane's full lips pulled into a smirk. "That is where you come in, Miss Dagon."

I scoffed, folding my arms across my chest. "I could try, but I doubt I'd garner any support." Leaning forward, I rested my elbows on the desk, emphasizing my point with the shift in posture. "In case you did not know, they call me the Witch Hunter. I've *killed* my own people."

Theron's knee brushed mine beneath the desk, and I couldn't help but think it was an encouragement. He knew the truth of my guilt—the way my actions ripped my soul in two.

"We have to try," Bloodbane said—almost a plea. "You may believe me manipulative—"

"Because you *are*," I interrupted.

Anger twisted his features—an emotion I'd yet to truly see on the man. "Everything I do," he declared, "I do for those I love."

That last word—love—hung in the air between us, and for a moment, I saw the vulnerability in his gaze. I remembered the way he'd looked at Akari—his wife. I thought of the tapestries in the hallways; the owls carved into numerous corners of the house.

One thing I could believe was that Amias Bloodbane loved his family—fiercely. It was something I could not fault him for.

And truth be told, if there were witches in the Waldwood, we *would* need them. Regardless of how we got here, King Wineslowe's reign needed to end. I just didn't know if I was the one to do it.

"The witches won't be enough," Theron mused. "We will need something more. If I know anything, I know my father's army." Theron's voice dropped low with the intensity of his words. "I know what we are up against, Lord Bloodbane, as I'm sure you do as well."

Bloodbane sighed, grabbing his glass and downing the last of his drink. "That is where my failures come to light," he said, looking more tired. "We have support here, but I believe the witches using their magic will give us the boost we need in a war. It will give us a chance."

"My father uses old witch magic," Theron revealed. "In the dungeons, in his own life. Any power he can get his hands on he's taken for himself—twisted into something gnarled and ugly. I'm afraid the magic from the witches will not be enough."

I hated it, but I had to agree with him. "We've suppressed our magic for years," I added. "That weakens it. I…" I swallowed, unsure of how much I could reveal to the man, but chose honesty as we had little else to lose. "I couldn't hold onto my illusions in the arena. I can craft when I'm focused, but the moment I lose focus, it's gone. My magic tires easily."

Bloodbane's brows furrowed as he traced a finger along the rim of his glass in thought.

I hated the truth of what I'd said. It made me feel weak—useless. What was my magic for if I couldn't use it properly? Sure, I could get witches out of the dungeons, but when it mattered most, when Theron had been caught in the maw of a giant beast, I had slipped.

"Speaking of witch magic," I started. "That bear—"

"A mender's mistake," he admitted. Lord Bloodbane kept his eyes fixed on his glass. "We thought we could...create weapons," he admitted, wincing. "Unfortunately, we have no control over whom the beasts lose their minds toward. They tried to tear apart everyone—not just our targets."

Theron's finger tapped on the wood of the desk, keeping time with the clock that hung in the corner. "Eirhiondus," he stated.

Bloodbane's brows rose. "The kingdom to the north?"

Theron pushed away from the desk, his chair screeching across the hardwood. When he paced the length of the office, he held his chin, deep in thought. "The Waldwood bleeds into their kingdom," Theron said. "I hear the king is looking for a marriage."

"Are you offering your hand?" Bloodbane asked, one corner of his mouth quirking upward.

"I'm just thinking," Theron snapped. "The king is establishing himself as a leader, marrying, molding what his rule will look like. We could use that desire—offer him something worthwhile. Land?" he questioned, shaking his head as if deciding it wasn't good enough.

Theron continued to pace, and I swallowed.

In the palace, I'd had no real plans for my future. My focus had been on survival, and survival alone. As it stood, I had little to lose and everything to gain.

If we could beat King Wineslowe—win a war and place a deserving king—Theron, on the throne, I could return to the Waldwood.

I closed my eyes, breathing deeply. If Bloodbane could see me as a representation of the witches, I was certain that it extended beyond.

"You could offer me," I said, nearly a whisper.

When I opened my eyes, Theron had stopped pacing, mouth agape, and anger burning in his eyes. "No," he said, his voice carrying a finality I hadn't yet heard from him.

"This could work," Bloodbane said. "The rebellion already views her as a figurehead for the witches. We could—"

"No," Theron repeated. "I will not sell a woman to a neighboring country for the sake of winning a war. I will not sell *Rialey* for an alliance."

The way my name rolled off his tongue sent goosebumps rising on my flesh.

"It may be the only option," I said. "We will offer something else. Trade, possibly."

"Our kingdom struggles to produce food as it is," Bloodbane countered. "Only the southern cities have crops worth trading, and we need those for our own people, so unless the witches residing in the Waldwood have something to offer—"

"We will see what happens when we get there. Half of the Waldwood exists within their border. I'm certain we can make an arrangement. I just need time." Theron stalled pacing, planting himself in the chair next to mine once more.

My anxiety spiked, and I grabbed the glass of wine, downing it to the last drop. "Is there anything else we should know?" I asked Bloodbane, setting the glass down in front of us.

With eyes wide, Theron watched me. I could feel his gaze kiss every part of my heated skin. I wanted to blame the wine, but I knew the memory of his kiss lingered on my mouth—making my cheeks heat.

Bloodbane cleared his throat. "There is the issue of continuing to keep a presence as our king," Bloodbane began, and I tensed. Theron sat stock-still. If he had a reaction to the title, he hadn't shown it.

"What are you suggesting?"

I stared at him, trying to read whatever thoughts flickered behind his gaze. I ground my teeth together, connecting the dots. Bloodbane had allowed us into his home, gathering the Guild mere days ago in his city.

"Have they left?" I asked, the words burning in my throat.

"Who?" Theron questioned, his head whipping in my direction.

I kept my focus fixed on Lord Bloodbane, noting the tick of his jaw, the tense line of his shoulders. "They haven't, have they. You have gathered as many members of this rebellion as possible to your city. The goal is to establish a capital — a stronghold. Keslow is meant to fall first, with Theron leading the initial strike to ignite the uprising. Without the witches' alliance or an army large enough to win, you mean to start this war."

"Not all wars are won in a day, Miss Dagon." Bloodbane blinked. "The king suspects my treason, and we need a place to establish ourselves. We have what we need to take the city—to push the soldiers out. And there are more," he swallowed, "Animals that we can release beyond the wall."

"That's a huge risk," Theron said, his mind spinning with possibilities, plotting what was to come. "But," he started.

My heart picked up to a gallop as I watched him, fear and dread icing my veins. "But?" I questioned, voice aghast.

"If we have no army to begin with—no standing to start—then why would the covens join us? Why would the King of the North join us?"

My stomach dropped, bile crawling up my throat. I knew exactly what Theron had decided before he spoke it.

"We will take Keslow," he said, his voice sounding more a king than a prince. "We will take Keslow, and then we will push north to the Wald-wood. While I still harbor bitterness toward you, Amias, you are right in your assessment here. It is time to start a war."

Lord Bloodbane dipped his chin, crossing one hand over his chest and placing it on his heart. "Let it be so," he said, his voice carrying a gravity that pushed the air from my lungs—from this room. "My King."

CHAPTER FORTY-ONE

VERENA

As I walked to my quarters in the temple, I focused on my breathing, sucking in a slow breath through my nose to fight off the sting of tears.

The more time I spent cleansing the temple and reorganizing the library—my newest task delegated by Narela—I found my past was catching up with me.

Sometimes, in the middle of the night, when I would wake up to darkness, placing my feet on the cold stone floors, I'd remember the stone floors of the dungeons I'd spent time in. I would remember the deep pang of hunger squeezing my stomach, the way my body withered into a weak and fragile thing.

Many days, I spent my time in the temple's courtyard. In my melancholic state, I'd started talking to the owl. She seemed to follow me there, watching with those dark eyes in the dappled sunlight.

I told her about Caius, of a heart grown too fond of the temporary. I told her of my mother—my memories of the Waldwood. And beyond that, I spoke of my sadness. I spoke so much that I started to believe that she was listening as intently as the gods Narela seemed convinced existed.

The plain wooden door to my rooms felt warm to the touch when I pushed it open. The creaking hinges echoed through the nearly bare room.

A crackling hearth sat on the right side of the room, my bed on the left beneath a frosted window overlooking the forest. The wardrobe pressed against the wall near the door held very little, considering I had come with little. My three priestess robes, one dress I'd brought all the way from Ahvi's, a tunic and pants, and a soft pair of wool pajamas hung just inside the intricately carved wooden doors. The wardrobe was the only piece of the room made to be beautiful. The bed was practical, but I was thankful for a mattress all the same.

I stripped out of my robes, folding them neatly at the base of the wardrobe to be washed in the morning. I pulled on my wool nightclothes, thankful for the modest dinner on the silver tray delicately placed atop my mattress. The hot cup of tea emitted steam from its perch, calling to me like the forest's magic called to my blood.

"Knock, knock."

I spun, abandoning thoughts of tea to find Rona in the doorway to my room. Her lanky figure stood a good seven inches taller than mine, practically towering over me. Her pale skin still held a translucent quality, but she looked better—healthier than she had the night she'd healed Caius.

I hadn't talked to her since—hadn't seen her—and at the sight of her standing in the doorway, my throat closed up. There were a thousand words of gratitude I longed to give her, but they would not come.

Rona walked through the threshold, welcoming herself into my space and looking around. Her intense gaze hopped from the hearth to the bed and back to me. "I didn't mean to interrupt your dinner," she remarked.

"It's fine," I said. "I wasn't hungry, so I stayed out late spending time in the—"

"The courtyard," she finished. "I am aware. Narela says that is where you spend most of your free time."

I looked down, nodding as heat flooded my cheeks. For whatever reason, I felt embarrassed, as if her knowledge of my time in the courtyard would reveal the secrets I'd spilled to the owl there.

Rona's jaw tightened before she spoke. "I heard you spent time in the dungeons at Marmere."

I nodded, the memory of damp stone and sleepless nights returning just as it had in the previous days. "I did."

"I thought..." She paused. "I thought that maybe you'd want someone to talk to about that." Swallowing, Rona looked ashamed before she amended her words. "I mean to say I might like to discuss it with someone who has experienced it. It might be good for me."

"Oh," I said, somewhat surprised at her confession. Rona, despite the fragility of her state, came across cold as the winter beyond the walls of the temple. In my limited interactions with her, she didn't seem one to be emotional. "Would you like to sit?" I asked, gesturing to the mattress where my dinner still sat undisturbed. "There's only the bed. I didn't ask for a chair. After Caius left, I—" My words fizzled out, the echo of his name haunting in the dim firelight.

"Caius, it was?" she asked, a small smirk curling the corners of her thin lips. "Your lover?" she questioned, and my eyes widened in shock.

"No!" I said, a bit too hurried. "No, we haven't—" I winced, and Rona managed a chuckle before striding to the bed, delicately moving my dinner aside to sit.

"It's okay," she said. "I was merely joking."

I breathed a sigh of relief, joining her with my back stiff, unsure of what we would discuss. Out in the courtyard, my words came easily. I'd spoken about the dungeons, but here? It was more difficult.

Rona's brow furrowed before she began. "The Witch Hunter," she remarked. "Was that who came to collect you?"

I swallowed, remembering the night I'd been released to the forest—left to dissolve beneath the trees. "Yes, but she only got me out of the palace. I was passed off to another man afterward. Eryx, I believe." I rifled through the memories, trying to recall the details. I'd been so tired then—using the last of my strength to escape. "He was kind," I offered, "but I don't remember much of that night. It was a bit chaotic."

"Eryx is Prince Theron." Rona stared at me when I let out a small gasp, my heart speeding up at the revelation. "The night I got out, he was revealed on the street." Rona shook her head. "Theron Wineslowe. I'd helped them—helped the Witch Hunter before I ran." She took a deep breath. "I'd felt guilty for fleeing, but I just got word that the Traitor Prince is part of a rebellion. They've taken Keslow, and I—" Rona shook her head. "I'm not sure why I'm telling you all this. I think I just needed to speak to someone who had touched the same ground—walked where I'd walked. You know?"

With each breath I dragged into my lungs, my shock still pulsed through my veins like ice water. "That was Prince Wineslowe?" I questioned, staring at my hands where they sat in my lap.

Rona placed a hand on my shoulder, and I startled, wondering what she saw when she looked at me, and her eyes softened. "Are you alright?" she questioned. "Maybe I shouldn't have—"

"No!" I asserted. "I deserved to know. I..." I shook my head. "I want to know."

Rona stood up, straightening her robes before striding to the door. Her blonde hair had been braided down her back, neat with no hair out of place. "I will leave," she said. "I've upset you, and I take responsibility for that."

"Wait," I said, and she halted.

A part of me didn't know if I was ready to talk about the dungeons with someone who had been in them. I didn't know if I was ready to learn all the details of the escape I continued to grapple with—the thing that nearly killed me. My chest tightened at the thought. Still, a yearning bloomed deep in my soul—one that recognized how lonely I'd been—how much I craved friendship.

"You could come back?" I said, the end of my sentence sounded like a question. "Tomorrow. I think I'll be ready to talk then."

Rona smiled, nodding. "I'd like that," she said. "I'd like that a lot."

Chapter Forty-Two

Caius

My stiff fingers fumbled with the papers in my cloak pocket as my horse approached the wall. The first time I'd done this, Verena had been with me. Her presence steadied me, but in her absence, my nerves pushed to the surface.

I wouldn't be able to pass through the gates with fake papers if I couldn't control my body's reactions, so I shoved it down and did my best to steady myself.

"Name?" the guard asked, holding a hand toward me as I approached.

Surprisingly, I had tamped down my nerves enough to hand him the parchment with steady hands. "Gideon." My heart raced, mind swirling with all the ways this could end poorly.

I glanced at the sword strapped to his hip. The metal glinted in the light of the sconces lit on the city walls. Dusk had fallen, and something about the looming darkness set me on edge.

"Right." The guard glanced over the information. Gideon McGrath, twenty-nine and single. Visiting family within the city.

The guard thrust the paper in my direction with irritation. I imagined he'd grown tired of checking these things, though it certainly didn't stop them from capturing young witches or sympathizers and throwing them in the dungeons.

"Go on," he said, nodding toward the opening gates.

Relief washed over me, and I steered my mount into the city streets.

I meandered down cobbled streets, my horse's hooves keeping a steady rhythm. Shouts rang from either side of me as merchants discussed today's sales while packing up their stalls.

As I found myself further in the city, the sun dipped below the horizon, plunging each building into darkness. They loomed over us, lights from the lanterns within shining in the windows.

The tavern, a beacon among the homes and businesses, stood just as I remembered it. If there was anywhere I'd find Ahvi, it would be in the apothecary with Florence. Without attending meetings, I had nothing to inform me of the rebellion's progress, and now that we'd left the cabin, my focus could narrow in on what I'd promised myself I'd achieve. I would avenge my parents—make a better kingdom.

Still, I didn't want to face the question of where Verena was. I would have to answer, and my heart clenched at the reminder that she was not here. I'd left her to the Waldwood—chosen to return to an empty cabin, and a brewing war that still seemed so far away. My soul pulled in two directions.

I shook it off, stepping up to the tavern entrance. As the wooden door opened, laughter and shouts spilled into the street right along with the glow of firelight. I sucked in a deep breath, smelling the stale beer and stew before striding to the bar.

A bartender I didn't recognize filled a glass to the brim with amber liquid before sliding it down the bar top.

"Can I help you?" he said, his thick northern accent surprising me. I fought the urge to widen my eyes and held a steady gaze. His black hair had been neatly styled, his black tunic open at the collar to reveal ivory skin, cleanly shaven.

"I'll need a room for the night," I said, digging in my pockets for what was left of the coin I had. It wasn't much, and I knew I'd need more to get along. "Also," I started. "Is the healer still here beneath the tavern?" I asked, and his soft features hardened.

"Why do you ask?" he questioned, his tone biting.

I swallowed, questioning what had made him so uncomfortable. "I helped her the last time I visited Branwood. Just wanted to say hello."

The barkeeper dug beneath the counter to fish for a key, sliding it across the wooden surface with a harsh scrape. "She is out," he said, his voice carrying a finality that told me I should not go looking for Florence.

It was all the confirmation I needed.

I tossed the coins on the counter, plucked up the key, and glanced at the room number etched into its surface—different from the room I'd stayed in with Verena.

"Right," I said, holding the key aloft in emphasis. "Thank you." I turned, walking through the bawdy conversation and loud clatter of dishes to the stairs at the far end of the tavern.

The barkeep's eyes burned at my back, and I knew better than to go down. He'd know exactly where I'd gone. Instead, I went up to my room, tossing my bag on the bed and shedding my cloak before warming by the fire. After a few moments, my stomach growled, hunger squeezing my insides until the urgency to earn more coin became all too real.

I grabbed the last of the dried meat from my pack, eating it before descending the stairs at the back of the tavern out of sight.

If Florence were away, I'd find it out for myself.

The door sat slightly ajar when I made it to her apothecary, the scent of herbs and incense wrapping around me in the hallway. Muffled voices leaked out of the room when I approached, and I felt my heart pick up its pace in my chest. Whatever was happening in the healer's room, I wasn't meant to be privy to it.

My hand gently settled on the wooden door as I peered through the crack, careful not to make a sound.

"The prince has taken Keslow," a deep voice rumbled from the center of the room. I couldn't get a good look at its owner or who he was talking to. "It was not an arduous task considering most of Bloodbane's men held the same sentiments as the Guild. My guess is they will push north, but we await Florence's return for more information."

"And King Wineslowe?" a feminine voice questioned, wise and familiar in a way that had my breath leaving my lungs in a whoosh. I'd know the voice anywhere—had lived with it since childhood.

The man stepped into view; his arms crossed firmly across his muscular chest. His dark features and fawn-colored skin glowed warm in the light of the lanterns around the apothecary, eyes wrinkled with age. "Word is he will send more forces to the Waldwood in retaliation. There's little we can do. The war has begun."

"And do you believe we are ready?"

"I—"

My hand slipped on the door, the creaking sound drawing the attention of my grandmother and whoever she'd been talking to.

With my pulse in my ears, I stepped forward, watching the panic turn to warmth in Ma's gaze when she saw me. Her gentle gasp, the way her dark eyes lit to a lighter copper behind the sheen of tears covering them.

"Caius," she said with a fondness that clogged my throat.

I stepped into the room, noting the way her companion watched me.

Ma met me in the middle of the room, wrapping me in her warm embrace with the scent of tea and woodsmoke drowning my worries. Tears burned my eyes, and I shook with the force of them.

I hadn't realized how much guilt I carried—how much worry I harbored for my grandmother until I could feel her heartbeat for myself—a confirmation that she was alive.

She pulled away as my shaking ceased, and I wiped my eyes. Her firm grip remained on my shoulders when she looked at my face, eyes catching on every scratch or smear of dirt I'd acquired in my long travels.

"What are you doing here?" she questioned, her features a war between relief, joy, and worry.

My brows creased. "Looking for you. I'm ready to—"

Ma shook her head, tears still lining her eyes. "Loyal to a damn fault," she muttered. "Where is Verena?"

My stomach plummeted to the scuffed wooden floor below, blood draining from my face. "I...in the Waldwood," I stuttered. "She joined the temple there, and she—"

The worry etching itself into the creases of her face cause me to pause. My breaths came sharper—shallower as I watched the worry tip to fear.

I nudged her hands off my shoulders, stepping back as panic tightened my chest. "What?"

"The rebellion," she started, and I shook my head. "The Waldwood is about to be a war zone, Caius. With the prince taking Keslow, leading the Guild of Eirdis, Wineslowe is certain to send out forces, and we will fight, but Verena is now alone with the priestesses. We worry we won't..." she swallowed. "Worry we won't get there in time."

My vision tunneled, realizations hitting me blow after blow. War was starting, and I'd left Verena there in the temple.

I'd been there—healed there. The temple of Eirdis had limited resources. Narela had taken the sick and wounded who found their way to the forest, but the village that once was Eirdis's was long gone—void of the coven that had existed there in the past.

"I—" Panic pushed the blood so fast through my veins, I could hear it rushing like waves of a mighty sea. "I have to go back," I nearly whispered.

The door clicked shut behind us, and I turned to find Florence striding directly to her desk. Her snow-dusted cloak dragged against the floor as she pulled off her gloves, setting them on the wooden desk's surface. Her white hair appeared matted and dirty, as if she'd been traveling as well, and I supposed she had.

"You do," she said, eyes blazing when she looked at me. "And I'm inclined to go with you."

Chapter Forty-Three

Caius

The frigid temperature pushed me to scoot closer to the fire. A thick covering of clouds shielded the night sky. While the kingdom had been plunged into a perpetual winter, I hadn't known it to be quite this cold.

I shivered, pulling my cloak tighter around my body and dreading when we'd all retreat to our tents. Ma, Florence, and Asa, the man who had been talking to my grandmother, sat around with me looking just as cold and miserable.

I'd left the mount that had traveled to the Waldwood with me and Verena back in Branwood, trading it in for a well-rested animal. The horse needed it, to be sure, but I missed the damn thing.

"They should be moving north," Florence said, continuing her conversation with Asa. Ma listened intently, and my eyes fixed on the dancing flames of the fire. "There's no telling if the prince and the executioner will get there before us or not—no telling they'll end up at the same coven, either."

My eyes met hers. "This executioner," I began. "The Witch Hunter; she's the one who aided the witches escaping the dungeons?" I asked.

Florence nodded before using a stick to poke one of the logs. It cracked, sending sparks up into the icy night air. "As far as I understand, she'd get them out of the palace. It was Prince Theron Wineslowe who got them out of the city."

"And then what?" Anger burned in my chest, the memory of Verena, hollow and broken as she lay in the snow. Her breaths were shallow, papery skin turning purple against the winter. If she'd been out in the forest in these temperatures, I'm certain I wouldn't have found her in time.

"They let them go," Florence answered, her brows raised, a curious expression on her face.

I couldn't help the tension in my shoulders, the way I ground my teeth together against my anger. "They left them to die," I muttered, tone laced with the bitterness that grew within me.

The prince had no business leading the Guild—not when he proved himself to be so shortsighted.

While his father took a more active role in killing the witches, Prince Wineslowe had still done the same. His way, however, allowed him to absolve himself of the guilt.

It didn't make him any less of a murderer.

Asa shifted where he sat in the snow. "Or gave them a chance to live," he said. "Depending on how you look at it."

I scoffed, noting the way Ma sat still, not adding to the conversation. She'd seen Verena, too, and I couldn't imagine she didn't feel some of the same emotions that ensnared me.

I hated King Wineslowe for what he'd done to the witches—to the people I cared about—*my* people.

And the more we discussed the prince, the more I loathed him, too—rebellion or not. He lived in the palace, closest to the evil of his father, and did nothing save for risking the lives of those he proclaimed to have saved. An arrogant bastard, and I wasn't keen on the Witch Hunter either.

"The witches are weak," Florence started, picking the conversation back up. "Most of us have suppressed our powers for so long we hardly have a hold on them. Not to mention our distance from the Waldwood. Menders pay a high price for their magic, and dreamwalkers are confined to the realm of sleep. With the illusionists weakened too, I'm not...hopeful."

"You do not believe we will win the war?" Ma asked, her expression fierce and determined, an image of the woman who'd done so much for herself—her family. A true picture of strength, she raised her chin, clearly disagreeing with Florence's assessment.

"The war has started whether we like it or not," I said. "If they've taken Keslow, they've initiated it without the backing necessary to win. Foolish leadership, if you ask me, but I'm not surprised based on what I know about the Traitor Prince."

"He's the only hope we have," Florence asserted, almost defending him.

I couldn't help how my tone took on a bitter edge—just like the air around us. "You just said you do not have hope that we will win this war."

She stood, eyes cutting when she looked at me. "Our chances are not good," she confirmed. "But I did not say I was without hope entirely, Caius. Maybe if we had more willing to fight and less longing to judge the actions of others, we'd have a better chance."

Properly scolded and wholly disagreeing, I sat with my thoughts as the others retreated to their tents. I'd spent most of my life training to fight the best I could—channeled my anger into something useful, but I'd hardly had enough opportunity to use it.

We had been a part of the Guild; which until now, did not mean much, I supposed.

Ma gave me a gentle squeeze on my shoulder before leaving—her thin smile showing she knew my thoughts and warring emotions.

She knew how much I cared for Verena.

And deep down, I knew it too. It just took me this long to truly realize.

When we crossed into the Waldwood, I felt the familiar buzz of magic across my skin, the horse stepping in the icy snow. After the cold temperatures over the past few nights, a layer of ice had formed across the surface, making travel more difficult.

I'd been haunted by my mind. I'd lived a quiet life—focusing on caring for Ma. Maybe it was to pay her back for what she'd done in caring for me after my parents died. I'd known her strength—seen it firsthand. After all, she'd lost her son all those years ago. I sometimes wondered if she saw him in me—the remnants of the father I barely knew.

The more I watched her with Asa and Florence, the more I realized that she'd wanted to do more—held herself back for my sake.

We had been a part of the Guild, but confined by a stagnant rebell ion.While growing in numbers, there had been a disorganization during training—a lack of leadership. The Guild survived on ideas and nothing more, and with the Traitor Prince, I assumed there could be...something.

My anger had not softened toward the prince or his executioner, but there was little I could do. I would not leave a rebellion out of spite—not give up what I'd worked so hard to achieve.

"There," Florence said, pointing at the stone emerging through the trees.

My heart sped up in my chest as I saw the dying ivy climbing the walls of Eirdis's massive temple. She was close—here.

After weeks of being apart, I'd filled up with stories and confessions. I'd hardly spoken of the rebellion, hiding that side of myself for fear she would...I didn't even know.

When we returned, would she care to see me? Did she care that I'd left? Did she understand why?

The sword across my back felt heavy at our approach. We'd stocked up on weapons in anticipation. Knowing that the King's army would push to the Waldwood had my nerves skittering along my skin, that rage burning deep in my chest. There was a good chance they would retaliate after the news from Keslow.

When we approached, Narela stood at the entrance to the temple, as if she'd been expecting us. She did not smile; she merely watched with a curious gaze as we dismounted our horses and walked to the entrance.

"We came as quickly as we could," Asa said. "We've much to discuss, starting with what the witches, here in the temple, are prepared for."

Narela's brows furrowed, a crease forming between them in concern. "What do you mean?" she asked.

"War, Narela." Florence walked up behind Asa, carrying a bag over her shoulder. In the cold, her pale skin had flushed pink across the bridge of her nose, lips nearly purple. "We mean to ask if you are prepared for war."

Narela nodded, gesturing to the inside of the temple. "Please," she said. "Come inside, and we can chat."

When we passed through the entrance to the temple, my gaze flicked wildly down every hall and into every corner, hoping to glimpse blue robes, soft brown strands of hair, a smattering of freckles.

Narela hung back as we walked a death march to one of the rooms deep in the temple. "She's spent a lot of her time in the courtyard," Narela said, a small smile forming on her full lips. "Welcome back, Caius. It's nice to see you alive."

A warmth washed over me like the heat from a hearth fire. When I'd returned to the cabin only to find it empty, the comfort I'd felt there for so long had disappeared, but here, in the temple, I felt a small glimmer of it again.

"We will see you after," Ma said, glancing back with a knowing smile.

I nodded once, my heart hammering as I disappeared through the winding halls, past the owl statue, and into the sunny courtyard just beyond the door.

There, in the center, sat Verena on her knees in the snow, looking up to the trees with the sun dappled over her face.

She looked ethereal. It was as if she'd learned to commune with the trees—made one with the magic of the Waldwood.

In her presence, I hardly felt worthy of her attention. She was stunning—strong. I'd watched her heal, and not once over all that time after she'd been tortured in the dungeons did she ever lose the kindness she held so close. It was a part of who she was—a part of the person I'd grown to care for.

"You look well," I said, my nerves making my voice breathier than I had hoped.

Verena stood quickly, a gasp leaving on a cold cloud from her parted lips when she turned to see me.

We stood frozen in the courtyard, watching one another until she broke the silence. "What are you doing here?" she asked.

"Helping a rebellion," I answered, chuckling at her widening eyes.

Drawn to her like a magnet, I took a step forward. I ached for the warmth of her presence, the comfort of companionable silence. Cups of tea, quiet nights beside her, the steady rhythm of her breath easing my worries—I longed for it all.

"I've missed you," I said, taking another step forward.

Verena stood—staring as if she didn't believe I was real.

"I..." Her eyes lined with tears as I approached, each careful step bringing me closer to the woman I'd left behind. "The rebellion has come here?" she asked.

When I'd moved close enough to touch her, I let my fingers skate gently over her cheek, watching the fluttering of her pulse at her neck. "There is a duty to protect," I murmured, eyes closing as she leaned into my touch. "I have done nothing worth speaking about in my time as part of the Guild, you should know. Ma and I would meet with others—train, but aside from offering healing herbs for no fee, there has been no movement in the rebellion as a whole." I paused, thinking of all the reasons I had to win this war. "But I think it's time I do something to change the fate of the kingdom. I lost my parents," I said. "I almost lost you—before I even knew you were something to lose."

Her eyes opened, near hazel in the light of the courtyard. "And am I?" she asked on a breath. "Am I something to lose?"

"No, Verena," I said, moving so close our breaths mingled in the cold air. She smelled of incense and herbs—likely from her time in the temple. "You were something to find."

Verena tipped forward, her lips pressed to mine, breath leaving on a gasp when I kissed her back. My hand tangled in her hair, the other gripping her waist and pulling her closer, regretting the moment I'd left her.

Her soft lips parted, and I swallowed the small sound she made when my fingers closed around the strands of hair they were tangled in, gently tugging her head back so I could get more of her.

When the heat eased, I pulled away, my forehead resting on hers.

"You came back," she whispered.

"I had to."

Wings fluttered above us, and we both looked up to see an owl plunge in our direction, causing us to crouch before it veered upward, disappearing over the trees and leaving the courtyard. Another swoop, and we found ourselves ducking away from the bird.

Verena's brows stitched together in concern. "Something's wrong," she said.

"What?" I asked.

"The owl." Her eyes stayed fixed on the sky as a scream rose into the daylight, high-pitched and fearful, causing my stomach to drop. "No." Verena took off through the courtyard, hauling the door open into the temple.

Worry gripped me, holding me tight as I found my sword, the blade sliding from its sheath with a smooth sound.

My boots pounded against the stone floors, blood roaring in my ears as I chased Verena through the halls.

"Verena!" I screamed, panic tightening my chest. "Stop!"

The flash of metal in her hand did nothing to ease my fears. She carried a small dagger and ran toward the entrance to the temple.

When I caught up with her on the steps, we stood to look out at the forest, crimson-stained snow, and the clanking of metal.

I watched as a soldier pushed forward, Rona's hands outstretched, fingers contorting at odd angles as the guard's joints cracked, forcing him to drop his sword, his elbow sticking out at an odd angle.

Narela followed behind, driving a dagger into the man's back, her eyes blazing when they briefly caught ours.

"No!" Verena screamed, and I reached for her arm, keeping her from joining the fray.

Panic stole my breath as I watched Asa, Florence, and Ma with swords out. There couldn't have been more than twenty soldiers, but considering how few witches lived in the temple, it wouldn't take much more to overpower them.

"Do not," I commanded, my grip tightening on Verena's arm. "Run," I said, before barreling down the steps, sword out and ready.

The first soldier collided with me, my breath leaving in a harsh grunt as I pushed him back, placing my sword between us. His amber eyes flicked left to where his weapon sat buried in the snow. I took the opportunity afforded to me and struck, plunging the metal through his stomach, the memory of a similar wound heating beneath my tunic.

Another soldier came at me, eyes blazing and sword arcing downward. I caught it just in time, the brutal clank of metal rattling my muscles as I held my weapon horizontally to ward off his attack. He brought his face closer, pushing with everything he had as sweat beaded on the back of my neck.

I shoved him away, and he stumbled back, holding his weapon the entire time. The emblem on his uniform told me these soldiers had come from Branwood—not from Marmere.

Had we led them here?

Had they been following us?

Florence screamed, blood staining the arm of her tunic as she crouched in the snow. The soldier in front of her, looking at his own arm, eyes widening with fear. He paused a step, just long enough for Asa to come up behind him, dragging his blade across the soldier's neck. His body fell into the soft snow, staining more of the glittering white a deep red.

I turned, kicking out at another as they attempted to sneak up behind me. He fell to his knees, and I spun, gripping the hilt of my sword and plunging the weapon downward, the cracking sound of bone and flesh deafening amidst the surrounding battle.

The soldier fell, and I leapt over his body, looking outward as Ma stood with her back pressed to a tree. She held her blade firmly between herself and the assailant, who kept her own sword across Ma's neck. The only thing keeping her from slicing through flesh was Ma's strength and determination to hold her sword with another.

Ma!" I screamed, pain lashing across my chest. The split-second distraction had her glancing toward me—just long enough for her eyes to go glassy as the soldier drove a dagger straight through her chest. A painful scream ripped from my throat as I watched her dead gaze as she fell to the ground, her blood mingling with that of the others who'd died.

Time slowed, and I turned to see a soldier running toward me, his own sword pointed in my direction.

I wanted to move—to react—but in my shock, I felt nothing, saw nothing.

Just before he got to me, a look of fear overtook him, and he jerked back, falling into the snow and frantically crawling away.

I looked around the forest, watching as every soldier left battled with their own mind, seeing things that didn't exist.

They began retreating until one turned her own dagger inward, shoving it between her ribs, thick blood pouring from her lips.

"What...?" I whispered, turning slowly to find Narela, her eyes fixed on the steps where Verena was on her knees, her head in her hands as she unleashed a scream of rage.

"No," Narela said. "No!"

She took off sprinting, and I watched in confusion, soldiers turning their weapons against themselves—against each other as Verena's voice cracked through the trees.

"She's going to burn out!" Florence yelled from across the graveyard of blood and bodies. "She's in their heads! It's too much!"

Fear jolted me from my state of shock, and all I could think to do was run. Blood and snow coated my boots as I tried to get to her.

Watching Narela kneel next to Verena's crumpling body.

She screamed her name, but Verena had lost herself to her mind—to her power.

I stopped at the bottom of the steps, frozen and longing to get to her—to touch her.

The sounds of metal ceased, replaced by a pained cry.

"She can't hear us!" Narela shouted. "Verena!"

I moved on instinct, my hands coming to either side of Verena's heaving shoulders. She lay on the steps, eyes squeezed shut against whatever she saw.

Grappling with my emotions, I tried to force calm into my voice—tried to bring her back to me the way I once had.

"Long ago, there was a beautiful witch who lived in the Waldwood." My voice broke on the final word.

With one final scream, her tense muscles relaxed before convulsions took over her small figure.

I fought the stinging burn of tears, panicking as I reached for her, grabbing at her arms, her hands. There was nothing I could do.

When the shaking ceased, Verena lay still.

One breath.

Two.

I waited for another—waited for her to wake up.

But it never came.

I knelt on the steps beside Narela, the rest of the coven, and what remained of our small group surrounding us. An eerie quiet took over the forest—the silence deafening amidst the remnants of battle.

I couldn't look away—couldn't stop staring, waiting for her to breathe again. Minutes passed, hours maybe, I didn't know.

A soft hand gripped my shoulder, and I slowly turned to see Narela there—silver streaks pouring down her face from the tears she spilled.

"Caius," she whispered. Somehow, my name told me everything I needed to know. It didn't stop Narela from continuing—saying the thing that would be a blow worse than the dagger I'd taken to my stomach.

"Caius," she said again. "She's gone. Verena is dead."

PART THREE

The kingdoms of the wicked drank the blood of innocents.
And so, a rebellion could never be bloodless.
It would always require sacrifice.

Chapter Forty-Four

Caius

We placed the bodies of our own in the temple's courtyard as an offering to Eirdis.

With the ground still frozen, we could not bury them until the temperatures became warmer.

Three days after I'd felt the heavy weight of Ahvi in my arms as I carried my grandmother into the temple, and then Verena, I struggled with the thought that corpses remain within the walls of where I was staying.

On night two, the tears had come. I'd cried and screamed—cursing the very gods the covens worshipped until I had nothing more to give—until I was hollow, haunting the halls like a phantom.

"There's much to be done," Narela said, standing at the entrance of my room with a tray of food. Her blue robes, now clean, draped over her body and spilled onto the stone floors below. With her white hair braided at her back, she looked at me with pity.

I hated the pity.

"I know," I said quietly. A rebellion still simmered beneath the surface, and King Wineslowe deserved to answer for his crimes. The bitter anger I held toward him would return in time—I was sure of it—but for now, grief lingered heavier than rage. I needed more time to face what I'd lost.

"I'd be happy to carry your tray for you," Narela continued. "Should you wish to eat in the commons with the rest of us."

"Too many are missing," I responded, my tone flat. When the temple only consisted of fourteen witches before our arrival, four deaths made a difference. I had no desire to be reminded of their absence.

Narela's voice dropped to a whisper. "I know."

When I looked at her then, I saw the heartache etched into every worried line creasing her forehead, the way her mouth turned downward in a permanent frown. I wondered what kind of loss Narela had experienced during the battle. Had she cared for one of the women? Two witches I hadn't known had been slain. Were they of importance to her? A lover, perhaps.

"I would like to be alone," I said. "But you go—be with those who can support you."

"Caius." Narela stepped forward, setting the tray on the chair by the fire before joining me in sitting on the bed.

We sat in silence for a while, the air thick with all the unspoken words—the heaviness of grief. "You need support, too," she finally whispered.

"I will be fine."

"She wouldn't have wanted you to be alone. Neither of them would have."

My chest felt like a chasm, a deep void of numbness that I somehow couldn't get rid of.

I stared at the floor, unable to speak or move. Giving up, Narela took her leave, the door clicking shut behind her.

I looked to the food with the knowledge I should eat, but I could not bring myself to touch the stew.

I pinched the bridge of my nose, squeezing my eyes shut until I couldn't see Ma's face as her eyes glazed over—the way she'd fallen to the snow. Until

I could no longer see Verena, lost to her own mind and screaming as she curled in on herself from the stone steps of the temple.

When my eyes finally opened, I looked out the window to find an owl perched in one of the snow-covered trees, black eyes watching as if I were something of importance.

Magic hummed over my skin just as it had the moment we'd stepped into the Waldwood. In the quiet, I assumed I'd become more attuned to it.

If King Wineslowe wasn't purged from the land, a war would likely fail. How many dreamwalkers were willing to exhaust their power the way Verena had?

I'd been around witches in my early childhood, seen them pass through the forest, hidden within the city walls. I'd never seen anything like what Verena did. The horror on the soldiers' faces would go with me, along with the other memories.

Another knock on my door sounded before it opened. Florence stood with the firelights in the hallway flickering behind her. Her gray eyes sliced through my sadness, stirring something within.

"What ails you?" she asked, and I frowned.

"Nothing, I—"

Florence stepped forward, the priestess robes she borrowed swirling around her ankles. "Then why," she asked, tone biting, "are you acting as if you cannot move from this place?"

She was angry with me, something I found wholly unfair considering the circumstances. Had she cared at all?

Anger stirred—the first thing I'd felt in days. "I am allowed to mourn."

Florence inched closer, her lip curling up in distaste. "We all carry sorrow in our bones. The question is, is the storm you feel *here*..." She pushed her finger into my chest with bruising force. "...strong enough for you to *do* something about it."

I pushed her hand away. "What is it you want?"

"This rebellion *needs* you. You can wield a sword well enough, and we are already at a disadvantage. Lord Bloodbane, the lord in Keslow, is already pushing things along faster than the Guild can withstand. If we are to be consumed by sadness, we are to be consumed by the pyres King Wineslowe lights."

Florence stood straighter, icy as the winter beyond the stone walls of the temple. "Sit in your sadness one more night," she seethed. "Then *do* something about it."

This time, when the guest who'd let themselves into my room left, I felt something swirling in my chest—a storm of rage for the suffering of my people.

When I looked back out the window, the owl had disappeared.

Without another thought, I picked up the bowl of stew and forced myself to eat.

CHAPTER FORTY-FIVE

RIALEY

Hot blood spurted across my face when I slammed the blade of my dagger into the soldier's throat as screams sounded from just outside the alleyway in the heart of Keslow.

Marmere's emblem stained red on his uniform; his teeth bared when he'd charged toward me.

Chaos had erupted in the streets during the weekly witching. In our last meeting with Lord Bloodbane, we'd found that his city had used similar tactics in their attempt to avoid the weekly witchings at the city center.

As Bloodbane's executioner paraded this week's sacrifice to the platform, we'd struck. Trained guild members turned against the soldiers scattered in the crowd, who had been sent either to search for Prince Theron or had already been stationed in Keslow to ensure weekly witchings took place per the king's decree.

I kicked at the heavy body of the soldier, barely moving his corpse when I gave in, deciding to leap over the lump of flesh and sprint towards the crowd.

Metal clashed against metal, the shouts growing louder the further I ran toward the streets. My boots slapped the snow-dusted stones until I found my way out of the alley.

There on the platform stood a tall figure with his face covered in a burlap sack. The man did not struggle, merely stood with Bloodbane's favored ex-

ecutioner keeping a light grip on his upper arm. The fighting did not cease, and I looked left, pulling the sword from the sheath at my back and slashing it across another soldier's neck. He'd pinned a woman—a witch—to the ground, the tip of his weapon drawing a bead of blood from her neck.

When he slumped on top of her, I helped to move the body, civilians now fleeing from the square.

I looked up just as the plan unfolded before the king's sympathizers. Bloodbane's executioner pulled the sack from the face of the man on the platform, the flames of the pyre melting the snow surrounding.

Theron stood with a devilish smirk on his lips, watching as the crowd gasped.

A soldier scrambled toward the steps of the platform, only to be struck down by those waiting there.

"Consider this an announcement." Theron's voice boomed across the city's center, and I tried to stay focused on the chaos. "The version of Alphaird my father has built will fall—only to be replaced with a new version—one that values the Waldwood for the magic she holds."

An arrow whistled as it flew through the air, striking Theron in the left shoulder.

Without a thought, he pulled it from his arm, staring out at the crowd that seemed to hold its breath. "Until next time," he said, the executioner guiding him down the platform, behind one of the buildings, and into the sewers where I was meant to meet him.

I ran for the other alleyway, wiping the snow away furiously before ripping the grate out of its spot and slipping into the darkness.

When my boots splashed in the sewers beneath the city, Theron came into view, his face pale as he collapsed into the disgusting mess below.

"Get Florence," the executioner shouted, his voice panicked.

I nodded, sprinting away from Theron to find a mender, hoping like hell this would be the last time he looked death in the eyes.

My eyes opened to the inside of the tent, my breath leaving me on a cloud as my heart rate slowly settled.

The wind howled outside, the memory of Keslow haunting along with all the others I carried.

"Rialey?"

I turned my head to find Theron next to me and lying on his side with his elbow holding him up. His features were hard to see in the darkness, but my memory filled in the blanks.

"A dream," I whispered, eyes flicking to the spot on his shoulder where the arrow had struck him. Theron played the part—a traitorous prince paraded to the top of the platform of the pyres his father used to kill witches. When the arrow had struck him, he'd acted as if he didn't notice, pulled it out, and walked down the steps.

It wasn't until we got beneath the city that he'd collapsed.

"Keslow?" he asked, his voice soft.

"You were a fool for pulling the arrow out," I said, reaching for the wound on instinct. "And for collapsing in the sewers with an open wound."

I could hear the smirk on his lips when he spoke, the way he made light of nearly dying...again. "Florence took care of it."

"I wish you wouldn't do that," I said, turning to look up at the ceiling of our tent. "You act as though none of this has bothered you, and here I am, waking to bloody nightmares." Shame taunted me as a flush bloomed across my face and chest. "It makes me feel weak."

I closed my eyes against the feeling, listening to the rustling of our blankets as Theron shifted closer. His cool fingers on my cheek had me sucking in a sharp breath, his nearness pushing my pulse into a gallop.

"Forgive me," he murmured, so close I could feel his breath fan over my face, the scent of juniper berries and smoke engulfing me. "I do not wish to make you feel anything but what you are," he continued. "You are strong,

Rialey." His fingers traced down my jaw before he removed his hand, only to trace the same path over again.

I breathed deeply, leaning into his touch. "I like…" I shivered, a confession sitting at the edge of my lips. "I like when you touch me."

Theron's fingers halted, as well as his breathing. The stillness had me opening my eyes. With parted full lips and hooded eyes, he looked at me in a way that sent heat barreling through me.

We stared at one another, breaths mingling as the words hung between us. For a moment, I thought I should be embarrassed at my confession. Though true, we hadn't so much as talked about the kiss—hadn't touched one another until now. In the back of my mind, I wondered if whatever passed between us before had resulted from what we experienced in the arena.

"Do you?" he asked, bringing his finger and thumb up to my chin, guiding me to look at him.

As my eyes adjusted, I could make out the subtle dip to his full mouth. His blonde hair had been pushed back, as if he'd been running his hands through it.

Awareness spread over my skin, and I could feel every lift and fall of my chest, feel my pulse fluttering at the base of my neck. Despite the cold, my cheeks and body had warmed, made more intense by the warmth radiating off the prince.

With my mouth slightly parted, I nodded, hoping he would see the encouragement for what it was: an invitation.

Theron watched me, eyes darkening when his fingers gently skated across my skin, moving from my chin, down my neck to where my pulse still fluttered, and then lower as he slowly glided his touch over my tunic to move down between my breasts.

A small sound escaped me, and he tipped closer, his mouth centimeters away from mine as his hand continued to migrate. Between my ribs, down to my bellybutton until one finger pushed the hem of my shirt aside, his touch at my lower stomach burning right through me.

"Do you want me to stop?" he whispered, the question fueling the fire burning inside me even more.

I shook my head, unable to speak. "I will," he said, his voice rasping in a way that scratched over my skin.

It was as if I could feel him everywhere—consuming me so entirely I didn't know where he started and I ended.

"No," I answered, only to be met with a low groan.

The tip of his finger dipped beneath the waistband of my pants, a taunting movement that had my blood boiling, the anticipation sending every inch of my skin buzzing.

"Have I told you how beautiful you are, Rialey?"

My back arched as his touch moved lower, so close to where I needed him, I considered begging. I didn't respond, merely soaked up his praise as his lips skated along the scar at my cheek before he kissed the corner of my mouth.

"Breathtaking," he murmured, his fingers finally finding me—stroking—moving in a way that had me squirming beneath him. When his fingers dipped inside me, his palm sliding against my most sensitive part, I gasped.

Theron's kiss was slow and languid, as if he longed to drink every sound that pushed past my parted lips. He moved and worked, pushing closer until I could feel him against my hip, hard and strong.

My body tensed, eyes squeezing shut as he kissed me deeper. I shuddered until his kisses turned light, his hand sliding from beneath my trousers.

When I opened my eyes, he looked completely satisfied, though I knew better. I reached for him, but he shifted away, a small smirk forming on his lips.

"Another time," he whispered. "No more nightmares."

Theron pulled me closer until my head rested on his chest. The steady thump of his heart calmed me as it reminded me he was alive—*we* were alive.

The goddess of death had not taken us yet.

Chapter Forty-Six

Caius

As night carried on out in the forest, I found myself restless in my room, running over Florence's words. The intensity in her tone needled me.

I paced, sorrow and rage dancing inside of me as the fire crackled in the hearth.

Giving up on my sleepless night, I pulled my boots on and took to the temple's halls. I wandered amidst the shadows and moss. The stone building had become one with the forest over the years. So much so that I could feel the magic in the walls when I skated my fingers across the smooth dips and curves.

I found myself in the largest room in the temple, the ghost of incense wrapping around me when I stared at the owl statue toward the back of the room.

Taking a deep breath, I walked to the door behind the statue. Magic buzzed over my skin, making the hairs at the back of my neck stand on end. There was something powerful here—something I'd never experienced before.

I pushed the door open to the courtyard, my boots stepping onto the squelching moss that had formed. Cool air kissed my skin, with the smallest glimmer of light peeking out in the distance as dawn approached.

The bodies I'd expected to see were nowhere to be found, save for one at the very center.

Verena lay on mossy roots, her brown hair fanning out beneath her. Ivy crawled over the priestess robes she wore. The bloodstains were nowhere to be found.

Wings fluttered overhead, and I looked up to find an owl swooping low, white feathers standing out in the now green courtyard. The creature swooped low, carrying something golden in its mouth.

I stood stunned as the owl lowered, leaving the golden artifact in Verena's hand and gliding upward to perch on one of the low branches, black eyes watching for whatever would come.

In the blooming morning light, the ivy and moss began crawling toward Verena, the forest swallowing her body until there was nothing but spring left in her absence.

Flowers bloomed where the corpse had been, violet and blue as the sun rose over the foggy landscape.

A gasp sounded, and I turned, almost in slow motion, to see Narela at the entrance to the courtyard, a hand clasped over her mouth.

With eyes wide, she would not look away from the forest floor.

"What?" I asked, almost frantic. This was magic I'd never seen before, and by the looks of it, Narela knew what it meant.

"A Queen of the Wilds," she whispered. "She's been chosen by Eirdis."

Chapter Forty-Seven

Verena

Death tasted sweet, like honey and herbs. It stuck between your fingers—lingered on your skin so that you'd remember her gentle whispers—the quiet that overcame you when she made you hers.

Death was warm like the sun, gentle like seeds of a flower floating through the air.

She reminded me of spring—rebirth. For she did not whisper dark secrets of the end but yearned for promises of the future.

My skin prickled with awareness. The cool press of moss and soil sticking to me like lingering death.

Roots crawled through the ground to reach me, to seek a source of life, but in me, they'd find none.

Each pierce of my skin stung, but I kept my eyes closed until I was moving toward the surface, as if the forest was breathing life into me—or I was breathing.

The sun warmed my skin, and I gasped, now lying on the surface of the forest floor, surrounded by small flowers and dappled sunlight as the roots shoved deeper, pushing themselves into my veins, drinking whatever blood remained there.

My panting breaths.

My beating heart.

Whispers and the rustling of leaves.

The roots receded, and I crawled to stand, unsteady on my shaking legs. I looked at my palms, noting the green tint to my veins and the moss still clinging to my skin like sticky death.

"I—"

I gasped, looking out at the courtyard of the temple. A dozen witches bent at the knee, their heads bowed in my direction.

My eyes locked with Caius, his gaze holding mine, full mouth agape in shock.

"I'm alive," I whispered, hoping it to be true.

Flashes of my decision entered my mind. The way my power screamed inside of me, begging me to release it. Still, I held on, molded the minds of the soldiers to my will, losing myself entirely.

Slowly—so slowly—Caius tilted his chin downward, lowering until one knee touched the mossy soil.

There were no remnants of winter here, only the thawed possibilities of spring.

A small smile found its way to his lips, and I stared, my beating heart going strong and steady.

"My Queen," Narela whispered, looking up until her silver eyes found mine. "We've been waiting for you."

Chapter Forty-Eight

Theron

I awoke to soft earth and yellow light, my eyes cracking open to see the inside of our tent.

Rialey stirred where she'd been on my chest, her dark hair kissing the sides of her cheeks—dark eyelashes fluttering before she looked at me.

I shifted, sweat sliding down my spine. It was warm. *Really* warm.

As a child, I'd never known anything but stories of seasons depicted in the paintings hung around the palace. I knew there'd been a garden in Marmere—knew the strife Alphaird's endless winter had caused its people. My father seemed to curse the land more for what it had done to the kingdom. Working hard to find a solution to famine, he'd found the southern part of the kingdom, the area furthest from the Waldwood, could produce food—but never enough.

I'd never been lacking, though. My father ensured that the palace would never feel the struggles of the kingdom. Maybe it would be a reminder of his failure, or maybe he was merely selfish.

Rialey closed her eyes, nuzzling closer. "You're so warm," she murmured, her words causing me to snap out of my sleepy haze.

I shook her shoulder gently. "Rialey, wake up."

Something was off, though I didn't believe we were in danger.

Rialey seemed to realize as she stood up, feeling the fabric of the tent beneath us, realizing what I'd realized only moments ago.

"It's..." She looked around, eyes frantic. "It's warm," she said. "The ground is soft, too."

We scrambled to the tent's entrance, unzipping the fabric to reveal a forest filled with melting snow. Most of the white powder had turned to liquid, the trickling of water sounding somewhere in the distance. Birds chirped overhead, and I knelt. The wet soil squelched where my knee landed as I fingered a small flower bud sprung up from the ground.

"Something's happened," Rialey said, her tone tense.

I tugged at the sleeves of my thick tunic, rolling them to the elbow. "Do you think the forest would lend us its magic in a rebellion?" I asked, tossing a smirk over my shoulder. I still felt a tightness in my muscles—the tension of uncertainty—and knew my smirk was only halfhearted.

Rialey's stony expression matched the worry I felt. Something had changed, certainly. It could be felt in the warm breeze rustling newly sprung leaves. The pines held their needles, but growing in their midst were trees that had sat dormant for nearly thirty years.

When Rialey came to stand next to me, my smirk fell. "Not likely," she answered, "But we should figure out why this curse has been lifted."

We rode in silence, stopping every so often to let our horses eat grass whenever we found a small clearing. I tugged on the reins, pulling my horse's head away from the rich foliage that had seemingly grown overnight.

The magic of the Waldwood hummed in the air, swirling around us when we passed over the border, but we'd found nothing of interest save for the beauty of the woods.

Thick tree trunks stood tall, boasting of wisdom and age. Their roots burrowed deep beneath the ground, thick as the smaller trees in the forests around Marmere.

The deeper we plunged into the Waldwood, the more prevalent the change in weather. Moss coated the bark of the trees and the forest floor. My horse walked steadily as I looked at the mushrooms jutting from fallen logs and the small violet flowers that had bloomed.

This was the beauty King Wineslowe had leeched from the kingdom.

I'd long since known that our chances of finding the covens were small. They'd grown so few following my father's initial attacks, but Bloodbane seemed to believe there would be witches deep in the woods, ready to fight for their freedom.

It didn't stop the knot of worry that tangled in my chest. There were so many factors to consider, and as the kingdom's future king, I'd need to take on the responsibility of puzzling the pieces—winning this war.

My shoulder ached as the memory of Keslow surfaced. Amias had suggested extravagance—something to make a statement to the soldiers who'd retreated.

I could imagine the anger my father would feel and the way his face would redden, veins popping out at his neck. As a child, such an image frightened me, for I did not want to be the victim of my father's wrath. As an adult, though, I'd found that the entire kingdom had fallen victim to the evil king, and I wanted nothing more than to be a part of healing Alphaird, though I lacked the confidence necessary to voice the ideas I'd been conjuring.

We'd taken Keslow, but there was still the matter of Vespahr and his loyalty to my father. That loyalty only stretched as far as his own personal gain. The second my father fell, Vespahr would be there lurking—waiting to make himself king. A Vespahrian rule would reap nothing but sorrow, and I had it in mind to take Branwood next. Assassinate the lord when he'd least expect it. It would weaken my father, but more than that, it would protect the kingdom from the man most likely to capitalize on its weakness.

"Do you think there's anything left?" Rialey mused from her horse walking beside mine. She shifted uncomfortably in the saddle, the corners of her mouth pulling downward.

"I'd like to hope there are covens hidden here. If I did not believe that, I never would have sent those girls beyond Marmere's walls."

Rialey winced.

"Did *you* not believe there would be anything here?" I questioned; my eyes sliding to her.

A somberness took over her features, and I longed to kiss it away.

"I liked to believe I was helping," she answered. "Though beyond that, I couldn't allow myself to think about what happened after. It would demolish the illusion I'd conjured."

I swallowed, understanding her meaning fully. Maybe helping the witches escape the dungeons had been a feeble attempt at assuaging my own guilt after the witch hunts. I liked to believe it was more than that, and maybe it was. It very well could have been both. Selfishness and altruism were not always mutually exclusive.

"Do you ever think about it?" she asked. "How many witches died because of us?"

I cleared my throat. "Do you ever think about how many survived?" I watched her carefully, looking beneath the layers. She felt guilt about a lot of things—unsure of her ability to gain an alliance with whatever covens existed in the Waldwood, but I was certain she could do it.

I did not want Rialey to pick herself apart until there were no pieces left. I'd been a victim of that once, and it left me hollow—drowning in my own nightmares from the past. If she did not believe herself worthy, her past mistakes would keep her from her potential.

"You need to forgive yourself," I said.

Rialey turned away, her voice barely audible above the wind. "What I've done is unforgivable."

My brow furrowed. "Then you should have compassion for the version of you who did it and recognize who you are becoming."

She stayed silent, so I carried on. "We will win over the Waldwood," I asserted. "Regardless of your belief in yourself, we will. And then we will take Branwood. We will secure an alliance with Eirhiondus. We will win the war we've started."

Rialey finally looked at me, and I breathed deeper. "You sound like a king." She tossed me a small smile, and I drank up the way her somber expression shifted. "I hope you're right."

CHAPTER FORTY-NINE

RIALEY

Misty fog stretched out over the forest floor, swirling above the moss and flowers that had appeared upon our waking.

I'd never seen a spring—not truly, and I found that with every step my horse took through the woods, I couldn't stop taking in the world around me.

My favorite part was the sound of trickling water that became a constant companion as we rode. We'd stepped over the source of its sound, a small creek with smooth rocks and pebbles next to a steep bank. Trees encased us, and small purple flowers hung like bells from their curled stems.

Trees that had once appeared dead and barren suddenly held small leaves and buds.

The kingdom had woken up, and I was thankful for the distraction.

While we didn't know where we were headed, the further we descended into the Waldwood, the more my nerves grew. In the past months, I'd longed for home, but home would not be what it once was. It was difficult to walk through a place I'd belonged to so fully, realizing there may no longer be space for me here.

The covens had moved on—changed in the way King Wineslowe had forced them to, and I'd been left on the outskirts, creating a name for myself that might not serve me well where we were going.

The horse beneath me jolted, stepping to the side so quickly my calf was wedged between the horse's side and a tree, the rough bark scratching through my clothing. With a firm grip on the reins, I pushed my hands forward and squeezed the horse's sides, encouraging her to walk.

Theron's mount halted, ears jutting forward as if his gelding were listening to something.

"I don't know what she's spooked at," I said, voice breathless. "Can you see anything?"

With a grunt, Theron steered his horse around a tree, over a log, and then halted. "Come on," he warned, but the horse did not move.

Finally choosing to dismount, I followed his lead, dismounting my horse and leading her across the forest floor.

"There," Theron said, pointing through the trees to ivy-covered stones. The temple stood as a beacon in the distance, sending my heart into a gallop.

We hadn't passed a village on our way to the temple, but this temple's coven could be long gone.

Every step toward the structure sent an odd mix of anticipation and dread out from my chest and to my limbs. I didn't know if I should be afraid of what was to come, or if I should be relieved—grateful that I finally found my way back to the Waldwood.

Above us, a crow swooped from overhead, black feathers gliding up into one tree where it perched next to an owl. The owl's black eyes sent a shiver down my spine. It appeared to be watching me—us. And the crow—

The heavy front door of the temple creaked open until a small figure emerged. A golden leaf pin stuck out from the back of her brown hair. She stared at me, brown eyes searching with an eerie calm.

I reached for my magic on instinct, but there was little I could do now that we approached as ourselves. Her pale skin contrasted against the smattering of freckles across her nose, a distinct gap between her front teeth that had me searching my mind for why she looked so familiar.

"Rialey," Theron voiced, nearly a whisper. There was something in his tone—something he wished to tell me but didn't.

It wasn't until we left our horses near the wall, and I stood at the base of the temple steps, that I realized who stood before us.

The last time I'd seen her had been months ago. Since then, she'd filled out, her skin looking less sallow, and her cheeks carried a natural flush high on her cheekbones.

My mouth dropped open, my emotions clawing their way to the surface, tearing into my lungs and making it difficult to breathe. Of all the witches we could have met, I didn't expect the one that stood before me.

A man joined her at the top of the steps, shorter than Theron, but broader. He carried two swords on his back and kept a stony expression as his eyes never left Theron's. I recognized a hint of disdain in his gaze. This man knew who Theron was and believed him to be worthy of the title he'd received since our escape from the palace.

If the witches saw him as the Traitor Prince but would not accept his leadership or the Guild, there'd certainly be no hope for me.

My stomach soured when Verena stepped closer, tipping her chin down in acknowledgement just before her brown eyes cut to mine.

"Welcome home, Witch Hunter."

I winced at the name but shoved the beast inside down. Guilt would not consume me. If I were to make an impact and gain an alliance here—one we desperately needed—I'd need to believe that I could be forgiven. If not by myself, by those who saw the glimmer of good I'd done.

"It's good to see you, Verena." Theron stepped forward, only to be met with the man's blade at the tip of his throat. He'd moved from the steps so swiftly, I'd barely had time to react and grab my dagger.

Sweat beaded on his upper lip as the man glared at the Traitor Prince, and I regretted reaching for my dagger instead of a sword. I still clenched it. The cool metal bit at my palm—ready to be used.

"I recommend not killing the future king," I warned, only to be met with a scoff.

The man kept his sword steady at Theron's neck even as he looked at me. If Theron used the distraction, he'd undoubtedly win, but we weren't here to initiate a war with the Waldwood.

"He will be no king of mine," the man snarled.

The scent of dried lavender and honey hit me, dragging a memory up from the far corners of my mind. I'd been sitting in a small shop off the city square in Marmere, head throbbing as I sipped on a cup of tea.

The night prior, I'd watched a witch die in the street—blamed myself for my own inadequacy. Every emotion I'd had that morning surfaced. The guilt and shame I'd felt, the anxiety that struck as a man approached me, face shielded by a cloak and mask. He'd sat across from me with a proposition—a way to right our wrongs.

He called himself Eryx, and in my desperation—my sorrow—I'd agreed.

Verena walked slowly from her perch atop the stone steps. The climbing ivy that trailed up either side of the temple seemed to whisper her name as she moved. There was power here—magic, but it did not feel like my own.

I'd been around dreamwalkers, and theirs didn't feel like this either—this was something new. It was something powerful.

Verena placed a hand on the man's shoulder. "Caius," she said, "he has good intentions. I've *checked*."

The last word echoed through the trees, my brow furrowing. "You've...*checked*?" I asked, keeping my attention on the man who'd threatened Theron.

"It's intrusive, and I don't like doing it, but after what happened here a few weeks ago..."

My head snapped toward her, brows furrowed. "What do you mean intrusive?" Horror washed over me—the feeling of being violated so completely as I put the puzzle pieces together. "Were you...were you in my mind?"

Verena's mouth pressed into a thin line as if she were displeased. "Only for a moment. We have a lot to catch up on, Witch Hunter." She looked to Caius and back again. "Please," she gestured to the doors. "Narela waits inside. She has been rather helpful since so much has changed." A smile lit in her eyes as she gestured around to the area surrounding us. "Spring, goddesses, power, and all. We should speak more in the temple."

Theron smiled, the one meant to charm and win over the company we held. I did not believe it would work here. "Then we should await your answers with bated breath." He, too, gestured to the door. "Shall we?"

We followed Verena and Caius up the stone steps and crossed into the temple. Vines climbed up the walls, covered in moss and growth as if Eirdis's temple was one with the Waldwood. The goddess of wild things, the hallway. It was strange the Guild had picked this particular goddess for the rebellion. Growing up, my family had lived in the coven near Abellona's temple—the goddess of death. Dark gray stone made up her temple. At night, shadows seemed to kiss the archway leading to the entrance.

I'd been in the temple before—learned the stories of such a goddess. Represented by crows, the goddess of death was said to have possessed equal parts wrath and gentleness. Abellona ruled the afterlife, protecting the burial locations where witches were laid to rest.

What I wanted to know as we descended the stairs of Eirdis's temple before walking through the double doors was if Eirdis possessed the same wrath as the goddess of death, and if that wrath would be turned on us.

The library opened before us with ornately carved stone archways leading to the different rooms. Tucked against the walls, stacks of leather-bound books lined the shelves.

Magic hummed from every inch of the library. We walked through different rooms as I soaked in the owl statues and plants sprouting from where the stone floors met the stone walls.

We stepped down a set of three stairs into a room with lush furniture. The green couches sat around a small coffee table. On one, a priestess sat watching us enter, standing at our arrival. Her white hair reminded me of the disguise I'd donned in Keslow, but her dark skin and silver eyes reminded me of the stories I'd heard about the moon goddess when growing up.

Behind her, a tapestry hung the entire length of the wall, thread stitched to show Eirdis with a bow in hand, flora and fauna surrounding her as she looked out between the trees.

"Please, sit." Verena gestured to the empty couch where I hesitantly lowered myself next to Theron. I inched closer on instinct, clinging to the only being in the room I trusted.

My eyes hopped to the woman who'd been waiting for us—Narela, she'd said—to Verena.

"Explain," I urged, wondering how much of my thoughts she could decipher. I'd never known dreamwalkers to enter the minds of those awake, and found her abilities entirely unsettling. Invasive was not a harsh enough description for the violation I'd felt. While I understood the need to know we were not a danger, I deserved to know why she'd suddenly obtained a level of power I'd never seen.

"If you're referring to how I ended up in the temple," Verena started, her back straight where she sat on the couch across from us. Caius refused to sit, but stayed by her side, arms folded across his broad chest. "I have Caius to thank for that. If your question has to do with my position among the witches, the title is rather new to me. I feel Narela could explain better. And as for my magic?" she said. "I tried to enter the minds of those awake once, and it cost me my life the first time. I tend to use the ability sparingly now."

My brow furrowed. For what it was worth, Theron did not seem phased by her explanations—or lack thereof. He shifted forward; elbows resting on his knees. "I'm anxious to hear more about this new title. As you may realize, we've come representing the Guild of Eirdis. I'd like to be very forthcoming in the information I offer you in the hopes that it should, at some point, lead to an alliance. We are looking for aid in removing my father from the throne."

Caius scoffed, looking toward a golden owl statue that stood in the corner.

"Then you're talking to the right people," Narela said, her smile wide as she gestured to Verena. "You are, in fact, speaking with our queen."

All eyes flicked to Verena, a slight blush forming high on her cheeks.

Nerves stirred in my gut. Verena didn't just speak for this coven; she now spoke for all the Waldwood. While this was great news for the alliance, this would be fatal news should she or anyone she trusted choose to harbor hatred for me or Theron. Looking at Caius, I had a genuine fear of the latter.

Theron tilted his head downward. "I apologize," he said. "I would like to extend not only my respect but my congratulations."

Verena shifted uncomfortably in the chair. "Thank you," she nearly whispered.

"I've been asked to relay information regarding the temple, Verena's chosen position, and her magic."

"It is not because I do not know," Verena interrupted. "It is merely that this is new, and I feel Narela has a better grasp of things pertaining to the gods."

Narela smiled, nodding her agreement. "That being said, I have some genuine concerns about where you stand. A traitor prince is, in fact, still a prince. Should you become king, I'd like to know a bit about your vision for your rule—for the Waldwood."

Caius grunted, and frustration bubbled up inside me like a kettle ready to scream. "Do you have a question?" I shot him an icy glare, but he didn't balk.

"Lord Bloodbane has been orchestrating this rebellion for years, so you can imagine my surprise when I find out the prince of this land has suddenly been chosen to not only lead but become the future king."

Theron took in every inch of the man, his assessing gaze almost frigid. "I take it you do not agree?"

Caius stepped forward, and I instinctively reached for my dagger, only to be met with a warning look from Verena, her soft edges turning to something sharper—a blade in her own right.

"What of your history?" Caius questioned. He stepped right up to Theron, who remained seated on the embroidered fabric of the couch. The prince did not back away, keeping his chin raised as Caius spat in his face. "You went on the witch hunts," he seethed. "I'm not convinced that a traitor to the crown wouldn't later become a traitor to his own kingdom." Caius snarled, a hatred so deep it had grown roots—sprouted from something much deeper within him. "Your loyalties are inconsistent, and your strategies for helping the kingdom—helping our people did far more harm than good."

"I understand," Theron said, his tone even. "War has already begun, and we will need all the help we can get. Witches have spent so much time suppressing their magic, they've become weakened. Regardless of what you believe about me, I've come to the Waldwood to gather the witches to strengthen a rebellion with which *your* loyalties lie." Theron's tongue rolled along his cheek, the only sign he was thinking about his next words carefully, tasting them to see how they'd fare in this negotiation. "If you do not trust me to be king, so be it, but for now, consider working with us toward a common goal, and maybe I can earn your trust along the way."

"You will never have my trust," Caius nearly growled.

Theron tapped the carved wooden arm of the couch we sat on, one brow raised. "If you have another recommendation for who should rule this kingdom once the Waldwood has her independence, I'd love to hear it—in fact, I'd be happy to step down and allow someone more equipped at leading to do so."

A lie. Theron longed to be king—he was fit for the role as well. I also did not believe he'd step down so easily, considering his blood oath.

I sat in silence, still as the books lining the surrounding shelves.

"I fear that some choices," Narela began, "are simply not ours to make."

We all turned to her, a true priestess, as the firelight from the sconces kissed her cheeks. "The gods make their own decisions, this we know. The coven of Eirdis has been empty a long time, but other covens still remained—though far deeper in the forest." Narela looked to Verena as she cleared her throat, shifting in her seat. "The temple is all that endures, but the message was clear. When Verena passed along with the others, we laid our dead at the temple's center, among the wild things as an offering to Eirdis."

Her words came slow like thick honey dripping from a spoon—sweet and rich—crafted from the wisdom of an entire kingdom. "The forest..." she paused, leaning forward. "The forest swallowed her, and when she came back, so did her magic, but it is *more.* We've no prophecies here, but an owl swooped low and dropped something in the soil, and we *felt* the ground tremble—the seasons changed outside of the courtyard following. As you know," she glanced at me, "Above the goddesses, we live by the magic of the Waldwood—and she has taken an offering and chosen us a queen. We will need to find the others."

I lifted my chin, watching Verena smooth down the fabric of her robes. "And what did *you* experience?" I asked, wanting to hear from the witch herself.

Verena's eyes held mine, unwavering. The blade had returned, her magic rushing over me until I felt the scratch of wood on my spine, the ache of sore muscles, and the sting of a blade carving into my cheek. Hot breath, rancid and foul, blew on a cloud toward my face as a sob broke free.

"Such a pretty face," he whispered, the soldier's dark eyes swallowing the light from the window in my childhood bedroom. "And now it bears my mark."

The door swung open, my father's figure filling the doorway. His firm hand squeezed painfully around his axe just before he barreled forward, shoving the man off me.

I stood frozen, watching the men fall to the ground, grappling with their weapons.

An arrow through my father's chest.

My mother in the doorway.

An illusion to distract as a sword slashed through mist and shadow.

One word from my mother's lips.

Run.

I blinked; the memory ripped from the deepest parts of my soul as Verena stared at me. I felt her then, in my mind and all around.

Death, she whispered, but her lips did not move.

Her magic retreated, and I sucked in a lungful of air. Theron stayed focused on me, his brow pinched in concern.

"I've decided," Verena said, and the entire room stilled to listen. "Your magic is weak. You will work with Narela." Verena stood, movements graceful as she smoothed down her robes once more. "As for your plans to ask Eirhiondus for aid, I happen to agree, though we will not offer them a piece of the Waldwood, Prince Theron. First, we should get word to the other covens, spend time regaining our strength." She gave me a pointed look. "Being in the forest will help with yours, Witch Hunter.

"After, we can travel north, but I must tell you, I should need to rest. My magic is not infinite, even as I channel from the Waldwood, and what I've just done has worn on me."

Verena turned to exit the room, but turned just as one foot touched the stone step leading out of the sitting area. "I have seen your weaknesses, and now I show you mine," she said, her skin taking on a pallor. "If we are to begin trusting one another, it's important we know nothing but truth. I will not play negotiation games. We have a common goal, and we should see it through."

Without another word, she left, leaving us behind with the ghost of her magic lingering on our skin.

"I will prepare a few rooms," Narela said, standing abruptly.

"One," Theron corrected, and I sucked in a breath, coughing gently. "One should be fine."

Narela nodded, gesturing for us to follow as we were led up the stairs and toward the heart of the temple, anxiously awaiting a more private arrangement so we could discuss what we had seen.

Chapter Fifty

Rialey

Thick vines climbed up the stone walls of our bedroom, reaching as high as the ceiling where delicate purple flowers hung above us like the limbs of a weeping willow.

Moonlight streamed in from the window on the far wall, and I turned over, looking at the thick leaves that had sprouted in mere days. Theron's deep breathing behind me grounded me as I gazed at the forest.

My magic already felt stronger—as if the Waldwood was feeding my power. It made my skin itch—eager to test out a muscle long since ignored.

In the quiet, the memory I'd almost forgotten crept to the front of my mind, and I saw gold. My power called to me just as the longing to see my parents did—a deep need gripping me like a vice.

I crafted the vision, careful to get the details just right as I pulled on the thread of my magic. It brushed over my skin, cool and soft like paint on a brush as the image took shape. My mother sat by the window in a chair, her long hair as dark as mine, with a slight wave that reminded me how much she loved the sea. Her delicate hand rested below her chin as she gazed at the forest.

My father took shape behind her, his features echoing my own. I was sure to include the light freckle on his jaw. In childhood, I'd always felt it softened him—just like my mother. Maybe the mark was her doing, a kiss she'd left on him that lingered and reminded him the world did not always require a blade.

They talked to one another in my illusion, but there was no sound. My power, though strengthened by our time in the forest, had limits. They felt more like phantoms than the real thing, and part of that brought sorrow into my tightening throat.

"Do you want to talk about it?"

My focus slipped, as well as my magic; my parents dissolving like a memory. I turned to find Theron's brows pinched together in concern.

"Talk about what?" I asked, my eyes stinging with the memories of my childhood.

"Rialey," he whispered, fingers gently skimming the side of my cheek. "I saw what happened."

The stinging in my eyes gave way to tears as I watched him, emotion pouring from me like a cup overflowing.

I'd sat with it for too long.

Lived with all of it for too long.

"Rialey," he repeated. "I'm so sorry." His hand moved to the back of my head, warm and gentle as he pulled me to his chest. I buried myself there as he became the grave to my sadness—a place to let it rest—to come back and remember when the world became too much.

"I didn't mean to, but when Verena entered our minds, I saw—"

A sob broke from my lips as I *felt*. My guilt and shame, the sorrow of loss, the painful ache of grief came out until time vanished. I didn't know how long he held me there, but I cried until I felt empty—until my breathing slowed, and I could think clearly.

Theron had always known more truth about me than anyone. As Eryx, he'd known about my magic—seen me night after night fight for something *good* in a kingdom of evil. And as Theron?

Theron had now seen it all.

"The nightmare the other night," Theron began as I pulled away from his chest. "Do those happen often?"

I shook my head. "That was just about Keslow. The other stuff...I've tried so hard to forget it, I thought I'd succeeded."

My hand came to his chest, and I felt his pulse beneath my fingertips.

"My father thought me too soft when I was a child," Theron admitted, blinking as if the confession surprised him. "That's why he forced me on the witch hunts. I'd killed despite every fiber of my being screaming at me not to. And even as I learned more—did better—I still carried that guilt with me." Theron gently brushed back a strand of my hair, his eyes now boring into mine. "While I was in the Waldwood during the hunts, I—" he swallowed. "I'd come back from bathing to hear the men boasting of the atrocities they committed against one of the witches. That night, I'd helped her escape.

"It was my first act of rebellion against my father, and after I'd done it, I *craved* it. Maybe it was simply to assuage my guilt, but I *needed* to do something. I see taking the throne the same way. It is an act of rebellion—exactly what the Guild is looking for."

I soaked up his words, watching the fierce determination pictured in the hard set of his jaw, the way he believed what he said so fully, the force of it could be felt where my heart kept beating.

"You are going to be a great king, Theron."

He gave me a tight-lipped smile as silence hung between us, carrying the weight of all we'd walked through and experienced together.

"How is your magic now that we've been in the Waldwood?" he asked.

"Stronger." I didn't know how much of my illusion he'd seen, but the control I'd felt along with the details I could conjure gave every sign that the forest was feeding my magic. The black of night turned purple as the sun climbed toward the horizon, threatening the arrival of dawn. "I'm meant to train with Narela after breakfast."

Theron smiled. "Are you nervous?"

I scoffed, looking behind him at the wall near our bed. "There's hardly time to feel anything as it is. So no, I'm not."

"I'm meeting with Verena about Vespahr today. I still believe he needs to be dealt with prior to our departure from the continent. He's chaotic and forceful—a true opportunist."

I grinned, matching his expression as his heart continued to beat beneath my hand. "Are *you* nervous?" I asked.

Theron leaned in closer, my pulse kicking up at his nearness. "Yes," he whispered before his lips pressed gently to my forehead. "Yes, I am."

The wolf ran through the trees. With a coat white as the memory of snow, it scampered toward the edge of a log before bounding onto the moss-covered soil.

The threads of gold stayed in my vision, but instead of tugging on one, I wove them together, creating an illusion that was more fluid—more convincing.

My magic had always worked from a distance in the town square, but this was of a different caliber. With the Waldwood feeding its power into me, I could maintain focus and paint something greater.

"Are you ready?' Narela asked, and I nodded, gazing at the image as events unfolded before me.

Narela's wolf, with its brown coat speckled with white hairs, leapt toward my wolf playfully, pouncing and jumping until its mouth gently bit at my illusion's neck.

I slipped, the movements becoming choppier, the wolf tipping in the wrong direction, breaking the accuracy of what we were trying to do.

Sweat beaded on my brow, slowly dripping down until my eyes stung as my illusion struggled with the added element of another's.

Narela released her magic, and I took that as permission to release mine.

"We will need to work on that," she said, her tone flat.

When I glanced in Narela's direction, she gave me a forced smile, glancing away as if to avoid telling me my illusion was terrible.

It was.

"Where will we be going?" I asked, knowing there were talks of moving to another coven. I recalled the early morning, the memories I crafted in the privacy of my room. A part of me dreaded the possibility of seeing my old home, but yet, another part hoped for it too. Like a sore muscle you kneaded to the edge of pain, I couldn't stop myself from poking the bruise that was my past.

"Abellona's temple."

My stomach dropped, the breath leaving my lungs in a rush. My rapidly beating heart made me feel dizzy as I tried to maintain composure. "Are there..." I winced, hating myself for even asking the question. "Are there many left?"

Dappled light from between the trees moved with every gentle wind, floating around us. Narela tilted her head to the side in understanding. "Your patron goddess?" she questioned, her voice softer—gentler than before.

I nodded, unable to voice the answer, but giving it nonetheless.

"There's quite a bit left," she said, her eyes softening right along with her tone. "New and old, I'm sure it will be difficult for you."

I swallowed, neither confirming nor denying.

"You are strong," she said. Turning to walk back through the forest to the temple. Before she disappeared behind a thick tree trunk, Narela tossed a look over her shoulder. "But your illusions still need work when reacting to external stimuli. Keep practicing."

I blinked, watching her disappear before gold flashed in my vision. Despite the sweat still sticking to my skin, I wove another image—two. I made the wolves dance in slow motion, nipping and jumping like pups.

I smoothed the movements out until my mind was empty—until exhaustion wore on me, and I felt ready to return to the temple—ready to pack for a place I'd long since forgotten.

CHAPTER FIFTY-ONE

VERENA

The magic inside me felt wild and unstable. More than that, it left me weary and weak. In the library, I'd exerted more energy than I had since the battle outside of the temple.

My power, along with my influence, felt too big—like a pair of shoes that didn't quite fit. I walked as sure as I could, but deep down, I still had questions about the goddess and why I'd been chosen. I hadn't even *believed* in the gods and goddesses of the covens. Unsure and unsteady, I tried my best to feel right—feel normal as I circled the courtyard.

The owl sat perched high above, watching me struggle with every aching breath that rattled in my lungs. The warmer temperatures turned sticky and hot, something none of us were used to in a kingdom of constant winter. It echoed the slow and heavy feeling of my limbs when I stopped at the sound of a door opening.

I turned to find Caius waiting at the entrance, a wide smile on his face. The gentle pull of his mouth reminded me of who he was at his core. This side of Caius—the relaxed version of him—this felt as if it were a gift just for me. It was something I coveted.

"Can I help you?" I asked, my smile a mirror of his.

Caius pushed off the doorframe, stepping into the dappled light of the courtyard. The tree's shadows did nothing to break the sticky heat of the

Waldwood in summer. "I was hoping to go for a walk," he said, crossing his arms and looking toward the blazing sun. "But now I feel that walk would be much more pleasant in the library. It's always cooler down there."

I giggled, my exhaustion taking a backseat as I stepped toward him. He took my hand, his skin sending a jolt through my arm. "I would like nothing more than to join you in the library."

We walked in silence through the halls and down the steps into the heart of the temple. As we passed the neatly stocked shelves and made it to the back of the library, the sound of harsh breaths and soft moans sounded from behind one of the shelves.

I paused, my cheeks flushing at the realization. Caius stumbled a step, knocking the statue until it teetered on edge. He caught it, carefully placing it to rights, but the damage had been done.

From the other side of the shelf, Rona rounded the corner, lips swollen and blonde hair out of place.

I gasped when Florence joined her, looking just as disheveled.

"I'm sorry, I—"

Florence dropped low into a curtsy, her pale cheeks pink. "My apologies, Your Highness. We will take our leave."

Both women scurried out of the library, leaving me and Caius to stand dazed and somewhat shocked.

His laugh broke first, followed by one of my own pulled from the depths of my belly.

"That was—" he started.

"Quite the discovery," I finished, and we both laughed in earnest.

I felt lighter with him, separated from the chaos of my past. With Caius, I did not need to make the shoes fit; I could take them off, instead—forced to be nothing but the Verena from before.

Before I'd touched the goddess.

Before the Waldwood made her home in my marrow.

"You still look tired from yesterday," Caius commented, worry stitching his brow.

I turned toward the three steps that led to the couches where we'd spoken the previous day. I'd hated how easy it was for me to enter their minds, to rifle through their memories and see things I'd never been able to see before—before death had claimed me for herself.

The worst part was what I'd seen. While it was an effective tactic to prove myself to our guests, it still cost me to shoulder the burden of their pain. And that was what happened. You could not watch someone's nightmares unfold and fail to carry some of the weight. Their pain became mine, and I had to fight to keep hold of my own thoughts and feelings. It would have been easy to lose myself there.

"I am," I admitted, my fingers running along the carved pine furniture. The blue fabric covering the seat beckoned me, and I gave in, finding a seat.

Caius joined me, sitting close enough that I could feel the heat radiating off of him—my awareness heightened.

"I met with the prince this morning," I said, noting the way Caius stiffened beside me. His jaw ticked as he ground his teeth together. He hated the prince—something I understood, though I struggled with how deep that hatred seemed to run. I couldn't help but ask. "Has something happened?" I asked. "Between you and Prince Theron? I've never seen you this angry before."

"I've heard of him from the rebels—heard of the atrocities committed by his camp during the witch hunts."

There was something more—a layer I hadn't yet unearthed. "And?" I questioned.

Caius's sorrow-filled eyes met mine, his emotion clear. "He left you there," he nearly whispered. "When I found you, I—"

I nodded once in understanding. "He did," I confirmed. "But he saved me from a far worse fate."

"By chance," Caius answered, voice stronger. "You survived by chance."

My fingers moved to the base of my throat, feeling my pulse beneath thin flesh. I became aware of every breath, every rush of blood through my veins. I could feel it all—what it meant to be alive. The forest called to me there, an undercurrent of magic that thrummed right along with the pumping in my chest. It was as if she flooded me, as if I now shared a heartbeat with her.

"I did not believe in the gods," I admitted, "But after—" I couldn't bring myself to say the word *dying*. "I think that maybe fate did exactly as she pleased."

Theron had stayed true during our meeting, explaining Lord Vespahr's history and involvement in his capture. Motivated and greedy, the lord craved blood and power. I understood why Theron thought it important to deal with him—to make a statement in regards to the war.

"Prince Theron wishes to assassinate the Lord in Branwood."

"No," Caius's response was almost immediate.

I looked at him then, knowing he saw the determination in my gaze. "I agree with him," I admitted. "War has already begun. Vespahr and his guards are a powerful asset to the king. I believe it weakens the kingdom and makes a statement about the rebellion's intentions."

"So, you've decided to join him?" Caius questioned, his features twisting.

"I don't know if you realize this, Caius, but you are already a part of the rebellion he leads. While I understand your distaste for the prince you share a common goal. We would be fools not to accept what they offer. Whether he becomes king or not is not set in stone."

Caius turned, staring at the floor. His jaw ticked as he jumped from one thought to another. With some effort, I could find him there—enter his mind as easily as walking into the next room. It would cost me the little bit of energy I'd since regained, though, and I couldn't do it. The violation of it still didn't sit well with me, and I didn't wish to lose that boundary.

"Florence will need to get word to Bloodbane," Caius said. "We will need more than what we have here if we are to be successful. If we kill Vespahr, his guard will act accordingly."

"I know," I answered.

"How soon do you wish to leave?" he said.

I straightened my spine, hoping to force myself into the role I'd been given. I didn't know if it would ever feel a part of me. "As I said, war has already begun. We should leave within the week."

Chapter Fifty-Two

Theron

Every bump on the dirt road leading to Branwood jostled me as the covered, wooden carriage dug into my spine.

Along the back of the carriage, boxes of apples, supposedly grown along the southeastern coast in Portmorey, were stacked. When we passed through the city, Rialey would ensure that all the boxes appeared to be filled to the brim, and that we would each fit into her illusion by disappearing entirely. This cart was a produce cart, and nothing more.

With the newly changed season, it would make sense that merchant deliveries would increase. The likelihood that the cities and surrounding areas were no longer starving brought me a great deal of hope amidst all the sorrow.

Florence shifted where she sat next to Rona, looking just as uncomfortable as I felt. The four of us did not speak, merely waited for the shouts of the guards as we approached Branwood.

My heart beat wildly in my chest when we could hear the men in the distance over every creek of the wooden tires. With our actions in Keslow, there would be added security. Caius brought falsified documents, and Rialey would need to bear a good deal of the burden by using her magic to cast us all into a believable illusion.

If we were to fail—

"Whoa!"

Rialey's magic licked against my skin like a cool brush. All I could see were stacks of boxes and apples where my companions sat, but my rapid breaths gave it away. I did my best to quiet them. I could not be the reason we were stopped and discovered—not when we were so close to getting to Vespahr.

Muffled sounds drew my attention outside the carriage. I could hear Caius's deep baritone, explaining that he was a merchant delivering produce for the city.

Skeptically, the guard responded, but I could hear little save for his tone. The words were too difficult to make out.

From next to me, warm fingers clasped mine, and though I couldn't see Rialey, I could feel her there. The encouragement slowed my heart enough that I could breathe deeply—quietly as the back of the cart opened.

I stiffened, unable to see the guards through Rialey's magic. The voices were clearer, though.

"I suppose we couldn't take a crate?" The guard said as he grabbed one from the cart. The crate scraped against the wood, and I bit the inside of my cheek. We'd used what we had in terms of apples back near Eirdis's temple, but if they grabbed any more from the back of the cart, there was a good chance their hand would slip through an illusion like a blade through fog.

"Awe, go ahead!" Caius said, and I could hear the smile in his voice. "I pack a few extras just in case we lose something along the way, but just one. I'd like to have a few more to give out if I could."

I pinched my eyes closed, gripping Rialey's hand tighter until I swore she could hear my pulse—hear the truth behind the mask.

I'd always known I wanted to be king—believed I'd make a good one—but deep down, kings were only human. I feared for my life, doubted my abilities, and recognized that my position would be a gift should I obtain it.

And now, with Bloodbane's oath hanging over my head, becoming king would be more than a gift of power to make a difference—it would mean I kept my life.

Caius appeared at the back of the cart as the guard left with apples in hand. His tense jaw, the way he looked through the illusion as if he could truly see us, had awareness pricking at my spine. So much of this assassination relied on chance.

We'd stay at the tavern tonight. Florence would continue work at her apothecary, where she healed those from the city and surrounding areas. Just before dawn threatened to break over the horizon, at shift change, we would gain access to Vespahr's castle through a window on the south side.

The trees surrounding the castle the castle would be strong enough to hold me as I scaled them and gained access to his bed chambers while Caius, Rialey, and Rona infiltrated the dungeons to rescue any remaining prisoners.

Florence would remain out of sight in case we needed healing, but if the gods were on our side, all would go according to plan.

And the gods had to be on our side.

Even in Verena's absence.

"Are you ready?" Rialey said just as a shadow passed over the fabric covering of the cart. Sounds of horses' hooves on cobblestones and shouts surrounded us from the outside. We'd made it into Branwood.

I thought of Vespahr cornering me in my father's palace, desperate to gain favor and willing to betray the king to do it. I thought of his men on the streets of Marmere—my capture.

With the illusion gone, I could look at Rialey—really look at her. In the past months, she'd become the only person I felt I could truly trust.

I dragged my finger over the scar on her cheek, my chest tightening now that I knew—I'd *seen*—exactly how she got it. Her hand still clasped my other between us, and I allowed a small smile to pull at my lips.

"I am," I answered, but the statement felt weighted—heavy, like it carried more than at first glance. "I really am."

Vespahr's home resembled the palace of Marmere, but on a smaller scale.

Sweat dripped down my spine beneath my black tunic as I hauled myself up the tree nearest the building. When I got to the wall, I felt for the golden accents hoping they would create an adequate foothold.

I tested it, gaining my footing before hoising myself higher. Frustration gnawed at me with every stretch of my limbs and tug on my muscles as I scaled the wall. If I were to make it in this war, I would need to spend more time training.

Pale stones worked against me the higher I climbed, thankful for the blanket of darkness that kept me hidden. I'd donned a cloak, hoping the hood would aid in concealing my identity. If I were to be caught, it would be better for them to think me some opportunist thief than the traitor prince in charge of leading an entire rebellion against the king of Alphaird.

My foot broke through some of the ivy, causing my breath to rush out of my lungs. I shouldn't have trusted the fragil plant. With heart pounding, I held onto a loose stone and prayed to the gods of the Waldwood that it wouldn't crumble beneath my gloved fingertips.

The heat became unbearable, sweat slicking every inch of fabric on my body.

I found a different foothold just above one of the third-floor windows and pulled myself up by the remaining jagged stones to the window we sought.

Darkness consumed the little light from outside, giving me hope that Vespahr would be sleeping. With a pin, I carefully picked the lock and slowly pushed the window upward until a small gap formed. I shoved the window again, doing my best to remain quiet until the gap was large enough for me to push myself through.

I crawled onto the floor, gripping the sword at my thigh to keep its sheath from clanking against the windowsill.

When I looked up, the lavish four-poster bed sat empty. The fire in the hearth had been put out, no doubt on account of the warmer temperatures, but fear crawled up my throat as my gaze hopped around the room, expecting a shadow or monstrous creature to appear from some dark corner.

Vespahr wasn't in his room.

"Shit," I whispered, letting my eyes adjust more to the darkness before prowling to the door. The temptation to rifle through the lord's personal belongings pulled at my gut, but I snipped the thread. We came with one goal, and Rialey's safety, as well as the safety of all our companions, depended on my ability to complete this task.

The door to the bedchamber opened to a sitting room, dimly lit by candlelight and the frightened look of a pale servant, no older than twenty, standing with a tray in hand.

She startled when she saw me, my mind calculating a million ways this encounter could go wrong.

I should have killed her—slit her throat with one swift drag of my sword, but I shushed her, pressing my gloved finger to my lip.

"Don't," I whispered, though my tone still carried a biting edge—one I hoped she'd heed.

The girl stiffened, backing away toward the door with the candle gripped so tightly, her pale knuckles turned white. "And what will you do, *Traitor Prince?*"

"If you call the guards?" I asked, tilting my head to one side. I stood taller, stalking toward her in a predatory movement that I hoped would intimidate her enough to garner her silence. "I suppose I could drag this sword across your throat for betraying your king."

Surprisingly, her expression hardened, eyes icy like the tip of a dagger in winter. She carried her own blades, but they existed within her mind—in every spiraling thought I could almost see flash across her face. "You are no king of mine," she spat, before turning to slip through the heavy door and into the hallway.

I chased after her, losing her at the first turn where the hall split in two directions.

Cursing, I moved with little regard for silence through the palace, rushing to where I believed Vespahr's office would be.

Florence had debriefed me on the layout of Vespahr's palace. In my desperation, I ended up on the first floor, struggling to remember if his office would be to the left or right.

I tried a door to my right, wiggling the locked handle as footsteps sounded behind me.

The left proved more fruitful when the door opened to a dark room. I slipped inside, listening as guards moved through the halls.

My foot slipped, noting the stone steps behind me, shades darker than whatever stone was used on the outside of the palace.

Cool air greeted me along with the thick scent of rot and decay. I fought the urge to vomit, clenching my jaw and swallowing. Pulling the collar of my tunic over my nose, I listened for the sounds to stop—for silence to bring a sigh of relief.

"In his bedroom!" one guard shouted from further down the hall. "You, check the dungeons!"

My stomach churned, realization hitting me like ice water. I turned, my gloved fingers scratching over the stone walls as I plunged myself into the unknown.

With every panicked breath, I thought of Rialey's discovery when the guards poured downstairs—how I'd led them right to her.

I kept a firm hold on the hilt of my sword, my cloak flowing out behind me the deeper I went.

When a familiar, snake-like voice slithered across the damp floors, the hairs on the back of my neck stood up. I stiffened. listening as Vespahr taunted and teased.

"I've heard of you," he sneered, and I risked stepping closer.

Cloaked in shadows, Vespahr stood at the entrance to an opened cell. Behind the bars, Caius sat slumped on the floor, his hands shackled to massive metal nails in the stone overhead.

"You've been involved with the Guild for quite some time, now. A healer of sorts, but you have no magic." Dim light from the dwindling lantern on the ground highlighted Vespahr's contempt. His lip peeled back as if disgusted with Caius's lack of power.

"Magic is reserved for the women," Caius snarled, fighting against the chains.

Vespahr laughed, the sound throaty and vile. "So, you are a witch," he mused. "What a strange dynamic to only gift magic to the weakest among us." The lantern light flickered over the sharp, metal dagger Vespahr pulled from his belt. He examined it, picking the dirt from his nails with the knife's tip. "I'm afraid the Waldwood would not agree with my ambitions. No matter, though, I plan to drain her magic the moment I take my place as king over Alphaird."

Caius ground his teeth together, the hatred and anger radiating off every strained muscle.

"King Wineslowe expects his son at Marmere any day now. Which is why he waits at the northern border of Stromadale." Vespahr's shined boots tapped the stone floors with every movement forward. He crouched in front of Caius, whose chains rattled as he fought. "I plan to kill the king there. Trying times mean Alphaird will be desperate for a king. Of the lord's, I find myself to be the best fit." Vespahr tilted his head to the side, dragging his dagger across the stone floor in a menacing taunt. He clucked his tongue. "But that information dies with you."

The door at the top of the stairs creaked open, echoed shouts bouncing off the walls. We'd have to act quickly.

Without thought, I lunged forward, placing the tip of my sword at Vespahr's spine, shoving past the crack of bone and squelch of flesh until he fell to his knees, blood splattering across Caius's face.

Vespahr fell to the ground, his skull cracking against the stone. I kicked his lifeless body, wincing against the aroma of the dungeons.

"I would have liked to take longer doing that," I said, eyeing the key at his belt. "He really deserved far worse."

I plucked the warm metal from his belt, panic quickly taking hold as I fumbled with the cuffs around Caius's wrists. His sword, discarded or lost at the other end of the cell, gleamed in the faint light. My breath came out in a rush as the guards descended the rest of the stairs. They'd find us soon—all of us.

"Where's Rialey?" I demanded.

"Gone," Caius answered, rubbing his wrists once they were free of the iron. "She left with Rona and the two they had here for tomorrow's witching." Standing, Caius dusted off his pants and lifted his shirt to wipe the blood from his face. He rushed to the corner to grab his sword as shouts greeted us.

"Florence will treat them." His eyes widened as a guard barreled into the cell, sounding a warning to the others hidden in the depths of the dungeon. I spun, slashing my sword across his torso before plunging it forward, stabbing into the bellowing man as he sank to his knees.

The gurgling sounds from his mouth brought back memories of the witch hunts, and I fought to keep them at bay.

"The city will be crawling with men," I said, readying my stance for another attack. "Shit," I whispered, running a gloved hand down my face. "I let a servant go." The words came out like a confession, and for what it was worth, despite all his hatred, Caius didn't comment. He merely swooped in front of me, dragging his sword across the throat of the next guard to near us.

Chaos broke into the cell, more guards plunging into the darkness as metal met metal. My hand tightened on the hilt of my weapon, arm aching with every strike of the guard's attacking us.

Caius and I worked together as he held his weapon against another, and I crouched beneath them—a risky move, but one I took as I shoved my sword into the guard's chest. I yanked it from his corpse with a slick sound, turning as another guard, larger in size, charged me. His sword slashed across my chest, warm blood soaking into my shirt from the injury. I fought through the stinging, pushing forward to stab again—again—until my muscles felt worn and my vision became blurry.

With enough of the dungeons cleared, we bounded up the steps. I cradled my arm against my chest, fighting for breaths as the stinging turned to a sharp, decisive pain. Every inhale felt like nails digging into my lungs, but I ran through the awakened palace, finding my way to a back street with Caius at my side.

"You're injured," he said, his stony expression unmoving as his dark eyes found the tear in my tunic.

Shouts behind us had me shaking my head, commanding that we run.

Light broke over the horizon, early morning settling over Branwood. It would have been peaceful if not for the constant reminder that I'd been struck with a sword, and the fear that Rialey didn't make it out—that someone had caught up to them and—

I couldn't finish the thought.

We dodged buildings and dipped into alleyways until Caius pushed faster, running in front of me at full force to the wall. I grabbed his arm, eyes widening with the realization that he wanted to leave.

"We cannot leave without them!" I shouted, my breath serrated as it came out. We couldn't leave them—not in the city with Vespahr dead and his guards taking to the streets. There would be chaos.

Caius stepped forward, crowding my space. His eyes burned with the same intensity I'd seen the moment I met him as his nostrils flared. "I have someone to get back to," he asserted, no doubt speaking about Verena.

My chest squeezed for a different reason, memories of Rialey over the past few years breaking in—the way she looked on the streets of Marmere when my mask was removed. The feel of her hair slipping through my fingers, her breathless gasps in the forest on our way to the Waldwood after Keslow.

My voice lowered. "My someone is here," I said, jaw tight as Caius watched me.

When understanding softened his features, he nodded, turning to run down a side street toward the inn where we stayed.

I stood watch when he went in, the hilt of my sword heated against my gloved hand. I felt every dip and ridge in the spiraling handle and ran my finger across the twisted metal at the base of the blade.

Caius came barreling out of the inn just as the light turned from purple to a crisp gold. "They left for the wall," he panted. "The first thing that will happen is an increase of security around the city border. If we are to leave, we need to leave now."

Nervous energy zipped beneath my skin, making me restless as I tapped the hilt of my sword, shifted on my feet where I stood. "And if she is not there?" I questioned, my tone sounding accusatory.

"Prince Theron," Caius said, leaving no room for questioning."

"Rialey is strong. You have to trust her."

My gut churned, vomit threatening to rise up my throat at the thought of leaving her.

I swallowed it down, pushing my way to the walls of Branwood—pushing myself back into the forest surrounding us.

CHAPTER FIFTY-THREE

RIALEY

"We can't just continue on the road!" Florence shouted from her spot, driving the covered carriage.

With every stone, the carriage jostled, leaving the silver-haired woman moaning in pain.

Rona knelt in front of her, hands fixed to the gushing wound at her calf. Dark purple bloomed beneath her eyes, made stark by the yellow hue that had overtaken her wrinkled skin.

Guilt twisted in my gut at the likelihood we'd rescued two women just to lead them to their demise.

Vespahr's presence in the dungeons took us by surprise when we'd entered the darkened cell. If it weren't for Caius, we wouldn't have escaped.

I squeezed my eyes shut, fear winding up my throat like suffocating ivy. I was so tired of sacrifice and death—so tired of the destruction unleashed upon the kingdom because of one man. The scent of rot and decay had become permanent, and I no longer knew if I'd ever be able to outrun it.

"She can't walk!" I yelled out over the loud scrape and grind of wooden wheels across the road.

Rona looked up through sweaty strands of hair with a frown pulling at her lips and desperation shining in her eyes. "I can't heal her," she said, blood blooming on the fabric of her pants. "There's too much—" She shook her head. "There's more than just her leg. Things are *wrong*."

I glanced at the woman, eyes closed as she leaned on the wooden sides of the cart. Whether she could hear us or not, I didn't know.

Dirt marred her angular face, her lips taking on a blue tint. I ran my palm over her forehead, brushing matted hair away from her clammy skin. Pain sliced through me at the realization that we were watching her die.

"It's okay," the woman behind us rasped, clutching her stomach. Her olive skin appeared dull, brown eyes brimming with sorrow. "She knew her body was failing her. I'm surprised she made it this long."

The cart jolted to a stop, the latch clanking as it fell open, and the fabric of the cover was torn apart. "We have to go." Florence looked from Rona to me, to the half-dead witch before us. "We have to leave her."

The finality of it—the way we wouldn't have a chance if we didn't—struck me until my lungs burned with the icy fire of rage and sadness.

The witch who'd spoken, Kaida, she'd called herself, stood slowly before limping toward the woman lying in front of us. Pressing a gentle kiss to her temple, Kaida then gathered the tattered skirt of her dress, dirt smeared over her bare shoulders, and across the sleeveless fabric as she hopped off the cart. She leveled Florence with a stare.

"If I slow you down," she said, "Kill me. Don't let those men have me again."

Rona unhooked the horse from the cart, helping Kaida onto the creature's back before we ran through the trees. She gripped the horse's mane with a desperate need to survive.

Thorns cut through my pants, but I ignored the sting, my heart pounding with every hurried step—every pound of my boots into the mossy soil.

I looked back, watching Rona slow. She'd spent a lot of time trying to heal the other woman we'd left, and I didn't know what that had done to her body—what injuries she'd taken on.

Shouts rang through the trees, and the pit of my stomach twisted. I wanted to push faster—harder—to escape the chaos of the city and our failed mission. Escape the deaths that were now on my hands. Caius, the woman in the carriage we'd left, everyone else. It seemed all I knew how to do was bathe in the blood of those I wanted to save.

"Rialey!"

I turned, watching Theron and Caius push their mounts harder through the trees until they came into view.

When they slowed, the rapid beating of my heart slowed right along with them. I smiled wide, looking up at Caius, who sat atop a large bay mare. "Good to see you," I said, feeling the words deep in my bones.

His lips curled up into a small smile as Caius nodded.

The others gathered around us, but my gaze zeroed in on the tear in Theron's shirt and the angry, red gash open with seeping blood.

The color drained from my face before I walked to him, determined when I tugged on his boot in the stirrup.

"Get down," I demanded, and he chuckled, looking around the forest.

"I don't know if you know this," he teased, his voice taking on a rasp that revealed the truth of his condition. "But we are being hunted by a number of guards who stumbled upon Vespahr's body in the dungeons. We need to keep moving."

I tugged again. "And you need to be healed. Now get down."

He leaned forward, face coming closer to mine. The infuriating smirk never left his lips as he spoke. "Are you going to do it for me, Miss Dagon? I recall you being great with a bandage."

My cheeks heated just as Florence stepped around me.

Theron brought his hand to the wound, pulling his fingers away with sticky blood. The look on his face told me he understood the extent of his injury despite his attitude.

"You should refrain from chasing death, Prince Wineslowe," Florence remarked. "If you do not stop, you're certain to catch up with her."

"And how do you know death is a woman?" Theron asked, his gloved fingers squeezing on the reins.

"Ask your lover about her patron goddess." Florence reached for his arm, clasping his wrist as she closed her eyes. The magic tasted like blood, humming through the trees as a small amount of blood appeared at her chest, exactly where Theron's wound was.

Theron, however, kept his eyes on me. The burning intensity of it had my skin heating. Neither of us corrected Florence, and I'm not sure if I could have. I didn't know what the prince was to me, but it was certainly more than a friend.

The pit in my stomach whenever he came back injured, the way I longed to tell him my secrets and listen to his—it pointed to something more, though I'm not sure we'd ever name it.

Theron would be king if we got out of this war alive. At that time, I did not know what I would do—where I would go. With death surrounding us, I didn't have time to think of the future. If there even was one.

"We'll all be faster on horseback," Rona commented. "Three horses, six bodies. Two per mount."

Florence stepped back, making her way toward Caius as Theron gave me his hand.

"Would you like help getting up here?" he asked. "I can't promise I won't get blood on you. It seems to be a bad habit of mine."

I scoffed, but there was no malice behind it.

When we'd mounted and rode off into the forest, I was haunted by my own thoughts.

"We left her," I admitted once the risk of discovery had lessened. Birds sang in the trees as the sun glided across the sky, with the threat of dusk approaching.

All I could see was the woman's frail skin, thin as paper. It was as if it would tear the moment we touched her. Her slow breathing—the way she wasn't given a choice.

We'd left her to die in that carriage. Another body for the kingdom to burn, but I didn't know who was responsible.

"Left who?" Theron asked, his warm chest brushing against my back.

I was careful not to lean into him, cautious of his injury. "The woman we'd tried to save. She was older—hardly well." Emotion clogged my throat, but I pushed past it, whispering into the wind. "Rona couldn't heal her." I paused, squeezing my eyes shut against the image. "We left her to die."

Theron's arm came around my waist as he pulled me closer, crushing me against his solid form.

In the safety of his arms, I found it difficult not to cry—not to let my hardened exterior crumble away until I was a vulnerable mess.

"I'm sorry," he whispered, his breath tickling the back of my neck. "I'd like to believe there will be less death in the future."

"When you're king?" I asked, a knot forming in my stomach.

When you've no need of me.

Theron sighed, a breath that held the weight of all his worries. "If I even make it that long. You heard what Florence said about death."

A cloud hid the sun from view, the tall trees stretching up toward the graying sky. I squinted, feeling the mist in the air—the way the breeze quieted, and the forest seemed to tuck its most vulnerable creatures away. We were going to get rain.

"I heard what she said," I answered, keeping my eyes fixed on the sky. I did not clarify, but by the way Theron's arm tightened around me, I thought maybe he understood.

There was a long silence before he spoke again, his voice vibrating at the back of my spine, making my body more aware—aware of his presence, his breaths, the beating of his heart.

"You did not correct her," Theron commented, and heat rose to my face.

I turned slightly, still not looking at him. "You did not either." My voice was breathless as I felt his fingers tighten at my waist. The memory of his hands on my skin—the way he'd touched me in our tent lingered.

Theron leaned even closer, his lips brushing over the shell of my ear, voice dropping dangerously low. "I didn't think I needed to."

Sharp need struck me as my lips parted, heat pooling at my core. Every inch of my body that brushed against his had me fighting for relief. There was too much between us—clothes, a war, a future. I didn't know how to break through all the barriers—but I wanted to.

"Okay," I whispered, and Theron hummed at my back, his lips leaving an imprint where they gently pressed against my shoulder.

It was a mark that could not be erased.

"Okay," he agreed, and we rode on in silence just as the first droplets of water released from the sky—washing away the blood and gore and giving us hope of something new.

Chapter Fifty-Four

Verena

My robes brushed against the floor of the temple as I made my way past flickering firelight and the moss-covered walls. In the past weeks, the forest had taken more of the structure as her own, and it felt as if it was meant to.

I could feel the magic thrumming through my blood, as if the roots below ground extended to me. I could feel her there—the Waldwood—knew she was preparing for something.

My mind still struggled to wrap around the meeting I'd had. A representative from Onelia's temple arrived in the morning, thrusting me into negotiations I felt entirely unprepared for. Word of my rule had spread across the Waldwood, and the woman I'd met with hadn't questioned my power.

I'd been accepted as queen, yet somehow, could not fathom the weight of it.

Sagan, the priestess who'd come from Onelia's temple, expressed hope for the independence of the Waldwood. While her temple was located to the north in Eirhiondus where King Wineslowe didn't dare to cross. The rest of the covens existed further south.

Sagan had offered menders. Menders to assist Eirhiondus if they should enter a war on our side, and because of the potent magic, I believed they would accept.

What I didn't know was whether I should offer up this information to Theron or leave it as a last resort.

Ivy wound up the wall where I entered the wing of the temple, where the sleeping quarters were left. Near my room, Narela stood with her arms folded, a determined look on her face. My stomach churned with uncertainty. I didn't know how much longer my mind could keep spinning—how many more questions I could answer before falling into my bed and sleeping for the next century.

"You seem to be taking to the role well," Narela commented as I approached. Her white hair had been bound in a long braid, draped over one shoulder.

I bowed my head, bending my knees just slightly as I did in a sign of respect. "Thank you," I said, finding her eyes lighted with mirth when I stood to my full height.

"I was worried at first," she admitted, stepping away from the door so I could go inside. "When you asked me to participate in discussions with the prince and his..."

The cold metal of the doorknob seeped through my fingers, biting like the forgotten winter. I turned it, pushing the wooden door open to reveal the same room I'd inhabited before Eirdis had chosen me—before the Waldwood had entered my blood.

Narela followed me inside, still speaking. "You know," she mused. "I'm not sure what the Witch Hunter is to the Traitor Prince."

I smiled, finding a tray resting on my made-up bed. The teapot had been painted with delicate purple flowers. Their blooms framed the image of a fox on one side, and a raven on the other. The matching cup, decorated with more forest creatures, sat on a saucer with herbs sprinkled at the bottom. I poured the hot water, letting the tea steep as the scent of chamomile invaded my lungs. Sweet and apple-like, the herb brought with it a sense of a day's work ending.

I inhaled. "They're more than friends, I'm sure," I commented. For one, the prince had requested to share a room with her upon their arrival. I was not blind to the way they leaned toward one another—a small gesture while we spoke in the library.

"And you and Caius?" Narela questioned, my smile faltering.

"That is…" My stomach twisted. There had been nothing said between us—nothing to show our kiss had been any more than bubbling up emotion. "That is not a discussion." I finished.

I held the teacup to my nose, hardly able to wait for it to finish steeping. Outside the window of my room, massive trees stretched upward to the sky. Dusk had fallen, marking another day that Caius and the others had not returned. They'd been gone for over a week, and I still couldn't stand the not knowing.

There, in my chest, sat a flicker of *something*. Caius had to be okay. If he weren't, I'd feel it there, wouldn't I?

"You worry for his return." Narela stepped closer, the light from the lantern near my bed dancing over her dark skin.

We hadn't lit the fires—not since winter had turned to spring—and now summer. At least, that's what I believed it to be.

"Of course," I said, caving to take a sip of the tea. The herbs calmed my nerves, but only slightly. More than that, the drink brought with it a subtle sorrow—a memory of a small cabin in a winter forest where tea had been taken time and time again. The place Caius had brought me into his home—helped me heal.

Narela's head tilted to the side as she observed me with an intensity that prickled my skin. "You love him."

I turned, setting the teacup down on the tray with too much force. The clank echoed off the walls, vibrating the way my rapidly beating heart did. I turned my head in her direction, keeping my back to her. "Did I ask you to pry into my personal life?" I questioned.

Narela did not look surprised at the bite in my tone—nor did it halt her from barreling onward. "He'd make a fine king," she commented.

I did not doubt it, but my wants and desires were not the only pieces on the board. I felt as if I were playing a game of strategy—one much like what my mother had taught me as a child. With politics, a war, and my new role—the magic that still felt too large for me to fill, I had other worries.

Maybe I was simply too afraid of heartbreak.

I looked back out the window. I could almost see him there, riding toward the temple, returning home. If that's even what he would call it. "I should have gone with them," I admitted.

I lifted the tray, walking it to a small table that sat near the chair by the fire. Once I'd set it down, I returned to sit on my bed. Narela joined me, keeping a careful distance.

In all my time here, she'd become somewhat of a friend. I didn't know if she understood how much I appreciated her and her guidance. She should know.

"No," Narela said after a moment. "You shouldn't have. Abellona has the largest number of witches on account of it being so far within the Waldwood. Onelia's coven already knows of your rule and supports you. Word of your status has spread throughout the covens. This work was important, and you were needed here to see it through."

Doubt flickered in my chest as Narela placed a gentle hand on mine, leaning in with her piercing eyes. "You are a wonderful queen, Verena. You have been chosen for a purpose."

I looked at her, my throat clogging with emotion. "And what if Abellona doesn't accept me?"

Narela scoffed as if what I'd said was entirely absurd. "They will," she assured. "Plus, Rialey will need the time there to work on her magic. I have a feeling it'll be best served that far into the forest. The Waldwood has helped strengthen her in the time I worked with her, and another few weeks should do the trick before you all travel to Eirhiondus."

Silence hovered between us, and I felt the weight of it—the weight of words unsaid. As we approached a war, I knew I could not leave this stone unturned.

"Did I ever say thank you?" I questioned as Narela drew her hand back.

"What?"

Thank you," I asserted. "Did I ever tell you that?"

Narela chuckled, bracing her hands on either side of her where she sat on my bed. "I believe you did."

A soft smile found its way to my lips. "Well, just in case," I started. "Thank you, Narela."

She nodded once before standing to face me, dipping her chin low in respect. "It has been my honor."

Shouts sounded from outside, followed by the clanking of metal and the sound of horses.

My heart leapt into my throat as I ran to look. Not a ghost, but flesh, Caius sat atop a horse, Florence wedged behind him as they plodded forward. He looked wary, the same as the companions that trailed behind him, but he was safe.

I looked for injuries from my spot at the window, finding none. Still, I could be missing something.

"They're here," I whispered, standing to straighten my robes before moving toward the door.

Narela smiled, watching as I hurried away, barely able to contain my relief. "So they are," she whispered. "So they are."

Chapter Fifty-Five

Rialey

The journey to Abellona's coven took just over four days. We'd quickened our pace, but by the time we made it to the coven located around the temple, my bones were weary.

Theron and I stayed in a house built high in the trees' canopy. The one-room dwelling floated above the forest floor with wooden walls that barely kept out the heat.

I'd struggled as my childhood home came into view. Different from what I remembered it, the coven still sat nestled in the deepest part of the Waldwood.

Tall trees stretched toward the sky, dotted with white clouds. The afternoon sun had poked through the canopy, causing sweat to drip down my spine. In the wide bases of the trees, homes were carved out—littered among the houses built at varying heights overhead.

The coven, much like the others, had become one with the forest. Dark wood and black iron were used to construct the goddess of death's village.

Upon our arrival one day prior, we'd been welcomed on account of Verena's known status as queen. I'd found my way into the bed at the corner of our small cabin in the trees and drifted off into a healing sleep.

Misty morning light filtered through the trees as I sat on the small porch out front of our cabin. I looked over the forest, watching the quiet and breathing deeply.

When I'd last been here, snow covered every inch of the landscape. The limbs dropped fat flakes of snow to the ground I'd walked with my parents—now gone on account of the war we'd helped start.

The bones were the same—as if the deepest winter couldn't frost out the truth of what this place was.

"How are you?" Theron asked as soon as he stepped out onto the small porch. My feet hung over the edge, with nothing but an iron railing separating me from falling.

He handed me a cup of tea, his hair mussed, but clean after having had time to bathe yesterday. The black pants he wore hung low on his hips. My eyes flicked to his bare chest as he sidled up next to me, sitting with his own cup of tea.

I inhaled the sweet scent of lemon balm and mint. "Where did you get this?" I asked.

Theron nudged me with his shoulder. "You first," he said, eyes on mine in a way that made my breath catch. It was as if he really *saw* me—understood.

"I'm fine," I answered, breaking his gaze to stare into the cup of steaming tea. "Tired of death."

"Is Abellona not the goddess of death?" he asked, his voice soft.

"She is misunderstood," I answered before taking a sip. The warm liquid soothed my throat. Sweetened with honey, the only thing keeping me from drinking it all in one sip was the heat. "She represents death, but rebirth as well. Fate. Choices." I thought back to the fox I'd watched my father kill in childhood—the memory that our encounter had unearthed in Keslow. "My father once killed a fox with the same ailment as that bear we'd seen. I'd tried to stop him." Below, a lantern had been turned on in one of the suspended homes lower than ours. The warm light cut through the fog that drifted between the trees. "He'd tried to explain the nuance of death—how choosing that something or someone should live could have just as much of an impact as choosing one should die." My stomach churned. I could see the faces of all the witches we'd lost—by my hand and by circumstance. "As with most things of significance, there's always nuance. What did you say to me that first night in the forest? Morality is not always a binary?"

Theron chuckled, looking at his own cup. "Something like that."

"I'm supposed to work on my magic, here," I said, tracing my finger along the rim of my tea. "The Waldwood helps significantly, but I still need to work on how my illusions respond to movement. Most of the time, it looks unnatural."

My magic hummed below the surface, a cool brush against my arms and legs, begging to be used. I toyed with it, seeing the golden thread in my vision, and weaving it as I pleased. The strands of my hair turned from black to red, and finally, to a stark white. I let go of the illusion, finding Theron watching me with amusement.

"I like this look the best," he said. When he set his cup down next to him, he turned to finger the ends of my hair, watching the motion as if he was trying to puzzle something together.

"If we win this war," he started, "I will become king." He dropped the strands of my hair.

"Yes," I whispered, willing it to be so. His blood oath bound him to taking the throne. Any other option would lead to death, and I could not bear the thought of Theron dying. He'd come close too many times.

I set my cup of tea to the side as the air crackled between us, the forest stilling as if a storm were approaching in the misty morning light. I looked into his eyes, finding a kaleidoscope of history there. How had I missed it, back when he paraded around as Eryx?

Theron had once said something about kindness and eyes—how they showed the truth. There was still kindness in him, too, despite all the death and destruction—the betrayal and running. He, at his core, was kind. He wanted a better kingdom than what his father had created, and I couldn't wait to see it.

Something flashed in his eyes. "I will need to take a queen," he said, his voice so low I almost didn't register it.

"Of course," I whispered. I knew this to be true—knew that there would be a future beyond this war if we were successful. A seed of hope unfurled in my chest, shedding its coat as the very beginnings of roots broke through. "Lord Bloodbane recommended his daughter," I said, trying to keep my tone light. I smiled. "I *did* tell you to dance with her at the ball."

Theron chuckled. "I suppose my dancing was terrible?" he asked, one brow quirking up.

"No," I admitted. "Far from it."

With death haunting us at every turn, my entire life felt fleeting. What I wanted from Theron was not something I dared ask for, not even when I knew him as Eryx. It was never something I believed I could have, but with the forest still around us, the static floating in the air, the small seed in my chest grew and bloomed as my lips parted.

One soft exhale.

Another moment gone by.

"I've spent too many years alongside you, Rialey," Theron said, almost whispering. His hand came up to trace the scar on my cheek, and my eyes fluttered shut. "I cannot picture any without you."

With my breaths shallow, I leaned into his touch, craving his next words the way I craved his every breath—the way my own halted at the thought of losing him—ripped from my chest as if we'd shared it all along.

"Be my queen," he whispered, fingers cupping the side of my face. His palm was warm, probably from the tea. My eyes closed as I *felt*. I felt the forest's magic over my skin, the misty air, the quiet of the morning in the coven where I'd learned to exist. I felt my sorrow, my shame, my joy, my hope.

He was the place I could come back to—the one person in the kingdom I felt safe enough to show all of me.

"Yes," I whispered, feeling his warmth as he leaned in. "Yes."

Theron's lips met mine with gentle pressure. His mouth moved on mine, as if he were savoring the taste of my words—the confirmation that I wanted the same as him.

A better kingdom.

A lifetime with him.

He tasted of herbal tea and honey as my tongue traced the seam of his lips. His juniper berry and cardamom scent was worth drowning in as I leaned closer.

My fingers found their way to the ridges of his abs, tracing every muscle before they migrated to the scar across his chest, then the one on his arm. He shivered at the contact, deepening the kiss until I was near breathless.

With his hand threaded in my hair, he tugged gently, my body buzzing when my tongue met his, and a groan escaped his throat.

Heat pooled at my core, my body a live-wire waiting to be struck by the incoming storm.

Theron swallowed my gasp before pulling away. He stood on the porch, his hand outstretched toward me in offering. With hooded eyes, I watched him take in every inch of me, memorizing every curve below the cotton shirt and pants I'd been given upon our arrival.

His large hand felt warm in mine, calluses scratching with delicious friction as anticipation shot through me.

I followed him into the room, with dark wooden walls all around us. In the corner sat the double bed, blankets still rumpled from this morning.

The misty light of the forest streamed in from the glass overhead, high-lighting Theron's heated gaze as he closed the door behind him.

My breath caught as his mouth met mine again, urgent and needy. He backed me toward the bed, grabbing one of the built-in shelves on the wall next to the mattress when we stumbled.

I sat on the bed, fingers thumbing the end of my shirt.

His eyes flashed when I removed it, exposing my breasts to his hungry gaze.

Without hesitating, Theron knelt before me, kissing the heated flesh of my stomach as his hand rose higher until his thumb brushed over my tightened nipple.

When he groaned, heat flooded me, sparking a *need* so intense, I tilted my head back, moaning.

"Rialey," he whispered, running fervent kisses down lower, his finger tucking into the waistband of my pants to pull them until his tongue swirled over my hip.

My hands tightened in his hair, tugging him upward until he rose, looking me in the eyes.

"Don't make me wait," I whispered. "We could die at any moment, Theron. I don't want to die without knowing how this feels."

He silenced me with a kiss, tipping me backward until I lay on the bed, his body warm and hovering over me.

I wiggled out of my pants, pulling at his with demand. He stood fully, shoving them down his legs to bare himself fully.

I stared at him, mouth dry.

When he hovered over me again, my breath caught at the feel of him. Slick heat and harsh breaths, he kissed me with a new urgency, his hips cradled between my legs. I could feel him there, nudging at my entrance.

He slowed his kiss, staring at me in question. I nodded and held his gaze, mouths parted as he pushed forward.

The stretch of him—the *fullness* —took my breath away.

"Is this okay?" he asked, pausing once he was fully seated.

I nodded, hands grabbing at his back, his hips, desperate for him to move.

When he did, we both groaned. With every thrust, my body heated until I was certain flames licked at my skin. He ran a finger over my nipple, sending heat out over my skin as he moved. His other hand migrated lower, finding the bundle of nerves there.

Every stroke sent me closer to the edge. I felt as if I were standing on a cliff, eyes closed and taking in every kiss of wind across my flesh. Theron kissed my neck, my collarbone, muttering promises as he moved.

My pleasure peaked, and I found myself falling as his thrusts became erratic, a dark noise rumbling in his chest before he shoved in once more, releasing himself.

We stayed in the cabin, pressed together as sleep overtook us. Nothing but the quiet of calm before an oncoming storm.

CHAPTER FIFTY-SIX

CAIUS

Sore muscles were often the cure for internal turmoil.

Herbs could calm and relax, but nothing did as good a job of getting someone out of their own head as physical exertion.

It is why I'd chosen to practice beneath the canopy of trees just outside the coven.

Sweat slicked my spine as I jutted forward, plunging the wooden practice sword at the air. I turned, spinning as if to avoid a blow, and swung again. With every movement, my muscles burned. The heat of the day descended on the forest in a way that made my limbs feel sluggish. I pushed past it, quickening my steps to jab, duck, stab until the endless thoughts eased.

Verena had spent the last two weeks in the temple, introducing herself to the priestesses, discussing the future of the Waldwood, and the potential of war.

She'd stepped into the role so gracefully, it was like she'd been destined to be queen the entire time.

Now that the bubble we'd created for ourselves had been burst, I didn't know where I fit into Verena's life. I had no home to go to with Ahvi gone, and with menders joining the rebellion, my teas and tinctures hardly had a use. Plus, Florence knew just as much of the natural magic of plants that she could handle both magical healing and non-magical healing herself.

I didn't know where I fit anymore or what I would have to go back to should we win this war.

I jabbed the air harder.

"Would you like someone to spar with?"

I turned, panting as I let my wooden sword drop to the side.

Prince Theron stood with his own practice weapon, a challenging smile on his lips. The last time I'd really seen him one-on-one had been when he'd saved me—killed Lord Vespahr and unlocked the chains around my wrists.

I'd thought I would die, then. Knowing that Rialey and the others had escaped—knowing that my place in the kingdom was unknown. It had made sense to sacrifice myself, but deep down, I felt like there was something more. Call it foolish hope, I still felt as if I would find my place. Where it was? Now that I did not know.

"I suppose you would like me to thank you?" I questioned, my grip tightening on the sword.

Sweat already dripped down my back, no shirt to soak it up. The forest provided shade, but the heat of what I could only assume to be summer still leaked through.

"I would like you to fight me, actually." Theron looked amused as he shed his shirt and stepped forward, raising his sword and squaring his stance in preparation to spar.

I'd never been one to waste an opportunity.

While I wasn't as angry with him as I had been, there was still a simmering rage burning in my chest—a lightning storm threatening to strike at the soonest opportunity.

My hand flexed around the hilt of the sword before squeezing. The practice weapon was lighter than my sword, something that took getting used to.

I held my weapon aloft, the storm in my chest crackling like lightning before the rain. We circled, neither one of us willing to strike first.

Prince Theron kept a smug smirk on his face, and I longed to wipe the expression away.

"How's Rialey?" I asked, taking the opportunity to ask probing questions—hoping to distract.

Theron broke into a grin, the sword slashing towards mine until he struck. My arm vibrated against the force of his blow as his sword struck mine. I blocked and stepped back, meeting his attack with one of my own.

"Stronger," he said, spinning away from the jab of my weapon. "I was worried about her coming here, but I think it's been..." He grunted, holding his sword vertically as I shoved against it. "Healing," he finished through gritted teeth.

Sweat beaded on his temple, dripping down the side of his face. A sheen appeared on his chest where an angry scar still stood out above his pectoral. "All healed?" I questioned, nodding toward the remnants of the wound.

He smirked again. "All healed."

His next attack was relentless. I struggled to keep up with his swift movements. Though taller, Prince Theron still fought with agility and strategy instead of brute force. It made him a formidable opponent, and I tracked his steps, looking for any weakness.

"Where's Verena?" he asked, and I stumbled a step, awarding me a brutal strike against the base of my sword.

"Learning politics," I answered, returning his hit with one of my own. I grunted in frustration. "Practically living in the temple."

I hadn't meant for the bitterness to leak out—hadn't intended on baring any of my emotions so completely to a prince I hated mere weeks ago.

Hate seemed like the incorrect word since our time in Vespahr's dungeon, but hardly anything like friendship.

Mutual respect, maybe?

I spun away from his attempted stab, jolted back, dodged, and slid to the side until I was at the very edge of the area where I'd been training.

Luckily, we had an entire forest instead of a confined area. He didn't have me cornered.

Prince Theron paused for a moment, lifting his chin slightly. "Are you two…" The last word lingered, a question he didn't finish. I knew what he was implying, and I hated it.

The truth was that I didn't know.

I'd kissed her, sure. I had feelings for Verena—that I could not deny, but I still hadn't established what my role would be in the war without Ahvi—without need of me.

"No," I answered, forcefully arcing my sword down. Luckily, Prince Theron blocked in time—just barely. I quickened my pace. "Different rooms," I said, striking again. Every hit shot through my muscles like lightning.

"But you want that?" Theron questioned, his voice now straining as he fought to catch his breath.

I growled. "That's none of your business."

Another hit.

Another.

I nearly caught his left arm, and the high of that narrow miss sent a thrill through my blood. It was possible for me to beat him.

I fought harder.

"How long have you been with the rebellion?" he asked—now on the defensive.

"Since I found out…my grandmother was part of it when I…was fifteen." Panting between every breath, I watched Prince Theron's eyes widen, the way he realized I would not back down easily. "I don't have magic," I said, frustration leaking out as I stabbed forward, missing him by a narrow margin. "I acted as healer," I added. "Injured from the Guild…would come to our cabin."

Finally, I'd grazed his right calf, causing Theron to back up. His movements became less sure, and I fought harder.

Panting and dripping sweat, we sparred beneath the trees until our bodies were exhausted. When I spun, kicking out and causing him to stumble, I moved quickly. I shoved Theron with my booted foot, pressing him to the forest floor with the tip of my practice sword at his throat.

My chest heaved, face a stony mask. He'd already gotten enough from me.

Theron dropped his weapon, raising his hands in defense. One corner of his mouth ticked up. "I suppose this makes me an unfit leader."

The phantom touch of metal cuffs kissed my wrists. I remembered how we fought in the dungeons, feeding off each other's strengths and covering each other's weaknesses. We'd worked together toward a common goal.

Theron had positioned himself to be king—to lead a rebellion he'd hardly been involved with. He'd been willing to fight with his. He took responsibility for his plans to further the war, fought alongside those in the rebellion, and showed he truly cared for those who'd gone into battle with him.

"I fought alongside you," I admitted, taking my boot off his chest. Lowering my sword, I stepped back. "I wouldn't say you're unfit."

Theron stood, chuckling as he dusted off his pants. "High praise coming from you." He tossed his sword off to the side, leveling me with a stare. "We leave tomorrow for Liethaire to negotiate with the king."

My chest tightened at his words—the knowledge that Verena would leave to beg for aid in this war. I knew nothing about the king of Eirhiondus. The thought of leaving her to the wolves sent my pulse pounding—frustration swelling until I was certain I'd combust.

Theron's brows furrowed. "You will come with us?" he asked.

It wasn't even a question. If Verena would travel north, so would I. While I didn't know where I fit in the rebellion, I knew that I couldn't bear to see her leave without adequate protection. Despite her strength and the ease with which she'd stepped into her role, Verena needed someone she could trust—someone willing to protect her no matter the cost.

"Of course," I answered, warranting a nod from the prince.

He took one step back, grabbing his sword before walking backwards, his eyes never leaving mine. The intensity there gave me a glimpse of who he would be—what he would be like as a king.

"Good," Theron said. "Then I'll see you tomorrow."

Chapter Fifty-Seven

Verena

I thought I would have grown tired of traveling, but I found myself thankful for the fresh air and change of scenery.

Abellona brought a real sense of what fate had decided for my future, and I felt suffocated by the walls of the temple there. Where Eirdis's temple let in flickers of natural light through windows, much like the dappling of the sun along a forest floor, Abellona's temple seemed to be stuck in an eternal night. Dark masonry made the walls, while shadowed ivory pillars stretched up toward the vaulted ceilings at every open room. Above, the ceiling had been made to look like a blanket of stars, as if death and night were one.

While beautiful, I found I missed how close I'd felt to the Waldwood in Eirdis's temple. It was the one thing I missed as we rode through the shrublands. The air was cooler this far north, though the openness of the terrain set my nerves on edge.

We'd crossed the border into Eirhiondus just this morning, and Liethaire was fast approaching. While empty, the vast grassland dotted with shrubs and small trees had to give way to this kingdom's subjects eventually, and there was no telling if we would be welcomed or not.

I rode in silence, watching Caius's back in front of me. We had spoken little since before the Waldwood flooded my veins, and while I'd been so sure of our trajectory at the time, now I was thrust back into the uncertainty.

Pushing my mount forward, I rode to catch up until our horses walked side by side, distanced enough that the others who joined us could not overhear.

"Something is bothering you," I said, flexing my fingers around the reins. My nerves set me on edge, making my body buzz with restless energy—energy that had nowhere to go as I sat atop a slow-moving horse.

Caius's gaze slid toward me, and I could feel it everywhere, as if he could see through whatever mask I'd gained on account of my new title. I wondered if Prince Theron felt the same—if Rialey saw through him the way I believed Caius saw through me.

"Are you okay?" I asked when he hadn't responded immediately.

Caius took a deep breath. "Yes."

My brows furrowed, nerves burrowing their way beneath my skin until every fiber of my being felt jittery and insecure. "It does not seem that way." I pressed my lips together, frustration rising with my growing worries. I had done nothing to him. Why was he so distant?

"I—" Caius shook his head, trying again. "It has been difficult without my grandmother," he admitted, and my heart clenched at his words. I'd been so selfish—so blind to how he would still struggle with the loss. Grief seemed to last a lifetime—only to be dulled and renewed in a never-ending cycle. "I am...not sure what my life is supposed to look like right now."

The sting of tears threatened to escape as I watched him, his features less stony—more vulnerable now that he had confessed what had bothered him. I traced the bridge of his nose with my gaze, dipping down to his full lips, over the sharp cut of his jaw.

"I'm sorry," I said, letting the words carry the weight. "If it helps, I am not sure what my life should look like now either."

He stared at me then, his entire expression softening. "You are queen," he said. "That is your answer."

Though there was nothing but gentleness in his tone, I still winced. My magic sat just beneath the surface of my skin, begging to be used. With very little, I could invade his mind and read his thoughts. With a great deal of energy, I could parse apart his memories—rifle through his greatest fears.

That kind of power felt unmanageable. I'd been given authority over the Waldwood while simultaneously being given the magic of a monster.

"I did not choose this," I whispered.

"I...I know." Caius closed his eyes, wincing. "I'm sorry, too."

I shook my head, feeling somewhat ridiculous. Ahvi's death stung; the sorrow of it following me after I'd heard. But Caius? He'd watched her die. I couldn't imagine what he was feeling and couldn't fathom his worrying about *me*. "You shouldn't be," I said, straightening my spine. My muscles ached in the saddle, and I longed for a change in scenery. "You lost Ahvi, and I haven't been there for you." The sunlight dulled as a cloud passed overhead, bathing the shrublands in a tint of gray. "I have not had time to talk to you, and I have not..." My face twisted, realizing how consumed I'd been with my own life. "I have not been a good friend," I finished.

Caius's muttered word was almost lost on the breeze. "Friend," he mused, one corner of his mouth turning upward.

My heart rate quickened, our conversation coming too close to the truth I hadn't yet admitted. "A...close friend."

Caius's smirk turned mischievous. "Friends who have kissed."

My cheeks flamed as I fixed my gaze on my horse's mane. Each memory of his lips on mine warmed my blood.

Caius leaned toward me from atop his horse. "I rather liked it," he said, and I could hear the amusement in his voice. "The kissing."

I let out a small, choked sound, keeping my focus now on the terrain ahead.

"Have I scandalized you, Your Majesty?"

My brow furrowed. Certainly, he didn't think I hadn't been with another. "No," I said, somewhat defensively. "I am not scandalized. I *have* kissed men before."

"Men?" Caius questioned, his inflection going up at the end. "More than one." He lowered his voice as if sharing a secret. "Was this all at once or—"

"One at a time," I asserted, my entire body now flushed with heat.

"And you have *kissed* them."

My nose scrunched up. "Done more than that," I muttered. Silence befell us, and I thought I heard Caius let out a small chuckle. I turned my head toward him, somewhat aghast. "Why are you trying to—"

His chuckle morphed into a boisterous laugh, one that had Rialey and Theron looking back toward us from where they led our party.

"You are trying to make me uncomfortable," I said, realizing I sounded like a petulant child.

"Are you?" he questioned. "Uncomfortable, that is?"

I stared at him, watching the genuine concern—the way it tightened his jaw and pushed his eyebrows together. He looked as if he'd sincerely wanted to know—as if he were concerned.

Truth be told, I was not uncomfortable talking about kissing with Caius. I would not be *uncomfortable* talking about more. In fact, the more he stared at me, the more I thought I should like to do more than merely discuss such actions.

"I am not uncomfortable." My voice dropped to almost a whisper as the confession left my gently parted lips. "Not with you, Caius. Never with you."

As we left the shrublands, we approached the palace of Liethaire. Backed by mountains with caps cloaked in mist, the pale palace seemed to be built by a man who loved spires. The charcoal-colored roof boasted at least ten that I could count, all capped in gold. I wasn't sure if it was to flaunt wealth, or if King Faris Faolan merely wanted those approaching to know that they could be stabbed.

My heart thundered in my chest as the distance between our horses and the long bridge stretching out over the moat that surrounded the castle narrowed and shortened.

"Strategy?" I questioned, my horse falling into step with Prince Theron's. His eyes were hardened as he stared ahead, jaw tight with the tension that stiffened his posture.

"We..." He winced before finishing his statement. "Arrive."

Blood drained from my face, my limbs growing increasingly chilled with the cooling air around us. This far north, we found ourselves in a different climate entirely, leaving behind the newly found summer of Alphaird and all its familiarity.

As soon as my horse's hooves touched the stone of the long bridge, I felt something shift in the air. My skin prickled with awareness, the gut feeling of being watched so strong, it made me nauseous. We didn't know what their intentions were. Guards, most likely, but their instructions were a mystery.

My magic thrummed. I stared upward at the million spires, using my magic to *feel* for the minds of those awaiting our arrival.

With no balconies to be seen, I didn't know where they would be standing. Hardly on the roof unless they were excellent climbers who defied all logic by not sliding down the narrow slopes.

There.

At least twenty guards surrounded us. Some stood in the windows of the palace, while others ducked behind the smaller stone wall that surrounded the castle. I could feel their curiosity—hear their thoughts as my own. With so many voices, they became muddled, and I desperately tried to parse apart intention without using too much energy.

Go too far, and I'd be useless to those I traveled with. Florence could mend, but it would be senseless to make her take on exhaustion because of my stupidity. Putting more stress on Theron, Rialey, and Caius? I simply couldn't do it.

I closed my eyes, trying to focus, but the thoughts still jumbled. Words scattered like broken glass until a few broke through the mess. *Do it now. Best chance for capture.*

Caius yelled to warn the others as guards approached us from ahead on the bridge and behind, blocking us in. Below, in the water, I could make out a small boat with more guards, arrows pointed in our direction. If they felt confident, they could shoot us from such a low vantage point. The archers had to have exceptional abilities.

Locked at the center of the bridge, horses and guards, with swords drawn, surrounded us. Their uniforms are different from those of Alphaird. Instead, they wore deep red, almost brown, with the image of a fox stitched onto the breast. The color reminded me of dried blood.

My heart raced, fear taking root as I caught myself warring between using my magic and conserving my energy.

"State your business," a voice called from the group of six guards on horseback in front of us.

Theron straightened. "We wish to speak to King Faolan on behalf of Alphaird."

A guard scoffed, a muttered *Traitor Prince* sounding from somewhere behind us.

"Get off your horses." A man demanded as he dismounted. His long hair hung to his broad shoulders; a scar, angry and red, cut across his upper lip. He carried his sword with confidence as he approached. Theron looked at me, and I nodded in agreement.

If we were to win King Faolan's favor, we would need to follow his rules.

Each of us dismounted before the guards rushed at us. Strong hands gripped both my shoulders, tightening with bruising force. They spun me, and metal cuffs clasped my wrists in front of me. A woman far taller than me looked down with a sneer as she yanked me forward. "You will go." Her accent, thick and slow, seemed stronger than that of the guard who'd originally spoken.

I did as I was told, following the rest of our group as the soldiers parted and marched us into Liethaire Castle.

Blood roared in my ears, my breaths shallow as I fought to keep my composure. My magic buzzed, and I finally gave in. If they were going to imprison us or kill us, I needed to know. The guard, who still gripped my arm, the tall woman with the thick accent and red hair slicked back into a low bun, was easy to read.

Her thoughts, wide open, had nothing to do with orders. Instead, she was thinking about a young girl, hair as bright as hers, running along the sand of a beach.

I quickly felt for another guard, another, until their motive became clear. We were not being marched to the dungeons, but to King Faolan himself. I pressed my lips together, eyes flicking to where Caius was being led by two men. When his gaze met mine, I did all I could to communicate what I knew. We would be okay—we were not being captured.

I didn't know if he understood.

The massive door opened as we approached the entrance to the castle. The palace of Liethaire was entirely different from what I imagined. Long hallways littered with windows stretched out before us, the marbled tile just as pale as the stone used to build the castle. Bright and gold, I found the interior to be less threatening than the spires outside. Instead, the interior spoke of a king who loved lavish and expensive things—had an eye for beauty.

We were led through about a dozen different halls until I was certain the guards were purposefully confusing us. Only when we entered a large room, decorated much the same as the rest of the palace, save for the long table in the center, did I realize we were being immediately thrust into negotiations.

Across from us, separated by an ornate spread of food and red decor, sat a young man no older than me. His high cheekbones made him appear striking; his amber eyes bored as he looked to our emerging group. His curly black hair was shaggy, as if he'd been overdue for a haircut, but it was the golden crown atop his head that gave him away as he leaned back, running a long finger over his lips as he scrutinized us.

His bronze skin was smooth and clean; his clothes immaculate.

There was no doubt we were meeting with King Faolan himself.

He lifted a goblet of wine, swirling the crimson liquid in the cup before taking a long drink.

"Your Majesty," Theron began, bowing ever so slightly. "We have come from Alphaird. I—"

The king scoffed, gesturing for Theron to have a seat. "Please," he said. "I know exactly who you are. Have a seat since you have decided to so rudely interrupt my dinner." Theron bristled. "I assume you want my armies to kill your father, *Traitor Prince*."

My eyes slid to Theron as he blanched. The king, young as he was, had thrown Theron off—thrown us all off.

"It is you," King Faolan said, and when I looked at him, my stomach dropped. There at the end of the table, he held a finger directly pointed at me. "It is not the prince I am interested in," he continued, his eyes never leaving mine. "It is you."

Chapter Fifty-Eight

Verena

The hunger in King Faris Faolan's eyes reminded me of a predator. From his perch at the end of the table, he looked exactly like the fox depicted on his guard's uniforms. With amber eyes hiding a cunning mind, I could not tell what his goal was, but I swallowed down my emotion and tried to ignore the churning in my gut.

I hadn't been queen for long, and already, I was being used as a pawn—a bargaining chip with other countries. Was it my appearance that intrigued him, or something else?

Reflexively, my hand twitched, as if it could reach Caius from his place on the other side of the table, still shackled. I could feel his eyes on me—almost hear the shallow breaths—the flare of his nose. As if connected by an invisible string, I *felt* Caius's reaction without a glance his way. I would not make him a target in this game of kings.

"It has been said you were chosen by the gods." King Faolan tilted his goblet toward me, a drop of crimson wine spilling onto the cream tablecloth. "Is that true?"

Ensnared, I did not know whether I should lie to the king or tell the truth. Theron and I had discussed the importance of not making enemies in this country, but maybe there was something far worse.

I tilted my chin down, looking at him with boredom. "In a sense," I answered.

King Faolan cocked his head to the side, and though he remained seated at the edge of the table, I felt as if he circled me, toying with his prey. "Please sit," he said, gesturing to the five made-up plates on either side of the table. Three to his left, one to his right, I pulled out of the guard's grip to move first, edging toward Caius.

"I'd like you to enjoy a meal with me," Faolan continued, a sly smile stretching across his angular face.

I took my spot next to Caius, my wrists bound in front of me, preventing me from reaching for him. I shifted in my seat until the edge of his thigh met mine. Warmth seeped into my clothes—my skin. I sat straighter, the comforting presence giving me courage.

Theron sat across the table between Florence and Rialey, his lip curled ever so slightly as he looked down his nose at the meal before us. Red meat, rare and bloody, sat next to a mix of seasoned potatoes and green beans.

"It's not poisoned," Faolan remarked, his tone biting. When his eyes narrowed at Theron, I could tell the king had taken offense to our hesitancy. My pulse pounded, worry stifling what was left of the air in the room. "I am not cruel," Faolan asserted.

"You forget," Rialey started, one brow quirking upward. "We are still shackled."

Faolan laughed—a sound that skittered across the floor and crawled up my spine. "You are a killer," he said, pointing his goblet toward her. Had he put it down at all? "Would you expect anything less?" Faolan took another sip as I risked picking up my fork, moving the potatoes around on my plate as the chains rattled between my hands. It made eating awkward.

Caius nudged me, and when I looked at him, he shook his head.

Grabbing his own fork, the chains between his wrists dragged across his plate as he pierced a bean and brought it to his lips—the first to risk eating the food.

"Now tell me," Faolan continued, attention firmly fixed on me. "Did the gods choose you or not?"

I bit the inside of my cheek to the point of pain, quickly conjuring an answer that would satisfy. "I was dead," I said, moving another potato around the plate. It dipped into the runny blood of the meat. "Then I was not. The rest is up for debate."

"And your magic?" he questioned.

My stomach growled. I was hesitant to discuss my magic. Even being in the Waldwood, there was still a sense of danger whenever we spoke of our abilities. The king must have read me for it.

"Please," he scoffed. "I do not intend to burn you. We are not like that barbaric country you hail from. Witches are not considered abominations here, but gifts."

"Gifts?" Theron questioned.

"Treasured," Faolan answered. "Not to be used against their will."

A small smile tugged at the corner of my mouth, but I fought to suppress it. *Good.* This was *very* good. If we offered him menders from the Waldwood, it might be enough to entice him to loan us his armies.

"I suppose we will cut to the chase," Faolan said. "You." He pointed to Prince Theron. "Desire an army. Easy enough since your father cowers at Stromadale instead of his own palace. I would hardly have to move my men. They'd just..." He mimicked jumping over his plate with his fingers. "Hop over the border. The real question is what you plan to offer me, Prince Theron Wineslowe."

"An alliance," Theron answered, his tone more authoritative than I would have expected. We'd been tricked, surely—one step behind the young king who sat before us. If it bothered Theron, he did not let it show.

"I will take the throne. Alphaird has found a change in season that is sure to give us a surplus to trade. There is much we could offer you."

Faolan's smile cut across his face. "A given," he said. "And what will the Waldwood offer? I *am* helping the witches as well."

A mere moment to debate if I should withhold my offer until they were desperate allowed King Faris Faolan to continue without my answer.

He leaned back in his chair, slamming his goblet on the table as the wine sloshed over the edge. "I know what I want," he began with the confidence of a man who knew he would get it. "As you know, I'm looking to marry. I think that kind of alliance would bode well."

Theron ground his teeth together before interrupting. "I do not have a sister to—"

Faolan cut him off. "No." With eyes blazing, Faolan barreled on. "I do not wish to marry royalty from Alphaird, Prince Theron. We already have our deal. I wish to marry royalty from the Waldwood."

A slight gasp left my parted lips, dread washing over me. Caius tensed beside me, his fist strangling the knife he held as if he intended to throw it at the king from across the table.

Blood roared in my ears, the shock of his words seeming to slow time.

In an instant, Faolan snapped the haze and stood abruptly, gathering his plate and his goblet as his chair screeched across the marble floor. "Consider this my formal proposal, Queen of the Waldwood. I plan to offer my hand, and while typically I would tend to be more romantic, time is of the essence. We agree to trade with Alphaird once Prince Theron becomes king, but seeing as the Waldwood cannot give me her magic, I am willing to take her queen for a wife."

At his full height, King Faris Faolan was taller than I expected, shoving his chair toward the table with one boot. His white breeches appeared to be wine-stained, a similar color to the dark tunic that matched the color of his entire kingdom. With his crown askew, I backed toward the door at the back of the dining hall nearest his seat.

"I will give you a day to think about it," he said. "Now, enjoy your meal. I will have you housed in the west wing." His nose curled as he referenced the other end of the palace. "It is darker in decor—not my doing, but I find you'll be comfortable. Your cuffs can be removed." He gestured to the guards, who still stood around the table. "You all look ridiculous trying to eat."

And without another word, King Faris Faolan walked out of the dining hall, leaving us to our meal.

After dinner, we were led to our rooms in the west wing and given clothing for our stay at the palace of Liethaire. I bathed and donned the delicate dress left in my wardrobe.

The light fabric, pale blue and sparkling, dipped low at my back, making me wince. I certainly hoped the dresses in my rooms did not reflect King Faolan's tastes.

With the freedom to roam the castle, I settled on remaining in the west wing, learning from one guard that King Faolan often stayed in the north tower of the castle. More solitary than social, the staff didn't seem to know much about him either.

Darker stones made up this part of the castle, just as Faolan said. Their carvings boasted a simplistic design, save for the stone statues that lined some walls.

I quickened my steps, passing an older woman carrying a tray of hot tea down the hall for the second time. I'd seen her before, coming out of the west wing kitchens and giving me directions to the library.

My face flushed as I kept my gaze away from hers. Certainly, she would know I was lost. I didn't seem to be anywhere near the library—I wasn't near my rooms either.

Being on the first floor was about the only fact I knew.

My mind replayed tonight's exchange over and over. I held on to certain things Faolan had said. *The Waldwood cannot give me her magic.* I didn't sense loathing in him, further proven by the way Eirhiondus treated his witches, but I also didn't sense hunger either.

In Alphaird, there were those who coveted a witch's magic, longing for control in their quest for dominance. If that were the case, wouldn't Faolan force the issue?

He needed magic, but what for?

I walked through a large archway and into the cavernous room lined with intricately carved statues. At the center, the grand staircase spilled out onto the main floor like the long train of a wedding gown. My stomach soured.

There, turning the corner to rush up the steps, I glimpsed dark hair and broad shoulders.

My heart lurched, breath whooshing out of my lungs as I rushed to catch up. Caius stood halfway up the stairs when I made it to the base, calling his name just for him to turn around.

Gone was the softness of his features on our ride to Liethaire. A stony mask seemed to replace the expression—the same one he wore prior to our conversation.

"What are you doing?" I asked, my voice breathless.

Caius slowly stepped closer. One step. Two. Until he stood stock still, refusing to come any closer. "Going to my rooms," he answered, and I felt my entire chest cave with it.

"Are you...running from me?" I questioned, my voice cracking at the end. I cursed myself for such vulnerability, but maybe he should see it.

He took another step down, slowly inching closer with one large hand planted on the railing of the staircase. His mask cracked, revealing the stressed and disheveled man beneath as he let out an exasperated sigh. "I do not—" he started, cutting himself off to run a hand over his face as if he could wipe away whatever ailed him. "I do not know how to do what is right. The clear answer is no longer clear."

I took a step toward him, longing to close the space between us. I did not take any more for fear he would run. "I don't understand."

As if called to me, he took another step down, now mere feet apart. His eyes looked hardened as he glowered at me, his voice low in the cavernous hall. "Do you wish me to kill him?"

I straightened in surprise, my eyes widening. *Kill* him? King Faris? "What?" I questioned, shaking my head. "No! No, I—" We couldn't *kill* the man. We needed his armies, and I found saving Alphaird took priority over Faolan's rudeness. "It is the way of kings to negotiate marriages," I answered, brows furrowed. "I just...need to decide if I should accept—" My body fought the words, stomach twisting as bile climbed up my throat. I swallowed it back down.

"You mean to marry him?" Caius questioned, that mask now returning in the tightness of his jaw—the way his expression turned blank.

I didn't know how to answer him. It had been hours, not days, and while I had no intention of marrying King Faolan, I knew little about him—which was why I sought the library. He had to have a weakness, or at the very least, something I could offer him that he wanted desperately—something other than my hand.

I could not marry a man I did not know. Not when—

"If that is what you want." Caius turned to leave, but I caught him by the wrist, quickly letting go as if he'd burned me. He felt hot and angry—like a bottle filled with emotions he could not—would not release.

"It is not what I *want*," I scoffed, anger and hurt ripping through me in equal measure. "Is there a reason I should not marry King Faolan?" I asked, taking one step closer—urging him to answer. Caius looked utterly defeated, but I pressed on. "Is there a reason I should refuse him?"

There, for a moment, I saw his pain—a mirror of my own. It reflected all the moments—memories adding up to this one, pivotal moment. I saw him there in Ahvi's cabin, brewing tea and complimenting my drawings. I could feel his warm hands pulling me out of the hot springs. There were our long conversations—my death—our kiss.

The hope in my chest shriveled the moment he shook his head and opened his eyes. I knew—I just *knew*.

"There is not."

His words cut like a blade as I fought the stinging tears pricking my eyes. Gathering my skirts, I rushed around him, climbing the steps. Forgetting the library, I hurried down the hall to my rooms, slamming the door shut once I'd entered.

My back pressed against the hard surface as my tears released themselves, streams of pain and hope and sorrow streaming down my cheeks.

I took a shuddering breath. My chest cracked into a million pieces.

Against my back, a soft knock sounded at the door—unsure.

I spun, wiping my tears and gathering myself—shoving all that emotion down until I thought I could answer.

When the door opened, Caius stood before me, wearing every thought and feeling in the regretful slump of his shoulders, his brows pinching together in pain.

I backed away slowly, not knowing what to say.

Caius stepped into my rooms, closing the door with a soft snick.

My legs bumped the back of an ornate chair, caramel-colored fabric with golden accents, much like the rest of the seating area by the fire. It echoed the rest of the west wing and mirrored the bedroom just past the arch on the far wall.

"I lied," he said, and I sucked in a sharp breath.

"About what?" My storm of emotion rose to the surface, my voice wobbling as I continued. "About when we kissed? About how you felt?" He took a step forward. "About—"

I didn't finish my sentence. Caius silenced me with a searing kiss—his mouth meeting mine with firm pressure as he gripped my face between his big hands. It was as if he couldn't bear to let me go—as if I'd run the moment he released me.

I softened to it, stepping into his heat as he fully engulfed me. This was nothing like what we'd shared before—this was urgent and needy—an undoing.

He pulled away, keeping his hands on either side of my face as he looked into my eyes. "There is a reason you should not marry him, Verena."

My voice came out as a whisper. "There is?"

"Of course there is," he said. The scent of herbs and honey surrounded me, his warmth flushing my skin and making my knees weak as I longed to sink into him. "It is that I am in love with you."

My fingers found their way to the sides of his jacket, green like the mossy forests of the Waldwood in summer. I clung to him, my lips finding his as he claimed my mouth in return.

Heat simmered in my blood, blooming out from my core to every limb the way the seasons changed in Alphaird.

When Caius gripped my waist, pulling me closer until I could feel him hard against me, I gasped.

He pulled away, eyes filled with questions. This was one I longed to answer. "I love you too," I whispered.

Caius turned us as his mouth met mine, his tongue running along the seam of my lips. He slowly encouraged me backward until I found myself caught between the door and every hard inch of him. I gasped, arching into him when his hand trailed up my waist, his thumb grazing the side of my breast.

"Is this okay?" he whispered against my lip, and I nodded. When my hands found the pockets of his trousers, pulling him closer, he growled against my mouth. The sound sent vibrations over my skin—making me more aware of every spot our bodies touched.

My body cried out for his when his thumb flicked over my nipple, followed by the descent of his mouth. He pulled the V-neck of the dress to the side to suck and lick until my head fell back against the door.

"Caius," I breathed, my hands gripping the back of his head.

He groaned, tugging at the dress as if he couldn't get enough—as if his mouth could not find enough places to claim on my skin.

A rip sounded as he shoved the other side down, a tear cutting through the thin fabric of the gown.

Caius stood straight, putting some distance between us. The cool brush of air against my bare skin felt wrong, and I longed to pull him closer—allow him to consume me entirely.

"I'm sorry," he whispered, and I let out a breathy chuckle.

"Don't be," I said. "I care very little for the clothing King Faolan found fit to give me.

With a possessive grip at the back of my neck, Caius pulled me closer. His kiss turned claiming as I met him stroke for stroke. My own mouth claiming his, just as my heart had.

There was no question about the engagement—it would not happen.

Caius's hands found my thighs as he hoisted me up, turning to carry me through the sitting room, past the archway, and laying me on the bed.

I pulled my dress off completely, watching as Caius stripped down to nothing.

When at last, he hovered over me, he brushed the hair away from my face, planting kisses on my forehead, my nose, my lips, and my neck.

As he filled me, he moved with slow, languid strokes. Every glide stretched me as I arched. Our gentle gasps filled the room—the sighs escaped my parted lips as he pushed deeper until I was certain our lives entwined.

When we'd finished, I turned into the familiar warmth of his chest, praying to the gods for a brighter tomorrow.

Chapter Fifty-Nine

Theron

My reflection stared back at me as I rolled the sleeves of the white button-down I'd found in the wardrobe. Gray trousers and dress shoes had been stowed away in the bottom drawer, so I'd put those on too.

Behind me, two large windows leaked light from the thin, billowy curtains, brightening the stone walls of the bedchamber.

When I looked at my pale skin, the slouch of my shoulders, I attempted to straighten. It was a struggle to see in myself the king I'd always promised myself I would be. The prince my father had raised no longer existed—a mere memory that formed the hardened man before me.

A figure moved from the bed, stepping across the floor with bare feet, and with not a scrap of clothing on her body, Rialey wrapped her arms around my shoulders from behind, her hands gently smoothing down my shirt over my chest. As her fingers skimmed the scar through the fabric, her head peeked from behind me, black hair kissing her bare shoulders with the same reverence I'd used just last night.

"Come back to bed," she murmured, watching herself in the mirror as she placed a gentle kiss on my bicep.

My blood heated, rushing downward in a way that had me reminding myself of my duties. "We are to meet with King Faolan tonight, and I will need to speak with Verena beforehand."

Rialey smirked, her hands gliding slowly over my shoulders, down my arms. "Leaving me for another woman?" she questioned.

I turned, gripping her by the waist and pulling her in, planting a kiss on her lips. "Never, you foolish woman."

Nerves broke through my lust as I thought of what we had to do. Faolan was set on Verena's hand, something she should not have to give. With little else to offer save for my cooperation and aid after becoming king, I had little. And even my rise to the throne would be up for question if Faolan wanted to dig his heels in even more.

I felt powerless—a traitor prince who'd lost his crown.

Rialey took a deep breath in before speaking. "Are you okay?"

Swallowing my fear, I glanced toward the wall. Golden-framed paintings littered the stone, each depicting a quiet view from the countryside. The shrublands looked familiar, as we'd traveled through them for days. There were paintings of mountains, gardens, and even one that looked like a castle, much different from the one in Liethaire. "This is the second time I've come to a table to negotiate and appeared weak," I admitted, the confession burning my throat. My gaze landed on Rialey, concern clear in the pinch of her brow. "How am I supposed to prove myself as king while I lead a rebellion and carry very little power?"

"You carry influence," she interjected. "Bloodbane was sure to give you that."

I shook my head, hating the way she'd phrased it. Had I not done enough? Was *I* simply not enough?

I'd spent years under the thumb of my father, seeking to earn his approval by pleasing him. It led me to become a monster, too, for a time. And while my time with Rialey over the past two and a half years had been spent, first, by helping my father's wrongful prisoners escape, and second, by involving myself in this rebellion, I couldn't shake the feeling that I still hadn't earned my place on the throne.

"It is not your fault, Theron," Rialey said, gripping the sides of my face and forcing me to look at her.

"Isn't it?" I questioned, my voice barely audible.

I'd killed before—wrongfully. While Rialey knew the guilt I carried, she hadn't been the one preaching against feeling it. I had.

I believed what I'd told her around the fire during what felt like a lifetime ago. Morality could not be so black and white, but just because I knew the logical answer to forgiving myself, didn't mean the actual task would be so simple—and it didn't mean I wouldn't have to forgive myself again and again.

Rialey kept her hands on me, and I was thankful for their steadying warmth. "You have been dealt an unfair hand," she said. "We all have."

My gaze flicked down to her bare chest, a smirk tugging at the corner of my mouth. "I cannot discuss my insecurities while you are like this."

A devious grin appeared on her face. "Like what?" she questioned, and I pulled her closer, pressing my mouth to hers.

When she pulled back, I looked at the scar across her cheek, the mark that had stained her soul with grief. Those memories were hers, but I'd seen them—couldn't stand what my father had done to her family—to *her*.

"It's going to be okay," she whispered, pressing her head into my chest. "It has to be."

I kissed the top of her head, my hand stroking through the soft strands of her hair. With her so close, my chest felt full—as if there were something good awaiting just beyond the horizon—like dawn about to break.

"My Queen," I whispered just before a knock sounded at the door to the sitting room beyond our bedchamber.

I moved swiftly, closing the door to the room where Rialey sauntered to the wardrobe before crossing the carpeted floor near the seating area to open our sitting-room door.

"Florence," I said in surprise. Verena stood with her, eyes bright with hope.

"Can we come in?" the Queen of the Waldwood asked, and I nodded.

Florence pinned me with her icy stare before walking around me, muttering on her way to the small couch in front of the fire. "I know what ails you," she said, before sinking into the cushions.

I turned, not bothering to hide my confusion.

"We need to talk," Verena said, choosing to sit in the less comfortable chair angled toward the fire near where Florence sat.

"Yes," I said, stepping forward. "That is what I'd just been preparing for."

Florence folded her legs beneath her, adjusting the long skirt of her gown and getting comfortable. "I have spent time in the palace apothecary," she said, a smirk forming on her lips. "Unfortunately, for King Faolan, I got turned around on my way there, finding myself in the palace's *second* apothecary. The one located in the north tower."

I stayed standing, finding it a better way to deal with my anxious energy. "I cannot pretend to know the significance of that."

"I *do* wish you'd get to the point, Florence," Verena muttered.

"Your father," she began, those icy eyes cutting right through me. "He imprisoned the king's older brother some years ago—a strategy for demanding food from Liethaire during the worst of the famine." My stomach roiled at the knowledge of my father's evil. "I found them treating the king's brother in the north tower. He is..." she paused, trying to gather the words. "Not right."

I folded my arms across my chest, leaning against the wall near the fireplace. "What do you mean?"

"His *mind*," Verena clarified. "There is a reason Faris keeps to himself, a reason he was so young when he became king. Theron," she said my name with a brevity that forced me to listen closer. "He made comments indicating he longed for the magic of the Waldwood. When Florence came to me this morning, it all made sense. His brother has not recovered from the torture your father put him through." She tapped her temple. "Has not recovered here. We can, for lack of a better word, exploit Faolan's need for revenge against your father."

My brow furrowed. "And you believe that would be enough?" I asked. While anger and grudges made for great weak spots, many kings could find their way past such emotions, or, at the very least, acknowledge them and use them to their advantage. I wasn't confident in Verena's approach.

"There is something else," she said, swallowing as if her body fought against the very words she longed to speak. "It is risky, but I think...I *believe* I can heal him."

The room seemed still, save for the crackling fire in the hearth.

"We will offer menders from Onelia and Abellona. I've already worked out those logistics, but as for the king's brother, I truly believe I could heal him." She turned away, resting an elbow on the arm of the chair and bringing her fingers to her mouth, muttering, "Anything to not marry the man."

I thought back on that first meeting in Eirdis's temple, how Verena had so quickly invaded our waking thoughts. "You're going to enter his mind," I remarked, knowing full well how exhausted she'd looked after such a feat.

Verena nodded, her eyes meeting mine. "I am going to try."

"It will wear on you." I brought up, the true question lying between each word.

Verena gave me a knowing smile. "Florence should be able to help with that."

It seemed a good plan. Meeting with Faolan, we would surprise him with knowledge he did not believe we had, dig at what I assumed to be one of his deepest wounds, though one could never be sure, and finally, offer him a solution he hadn't hoped to find.

"If you are sure," I said, knowing that if she should change her mind, I would not fault her for it.

The door behind me clicked open as Rialey entered the room, wanting debriefed on our conversation, no doubt.

Verena's jaw hardened with fierce determination as she gave me an answer that sealed our strategy.

"I am sure."

My grip tightened on Rialey's hand as we were escorted toward the same dining hall we'd eaten in upon our arrival. Since then, meals had been brought to our rooms by the staff.

Now that I knew a bit about King Faolan and the way he operated, nerves skittered down my spine, causing me to stiffen.

He seemed to enjoy knowledge and using it as leverage when he could. Presenting that we may have known something he'd intended to keep hidden could come with a risk. Though clearly a drunk, and if what we'd heard of his kingdom was anything to go by, a fair and just king, King Faolan still had the makings of a predator.

Sly. Cunning. *Dangerous.*

We were not in Alphaird any longer.

Two guards walked paces ahead of our entire party, Rialey never leaving my side as she inched closer, determination evident in the set of her brows.

One guard turned, a tall and lanky man, far younger than I'd originally thought if his boyish features were anything to go by.

"King Faolan is expecting you," he said, placing one hand on the door keeping us in the hallway. "But should he change his mind, you should not attempt to stay beyond your welcome."

My stomach churned as the door opened, revealing the vast dining room we'd entered the previous evening.

The table, now set for each of us with those dark crimson napkins and decorations, stretched out to where King Faolan sat, leaning back against his chair with his eyes on the door and a smug smile on his face.

Verena was the first to walk in, and the rest of us followed. On our plates, a pile of pasta sat with a variety of vegetables and shrimp.

"Ah," Faolan said as Verena made her way to the side of the table. "My beautiful wife arrives."

Rialey and I took our seats, watching as Caius pulled Verena's chair out for her, tension woven in his shoulders, his jaw clenched shut. He sat nearest King Faolan, separating the king from the Waldwood's Queen.

"Interesting," Faolan mused, his foxlike eyes narrowing into slits briefly before he sat forward, elbows resting on the table, and his hands clasped in front of his face.

Despite my pounding heart, I kept my expression bored. I would not be a rabbit ensnared by a fox. "I'm afraid the Queen of the Waldwood's hand is off the table when it comes to our negotiations, King Faolan."

Faolan scoffed, gesturing to Verena. "I think the lady should speak for herself, should she not?"

I watched Verena carefully, surprised to find the picture of strength as she sat up straighter, turning her head toward Faolan with very little emotion. "I cannot offer you my hand." Her words, matter-of-fact in their delivery, hung in the air.

Faolan stood, slapping his hands on the table and causing the dishes to rattle. "That settles it," he says. "Unfortunately, we do not have a deal, and I ask—"

Now or never.

"How's your brother, King Faolan?" I asked, picking up my fork and twirling it in the pasta. We hadn't been told to eat yet, so I risked rudeness—but that was the entire point. We meant to throw him off balance—play with his emotions so that when the solution was presented, he could do nothing but take it.

Faolan's fists clenched as he slowly lowered into his seat. Anger rippled off him as he picked up his knife, twirling it between his fingers in a threatening motion.

"I apologize for my father," I said, feeling Rialey's hand gently brush the side of my leg beneath the table in encouragement. "As you know, I wish for him to suffer for his crimes." I paused, twisting the pasta around my fork to look the king in his eyes as his equal—as a king myself. "All of them," I finished.

King Faolan gritted his teeth. Gone was the sly and snarky king we'd met yesterday. In his place, an angry and vengeful king sat—one that acted out of what I could only assume was love for his family. I didn't blame him.

"How dare—"

"My father will be killed," I continued, interrupting him. "It will be punishment for what he's done."

Faolan held the knife in his fist, stabbing the table with one firm strike. So far, angering him was working. Whether we'd get the result we'd want was still up for debate. "Tread lightly, Prince," he warned, "Or you will not find yourself so welcome in my kingdom."

I did not acknowledge his threats. What we offered—it would be good enough. I had to believe it. "My offer still stands for an alliance with Alphaird. We do, in fact, owe you a great deal." My knee bounced beneath the table, and Rialey's hand quickly found it to still it. I was nervous, but I needed to do a better job at hiding it. "But it is what I've discussed with the Waldwood that may entice you despite the queen's rejection of your proposal." I gestured to Verena, allowing her to continue.

"We are willing to offer menders from Onelia and Abellona to tend to your subjects," she said, opening her mouth to continue, but Faolan cut her off with a brutal smack to the table.

"I don't need a fucking mender," he seethed. "Do you think I have not tried that?"

"I see." Verena kept calm as she spoke, her tone floating through the dining hall until it landed like a smooth balm. "I may not offer you my hand, but I can, however, offer you something else. You asked about my magic, King Faolan."

Rialey took a sip of water from her cup as Florence did the same from her position on the other side of me.

"I have been given," Verena continued, "unique talents; gifted by what we presume to be the gods."

Magic hummed in the room as Verena looked squarely at the king. A vein protruded at her neck, revealing the effort it truly took to enter one's awakened mind.

Faolan's eyes widened.

Moments passed where it felt as if we were all holding our breath until the thread of tension snapped.

Faolan blinked, one stray tear streaming down his cheek.

Verena leaned forward, menacing in her approach. "If you give your armies to fight for our cause, I am willing to heal your brother—provided my mender can come with me. Should something go wrong," she swallowed, the first tell of her true insecurities. "If something should go wrong, I will need—"

Faolan stood up, rounding the table in two quick strides and grabbing Verena's arm, yanking her to stand. Caius caught his wrist, his tone dark.

"Let go of her," he commanded, and Faolan's hand jolted back as if he'd been burned.

He rubbed his wrist. "We go now," he said, turning on his heel and leaving his dinner behind.

Florence and Verena pushed their chairs in just before Verena shook her head at whatever Caius whispered.

"I will be back," she said, straightening her gown. "And we will hopefully have what we need to win this war."

Chapter Sixty

Verena

The stained-glass windows just outside the winding stone staircase of the north tower painted a kaleidoscope of color on the walls behind us.

King Faolan hadn't said a word to us as Florence and I trailed behind, the fabric of our skirts creating a shuffling sound on the stone floors.

I swallowed my nerves, my magic coming to the surface, buzzing over my skin with such an intensity, I scratched at my arms.

Entering King Faolan's mind in the dining hall had been risky. I knew I'd need almost all my energy for what was to come—if I could even do it.

The anger the king carried remained when we descended the staircase into a room on one of the lower levels of the palace.

Faolan plucked a key from his pocket, placing it in the lock and turning until a sharp *click* echoed off the pale, stone walls.

When we entered, the entire room had been decorated with luxury in mind. Gold accents highlighted every intricately carved corner of the rooms. A lavish red curtain hung on the far wall where a window should be in the sitting room.

My brow furrowed. We'd gone low enough beneath the palace that no windows should be down here.

King Faolan stopped, noting my distraction. "The illusion of windows," he said, gesturing to the wall. "I don't like that Kaemon is housed in what is essentially a basement, but on the upper floors, he'd often use the windows when he felt the need to jump during his night terrors."

I turned to him, noting the resigned look he held as if he were used to the acts.

As we moved past a door and into the bedroom, we found Kaemon Faolan sitting cross-legged on a crimson comforter, facing the headboard with a stillness I'd never seen.

A statue, the bare-chested man riddled with raised white scars, did not move. Long, lanky limbs reflected a similar height to his brother, and when Kaemon turned, the sharp angles of his cheeks echoed that of his sibling, along with amber eyes, though Kaemon's were highlighted with deep bruising on the thin skin below—his skin far paler than his brother's.

"Kaemon," Faris spoke, his tone soft as he approached, steps slow and muffled by the red carpet. "I've brought—"

"I know." Kaemon turned, the light in his amber eyes wholly missing. "Have you come to break my bones again?"

My brow furrowed, not sure how to respond to such a gruesome assumption. Guards entered the room behind us, three strong men with weapons missing from their uniforms.

"Kaemon," Faris said, stepping closer. I swore I heard a slight break in his voice, saw the silver line his eyes. "Forgive me."

King Faolan looked to me, the weight of his hope held in my magic as he nodded once.

The guards stepped forward, grabbing Kaemon's limbs, fighting him as his screams rang out so loud, I swore the others could hear them at the other end of the palace.

When I realized I'd been shaking, Florence placed a gentle hand on my shoulder, and I closed my eyes. Sucking in a deep breath, I tapped into my magic, Kaemon's mind opening as if desperate—a dam with so many hairline fractures, it could do nothing but crack.

Memories assaulted me, thoughts swirling around like a twisting storm as I fought to catch my breath.

There was so much darkness—so much suffering.

I saw Marmere's dungeons. The king's wicked face as he stared down at what felt like me, though I knew I'd never lived this. I became Kaemon, my magic burning so strong in my chest, I found it hard to breathe.

"You know," the king began, "I've grown rather tired of housing you here. You'd think your father would learn and accept my arrangement."

I spat at the king's feet, rough stone scraping against my bare back. With heavy chains on my wrists and ankles, I struggled to move, the gnawing in my hollow stomach nearly unbearable.

The slap rang out in the dungeons as my head whipped to the side, a blade quickly at my throat.

King Wineslowe dragged the gleaming metal over my skin, down until he got to the spot just above my heart. Anger flashed in his cruel gaze, his pupils swallowing the little light of the dungeon. King Wineslowe traced the shape of a W, every cut burning as I forced my eyes closed, tears leaking out where I could not wipe them away. My arms were suspended overhead, completely numb and limp against my bindings.

"I could run this right through your flesh," Wineslowe spat, his hot breath fanning over my face. "You are a bargaining chip, nothing more. Things are going to get a lot worse for you, Kaemon. Much, much worse."

Every drag of Wineslowe's knife—every aching muscle, every hunger pain —knocked the breath from my lungs as I crumpled to the ground.

"Verena!" The voice sounded faint. I didn't know that name. I didn't—

"Verena!" My eyes snapped open, the images still in my mind but now separate—more distant. I didn't know how to heal such evil.

I'd suffered my own punishments in the palace dungeons—unspeakable things I did not wish to recount.

Tears streamed down Kaemon's face as the guards held his arms and legs. I touched one, wiping it away as our minds remained linked. Exhaustion settled over my weary bones.

"I don't know if—"

"Verena." Florence's sharp whisper sounded in my ear, her cool hand gripping my shoulder like a vice. "Think of how you healed. You cannot take all his memories, but you can overwhelm them with those forgotten. Dig *deeper*."

I strained against the darkness in Kaemon's mind—the thoughts that resulted from so much torment. Fighting, I pushed past them—looking for something, anything of the man that existed *before*.

Lavish ballrooms.

Diving off cliffs near the palace.

The icy sting of water mixed with the pleasure of adrenaline shooting through my blood.

"When do you think we will stop being followed?" Faris questioned, his eyes alight with joy as we kicked our feet in the icy water of the lake.

There, just atop the cliff, stood Regis, the guard assigned to ensuring we did not meet our demise. I was certain his reports were the bane of Mother and Father's existence.

"I am not sure," I answered, a laugh bubbling up in my chest. "Though I believe Regis is absolutely livid. Look at how red his face is."

Faris laughed. At fourteen, his face still carried the boyish roundness of his youth.

Five years his senior, he'd been the greatest gift my parents could have given me. When the stress of my duties became too much, there was always this.

It had started with sneaking into the kitchens for Aurelia's famous tarts. And now, I enjoyed nothing more than taking a break from negotiations and meetings—stiff ballrooms and a court of vipers chasing wealth.

"I'm certain they're only following you," Faris said, a wide smile on his face. His dark hair dripped water onto his bronze skin, made darker by his time in the sun.

"Nonsense."

"They don't follow me like that," he asserted. "It's because you are to be king, and they absolutely cannot let you kill yourself cliff diving into Feith Lake."

I laughed, a deeper, hearty sound that was pulled from the pits of my chest. "I'm certain Regis is supposed to keep you alive as well."

Faris's nose scrunched. "Not to be king, though." He turned to me, more serious. "I do not want the responsibility. I would not make a very good king."

"You would make a fine king, Faris." Something tugged at my chest as I kicked the cold water away from me, keeping my head above the surface.

Kind, generous, cunning. Faris would make a fine king should fate decide I am unfit.

"I should not like it," he answered, his eyes turning to a rich amber—the way they always did when he was about to say something particularly devious. "I should like to bed women and drink father's most expensive wine."

"You are fourteen," I said, rolling my eyes and skidding my hand across the water. "You should not be bedding anyone."

"Boys!" Regis shouted from the cliff just before Faris groaned.

"Times up, little rooster. Time for our very important dinner." I wriggled my eyebrows despite the hint of dread in my stomach.

"You think you will find a wife among court ladies?" he asked, and my chest tightened. I'd found someone perfectly suitable for marriage, save for her lack of status—though our parents wouldn't listen to that.

"Eh," I said, keeping my tone casual. "I doubt it."

I dug up memory after memory—piecing together the life of a prince—one from a kingdom that was nothing like Alphaird if his parents were anything to go by.

Well loved, well revered by those around him, Kaemon had the hope of being king—something taken from him by the man who had a habit of doing *nothing* but take.

"Faris?" Kaemon questioned, and I watched the predator king break, tears falling in fat drops.

"Yes," he said. "It is me."

Then Kaemon did the one thing I'd never expected—he smiled.

The hall just beyond Kaemon Faolan's room painted pictures from the stained glass as the sun set low on the horizon. Streaks of red and gold decorated Faris's face.

My muscles felt weak—my mind weaker as I gave up standing straight. I'd used everything I had and more. I was certain Florence would not have a good time taking my weakness as her own.

"King Wineslowe plans to leave Stromadale in two weeks." Faris looked at me, his expression more open than I'd seen it. "Heal well." His eyes flicked to Florence. "We will leave in the next few days. I do not wish for my army to travel all the way to Marmere if they do not need to."

"I fear it will not be over with the death of the king. The kingdom will have to accept Theron as king," Florence said, her arm gently tucking beneath mine as she helped me stand.

"Theron will make a fine king," Faris said. "And you..." His eyes found mine, an echo of the boy I'd seen in Kaemon's memories. "You, Your

Majesty, are a fine queen. I envy the man who has claimed your heart before I could win your hand."

"Thank you," I whispered, my eyelids growing heavy.

My steps swayed, and I could feel my mind going dark.

Just before I collapsed, I felt a firm grip catch me by the elbow. "You're welcome, Verena. You are very welcome."

CHAPTER SIXTY-ONE

THERON

The moment we'd passed into Alphaird, something had shifted within me.

I'd spent my entire life preparing to be king of a kingdom I so desperately wanted to change. For so long, my fear of my father drove my actions. Even on the streets of Marmere as Eryx, I'd been cowering in the shadows—pleasing my father in the daylight.

As we marched toward Stromadale—towards my father's demise, I knew that the rebellion had been formed, not just in the country I would someday claim as my own, but also within myself.

Hot rage burned in me like the fires at the city squares—desperate to consume and light the man who'd caused such fear and suffering alight.

I guided my horse, borrowed armor clinking with every step toward the castle, spires now visible above the tree line.

Florence had sent word to Bloodbane the moment we found ourselves in King Faolan's favor.

Bloodbane would lead the Guild's armies against Marmere as we marched toward Stromadale with Faolan's armies.

"Are you meant to ride at the front?" Rialey questioned as her horse appeared next to mine. Her black hair had been braided back, armor glinting over her heart, catching the sunlight poking through the trees. With sweat on her brow, and two swords sheathed at her back, Rialey looked fierce, marching along with the men surrounding us.

"I am," I answered, a smirk on my face. Our plan was to take the palace by surprise—to let them know exactly what had come for them. I would gain entrance into the castle, find my father, and claim my rightful place on the throne.

My head tilted to the side as I looked at her—memorized her features before our battle. "You, however, are not."

"And why is that?" she questioned.

A frown pulled at my lips, worry gnawing at my insides. "Rialey," I said, tone serious. "If I should not make it."

"You will make it," she asserted. "We all will."

Behind us, two thousand soldiers marched with the intent to take Alphaird—with the hope of a new rule.

Rona, leaving the moment word got to the Waldwood, had found us at the border, insisting on fighting alongside us as a mender.

Bloodbane, however, would be up against a larger army. With the goal of taking the palace, he'd needed more magic. Stromadale's lord, Rodric Cask, did not keep a large guard for his city this far north.

We descended the hillside, cloaked by trees, just before emerging in a large meadow that sprawled out to the palace entrance.

When our army broke, I could hear shouts from the palace wall, frantic warnings thrown out to the guards to prepare for an attack.

My hand wrapped around the hilt of my sword; the leather wrapped around the handle sticking to my gloves and giving me a better grip.

I gripped the reins tighter in my other hand, my body ready to push forward. "A better tomorrow!" I bellowed, the words ripping from my chest. "We ride on!"

Urging my horse forward, we pressed into a gallop, followed by the thunderous sound of thousands of hooves behind us. Wind whistled in my ears as we picked up our pace—closing the distance between the tree line and the castle until soldiers came into view, their arrows poised and ready to strike.

With a snap of string, the weapons went flying, felling two men at the front of the line.

We charged onward, our own archers pulling out their weapons and firing a counterattack at the wall just as soldiers poured from the palace doors, most on foot, while we rode on.

One man, with graying hair and a beard to match, did not hesitate as he launched himself towards me. With a firm grip on my sword, I swung low, the metal clanking against the metal of his as the tip of his blade nicked my horse's flank.

I dismounted quickly, letting the beast go on and holding my weapon at the ready.

All around us, chaos erupted, a mass of soldiers overtaking the guard with ease. It ignited something in me as I lunged forward, shoving my blade straight through the man with a guttural cry.

Rialey fought next to me, spinning away from another soldier as she arched her blade downward.

Another Rialey materialized, another—leaving the woman confused. During that brief stutter, I yanked my blade from the dead man at my feet, marching with the weapon slick with blood until I came up behind Rialey's opponent, and dragged my sword clean across her neck, her head rolling in the bloodstained grass below.

More soldiers appeared, pushing forward with weapons ready. My heart dropped at the thought of it—at the thought of abandoning the fray to find my father hidden away in the palace.

With a swift strike, Rialey felled a man three times her size, clearing an opening for me to run to a side door on the palace.

"Go!" she screamed, twisting with her blade to slash across a woman's arm. "Go now!"

I listened, sending a prayer up to the gods that she would be here when I returned.

Heart pounding, I ran for the palace, cutting through two men before making it to the old wooden door. I yanked on the handle, found it locked, and opted for a more rigorous technique.

I backed up, barreling forward to slam the full force of my body into the wood as it shuddered.

Again.

Again.

Until the door splintered and fell into a small room that appeared to be part of a servant's quarters.

I hadn't had the time nor resources to review the layout of the palace of Stromadale, but I knew there were a few places my father could be hiding.

First would be his bedchamber.

With heart racing, I ran through the halls past servants and shocked courtiers standing in their luxurious clothes with mouths agape.

Some screamed and ran off, but one particularly brave servant charged me with a candlestick. I quickly whacked it out of his hand.

"Forgive me," I pleaded, shoving my sword into his chest. I'd let a servant go before, and it had risked our capture back in Branwood. I would not make the same mistake again.

Climbing the stairs, my breath left in panting gasps by the time I emerged on the fifth floor, blazing down the hallway, and shoving at doors as I went. Most rooms sat empty, and frustration burned in my chest when I'd found myself in a large room, the scent of frankincense and patchouli reminded me of my father's cologne.

I grunted in frustration, aware of the time constraints on my task.

If my father got away—if he left Stromadale—our efforts would be wasted, and I did not know how much time King Faolan would allow us to use his armies before he saw some kind of reward for it.

I moved back toward the staircase, finding two soldiers running with weapons drawn toward me. Pivoting, I turned to find a smaller stairwell on the other side of the hall. Taking the opportunity, I took the steps two at a time as I descended to the first floor of the castle.

The staircase led me directly to the kitchens. One cook screamed as she saw me, holding a kitchen knife in her right hand as she backed away.

I pressed a finger to my lips, sweat drenching the tunic I wore beneath my armor.

Looking back toward the staircase, I waited, knowing the soldiers would be fast approaching, but found the doorway empty.

The cook ran in the opposite direction, fleeing through the doors and into another hall. I ran after her, finding the halls abnormally empty when I got out of the kitchens.

I paused, my hand tightening around my sword as I spun, observing my surroundings to learn what had gone wrong.

Where would he be?

The lavish tapestries covered nearly the entire wall all the way down the hallway—each with the symbol of Stromadale stitched into it with silver thread.

A loud popping sound echoed from near the kitchens, followed by roaring and heat.

I turned, finding a smoke cloud billowing down the hall—black, heavy, and followed by the orange glow of flames.

"Shit," I muttered, watching, one by one, as each tapestry lining the wall was lit aflame—as if Alphaird would rather consume herself than accept a new ruler.

I sprinted, my arms pumping as my boots pounded the stone floors. My breaths were shallow—hard. The tang of blood coated my tongue. When I'd reached the end of the hall, I found another servant's stairwell and took my opportunity.

The wooden steps would certainly burn, so I needed to ascend faster—work harder.

I pushed myself, stumbling out of the third floor as smoke surrounded me. Ducking, I tried to stay below it, my vision nearly lost against its thick veil.

Fingers fiddling with a door handle, I felt it give way and fell onto the floor of a second-story bedroom.

Flames threatened me at my back, the entire palace burning to ash around me.

I ran to the window, lifted the latch, and slammed it open.

I swallowed, sheathing my sword at my back before gripping either side of the window. The wood groaned beneath my fingertips—begging me to stay and be consumed by fire.

Without another thought, I jumped, my knees buckling on my landing until pain shot through my left leg.

I looked out over the field, the battle still raging despite the dead bodies that littered the landscape. I did not have time to feel sorry for those who had been lost.

Caius appeared, breaking away from the fray, sprinting toward the trees with a sword gripped in his hand. I watched as the others fought, Caius now fleeing.

My brow furrowed, but I didn't stand still. Deciding, I took off through the meadow, keeping away from the battle as I found the hole through the trees that Caius had entered.

I didn't take the man to be a deserter, but maybe I'd been wrong.

That, or maybe he'd found something—*someone*.

CHAPTER SIXTY-TWO

CAIUS

I broke through the trees, heart beating like a rabbit on the run. I looked between the tall pines, mist settling between the trees.

Wiping my glove across my face, I smeared the dirt and blood more than ridding myself of it, as if death had permanently stained itself on my skin.

Verena had struggled to recover after her time in Liethaire, her magic weakened by her distance from the Waldwood and overworking herself with the king's brother. I begged her to stay toward the back of our army, but didn't realize how much that separation would worry me.

The moment I saw King Wineslowe break for the trees, abandoning the castle of Stromadale, I took after him—seeing nothing but an end to the kingdom's sorrows—the senseless death that took those I love, and threatened the ones who remained.

A breaking branch to my left sent a murder of crows into the air, their dark feathers dull in the misty light of the forest. With a loud call, they sent a warning signal across the forest—alerting its creatures of danger. I ran straight for it.

A glimpse of black fabric caught my eye, followed by the king running from behind a nearby tree. I lunged toward him; the coward abandoning his kingdom to the wrath of a rebellion that would surely come for him.

I would come for him and be his demise.

Pain shot through me as I sprinted and propelled myself into him, slamming us both onto the ground and causing us to lose our swords.

King Wineslowe quickly twisted, his sword lost a few feet away as he scrambled to retrieve it. I threw my weight on top of him, clawing at his skin with rage burning in my belly—hot and angry, I cocked my arm back, landing a punch across the king's face.

Up close, King Wineslowe looked to be the mirror of Theron, but there was something dead hidden behind his eyes. He stared at me with no crown atop his head, small wrinkles forming on his face from age. Wineslowe was just a man. Another punch sent his face cocking to the left, blood spurting from his nose and mouth.

I inhaled the sharp, coppery scent, needing more.

Wineslowe shifted, trying to free himself as a smile cracked across his face, blood-coated teeth stained crimson.

"You've a good arm," he said, causing me to stutter, a moment I regretted as warmth and pain bloomed from the side of my calf.

Wineslowe dragged the blade from my flesh, and I felt every burning inch as it pulled out, crying into the trees. I scrambled off him, running toward my sword, discarded on a blanket of moss.

I turned, noting my weakness as I limped with each step, I took closer. Holding the sword like a lifeline, I pointed it in the king's direction.

His dagger, now slick with my blood, was sheathed at his belt before he retrieved his sword from the ground.

"Brave to think you could end me," he mocked, stepping closer. "And now look at you." He pointed to my leg with his blade as I ground my teeth together, sweat dripping down my face, stinging my eyes as I blinked rapidly. "A wounded animal ensnared by a wolf."

"You will die before this war ends," I warned, my voice stronger than my body felt.

Wineslowe laughed, the sound throaty and grating. I could feel it skitter across my skin, sending chills down my spine. "Is that what you truly believe?" he questioned.

Behind us, a snap sounded, and I turned, finding Theron there. His blonde hair had been stained with dirt and blood, soot covering his pale skin in a deep black, making his blue eyes even more striking.

"Caius," he said. "Go."

Theron never took his eyes off his father, anger burning along with the contempt written on his face.

"But—"

"Go!"

I jolted back, noting the way he spoke with authority. I'd seen it before—in the moments where Theron became more than a prince—became a king.

He'd prioritized protecting Verena in Liethaire, ensuring that she never felt pressured to offer what she did not want to give. He fought alongside his people—longed for a better future.

I stepped back, my leg stinging when I put weight on it. Theron looked to the wound, then back at me, tossing his head back toward the meadow. "Go," he said, softer this time. "Take care of our people."

Nodding, I obeyed, breaking into the clearing to find nothing but death. I watched as smoke billowed from the palace, rising like a thick fog over the clank of swords and shouts of soldiers.

With one glance toward the sky, I begged Abellona to remain true to what I'd heard.

Let this not be the end, but a new beginning.

Chapter Sixty-Three

Theron

"You've grown into a disgrace," my father snarled, watching me with the same haunting look I'd seen time and time again growing up.

I used to cower in the wake of that look—knowing the punishment that awaited. This time, however, I did not run. My father used to seem so large—so terrifying, but now, amidst the smoke and mist, he looked nothing like the picture I'd painted of him. Behind his arrogance, hidden by a mask now cracking, I saw the fear etched into the lines of his face, carved there at the realization that his own son would be his demise—the one to steal his throne instead of inherit it.

"A mirror image of you, I suppose." I smiled, goading him.

My father's lip curled as curses left his mouth. I pushed forward, my blade coming down to slam against his, the vibrations so intense, I could feel them in my bones—my teeth.

I released pressure, spinning away from the arch of his blade as I thrust the tip of my sword toward his back.

My father leapt back, narrowly avoiding my assault, and fueling the determination within me.

Gritting my teeth, I pushed forward, a relentless sequence of attacks. Every clank of steel on steel sent echoes through the trees. The ringing echoed to my ears until I heard nothing but metal and death, tasted blood and soot and sorrow on my tongue.

I pushed forward harder, faster, until my father stumbled a step and landed on his ass.

Without ceasing, I took the opportunity, sliding to my knees to plunge my sword deep in his stomach.

Blood splattered from his stained teeth onto my face, coating my lips with the copper taste of his demise. Pushing closer, I could feel his breath on my face as I looked him in the eyes. I relished in the resistance of flesh against my blade and shoved deeper, causing King Wineslowe to smile, a gesture that curdled my stomach, making bile rise in my dry throat.

My brow furrowed when he shifted, warmth blooming in my gut, followed by the sharp sting of pain.

I looked down, eyes wide, to find a dagger protruding from between my armor, deeply embedded in the flesh of my stomach.

"Wherever I should go in this afterlife," my father seethed, his breaths labored. "I am taking you with me."

He shoved deeper as time slowed, my vision tunneling into one narrow circle.

I watched the light leave my father's eyes, felt dizzy as I forced myself upright, dropping my sword and shedding my gloves to feel the weapon at my stomach. Blood coated my fingers, and I couldn't help the realization that it was mine.

Mine.

Mine.

Mine.

Rialey was mine, and I needed to get to her.

Icy dread coated my veins as I saw her, hair splayed out beneath her on a pillow we'd shared.

I saw Rialey's hope for the future—the confidence she had as we stood before a mirror in Liethaire. Not once had she doubted my ability to be king—not once had she given up on me.

Even in the face of betrayal, she'd been there—rescuing me from the dungeons of a man who now sat dead and alone in the woods.

I stumbled through the trees, the scratch of thorns cutting my bare hands.

Smoke billowed above the trees, the fires burning like the pyres set alight in the city square of Marmere—the city I longed to save.

"Rialey," I whispered, falling to my knees. Damp moss soaked between my fingers as I grunted, forcing myself onward.

My limbs were weak, vision narrowing the harder I pushed.

I crawled—crawled past the pain—past Abellona's kiss as she promised a sweet end.

When I broke through the trees, finding my way to the meadow, I saw nothing but death and destruction.

It was the last thing I saw as I closed my eyes, laid my head on the grass and soil with my hand clutched to my stomach.

Death tasted sweet, like honey and herbs. It stuck between my fingers—lingered on my skin so that I *knew* I'd remember her gentle whispers—the quiet that came as she made me hers.

My last thought being that even in death—I belonged to another.

Chapter Sixty-Four

Rialey

"Now!"

Gold flashed in my vision as I spun an illusion, masking Rona as she barreled toward two soldiers.

My focus strained as the image rippled—just slightly. Though not perfect, it was still effective when I watched heads roll, releasing my illusion just in time to spin, finding a soldier there with gritted teeth and a sword pointed towards my throat.

I smiled, my magic cool against my skin as I disappeared, appearing again behind him. He turned, shoving his sword through the apparition while I did the same. Instead of finding air, I found the grind of flesh and bones when I strained to push my weapon through his spine.

The man screamed as he fell to the ground, staining the grass with more blood.

When I looked up, smoke poured from the palace windows, winding up in a thick cloud that darkened the sky—an omen of death.

I looked through the chaos to Rona, the smell of blood and smoke invading my lungs.

Theron.

He'd been in the palace—he'd been.

I spun, searching the meadow for any sign of him.

Weapons rang out over the field, cries floating to the clouds above.

Straining my eyes, I squinted at the tree line, looking for any sign—anything that said he wasn't in the palace—wasn't burning like the fate that should have befallen me.

There.

Movement, low to the ground, came as I caught a figure crawling in the grass. Instinctively, I took a step forward—another, as if my body knew who I'd find there.

"Florence!" I screamed over the chaos, breaking into a run, sure it was him. It had to be him.

I pushed harder—faster, watching as Theron lay in the grass, his hand clutched against his stomach.

Dread coated my veins.

Something was wrong. *Very* wrong.

My knees slammed into the ground next to Theron's still body, my hands dragging him onto my lap. My fingers brushed across his face, trying to remove the blood and dirt—the soot I assumed was from the fire.

I pressed my hand against his chest, feeling nothing there.

"He has no pulse!" I screamed, tears stinging my eyes, mixing with sweat and dirt. "He has no pulse!" My voice cracked across the meadow, hot dread consuming me—cloaking me in darkness.

"Come on," I whispered, looking to the hilt of a dagger sticking out from between his armor. "Come on!"

I didn't know what to do—didn't know how to react as wind whipped over the field, bringing with it the scent of blood and death.

Florence found me, tossing her sword aside as she knelt on the other side of him.

My body shook as she spoke, but I could hear nothing save for the roaring in my ears—the ringing and cries of the dead and dying.

Looking at the dagger, my fingers brushed against the cool metal, shuddering as I realized how deeply it had been shoved into his stomach. Somehow, I knew his fate.

Clutching his body, I pulled him closer, noting the warmth. "You were supposed to be king," I said, voice low and shaking.

Florence looked up behind me, silver eyes hardened with determination.

Sobs racked my body, my shoulders shuddering beneath the weight of my grief.

I couldn't let go. I couldn't—

"He's gone." Rona stepped forward, placing a gentle hand on my shoulder. Her touch burned—branding me like the sorrow.

I shook my head. Refusing to believe it—accept it.

"He's supposed to be king," I whispered.

Florence leaned over, gentle hands unwrapping mine from Theron's lifeless body. Every fiber of my being fought her as she lowered his head to the ground.

Florence leaned over his body, grabbing my face with a firm hand. "Hold her back for me," she said, her voice low.

I blinked, voice shaking. "What?"

Her next words were firm—punctuated. "Hold. Her. Back."

Florence released me, her hands moving to Theron's side, eyes closed in concentration.

I turned, watching the horror wash over Rona's features, her face paling. "What are you doing?" she asked, lurching forward.

She made to step forward, and I followed her movement, blocking her with my body. "Don't," I warned.

Florence worked behind me. I could feel the magic in the air—feel what she was doing as she did. She was going to heal him—save him—and I didn't want Rona stopping her.

"What are you doing!" she screamed, lunging forward.

My arms braced against her shoulders as I pushed back, fighting with all I had left to keep her away.

"Rona, stop!" I yelled, watching as her shoulders shook.

Tears lined her eyes, a mirror of my own as I held her away from Florence and Theron.

"You have to let her try!" I begged. "She has to try!"

Rona shoved me, causing me to stumble a step. "Nature demands balance," she screamed through gasping breaths. "Do you know what she's doing!"

I turned, failing as Rona rushed forward, grabbing Florence and pulling her back, but it was too late.

Florence's eyes turned glassy, magic swelling like a soaked sponge around us.

I watched, horror finding me in equal measure when I saw what she'd done.

There on the ground, Theron's body rose and fell with the rhythm of his breaths. The dagger had been removed, discarded in the dirt.

Next to him, Rona gripped Florence, her eyes wild and bitter as she screamed—the sound echoing over the entire continent.

Florence lay still in her lap.

Not breathing.

CHAPTER SIXTY-FIVE

RIALEY

We carried Florence's body with us to the Waldwood, laying her to rest in Eirdis where the temple stood ready to welcome Verena into her home.

The sun shone through the trees, a warm breeze swirling with the fallen leaves of late summer. Rona was the first to step into the courtyard, moving closer to Florence's decaying body wrapped in white cloth. She lay over her lover's wrapped form, her tears dampening the rich soil—watering the Waldwood that would soon become her own free country, no longer under Alphaird's torment.

Flowers bloomed around her body as if the forest welcomed her sacrifice.

We stayed there, somber with the memory of loss. In the quiet night, I'd caught Theron tracing his fresh scar in the mirror at the temple, running a finger along the angry red line where death had been brought to him.

I hadn't had time to talk to him about it—nor did I think he was ready to share.

After our time in Eirdis, we carried on, leaving Caius, Rona, and Verena, bringing with us a small portion of the army. Word had gotten to Eirdis that Bloodbane had successfully led the rebellion to take Marmere, but that didn't mean we'd be welcomed in the city.

Night after night, we stayed beneath a blanket of stars, but even the calmest of nights couldn't quite rid my nostrils of the smell of blood—my skin of the stains I'd worn—crimson scars only I could see.

I curled into Theron, taking refuge in his warmth—his understanding. He'd killed his father, and while I knew it had always been his goal, even before he knew of it, slaying one's own, even for good, would always weigh heavily on the heart.

Two weeks after we'd set out, we approached the walled city of Marmere, my heart pounding in anticipation.

Would we be accepted? Find more death before we'd even seen our vision of a better life—a better kingdom—come to fruition.

I halted my horse, eyes stinging with the memories of this place—the knowledge of what it would take to erase them.

"Are you ready?" Theron asked, his kind eyes a comfort as I lost myself in their sea of blue.

I nodded, urging my horse forward until we stood at the gate's entrance.

The guards did not wear one uniform, but a mix of priestess robes from the Waldwood, civilian clothes, and uniforms from Keslow and Marmere.

The gates opened, the air stilling as we passed onto the cobbled streets of Marmere. Soldiers followed us when we turned down different roads, winding our way through the parting crowd to the palace.

Figures dotted the front of the palace when it came into view, my throat tightening with emotion. I wondered how we looked after two weeks of travel. Dirt had become a permanent fixture beneath my nails, across my skin.

Bloodbane stood at the front, his sword sheathed, and chin raised. Akari and his wife at his side, his eyes shone with tears upon our approach. When we'd gotten close enough, Bloodbane looked to Theron, tears spilling down his cheeks as he nodded his approval.

Without a word, he dropped to his knee, bowing his head low before the new King of Alphaird. Before King Theron Wineslowe, the traitor prince turned noble king.

As if a wave rippled through the crowd, Bloodbane's respect was followed by hundreds dropping to acknowledge our arrival, giving their respect.

While the group before us represented the palace staff and the Guild of Eirdis, I turned back to see others kneeling—and some standing with skepticism written across their faces. I was certain Theron would win them over—in time, they would see him the way I did—the truth of him.

Before the crowd rose, one sole figure stood first, standing in the center, wearing a simple dress, an apron tied around her waist. Visha looked just as I remembered her, wise and fierce. I'd expected her to scold me for leaving my bed unmade again—failing to rest through the night the way she once had.

"Hello," she said, her voice echoing over the quiet.

A sob broke me as I released everything I'd been feeling for weeks.

Visha stepped forward, walking around those who slowly raised their heads.

She made it to the front of the crowd, tears lining her eyes and a wide smile on her face.

"Welcome home," she said, her voice cracking with the same emotion that seemed to overtake me. "Welcome *home*, Witch Hunter."

Acknowledgements

This particular book has been years in the making. When I set out to do this, fueled by excitement, a Pinterest board, and a carefully crafted playlist, I knew that this would be the best book I'd ever written. As time went on, I soon realized that I might not have an IQ high enough to tackle this kind of story and do it justice.

Amidst my doubts, there were a number of people who reminded me that I was fully capable and talked me off every ledge in a ten-mile radius.

Nicole, thank you for being the first person to hear about this story in a Barnes and Noble Cafe. I think the original idea was a king's executioner, a hot prince who is actually blond, and a magic system that involves witches. It seems like forever ago, but I'm glad I really leaned into the hot, blond, male main character thing. The girlies are going to hate it.

Thank you to my husband for painstakingly criticizing every injury or physical task described in this book. Your knowledge since becoming a firefighter really benefits my action scenes. To be fair, I still believe Rialey could have dragged that guard's body without the using the belt. Thank you for showing me everything I know about love. Without you, the romantic subplot would have certainly fallen flat.

A special thanks to Barb for reminding me I'm not stupid, this book is good, publishing sucks, publishing is the best, and no, I don't actually want to quit. I simply could not navigate this world without turning every set back into a joke with you.

Thank you a thousand times to Shelby. The internet is a dangerous place, but we lucked out when we started planning a book event without ever meeting. I love getting to watch your successes and being able to share our story ideas. You stuck around even as I served frozen grilled cheese sandwiches to people without checking to make sure the center heated through. That's true friendship.

As always, I need to thank Wednesday, Ali, Kera, Kayla, Katelyn and all those who truly believe in my stories. Along the way, you've been forced to learn about this book against your will. However annoying that may be, I'm eternally thankful.

I owe a special thanks to Kristin and Jaynelle for taking the time to read this story before publication (assuming that Kristin finishes sometime soon). Your feedback, crying photos, and support have meant the world to me. Please move out of Texas and live closer. Also, stop meeting Ali Hazelwood without me. At this point, it's just bragging.

Reanna, thank you so much for combing through my complete misunderstanding of grammar. I know this story isn't my usual smutfest, but thank you for loving it anyway.

I cannot thank Sarah enough for simply being a friend. Without your support, I'd probably lose my mind.

Meghan, I cannot possibly express enough thanks to you for making this story happen. You took on a Kickstarter, worked on an insane amount of art, listened to every intricate detail, read scenes in advance, were tortured by a million audio messages, and you still somehow think I'm decently cool. This story feels like it also belongs to you. With every piece of artwork, you've left your fingerprint on these characters, and I'm so amazed by your talent and willingness to work with me on such a big project. You understood the vision for Faris (hot and slutty) and brought that to life for the special editions of this book. Thank you, thank you, and again, thank you.

And for my readers, thank you for believing in me and sticking by me all this time. I quite literally could not do this without you.

www.ingramcontent.com/pod-product-compliance
Lightning Source LLC
Chambersburg PA
CBHW022255310726
48973CB00001B/78